CW00702491

"I PROMISE I WON'T MAKE LOVE TO YOU UNTIL YOU ASK, JENNY . . ."

Make love to me? she thought as he laid back the halves of pale blue blouse to expose her camisole. *If this isn't making love to me, what is?*

Just the thought that he was seeing her in her undergarments and that he was so near and that he was going to kiss her again at any moment had brought on a strange and nameless yearning.

He kissed her again. Unbidden, her arms floated up to rest lightly on his broad shoulders, and he took this as a signal to proceed with his seduction.

He eased his lips from hers and began to rain soft kisses on her eyelids, her forehead, and down the sleek column of her throat.

A tiny sound escaped her as he gently teased her with his lips, his fingers seeking, touching, caressing.

She felt herself approaching something undeniable and unknown: something for which she had no explanation or definition.

Something beyond words.

As if struck deaf and blind, she was oblivious to her surroundings, sensing only his nearness and his touch and their mesmerizing effect.

DANA RANSOM'S RED-HOT HEARTFIRES!

ALEXANDRA'S ECSTASY   (2773, $3.75)
Alexandra had known Tucker for all her seventeen years, but all at once she realized her childhood friend was the man capable of tempting her to leave innocence behind!

LIAR'S PROMISE   (2881, $4.25)
Kathryn Mallory's sincere questions about her father's ship to the disreputable Captain Brady Rogan were met with mocking indifference. Then he noticed her trim waist, angelic face and Kathryn won the wrong kind of attention!

LOVE'S GLORIOUS GAMBLE   (2497, $3.75)
Nothing could match the true thrill that coursed through Gloria Daniels when she first spotted the gambler, Sterling Caulder. Experiencing his embrace, feeling his lips against hers would be a risk, but she was willing to chance it all!

WILD, SAVAGE LOVE   (3055, $4.25)
Evangeline, set free from Indians, discovered liberty had its price to pay when her uncle sold her into marriage to Royce Tanner. Dreaming of her return to the people she loved, she vowed never to submit to her husband's caress.

WILD WYOMING LOVE   (3427, $4.25)
Lucille Blessing had no time for the new marshal Sam Zachary. His mocking and arrogant manner grated her nerves, yet she longed to ease the tension she knew he held inside. She knew that if he wanted her, she could never say no!

Available wherever paperbacks are sold, or order direct from the Publisher. Send cover price plus 50¢ per copy for mailing and handling to Zebra Books, Dept. 3760, 475 Park Avenue South, New York, N.Y. 10016. Residents of New York and Tennessee must include sales tax. DO NOT SEND CASH. For a free Zebra/Pinnacle catalog please write to the above address.

PHOEBE FITZJAMES

RENEGADE'S ANGEL

ZEBRA BOOKS
KENSINGTON PUBLISHING CORP.

ZEBRA BOOKS

are published by

Kensington Publishing Corp.
475 Park Avenue South
New York, NY 10016

Copyright © 1992 by Phoebe Fitzjames

All rights reserved. No part of this book may be reproduced
in any form or by any means without the prior written
consent of the Publisher, excepting brief quotes used in
reviews.

If you purchased this book without a cover you should be
aware that this book is stolen property. It was reported as
"unsold and destroyed" to the Publisher and neither the
Author nor the Publisher has received any payment for this
"stripped book."

First printing: May, 1992

Printed in the United States of America

"But I don't want to go among mad people," Alice remarked.

"Oh, you can't help that," said the Cat: "we're all mad here. I'm mad. You're mad."

"How do you know I'm mad?" said Alice.

"You must be," said the Cat, "or you wouldn't have come here."

—Lewis Carroll
Alice's Adventures in Wonderland

One

August, 1870

"You look mighty happy, miss."

Jenny smiled. In one hand she gripped the shuddering rail of the car's rear observation deck; in the other she clutched the smallest of her two bags. "I'm going to . . . well, it's a reunion." The train ground to a halt, and the metal deck suddenly stopped its rattling vibration.

"Oh!" she said, a little surprised.

The porter grinned. He kicked the metal stairs down into place, hopped to the station's platform, and set the last step beneath them. "Yes'm," he grinned, offering his arm. "M'self, I gets so used to that shiv'rin' in my shoes that it don't seem quite natural when she stops."

Jenny took his white-gloved hand and stepped down to the platform.

"What sort of reunion, miss, if y'don't mind my askin'?" He handed over the other bag. "Must be a

7

good 'un. You look near to bust."

"I am happy," she confessed. "I haven't seen my father for a very long time . . ."

It had been six years—almost seven, in fact—and eighteen-year-old Jenny was ecstatic at the prospect of living with her father again. After her mother's death in the spring of 1863, Jenny's beloved father, a lifelong teetotaler, had discovered the bottle: it hadn't taken him long to turn drinking into a full-time career. Only after losing the Missouri homestead (and nearly everything else) did he regain the presence of mind to realize that while he could not halt his own slide into degradation, he could at least salvage his daughter's life.

He had sent her to his wife's sister in St. Paul, and it was there that Jenny had lived since she was twelve, helping around the house and caring for Aunt Victoria's three young daughters. She supposed she was fond, in a way, of starched Aunt Victoria and grim, humorless Uncle Homer, and she was honestly rather attached to their little girls. But they could never take the place of Jenny's gentle, soft-spoken father.

She had prayed that he would one day recover and send for her. She knew that he genuinely loved her, while her aunt and uncle seemed to value her only as an unpaid housemaid and a captive audience for their relentless proselytizing. So when her father's letter arrived (or rather, a letter the illiterate George Templeton had dictated to a traveling preacher) telling her that he had renounced the bottle and purchased a farm in Lancaster County, Iowa, she was more than willing to rejoin him as he requested.

She promised her aunt that she would stay until a suitable replacement could be hired to assume her duties with the children, thinking it would take no longer than a fortnight. But either Aunt Victoria was exceptionally fussy or Jenny was exceptionally difficult to replace, because that one fortnight stretched into six before her aunt finally settled on a successor.

The parting had been cool, but not bitter. As a going-away gift, the girls had presented her with her own copy of Mr. Carroll's *Alice's Adventures in Wonderland*. It was a book she loved, and one that she'd read to the children so many times that she'd practically committed it to memory. Her uncle had pressed his own battered copy of Cicero's *Orations* into her hands, solemnly intoning, "To uplift and purify."

Free at last, Jenny had bought herself a train ticket, packed her meager possessions into two frayed satchels, and traveled south to Fowlersville and her father.

She left her bags under the watchful eye of the stationmaster, and after asking directions to the sheriff's office, she tucked a few stray wisps of pale, straw-colored hair under her hat and set off down the street.

The sheriff was in, his feet propped up on his desk, a cup of coffee poised at his lips. When Jenny entered he snapped to attention. His boots hit the floor with a resounding thud. It was not often he had such a striking visitor. She stood about five feet four inches in her low-heeled shoes and was long of leg and full-busted. The pale green dress she wore brought out the deep, unmuddied emerald of her wide, thickly lashed eyes, and her skin was soft, poreless, and of a creamy complexion varied only by the soft blush of rose in her cheeks.

She smiled at him, her full lips revealing a row of small teeth, white and even. Sheriff John Trenton was a happily married man and had been so for better than twenty years, but it was difficult for him to keep from reaching across his desk to touch this girl, if only to make certain she was real.

"I hope I'm not disturbing you, Sheriff," she began in a voice that was sultry not by device, but by nature. "I wondered if you'd be able to help me."

Trenton, big and burly and carrying too many scars from too many bullets, grinned at her almost foolishly and jerked to his feet. He pulled a chair away from the wall, to the other side of his battered desk.

Jenny accepted gratefully, and after he had regained his seat, she began.

"My father recently purchased a farm not far from town, and I thought you could help me locate him. You see," she said smiling, "he doesn't read, so I couldn't write to tell him I was coming. We haven't been together in better than six years now, and . . . well, you can imagine how anxious I am to see him."

The sheriff nodded and ran coarse fingers through his graying hair. "Well, that doesn't sound like too tough a job, young lady. I reckon I know just about

10

everybody in the county. What'd be your daddy's name, then?"

"Templeton. George Templeton."

The smile left Sheriff Trenton's face and he looked away. He cleared his throat uncomfortably.

She leaned forward. "Is something wrong?"

It was a moment before he spoke again. "Afraid I've got some hard news for you, miss."

Jenny tensed. One hand left her lap to clutch at the edge of Trenton's desk. "What is it? My father . . . He's not—he isn't sick, is he?" *Have mercy*, she thought, *Papa's drinking again. He's the town drunk, and he promised, he promised me . . .*

"No, miss, he's not sick, he's . . ." He stopped himself. He couldn't come right out with it like that. He took a different tack. "Last month we had a holdup at the Mercantile Bank. The Denton gang, at least part of it. Ace and the Dodge brothers."

She'd heard of the Denton gang. They were thieves: robbers of banks and stagecoaches, and heirs to highwaymen of long ago like "Bad Bobby" Belkins and the infamous Arkansas Kid. The story went that during the War Between the States, some of the Denton gang, including their leader, Ace Denton, had ridden with Quantrill's Raiders, the same band that had included Frank and Jesse James. Like many of Quantrill's men, a bounty had been placed upon their heads at the end of the war. Now they stole for a living. But she had never realized they operated here in southern Iowa. This was the tramping ground of the James Gang and the Younger brothers, not the Dentons.

"I was out of town when they hit," Sheriff Trenton

11

continued. "Deliverin' a prisoner up to Fort Dodge. I wish to God I'd been here . . ."

"I don't understand, Sheriff," she interrupted. "What does this have to do with my father?"

Trenton sighed heavily. "After they took the bank, there was some gun play in the street. Three citizens wounded, two killed. I'm afraid your father . . ." He cleared his throat. "He died quick, Miss Templeton. He didn't suffer, if that's any comfort. Doc said he probably never knew what hit him. Witnesses said it was Ace himself that done the shootin'."

She was absolutely dumbfounded. She could only stare at the sheriff's sympathetic, weather-beaten face.

"I would have gotten in touch, miss, but nobody knew he had kin. He'd just moved into the old Faulkner place about a month before, and he'd only been in town two, maybe three times." His brow knotted, creating even more wrinkles in an already lined face. The poor little thing . . . He wondered if she had anywhere to go now that her daddy was dead.

"Perhaps," she said softly, her voice breaking, "perhaps you could direct me to his farm. There'll be things there that need—"

"I'm real sorry, miss, but I'm afraid there's no farm for you to go to."

"I—I don't understand."

"See, he put a little money down on the place, but he made a deal with the bank—lot of farmers 'round here do it—not to make no payments till he brought in his first crop. Seeing as how there wasn't goin' to be no first crop, well . . . Bankin's a business, too, I reckon."

She was crying now, silently, and John Trenton felt as guilty telling her this as if he had repossessed that farm himself.

"But *I* could work the farm. *I* could—"

He cut her off. It was better that she hold no false hopes. "You'd never be able to work it by yourself, Miss. Besides which, plantin' season's long over. It's practically harvest time."

He was right. There was nothing for her to do here. She would have to go back to Minnesota: back to Aunt Victoria and Uncle Homer. But first there was something she had to know.

"I don't understand, Sheriff." Her tears slowed as anger, at least for the moment, began to replace mourning. "I always heard that the Denton gang didn't shoot people. That they went out of their way not to hurt anybody."

"Used to be the case, miss, true. Lots'a folks called 'em heroes for that. Said Ace Denton was the Arkansas Kid all over again—all that 'steal from the rich, give to the poor' Robin Hood horseshit." He caught himself and made a face. "'Scuse me, miss. But they was outlaws none the less. Ace and his bunch've done 'bout as many jobs as the James boys and the Youngers put together. And the past few months they've picked up some real nasty habits. Like killin' folks. Pullin' off jobs in broad daylight and shootin' up towns, that sorta thing. The bounty on 'em—on Ace Denton, in particular—just went up considerable."

He reached into a desk drawer, pulled out a sheaf of wanted posters and thumbed through them. "These just come in the other day," he said. "Haven't had time to post 'em yet." He found what he was looking for, and handed her a printed sheet. At the top was an artist's rendering of a dark, rugged-looking man, beardless and scowling. Beneath the drawing was printed:

WANTED—DEAD OR ALIVE
* REWARD *
$5000.00 in GOLD
for information leading to the
CAPTURE and CONVICTION
of
ACE DENTON
(alias Marcus Denton, alias Mark Dirkson)
for Murder and Robbery
Height: About 6'0"   Weight: 175–185 lbs.
Hair: **Dark Brown or Black**
Eyes: **Dark Brown or Black**

A list of crimes was printed below, in small type, along with a terse description of each man known to ride with the gang. The drawing made Denton look cruel and dangerous, but it wasn't very specific—it could have been any one of dozens of men. Trenton noticed her quizzical look.

"Not much help, is it?" he remarked. "Nobody ever come up with a photograph of him."

"May I . . . May I keep this?" she asked, still clutching the poster.

The sheriff lifted a bushy brow. "S'pose so. I've got extras. But why do you want—"

"My father's personal possessions," she interrupted. "Who would have charge of those?"

Trenton stood up and went to his filing cabinet. "I would, miss." He handed her a large yellow envelope. "This here's what he had on him: coin purse 'n pocket watch 'n so on. And a few things we found out at the farm. Didn't seem to have much else. I've got a little trunk out in the back room with some things we found in the house. Clothes and the like. Everything else out there was the furniture and such that he bought along with the farm . . ."

"That doesn't surprise me, Sheriff. My father traveled light these last few years." She took the envelope from him. It was heavier than it looked and clanked faintly when she tucked it under her arm.

"There's just shy of ten dollars in there, too," he said. "My deputy found it in a coffee can out to the farm. Would'a been a few dollars more, but we took out for the funeral . . ." He paused and cleared his throat.

"Your daddy had a little bay saddle mare, too. Fancy thing for a farmer to have . . . She's down to Bill Seaver's Livery. Bill's been usin' her to hire out, so I don't reckon he'll charge you for her board. If he tries to, you just tell him to come talk to me. Your father hadn't paid up on the plow horses and the milk cow yet, so they—"

"—went back to the bank?"

"In a manner of speakin' miss."

She nodded as her eyes filled again. Ten dollars, one saddle horse and a small trunk in the back room. It didn't seem much to show for forty-three years of living. She straightened, sniffing back the tears.

"May I see the trunk?"

"Course." He led her out of the front office and

toward the rear of the building, past an empty pair of iron-barred cells to a padlocked room. He turned a key, opened the door, and pointed to a battered trunk in the corner.

"There she is, miss," he said. "Reckon I'll leave you alone for a spell."

She nodded, and after he had gone she knelt and opened the leather-bound lid. Inside she found her father's neatly folded clothes, an ancient humidor, two pipes, and a scratched tintype: her parents' wedding picture. His Sunday suit was missing, and she realized they must have buried him in it. His favorite whittling knife was there, as well as a partially carved block of cherry wood, half-formed into a small prancing horse. She picked up the little figure and stroked it, remembering the menagerie of toys he'd carved for her when she was little: fat pigs and stout draft horses, dogs and chickens and deep-uddered cows. She began to cry again. Gently, she set aside the carving and began to sort through the rest of the trunk's contents.

At the very bottom of the trunk, she found what she sought.

She pulled it out and turned it over in her hands: her father's old Colt pistol. It was as heavy and worn and second- or third-hand, but faithfully cleaned and cared for. He'd been such a gentle soul. She had never known him to actually fire it, but he'd always said it was a good thing for a man to have handy and ready.

She pulled out a pair of her father's trousers and two of his less-worn shirts, along with a fairly new pair of work boots. *He must have bought them just before . . .* she thought, and fought back a new surge of tears. She would have to stuff papers in the toes of the boots, but they would be all right. The trousers would be long, but her father hadn't been a tall man—probably three extra rolls in the cuffs would fit them.

She rolled the wanted poster, a box of cartridges, the half-finished cherry-wood horse, and her father's boots and Army Colt inside the clothing. Gently, she closed the lid of the trunk and stood up. "They won't get away with this, Papa, I promise," she whispered before she turned her back and rejoined the sheriff in the front office.

He rose when she entered.

"Thank you, Sheriff. Thank you for your kindness and your stewardship. I'd like to leave the trunk with you, if I may. I'll send for it later." She turned to go out the door, the parcel under her arm, the envelope in her hand.

"Miss Templeton!" he called after her. "You got someplace to go?"

She forced a weak smile. "Yes thank you, I do have someplace to go. And something to do. But first, could you tell me how I might find the cemetery?"

She did her homework. In the beginning, she spent long afternoons in dusty, small-town newspaper offices, her nose buried in their back files, her ears open and eager for any tidbit or rumor an employee might mumble about the Denton gang. But she soon realized that her first instincts had been right: the sort of information she wanted would not be found in print or official records.

17

She resurrected the clothing she'd taken from her father's trunk, packed away her petticoats, and began to drift from hamlet to hamlet: lingering in the shadows outside saloons and livery stables, eavesdropping on farmhands and town gossips and chatty drummers. With her hair tucked up, a hat pulled down over her eyes and her chest strapped down, she could pass—as long as the inspection wasn't too careful—for a young boy.

It was not the sort of existence she had ever dreamt of leading. It was rough and it was hard, but if Jenny Templeton was anything, she was stubborn. She would do what she had to do. And as the days and then the weeks went by, she metamorphosed, both mentally and physically, into someone Aunt Victoria, and possibly not even Jenny herself, would have recognized.

It was worth it, though. Anything was a fair price to pay to bring Ace Denton to justice, and that was precisely what she planned to do. Just exactly *how* she'd do it was another thing entirely, but if she could find him—something the local sheriffs didn't seem too interested in doing—she was certain she'd be able to find somebody to turn him over to. And then he'd pay for what he did to her father.

Down through southern Iowa and into Missouri, she traveled the back roads and cattle tracks. She purchased what supplies she could and slept in the woods at night. Hotels were too expensive, and the polite, small-town folk she'd meet in their lobbies wouldn't be the sort to have information about the Denton gang. The woods were deep and dark and filled with strange sounds, and the first few nights every owl's hoot and snapped branch found her trembling and blindly pointing her father's old handgun out into the murk.

Sometimes, when she'd been jarred from slumber by the passing of some unseen night creature, Jenny would try to purge the fear by spouting memorized bits of *Alice*. But it seemed that every time she'd get halfway through one of the poems, something else would scurry or scutter through the darkness and she'd have to start over.

Other times she'd bring out that little unfinished carving, running her fingers along the path her father's careful blade had traveled.

But anger proved a better shield against her fear than rhymes or even memories of her father. She would fix Ace Denton's poster to a tree and stare at it across the firelight, letting her hatred for him well and fester. She fantasized him, bound and gagged, riding ahead of her toward some marshall's office as she wielded her father's Colt. Sometimes she saw him dangling from a gallows. Other times, when she was feeling particularly brave, she envisioned herself standing over him, smiling: the gun smoking in her hand, his life's blood ebbing into the earth.

Her nights were a strange juxtaposition of magical Wonderland; misty thoughts of her gentle father, cut down too soon and in innocence, and those fantasies of violence. But she managed to hold to her purpose, however vague.

For when it came right down to it, she had no firm plan; and perhaps, she decided, she didn't need one, at least for now. She would find him first; there would be time enough for plotting later on. And if there were sounds in the forest that frightened her and stole her sleep, the knowledge that soon, one way or another, she would be responsible for Ace Denton's death made the lonely roads and the heat and the mud and the drizzling rain bearable.

She memorized his description and those of his cronies. There were the Dodge brothers: the boys who had been with him the day he shot her father. Andy Dodge and his younger brother Billy were both blond, blue-eyed, and of medium height. Andy was about twenty, and Billy, at sixteen or seventeen, was even younger than Jenny. Scar Cooksey rode with Denton, too, and he would be the easiest to recognize. The damning mark of his identity had been received during Quantrill's ill-fated raid on Lawrence, Kansas: a long, thin sabre scar that diagonially bisected his right cheek. The fifth most likely candidate was a quarter-blood Cherokee named Rafe Langley: a fast and dangerous gun whose description was as vague as Ace Denton's. There were others who sometimes rode with the gang, but these five seemed to be the core of the group.

On the deserted trails to which she kept, she met few other travelers. Most of the handful whose paths she crossed merely nodded or said "how do" and moved on. If she had any fear of bandits or ruffians, she told herself that she looked far too poor to rob. She was probably right. Her clothes were baggy, and soon so filthy that she could hardly bear to wear them. She refrained from washing them only because she determined that the easiest way to blend into the landscape was to wear as much of it as possible on her clothing and face. Early on, she'd purchased a long white duster to protect her against the wind and the rain. It soon turned to dingy, mud-spattered gray, and its long, enveloping folds hid what few of her curves escaped the bindings. Even the little mare she'd inherited from her father and christened "Fancy" was fancy no longer: the mare became as scruffy and untended as Jenny.

When she passed a town she'd amble in along a back street, moving slowly, clinging to the shadows. And she would watch and listen.

Her eavesdropping paid off. She'd heard plenty of rumors about the Denton gang: gossip and innuendo about the band was bantered freely in this part of the country. Some said that the Dentons, like the James boys, often took refuge in the caves and caverns that lay deep beneath Missouri's fertile fields. Some said they hid out in Kansas and never came this way anymore except to loot and kill. Some said they were dead and that another gang entirely had usurped their name and their territory. But the one recurring snippet of information that had a persistent ring of truth concerned Scar Cooksey's girlfriend.

It seemed that Scar had a lady love: a certain Miss Meg Sweetwater. They said Meg was a whore. It was a word Jenny'd never heard before, but then, she had learned many new words these past weeks, if not necessarily their definitions. But whatever "whoring" was, Meg did it in a place called Briarbirth House down in Banjo County, Missouri, just outside the little town of Green Mule. It was Jenny's single, strongest lead, and so she determined to take herself to Green Mule to find Meg Sweetwater and wait for Scar Cooksey and Ace Denton to rear their heads.

*　　*　　*

Just over six weeks after she stood at her father's graveside in Fowlersville and promised him she'd make it right, and three days outside of Green Mule, Missouri, it began to rain. Jenny was used to inclement weather by now. She and the little mare had plodded their way through many a late-summer shower. But on this afternoon, the storm showed no signs of abating. Gray clouds, then black, scurried too quickly across the sky, bringing twilight an hour early. The air, filled at first with fat warm droplets, was sliced and battered by cold, cutting sheets of rain.

Her sodden hat pulled down over her ears, the collar of her duster turned up about her neck, Jenny forged on. The woods to the right of the weedy, disused road she followed would provide her with no better cover against this downpour than she had here at their edge; and besides, she was too close to Green Mule and too stubborn to stop. But when the hail began to pelt down—pea-sized at first, then nearly as big as robin's eggs—she decided to search for shelter.

She was too late. Real darkness descended quite suddenly. It replaced the false night of the cloud-obliterated sky, and brought with it the height of the storm's fury. Thunder, only distant rumblings before, now crashed with such intensity that Jenny's sodden mare shied and darted every few seconds. No stars showed through the clouds, and even the moon could not force a feeble glow through those black, roiling thunderheads. Near-blinding flashes of lightning that came too often—and too close—were the only lamp she had to light her way.

She was afraid of the woods now, afraid that those tall spires of elm and oak would attract more of the lightning that had already crisped several of their kin. Three times she saw the burst of fire further back in the forest, heard the sick *pop* of exploding wood and the scream of the living tree, and smelled the green wood turned to smoke and cinders.

The hail was larger now, bigger than quail's eggs; and Fancy, frightened by the thunder and lightning and the stinging pelt of ice, was skidding dangerously in the muddy lane. Jenny couldn't go into the wood, and the overgrown field down the slope to her left would be even more dangerous. Riding through it, the top of her head would be the highest point in the treeless meadow, and the lightning would surely find her.

Then the lightning flashed again, and she saw it: a cluster of farm buildings, tumbledown and long deserted by the folk who had once worked those brambled fields. The house had mostly fallen in upon itself, but there were two barns. One was tall and broad with a gabled, hole-pocked roof and a broken weather vane; and beside it, the other, smaller, more snug, and not quite so battered. She reined in the mare and waited for the next flash of lightning to tell her that she had not imagined this haven; and when, seconds later, a burst of white, harsh light showed her it was true, she gratefully reined Fancy down toward the abandoned farmyard.

It wasn't far. Jenny dismounted and led the skittering mare through the soupy yard's maze of broken boards, then into the smaller barn. The structure had no doors. They had long since fallen from their leather hinges, and lay in muddy, decaying, hail-freckled pieces out front. There was a smell of mildew and mold spore and a faint, unpleasant underscent of decay, but aside from a half-dozen enthusiastic streams of water that cascaded through the roof, it was dry.

Jenny groped for her saddlebags and managed to find her little metal matchbox. With fumbling fingers, she extricated a sulphur tip, struck it, and looked about her. The barn, even though it was the junior of the two, was larger than she'd first thought. It was obvious that it had been reserved for someone's horses. There were six dusty, broken-boarded stalls along each side of the wide central expanse, and a sagging hayloft overhung the stalls. Toward the back was an inset harness or feed room, its door closed.

The match burned too close to her fingers. As she shook it out and struck another, she found herself swearing softly under her breath and smiled wryly. If nothing else, all those weeks of eavesdropping on the more unsavory elements of rural Iowa and Missouri had added somewhat to her vocabulary.

Fancy trailing in her wake, she walked back to the door and pulled it open. It was a large room, probably once used for feed or tack or both, but now empty except for rubble. At the back was another door which would lead to the rear yard, but part of the loft had caved in, blocking the exit with splintered boards and a tangle of discarded tack. As the second match expired, she heard the scutter and squeak of rats. Jenny slammed the wobbling door and jumped back to collide with Fancy.

"I guess we're safe enough here, girl," she

whispered shakily, taking some comfort from the sound of her own voice. "If the lightning comes this way, the taller barn'll take it for us." She stroked the mare's neck, and her hand came away dripping with muddy water. "We need to get you dried off. Me, too. And I'll bet you're hungry." As the thunder boomed and the hail and rain pelted into the swampy yard outside, she began to search through her packs for Fancy's dwindling bag of grain.

But just as her fingers touched it, she heard a new sound beneath the thunder's roll. Voices. Men's voices. And they were coming toward her. Quickly, she grabbed for the mare's reins and pulled her back through the darkness toward the storeroom door. She was off by two feet and groping blindly along the splintery boards when a God-sent bolt of lightning illuminated the barn just long enough for her to find the latch and yank it open. Dragging Fancy along, she lunged inside and pulled the door closed just as the voices, and the men to which they belonged, entered the barn.

There were several of them, four at least by the sound of their horses' hooves. "Christ," one of them grumbled. "Darker'n a sombitch in here."

Fancy tossed her head and tugged at the reins. Jenny clamped a hand over the mare's nostrils to keep her from whickering as a second man, younger than the first, spoke. "Youch!" he complained. "Watch where you're swingin' that horse, willya? What the hell's wrong with him, anyhow?"

A third voice, deeper and richer than the two before it, said, "How should I know? Do something productive for a change, why don't you? Clear a place and get a fire goin' . . ."

Then there was the muted scuffle of a boot kicking away moldy straw and scraping the dirt beneath, the dusty snorts of horses being tied into ancient stalls, and the low murmur of the men's voices as they spoke to their mounts rather than each other. Behind her in the dark tack room, Jenny heard a rat scurry along the base of the wall. She bit at her lip and tried not to scream.

"There," said the second voice. "She's goin' now."

Faint light seeped through the cracks of the tack room wall. One hand still cupped over Fancy's muzzle, Jenny leaned forward and peeked out into the barn.

There were four of them. They were too far back from the tiny blaze for her to make out their faces, but as one leaned forward to stoke the fire, she saw that he was light-haired and fairly young.

There was a pounding of hooves and the crack of splintering boards from within the shadows behind the fire, and the blond boy's head jerked up. "Jesus! How come he's so proddy all of a sudden?"

Behind him, a second youth, his hat pulled down over his eyes and younger by the sound of his voice, moved into the light. "Maybe you come into heat again," he laughed, "an' you got him all worked up. Why don't you go on over there and bend over for—"

"You little turd!" The blond boy leapt at him, and the two began to roll wildly on the floor, punching ineffectually at each other's midsections and cursing. Over and over they rolled, away from the firelight and toward the gaping outside door. Intermittent flashes of lightning illuminated them as if in a series of still photographs.

"Aw, knock it off." It was a dark man, tall and lean and cruel-faced, who emerged from the shadows. He stepped over the little fire and administered a sharp kick to the scuffling boys.

The younger one cried out, then jumped up, clutching at his ribs. A thin line of blood ran from one nostril, and he had lost his hat, exposing a shaggy mop of yellow hair the same color as his opponent's. "Whatcha have to go and do that for? We was only—"

"I told you before," the dark man growled, "I've had it with all'a your crap."

"Easin' up." It was the silky baritone voice she'd heard earlier. The owner emerged from the half-light into the fire's glow. He was dark, too, like the man who'd broken up the fight: black-haired and jet-eyed. They were about the same height and build, and while the soft-spoken man didn't look so hardened or mean, she didn't think he looked like someone you'd want to cross. He was also, from what Jenny could see in this light and at this distance, quite handsome.

"What?" It was the older boy.

"I said it's easin' up." He nodded toward the door. The rain was still coming down, but with much less insistence than earlier. Hail had ceased to pelt into the yard, and the night seemed a little less black, as if the moon had finally begun to win its battle with the thunderheads. "Clouds are movin' fast, and the horizon's clear. Oughta be able to move on out before long."

In the darkness of the tack room, Jenny allowed herself a quiet sigh of relief. It was all she could do to keep the mare quiet. Fancy had grown increasingly restless, and although she was obedient, Jenny could not keep her from shuffling her hooves in the decayed straw underfoot. She knew she couldn't stand here all night soothing the mare, and the sounds of the storm, which had so far masked Fancy's movements, were gradually becoming more and more distant.

"Speakin' for myself, boys, I ain't lookin' forward to the rest of this ride. Why don't we just bed here tonight and go on to Medford Springs come sunup?" It was a fifth man, one she hadn't noticed before. He walked out of the shadows as he spoke. He was slender, brown-haired and narrow-lipped. A long thin scar ran diagonally across his right cheek, from the outside corner of his mouth to the outer wing of his eyebrow. She recognized him immediately: Scar Cooksey. And if he was Scar, then the blond boys must be Andy Dodge and his brother, Billy.

Which meant that one of the two dark men was her father's murderer.

She clapped a hand over her own mouth, muffling a gasp. It was him, it had to be. But which one?

Her question was answered when both men turned into the firelight. There was no mistaking Ace Denton for the cold-blooded killer he was. True, both men were of the same size and build, but Ace Denton's face was leaner, harder, higher of cheekbone, and narrower of eye. A hank of oily dark hair swung across his forehead as he talked, and his words were punctuated by a slight sneering twitch that curled one corner of his mouth.

"Naw," he said, "he's right. We gotta get out of here. Got business to attend to." He smiled, and there

28

was something so cunning and almost deranged about that smile that Jenny's arms broke out in gooseflesh. "'Sides, Scar, I'd think you'd be more anxious than most to pick up that poke in Medford Springs so's you can get down to Green Mule all the quicker. Ain't you got a hanker to climb up 'top that little whore a'yours an'—"

"I don't know why you gotta always call her a whore," Scar broke in. "I mean, I know she, well—"

Behind them in the shadows, the stallion suddenly bellowed with such volume and intensity that Scar and the Dodge brothers flinched and Ace reached toward his holster. And immediately, beneath her hand, Jenny felt Fancy take a gulp of air in preparation to answer the call. Desperately, she jerked the mare's head to the side and pinched her nostrils.

She managed to stop Fancy from calling, but she couldn't stop the mare from swinging her rump up against the tack room wall.

"What was that?" Andy was on his feet now, and his hand was on the butt of his revolver.

"Christ, you're jumpy," Scar laughed. "Just the storm."

"No," said Billy. "I heared it, too. Come from back there. I been hearin' stuff from back there ever since we come in."

"You're full of it, boy," Ace sneered. "If you think somethin's back there, why don't you go look?"

"Why don't *you* look? How come I always gotta do everything? Huh? How come it's always 'Billy, fetch my horse' or 'Billy, pour me a drink' or 'Billy—'"

The man with the rich voice—who, by default, had

to be Rafe Langley—stepped between them. "Why don't you two save some of it, all right? It's just rats or a 'coon."

"Aw hell." It was Ace Denton. "I'll go look if it'll make Baby Billy feel better. Wouldn't want him messin' his diapers, now would we?"

He started toward the tack room.

There was nowhere to hide. The back door was blocked. She was trapped, and her father's pistol was buried deep within her pack roll.

Her father's killer stopped outside the door. Through the cracks in the wall, she watched, trembling, as he reached into his shirt pocket for a match, then popped it into flame with his thumbnail. He put his hand on the latch.

"She's quit."

The latch half-lifted, Ace Denton turned back toward his men. "What?"

"I said, she's quit." It was Rafe Langley. He was leading a muscular dark red horse out into the center aisle of the barn. Leading their mounts, the Dodge brothers emerged from the shadows behind him. "You coming with us, or you gonna go play with Billy's rats?" As he swung into the saddle, his mount half-reared, but he seated himself effortlessly, murmuring, "Easy, Trooper. Easy, son . . ."

Beside him, Scar Cooksey led out two geldings: a thin buckskin and a tall sorrel, nearly the color of Langley's mount.

"Make up your goddamn minds," Ace growled under his breath before he jerked his hand away from the latch and strode back to rip the red gelding's reins from Scar's hand. He mounted while Scar kicked out

30

what was left of the little fire, and the five of them rode out of the barn and off into the darkness.

Jenny was still shaking when, five minutes later, she finally mustered the courage to ease open the door and lead Fancy out into the aisle. *Well,* she thought as the adrenaline in her blood finally began to thin, *now I know what they look like, and where they're going. I'll make it right, Papa. I'll make it right.*

She stripped Fancy of her tack, tied her in a stall, gave her a measure of oats, and rubbed her as dry as she could with handfuls of musty hay. And at last, she fell sound asleep on a pile of ancient straw, her head propped on Fancy's saddle; a smile on her face as she dreamt not of Alice's adventures, but of her own vengeance.

Two

She rode into Green Mule still wearing her father's old clothes. She made a curious picture as she hitched her horse outside the hotel: a scuffed and smudged waif of indeterminate sex, her carpetbags tied to the saddle of a finely made bay mare whose white-splashed forehead she rubbed before entering the building.

She had less than two dollars left of her meager inheritance. After some deliberation, she used a dollar of it to pay for a room and a bath and, toting her own bags, climbed the stairs. When she emerged three hours later, the heretofore indifferent desk clerk snapped to attention. The scruffy urchin he'd checked in had been transformed by soap and water and a pale pink dress into a vision both rare and beautiful.

He beamed at her broadly. "Why, you're—I mean,

good afternoon, miss!"

She returned his smile. "Good afternoon. Perhaps you can help me," she began. "I'm looking for work. Would you know if anyone in town is hiring right now? I'll do almost anything—clean, wash dishes, wait tables . . . I'm very good with children, and I can cook a little." She looked at him expectantly.

The clerk, more than a little mesmerized, gazed into her eyes. Never had he seen any girl with skin so pale and flawless, one who radiated such purity as did this girl. Her golden hair was simply plaited into a thick twist at the back of her head. The soft blush in her cheek matched the soft pink of her gown, and set in that heart-shaped, ingenuous face were the biggest, clearest, greenest eyes he'd ever seen. She looked as if she might have been crafted in porcelain rather than grown of flesh and blood.

"Sir?" she said, shaking him out of his reverie.

"Jobs. Jobs . . ." he muttered, wracking his brain. He really *did* want to help her. She was someone you automatically wanted to help, he thought, someone you wanted to take care of . . . But nothing popped into his mind. Even though Green Mule was the county seat, it was a small town. If anyone was hiring, he would have known.

"Sorry, miss," he admitted. "I can't think of no one, 'cept maybe . . ." He paused, his cheeks flushing slightly. "But you wouldn't be interested in that . . ."

"Interested in what?" she pleaded. "Please, I really do need the work, sir."

It was the "sir" that got him. Or maybe it was the way her wide green eyes seemed to grow even wider, deeper. He'd kick himself for it later, he knew, but he seemed unable to withhold any information from her.

"Well, it's just that Miss Liz McCaleb's servin' girl, she . . ." He hesitated, blushing, but Jenny continued to stare at him expectantly. "Miss Liz, she runs kind of a gamin' house. You know: hot dime dinners, liquor, gamblin' and, uh . . . It's a couple miles out of town. And her servin' girl, she . . . Well, she's workin' upstairs now, instead of downstairs, if you get my drift." He wiped at his brow. He couldn't remember ever being this uncomfortable.

"It really ain't the kind of place a nice young lady like you . . . I mean . . ." He was blushing brightly now, and turning redder by the second. If only she wouldn't roll those big innocent eyes at him! "As much as I'd like to have you—I mean, as much as we'd *all* enjoy having you—I mean, as much as the town would be love to—that is, be proud to have you. As a new citizen, I mean . . ." He leaned on his elbows, exhausted. "Shucks, miss! Briarbirth ain't the place for you."

It was perfect. It took all her willpower not to grin triumphantly. What better place to wait for the spider than in the middle of the web!

"I appreciate your concern, sir, but I'm in desperate need of a job, even a temporary one. How do I get to Miss McCaleb's?"

The clerk had told her to take the road south of town and go about three miles. "How will I know it?" she'd asked him, and he'd answered, "Miss, ain't no way in Hades you can miss that place."

He'd been right.

Briarbirth House faced north, and it was huge, bigger even than the Summit Hill mansions she remembered ogling in St. Paul. Three and a half stories of crisp, whitewashed clapboard and gray, mortared rock rose up to meet the gabled roof, and the style of the house was something which she decided not even Lewis Carroll could have invented. It was a curious mix, as if it had been designed by a quixotic drunkard: part English manor house, part Greek revival, part Queen Anne, and part something else she couldn't quite put her finger on.

The architecture was eccentric enough to own a curious charm, but somehow its odd blend of pillars and gingerbread and stained glass and turrets seemed foreboding. It stood alone, far back from the road, in the center of five acres of rolling meadow; and even if she had now known it at once, the weathered, tilting granite marker to the left of the drive would have named the place for her. BRIARBIRTH, it announced, in deeply incised, half-mossed letters.

Hidden from her view until she came even with the house were several outbuildings. They lay to the east, at the base of a long, grassy slope.

The nearest was a neat red stable, trimmed in white. There was a big attached corral on the side that faced the house. A smokehouse and a chicken coop with a fenced yard were on the other, as well as a pig sty that held a small shed and four chubby, half-grown hogs.

Farther down and back, at the edge of a deep wood in the first stages of autumn, was an old monster of a barn, abandoned and decaying. Its once white paint was gray and peeling, and its wide front door yawned like an open mouth. Something about it made her shiver despite the warmth of the afternoon. By contrast, it made the macabre design of Liz McCaleb's big house seem warm and friendly.

She sat in the road for a few minutes, staring at the house and chewing at her lip and wondering just what sort of rabbit's hole she was about to leap into. At last she decided it didn't matter; she'd come too far to back out now. She took a deep breath and urged Fancy forward, down the long drive toward Banjo County's most notorious bordello.

Two of the girls, clad only in their underthings, were lounging about the garishly appointed receiving parlor. One, a mousey, long-legged, wide-mouthed brunet of nineteen years, was sprawled on an overstuffed, Chinese-red divan. She was playing with the ribbon on her camisole. The other girl, a pink-skinned, plain-faced sixteen-year-old whose generous bosoms were barely encased by the paper-thin material of her chemise, stared absently out the window.

Quite suddenly, she sat up. There was a visitor coming down the drive: an angelic but determined young woman in a pale pink dress, who looked as though a band of angels might be invisibly fluttering over her shoulder.

"Well, I'll be jiggered!" Pearl exclaimed. Her bosoms heaved as she got to her feet and clamped her hands on skimpily clad hips.

The brunet, Mary-Rebecca, did not look up.

Pearl grabbed her hand and hauled her to the window. "Looky here," she said, pushing lank, white-blond bangs out of her eyes. "Looky what we got comin' up the walk. Reckon she's here to enroll us in Bible school?"

Mary-Rebecca laughed. "Looks to me like somebody give her the wrong address."

There was a knock at the front door, and Mary-Rebecca went out in the hall to answer it. Giggling into her hand, Pearl hung back and pressed herself into the parlor doorway.

Mary-Rebecca peeked through the leaded, stained-glass panes of the wide front door before she opened it with a flourish. She leaned provocatively against the frame. She was still playing with the ribbon of her camisole. "Looks like you're in the wrong place, honey," she cooed, intending to shock. "'Fraid we don't cater to your kind." She jabbed her thumb toward the road. "You must be lookin' for the First Methodist, five miles yonder. We got no truck with missionaries 'round here." She pursed her lips into a contrived pout, then added, "Course, we're kinda fond of their position."

Behind her, in the hall, Pearl tittered.

But Jenny Templeton stood her ground, as if it were the most natural thing in the world to be greeted by an overrouged tart wearing nothing but her underwear. "Good afternoon," she began, hoping she didn't look as flustered as she felt. "I should like to speak to Miss McCaleb. Is she in?" She smiled at Mary-Rebecca: it was a friendly smile, but one that got the point across—she meant business.

Mary-Rebecca understood. She pulled away from

the door frame and shrugged, all the fun gone out of her game. "Hey Pearl!" she yelled back down the hall. "Find Miss Liz, will ya? Lady here wants to talk to her."

With that, Mary-Rebecca turned on her high heels and walked away with a swish of her generous hips, leaving Jenny standing in the corridor to await the madam.

Briarbirth's interior seemed even more incredible than its exterior. The main hallway, in which she'd stood for almost fifteen minutes while she waited for the madam, was fifteen feet wide, papered in a flocked floral of white and gold and green, and hung with expensive-looking paintings in gilt frames. The lower half of the walls—which Jenny had first thought to be panels of rather oddly patterned burlwood—proved, on closer inspection, to be covered in thin sheets of tooled leather.

The huge front parlor from whence Mary-Rebecca and Pearl had emerged opened to her right. There were two other sets of double doors further down that mirrored portals on the left, and just before the foot of a massive grand staircase there was a cross hall. She guessed that it would, with the main corridor, evenly quarter the first floor of the house. Three chandeliers, dripping with cut glass baubles, hung down the center of the corridor at ten-foot intervals. The last was near the foot of the stairs, where the hall narrowed to more normal proportions before it disappeared into darkness. The house was silent except for the ticking of the elaborate grandfather clock that stood behind her, near the front door. Jenny began to relax, and stared upward, into one of those cascading chandeliers, while she waited.

She nearly jumped out of her shoes when a raucous squawk erupted from the parlor.

Bugger off!, it croaked. *Heave to!*

Her hand to her heart, Jenny peered into the room. *Bugger off!*

It was a parrot, and even if Jenny had ever seen a real live parrot before, this would have been the most amazing of them all. Bright scarlet and nearly three feet long from its head to the tip of its tail, it sat atop a heavy wooden perch in the far corner. There were patches of yellow and blue on its wings, and it had a great hooked bill and pebbly bald circles around its beady eyes. There was a leather cuff around one of its horny legs that tethered it, by a chain, to its perch. It looked straight at her, and half-spreading its wings, opened its beak wide and let out a guttural squawk.

A hand touched her shoulder and she jumped again.

It was the madam, a darkly beautiful woman of about forty-five. "That's Onan," she said. "He doesn't talk very often, but once he starts, we can't shut him up." She smiled warmly. "How can I help you, dear?"

Miss Liz was dressed, unlike the scantily clad girls, in an expensive, well-cut gown of deep ultramarine blue. Her glossy black hair was untouched by gray, except for a neat, narrow, shimmering streak of silver that began just above her left temple and ribboned through the coiled plait at the back of her head. Her only jewelry was a pair of dangling gold earrings and a heavy gold bracelet thickly fringed with what Jenny's father would have called "gew-gaws." Miss Liz twisted and fussed with the charms as she talked.

She seemed quite nice, Jenny thought: well-spoken and sympathetic. But she couldn't seem to understand why Jenny was so insistent on working in the scullery. "My dear," she purred as they sat together in the overstuffed front parlor, "you're a lovely child, just lovely. You'd do very well here. And my girls make a great deal more than I can pay you as a housemaid."

"No, really, ma'am, I'd be very happy helping in the kitchen. Honestly I would."

"Well, dear, that will be up to Mrs. Bramley. But I imagine she'll take you on. If she does, you'll be on trial for two weeks. That'll take you up to your first payday. Your wages'll be two dollars a week on top of whatever tips you pick up. And your room and board, of course. And perhaps after a week or so of dirty dishes and muddy floors, you'll look more favorably upon moving upstairs," the madam explained, smiling. "Bertha will tell you what she needs from you in the kitchen, but you'll have duties in the house, too. First of all, there's the dusting . . ."

As Miss Liz listed her chores, Jenny listened only halfheartedly. Never in her life had she felt more out of place. And what was worse, she felt ignorant. She was a bright girl, a quick study, and it irked her to feel that there was something she didn't grasp: some really basic, important thing that everyone else in the world took for granted and that she—who was one of the best geography students Mr. Peabody at St. Mary's Academy for Young Ladies of Good Family

41

claimed he had ever had the privilege to teach, who had received straight A's in algebra and taught herself to read Latin—did not understand. Because quite honestly, she had no idea just what it was that Miss Liz's "girls" did to earn their keep, or what "working upstairs" might entail.

Although she'd started life as a farm girl, Jenny had been carefully sheltered: kept away from the breedings and birthings of the livestock as well as any discussion about them. Once, when she was about ten, she'd overheard her father remarking that one of his plow mares was in season, and when she'd asked what that meant, he explained—with no small degree of embarrassment—that it meant that if he turned Old Dolly out in the pasture with the neighbor's stallion, the horses would "get together" and Dolly would have a foal next year. And this terse and mysterious observation was the sum and total of her understanding of animal husbandry. She had it in her mind that somehow, by being in the same field, the animals became mated; that they had some sort of wordless, mystical animal wedding, and later produced offspring.

Her mother, a beautiful but nearly maniacally tight-laced woman (who had, for as long as Jenny could remember, dressed only in black and called Jenny's father "Mr. Templeton"), refused to answer any of bewildered Jenny's questions as to just *how* the horses would get married. She had, in fact, washed Jenny's mouth out with soap when she brought up the issue for the third time, effectively and forever closing the subject.

This same mother schooled Jenny at home, so she

had been denied even the gossip and schoolyard talk of other children. And later, when she was sent away to her aunt and uncle in St. Paul, she had entered a strict and starched household where sex was neither mentioned nor alluded to.

She had been allowed to attend only sporadic classes at St. Mary's Academy during her first year with Aunt Victoria. She'd come home one day and announced to Uncle Homer that Stevie Moore had stopped her on the way home from school and offered her two steelies and an aggie if she'd pull down her panties and let him look. She hadn't, of course—she wasn't much interested in marbles—but why, she asked, would he want her to do that? Uncle Homer's reply was to slap her across the face and stride out of the room, twisting his hands and bellowing for her aunt.

Later, and with a great deal of embarrassment, Aunt Victoria explained that boys and men might try to see her underthings, or worse, want to see her body. This was a bad thing, Aunt Victoria said, a very bad thing indeed: something for which a girl would burn in hell forever. When Jenny asked *why* they would want to look at her, the only answer she received was that all men were wicked, with the possible exception of a person's own husband, and even *they* weren't to be entirely trusted.

Thus, upon Uncle Homer's announcement that he would not have his niece "tainted," Jenny's days at St. Mary's Academy came to an end. After that, her education had come from the books and church tracts she found in their home.

When her first menses came, she'd run weeping to

43

her aunt that she was hurt, she was dying, she was bleeding to death. But Aunt Victoria had advised her that it was a punishment from God on High that all women must bear, and that it had come to Jenny in particular because little Stevie Moore had lusted to see her naked bottom; that she must never, ever speak of it again, and that when the blood and the pains came each month, Jenny was to keep to her room and devote herself to prayer and fasting until she was "clean." No explanation was given as to where the blood came from or why. God, it seemed, did not need a reason to make her suffer.

She'd never had a beau—two or three boys had asked to "go walking" with her during her six-year stint as unpaid nanny to Aunt Victoria and Uncle Homer's children, but Uncle Homer had sternly forbade it.

Jenny's life had been as cloistered, at least in this respect, as the most carefully guarded novice nun. And now she was eighteen, and totally innocent. She had never even been kissed.

So when Miss Liz tried to convince her that she should be working upstairs with the other girls, Jenny heard her urgings with mixed emotions. She was flattered that anyone as elegant as Liz McCaleb thought she was pretty enough to do whatever it was she and the other women did, but she was a little afraid to find out just what that thing was—that thing that seemed to entail the "girls" walking about the house in their underwear.

She thought that it probably had something to do with this inexplicable urge men had to look at women without their clothes. It might even have to do, she thought, with mating—she knew, vaguely, that both people and animals had to mate to have children, and she'd managed to gather that men were more avid for it than women. But she had no idea how this might be accomplished, or why men would pay money to look at (or mate with) women other than their wives. Or why, if all this mating was going on, the house wasn't filled with babies. And she was too embarrassed to ask.

". . . and this is Bertha's domain," Miss Liz was saying.

She had just given Jenny a quick tour of the first floor that ended in the cavernous dining hall, and now she swept open the door at its rear to usher Jenny into the largest, most amazing kitchen she'd ever seen. It was white and high-ceilinged, and lined along two walls with ornately carved cupboards. Waist-high marble sideboards topped banks of drawers and cabinets below. Above, leaded-glass doors that reached nearly to the ceiling protected stack after stack of plates, saucers, soup bowls, and cups, as well as a galaxy of glassware.

Along the outside wall were three hulking, wide-doored ovens spanned by a gargantuan, pot-covered cooktop. Where these left off, a long work counter, centered by a white-curtained window and a deep double sink, began. The pump was brass, or at least brass plated, and the countertops matched those of the sideboards: pink marble trimmed with alabaster insets in the shapes of posturing gryphons and unicorns.

On the opposite side of the room, at the other end of the counter, was another door beyond which lay the pantry, the back service hall, and the rear porch. In the center of the kitchen's polished, oak-planked floor stood a long, heavy teak table flanked by fourteen chairs. The kitchen smelled of baking bread, apple pies, and roasting beef.

"And this is Bertha Bramley," Miss Liz continued as a frowning, mountainous woman came toward them. "She runs this kitchen and she'll be your boss if she decides to take you on. It's her kitchen as far as I'm concerned, and she has the last say."

Mrs. Bramley, all two hundred and forty pounds of her, scowled at the petite would-be waitress. "Hmph," she snorted, wiping floury hands on the soiled apron that covered her broad belly. "Won't last long in the kitchen." She looked Jenny up and down for the third time. "Be workin' on her back inside a week."

Miss Liz shook her regal head. "I've been trying to talk her into it, Bertha, but she's not having any."

The cook addressed Jenny personally for the first time. "You're too purty to spend your time turnin' your hands red in hot dishwater, missy. Take advantage of what the Lord gave you while you still got it, and save your money. If you don't, you're stupid. I was stupid." She turned her broad back momentarily to rescue a pan of steaming golden biscuits from one of the huge iron ovens. "I didn't save nothin'. And now look at me."

"Bertha used to be top girl at Trish Gallagher's place in Chicago," Miss Liz said somewhat routinely, as if she'd given Bertha Bramley this same introduction many times before.

"I sure was." The cook smiled for the first time since Jenny and Miss Liz entered the huge kitchen. "Top girl, that was me. They used to pay fifty a night for the pleasure of my company. Sometimes on Friday and Saturday nights they'd bid; kinda auctioned me off, you might say. Once I brung near two hundred."

Jenny nodded and kept silent, not knowing quite how to respond to this revelation. She had a hard time picturing the massive, doughy-faced Bertha Bramley as a slim young beauty worth a small fortune a night. And frankly, she wasn't quite sure just what Mrs. Bramley could have done in one evening to earn two hundred dollars: nearly enough money to buy a small house.

"Really, ma'am," she insisted, "like I told Miss Liz, I just want to work in the kitchen. I'm very handy, honest I am. I'm a hard worker, and I'll try to do a good job." *Please,* she thought, *you've got to let me stay on. I have to be here, because* he *will be coming here . . .*

Mrs. Bramley stared at her for a long minute. "All right," she finally pronounced, her scowl back in place. "I s'pose she'll be as good as any. But don't stop lookin' for a gal for me, Liz. This one won't last long. Just too damn purty."

Before Jenny began her official duties, Miss Liz introduced her to the people she liked to call her "family." There was wizened little Harvey, who looked seventy-five, although Jenny suspected he was only in his early sixties—life with her father had familiarized her with the ravages of chronic drinking, and Harvey bore all the signs of a longtime tippler. He played the piano in the receiving room each night, and Miss Liz told her later that if Harvey didn't play with much expertise, at least he played good and loud, and that seemed to be what the customers liked.

Next she met Agnes Valdez, a wholesomely pretty, chubby, happy woman of slightly less than thirty. She was, Jenny was told, in charge of the parrot.

"Onan's not very friendly," Agnes explained. "But he likes me, so I tend to him and clean up his mess. He's very messy, you know. That's how he got his name."

Jenny looked at her quizzically. "I beg your pardon?"

"Because he spills his seed upon the ground," Agnes smiled slyly. She had explained this before.

Jenny still didn't understand, but before she could ask Agnes to define that cryptic remark, Shirley Mae Vinton presented herself for introductions.

Shirley Mae seemed to be the oldest of Miss Liz's "girls": in her late thirties or early forties, Jenny thought, though she looked a good decade older. Makeup was caked on her lined face, and her carrot-orange hair was shot through with gray: not in an attractive way, like Miss Liz's distinctive silver streak, but grizzled to salt and red pepper. She continually touched and fussed at her breasts, tugging her robe at the waist as if to accentuate her bustline, to prove that she still had something to offer.

She had already met Pearl and Mary-Rebecca, if

fleetingly, and she learned that the pink-skinned, platinum-haired Pearl had been her predecessor in the scullery.

She was introduced to Meg Sweetwater, the girl whose name she'd heard in connection with Scar Cooksey. Meg was a pleasant (if not too bright) strawberry blonde of twenty-two. She was brown-eyed, lightly freckled, and pretty in a sort of vague, absent way.

Meg took Jenny's hand, shook it shyly, and whispered, "Pleased to meet you, Miss Jenny." Then she reached out to touch Jenny's plaited hair. "Oh," she said, "that's so pretty! Maybe sometime you could show me how to do that?"

Jenny liked her immediately, but she couldn't help but wonder just what there was that made this girl the sort that would fall in love with an outlaw. Or that could make an outlaw fall in love with her.

The last two women, Iris Jakes and Belinda Critchley, made an appearance after the others had filtered out and Jenny was heading back toward the kitchen. It was dusk by then, and the girls appeared to have just risen. They were in their middle or late twenties, and were both from somewhere further south; their drawls were pronounced, although Iris's was by far the more nasal and irritating of the two.

Belinda was short and chubby and dark-haired, with narrow dark eyes set a little too close together. She was pug-nosed, olive-skinned and haughty-looking, and when she walked in her high heels, she affected a little strut that made her bottom stick out behind her in a most peculiar way.

Iris was taller and narrower, if a little coarse

around the middle. Just shy of beautiful, her face was an aquiline, narrow, high cheek-boned oval. There was a tiny crook midway down her thin nose, as if it had been broken long ago. She was blue-eyed, and had long, sweeping lashes and a thick head of wavy, setter-red hair that curled about her shoulders in a wild tangle, as though she had not bothered to comb it since the day before. Both girls, looking bored and superior, slouched against the bar in the wide, fresco-ceilinged dining room.

Miss Liz had juste completed the introductions when the front doorbell jingled, indicating the arrival of the evening's first gentleman caller. Hastily, she excused herself to answer it, leaving a nervous Jenny alone with Iris and Belinda.

"So you're gonna work for the fat hag in the kitchen, are you?" Belinda began. She walked behind the polished, beer-barrel-flanked bar and poured out a healthy shot of rye. She wore only a short silk robe, and when she reached behind her to put the bottle back, it fell open to expose one small sagging breast. She made no attempt to cover herself as she tossed back the liquor. Jenny, embarrassed, looked away.

"Kitchen, huh?" Belinda repeated. The fresh influx of whiskey seemed to fuel her surliness. "What's'a matter, sugar? You too good to work on your back?"

Confused, Jenny stared at the floor and wished they would go away.

Iris's nasal laugh was cruel. "I do believe you're embarrassin' our new little flower, Miss Belinda. Why, she's all a'blush!" She laughed again, and Belinda, pouring herself another two fingers of rye, joined in.

"You know, Miss Belinda," Iris continued, "I do believe that Pearl was right. Didn't she tell you that this one looked fresh outta Bible school?"

"That was Mary-Rebecca," Belinda smirked and tilted the bottle to her glass again. She lifted it to her lips, pausing before she gulped it to add, "'cept I never saw one of them Bible school sweeties with jugs that big. Those yours, honey, or you got your laundry in there?"

Jenny felt rooted to the floor, and she knew hot color was rising in her cheeks. A normally enterprising and forthright girl who had never had the slightest trouble controlling either herself or the small children in her charge, she suddenly felt—even more than during her interview with Miss Liz—terribly inadequate and stupid. And monumentally out of place.

She was seized with a sudden impulse to just turn around and leave and never come back, to return to the familiar safety and sanity and propriety of St. Paul, of Aunt Victoria's dark, cool, quiet house, where people were soft-spoken and circumspect and nobody walked through the house in their underclothes. But her desire for revenge was greater than the unsettling fear she'd felt since entering Briarbirth, greater than the embarrassed discomfort she was feeling as the two girls taunted her.

It was little enough to endure if, in the end, she would see Ace Denton taken to the gallows.

"What's the matter, sugarpie?" Iris purred snidely. "Cat got your tongue? Or maybe you ain't as pure and precious as you let on. That it?"

51

Jenny was past the point of blushing. All the color drained from her face. She tried to move her feet, but they wouldn't budge. And then, just as Iris began to spew some puzzling new obscenity, Jenny heard the creaking swing of the kitchen door, followed by the boom of a male voice.

"All right, you two. Hop to it. Iris, you're a rat's nest! As usual. Comb that hair and get washed up. And Belinda, how many times have I got to tell you to quit runnin' around the house with your merchandise hangin' out!"

The girls seemed to hesitate for a moment, and the voice boomed again. "I said, move it!"

Iris snorted disdainfully but both girls exited, and Jenny turned around to see the face of her savior.

He was a tallish man of about fifty, dark-haired, dark-eyed, and graying at the temples. He would have looked distinguished had he not been wearing workman's clothing, and he smiled warmly at the ashen and obviously unnerved Jenny. *She looks like a little angel,* he thought to himself. *Like a little blond girl angel out of a painting. She's got no business here, none at all . . . Looks like I've got a new chick to look after.* "You'd be the new kitchen help, then?" he inquired.

She liked him immediately. He seemed sort of, well, fatherly; a little like the sheriff back in Fowlersville. "Yes sir," she answered, shyly returning his smile. "I'm Jenny. Jenny Templeton."

"Glad to meet you, Jenny." He took her small hand in his and shook it warmly. "My name's MacCauley, but everybody calls me Mac. You'd better, too!" He grinned. He could see he was going to have his hands full keeping the vultures off this one. He almost asked her what in the world she was doing here, but thought better of it. It wasn't the sort of question he'd want anybody to ask him, and he hadn't the right to ask it of anyone else.

"I'm kind of the handyman around here," he continued. "Take care of the milk cows and the chickens and the horses and the garden and such. Fix whatever breaks around the place. Throw out the rowdies. You have any trouble, you just call for Mac, and I'll take care of it, all right?"

She grinned at him. "Yes sir, Mister—I mean, Mac. I guess you'd be the one I should ask about my mare. I left her out front. Do you think it would be all right if I kept her here? I saw the two big barns from the road when I rode up and—"

"Don't worry, child. Miss Liz won't mind a bit. I'll go out right now and get your mare set up. She'll be in the first barn, the red one. We don't use the big cattle barn down the hill. It's left from when this place used to be part of a workin' farm."

She looked at him gratefully, not only because he'd offered his assistance, but because Fancy wouldn't have to stay in that big, frightening barn at the edge of the wood. "Thank you, Mac. Thank you very much."

"You bet, honey. Now tonight, when you're servin', just try and stay at arm's length from the customers as much as you can. I'll be around, and I'll make sure they know you're not one of the . . . the girls. But you'll have to watch 'em just the same. And like I said, if you get into trouble, just holler."

He poked his thumb over his shoulder, toward the

kitchen. "For now," he said grinning, "you'd better get out there and give ol' Bertha a hand before she starts raisin' the roof."

Mac watched Jenny walk through to the kitchen, then he strode out of the dining room, crossed the hall, and tapped at the office door. He didn't wait for an answer before he entered.

Liz McCaleb was alone in the dim room, seated at her desk and scribbling in a ledger book. She did not look up. "What is it, Mac?"

He pulled up a chair and sat down.

"You had no business hirin' that little blonde," he said.

Liz shrugged and glanced up at him before she went back to her figures. "Why? She wanted the job. She'll do fine."

"I'm sure she will. I'm sure she's a real good worker. I'm also sure she doesn't belong here, in a place like this. She's—"

"Everybody's a virgin once," Liz cut in. "Even I was, believe it or not." She smiled grimly, and turned up the lamp slightly before she began totting up another column of figures.

"It's more than that, Liz," Mac sighed. He hoped she'd understand. He knew she had a heart in there somewhere, if only he could find a way to it. "She's more than that, I think. She's . . . she's innocent," he added, remembering the conversation he'd just overheard, and the confused, embarrassed, helpless look on Jenny's face when he'd interrupted it.

"Nobody's *completely* innocent, Mac." Her voice

had taken on that cutting, sarcastic edge he detested.

Mac MacCauley stood up. "Just the same, I'm gonna keep my eye on her, Liz. And you'd better tell those girls to lay off her, too. Belinda and Iris, in particular. I don't like those two."

"They're popular girls, Mac. They turn more business a night than any of the others, and they're not fussy who with. I swear to God, either one of them would take on a barn rat for two bits." She paused and looked up. "They bring in a lot of money, Mac. As if it was any business of yours."

"I still don't like 'em."

"You don't have to, do you?"

"Just the same . . ." he said again, opening the door and stepping out into the hall, "I'm keepin' my eye on her."

The door closed softly behind him. Still seated at her desk, Liz McCaleb tallied another column of figures.

"Me, too, Mac," she muttered absently, never losing her place. "That little angel might just turn out to be worth a lot of money to me. All it takes is time . . ."

Jenny's first night in Mrs. Bramley's kitchen was both disturbing and exhausting. She carried out plate after plate of steaming, greasy food to cowboys, farmers, and merrymaking businessmen who seemed more intent on patting her fanny than on eating the gravy-smothered dinners she laid before them. For each plate she served, she collected a dime that went into the big glass jar at one end of the kitchen counter. At least, she thought, she couldn't confuse the orders, and there was some mercy in that. Every plate that emerged from Bertha Bramley's kitchen was exactly the same, no substitutions. Tonight she was serving fried chicken, mashed sweet potatoes, stewed onions and peas—or so Jenny thought. It was hard to tell what was under all that gravy.

The evening thundered by in a blur of deafening sensations: the unrelenting din of the piano as Harvey assaulted its chipped, worn keys; the snatching, moving hands both calloused and soft that seemed to snake out of nowhere, reaching toward her to clutch at her sleeve, her hem—trying to touch her in places where they had no business; the scantily clad, painted women draped lewdly over grinning, grimy farmhands who smelled of manure and tilled earth; the staccato clack of the whirling roulette wheel down the hall; the constantly changing, leering faces; the odors of heavy food, spilled beer, and vomit; and the thud and clatter of heavy boots and high heels traipsing up and down the big staircase just outside the dining room.

The men must have come in from all over the countryside, for during the evening it seemed to Jenny that she was serving more customers than the total population of Green Mule, Missouri. Mac stuck fairly close around the dining room and bar during the evening, and although several times he tactfully extricated her from a physically threatening situation, he could not prevent those whiskied, whispered innuendos he could not hear.

Men said things to her that night that she did not understand, words she'd never heard. Over the din of

56

raised voices and laughter and the unrelenting battery of old Harvey's fingers on the upright, they suggested situations that she could not even begin to imagine, and she ended her night's work tired, confused, and flustered.

It was past three in the morning before she finished drying the last dish. The crowd had thinned considerably by the time she climbed the back stairs, although, as she passed the second floor landing, she could hear a few muffled giggles interspersed with groans and the creaking of bedsprings. She was far too exhausted even to tend to Fancy, and as she sank into the narrow bed in her tiny, windowless, third floor room, she hoped that Mac had fed the little mare and bedded her down properly.

Three

Too tired to dream, Jenny slept through the night until the cook's fat fingers poked and prodded her awake.

"It's nigh on nine o'clock, missy," Mrs. Bramley admonished her, her perpetual scowl firmly in place. "Them whores may be able to sleep in 'til afternoon, but you 'n me's got work to do."

She turned loose of Jenny's aching shoulder and thudded across the room to the door. "Now get crackin'! I got a ton of sheets biled up out back, and you've gotta get 'em strung up on the lines 'fore we start cookin' for the day."

She slammed the door behind her, leaving a groggy and bewildered Jenny to drag her sore and still-exhausted body out of the small hard bed.

Jenny dressed and washed up as quickly as she could, donning a shirtwaist and skirt over her underclothes. She wore no corset. After leaving

59

Fowlersville and her father's grave, she had tossed them all away. Although she had worn them during her stay in St. Paul to please Aunt Victoria, she hated them. And she certainly didn't need to wear one. Her body was young and firm, and at barely twenty inches, her waist was tiny. But right now she wished she hadn't been so eager to discard them. A nice whalebone corset would have provided an impenetrable barrier to the roving hands she'd have to dodge again this evening.

The pink dress she had worn the day before had been her best, but now it was nearly ruined: spattered with grease and gravy stains and grime from the snatching fingers of Miss Liz's customers. She had another dress, pale green, plus three skirts and five shirtwaists to her name, and decided that the separates would not only be easier to launder than either of the dresses, but possibly less inviting to the customer's wandering fingers.

She began to dress her hair, but when Mrs. Bramley's bellowed "Jenny!" boomed up the back stairwell, she simply pulled her shining, straw-blond tresses up into a long horse's tail and secured it with a ribbon of the same pale blue as her shirtwaist. Casting a final glance at herself in the cracked mirror, she decided that she looked washed-out, tired, and undeniably plain.

"Gaw*dammit*, girl!" came Mrs. Bramley's exasperated roar.

Dropping the hairbrush, Jenny scurried out the door and down the back stairs.

*   *   *

When Mrs. Bramley said that she had a ton of sheets "biled up," she'd been serious. Briarbirth's backyard was now home to three steady fires, over each of which hung a big black kettle. The kettles were filled with bed clothes boiling noisily in an acrid roil of water and lye soap. Mrs. Bramley was in the side yard, bent over a wringer and cranking its handle, squeezing steaming wash water out of another load of sheets. She pointed at several baskets of linen she'd already run through the wringer, then to the rows of clothesline further down the slope.

"Get crackin', missy," she said before she threw the not insubstantial weight of her shoulder against the crank.

Jenny hung towels and sheets, and more sheets still until the steaming black kettles and Mrs. Bramley's baskets were emptied, and then she went back to the beginning, taking down the linens that had already dried in the bright sunshine. Several times she glanced longingly down the slope toward the red barn where Fancy would be waiting. In the past weeks, the dainty bay mare had become her only friend, and she pined to pay her a visit, to make certain that she was comfortably fixed. But there were so many sheets, and she could just imagine the scope and tenor of Mrs. Bramley's wrath if she were to come outside and find her gone. She sighed and tugged at another one of the seemingly thousands of wooden clothes pins.

It was well past lunchtime when she pulled the last fluttering linens from the line.

Mrs. Bramley had long since disappeared inside the house, and after Jenny lugged the final basket of sun-dried sheets up the steps to the back porch, she went in the creaking back door, through the rear hall and into the kitchen. She'd had no breakfast, and she longed to get off her feet and have something to eat, even if it would more than likely be dripping with lumpy gravy and floating in grease.

She found a red-faced Mrs. Bramley leaning over the stove top, stirring something thick and white. After a moment, Jenny recognized the odor as oatmeal.

"Took you long enough," was the cook's only comment as Jenny, bedraggled and hoping for lunch, slumped into a chair at the wide kitchen table.

"I'm sorry," Jenny said. She rested her forehead in her hands. "I went as fast as I could. They're all dry now. The baskets are out back on the porch."

"Hmph," Mrs. Bramley snorted, banging the white-coated spoon on the side of the pot. "Well, don't get comf'terble. Girls'll be comin' down any time now. Soon as Mac gets his butt in here with the—"

"Somebody mention my name?" came a voice from the back porch, followed by Mac himself. He was carrying a basket of freshly gathered, still-warm eggs and a small ham. He plopped them down on the counter top and winked at Jenny.

She grinned back. She did have one friend here, she thought, and she was grateful for him.

"Get off your duff, missy," Mrs. Bramley broke in. "Break out some plates and silverware. Got to get that table set. Them whores'll be driftin' in here any time now, and they're gonna want breakfast. Hope you're faster settin' table than bringin' in sheets."

She dropped thick dollops of freshly churned butter into a mammoth cast-iron skillet. The butter sizzled on contact and melted into a bubbling yellow pool.

Jenny pushed away from the table and began to gather plates, saucers, cups, and flatware, as Mrs. Bramley cracked egg after egg into the frying pan.

"Speakin' of laundry, Bertha," drawled Mac, leaning casually in the doorway, "I can't remember you ever havin' Saturday linens done this early." He winked at Jenny again.

"Don't remember askin' your opinion, Mac," the cook growled. She shot him a nasty look before she sank a long, sharp knife into the ham and, muttering, began to cut it into thin slices.

Meg Sweetwater and Shirley Mae Vinton came through the far door. Meg seemed cheerful and somewhat expectant. She was freshly scrubbed and humming softly to herself.

Shirley Mae appeared to be wearing last night's makeup, and the greasy black goo she used to line her eyes had smeared into dark and drooping half-moons beneath her lower lashes.

"Good mornin', ladies," Mac said cheerfully as Meg slid into one chair and Shirley Mae slumped into another.

"That's your opinion," scowled the prostitute with the ruined face. "Ain't nothin' good about any mornin', far as I can see."

"First of all," Mrs. Bramley interjected, "it ain't mornin', it's halfway into the afternoon. Second, I don't know how you can see anythin', Shirley Mae." She slid a pair of slippery fried eggs onto the grizzled redhead's plate. "Don't you ever wash your face?"

Shirley Mae scowled at her. "Clean or not, it's a sight better than yours, you fat old cow. Least I've still got my figure."

Mrs. Bramley spun around with surprising lightness of foot, the spatula raised in her hand. "Listen, you two-bit drunken hag, even on your best day, you couldn't—"

"Ladies! Ladies!" Mac stepped into the breach. "Let's not start this again, all right? For once, let's just all have a nice quiet breakfast . . ."

Grumbling, Bertha Bramley lowered the raised spatula and went back to her stove. She began to slap slices of ham into another pan.

Jenny found that she'd unconsciously pressed herself back against the sideboard. Never had she met such a bizarre and volatile collection of people. She didn't know which group disturbed her the most—the customers or the staff.

She felt Mac's big hand on her shoulder and looked up at him. He nodded at her reassuringly, smiled, and pointed wordlessly at the remaining dishes she still held in her hands.

She went back to setting the long table as a few more girls trickled in, yawning and rumpled. When she came to the place next to Meg, the brown-eyed strawberry blonde was still humming to herself, slicing the ham Mrs. Bramley had just slapped onto her plate into tiny pieces and dipping them into running yellow egg yolks. She smiled up at Jenny, and in a tiny, birdlike voice she half-chirped, half-whispered, "Good mornin', Miss Jenny. Could I trouble you for some coffee?"

*   *   *

She was washing the breakfast dishes when she heard the slide, then slam of the dining room's double pocket doors, followed by Agnes's voice. "Heads up!" she shouted. "Loose bird!"

"What in the world?" Jenny pulled her hands from the soapy water to go investigate.

"You just keep doin' what you're doin', missy," the cook growled. She left the table, where she'd been rolling out dough for pie crust, and set a chair against the swinging door to the dining room. From the other side, Jenny could hear a swoop and a swish and then *Howdy, cowboy! Bugger off! Howdy, cowboy!* Then there was the sound of a chair toppling over and Agnes's voice, cursing.

"Gawdamn bird," Mrs. Bramley grumbled as she returned to her pie crusts. She dusted flour over the expanse of dough before she attacked it with the rolling pin again. "That Agnes turns him out in the dinin' room couple times a week. Says he needs the exercise." She snorted derisively. "Exercise, my butt! Sombitch flew straight for that door last week, banged it open, and flew right into a four-layer cake I'd just got the icin' on. He does that again, an' so help me Hannah, he's gonna find himself on the menu . . ."

Evening came, and with it an even larger crowd of men than the night before. Friday and Saturday nights were the busiest of the week, Mac told her. She'd already made it through Friday, and if she could manage to last through this evening, she'd have the rest of the week to get her bearings.

By this time, she was almost accustomed to the din

and the smells, and was fairly adept at scurrying through the bar and dining room, moving swiftly between the tables just out of arm's reach. She tried, when she could, to sneak up on the diners from the rear, serving them quickly over their shoulders so that they could not reach an arm out to grab at her; and for the most part, the ploy worked fairly well. That was, until one drunken farmhand surprised her by raising his head abruptly and playfully attempting to bite her breast. With a shriek of surprise and indignation, she pulled back just in time, but his slobbery lips left a wet whiskey stain on her shirtwaist. Mac appeared from out of nowhere, and as Jenny scurried, blushing hotly, back to the kitchen, she could see him scowl as he lectured the farmer.

By ten o'clock the activity in the dining room had slowed somewhat, and Mrs. Bramley pulled her away from waitressing to wash dishes. She was standing over the basin, her hands immersed in hot water, when she heard men's voices coming from the back hall.

She was frightened. Customers were supposed to come in the front of the house, not the rear, and she was alone in the kitchen. Mac was out by the bar, and Mrs. Bramley had deserted her, probably for the quiet and solitude of the lady's privy.

And they'd come in so quietly; she'd heard no scrape of boots on the back porch, no creak of the door. She stiffened, ready to bolt for the dining room and Mac. But instead of coming straight ahead through the pantry and into the kitchen, the men turned down the dimly lit rear hall, toward the back staircase. As they rounded the corner, she caught a glimpse of two faces. Meg Sweetwater's beau, Scar Cooksey, was unmistakable. Meg must have known they were coming tonight. It would certainly explain her detached cheerfulness at the breakfast table.

The other man whose face she saw for a flickering instant could be none other than Billy Dodge. At a distance, the Dodge brothers had seemed quite similar: both were about five feet ten inches, and both were blond and blue-eyed, but at this range young Billy could not be mistaken for his older brother. The cocky grin of youth broke up the otherwise blank, unlined surface of his face, and his cheeks were downy and smooth.

There were three other men whose faces she could not make out in the gloom, but she knew that Billy's brother Andy would be there in the shadows, along with Rafe Langley and the reason she was here—Ace Denton.

When the realization hit her that she was standing not fifteen feet away from him—a murdering, ruthless outlaw worth more, dead or alive, than many farmers would make in a lifetime—a wave of cold shivers ran up her spine. For now that she was this close to him, this close to taking her revenge, she realized how ill-prepared she was.

She was in the right place and she had a gun upstairs, but she had never determined just exactly *how* to accomplish her revenge. If this was a frequent hideout of his, how could she be certain the local law didn't already know it and simply look the other way? And if the law couldn't help her, then what? Was she capable of shooting him in cold blood, even if she could find the opportunity? She honestly didn't know, and once again—even more painfully, this time—she wondered what in the world she had gotten herself into.

An hour later she was distractedly clearing off a particularly disgusting table in the dining room when Mrs. Bramley called her out to the kitchen. The cook, lobster-faced and sweaty from a long evening over a hot stove, pointed Jenny toward a gargantuan tray on the breakfast table.

"Private party upstairs in the playroom," she growled curtly. "Get that up to 'em. Keep your mouth shut while you're up there. Just serve 'em and get back down. Got more dishes for you to do."

Jenny eyed the tray. It was the largest in the kitchen, and it was piled high and draped with a red-checkered linen. She wondered if she'd be able to lift it, let alone carry it to the second floor. And she wondered to whom she'd be carrying it. She could only think of one group of people in the house who might be holed up in the playroom and classified as a "private party."

"Yes, ma'am," she said with some trepidation, and bent to pick it up. Fortunately, it was not so heavy as it looked. The food beneath the cloth must be sandwiches and cold cuts rather than a collection of Mrs. Bramley's usual rock-heavy hot dinners. She started toward the dining room door.

"Hold it, missy," the cook called, stopping her just before she pushed the swinging door open with her hip. "Use the back stairs."

Jenny shrugged and trudged back across the kitchen. If Mrs. Bramley didn't want the other customers to see the tray going up, it must be for Ace Denton and his bunch. By the time she reached the landing and started up the stairs, her knees were shaking. At last she would see—close up—the face of her father's killer.

The upstairs service corridor was dark, and she had to feel her way until she turned the corner into the gallery, and into what was not light, but filtered gloom.

The second floor of the house contained eight bedrooms, one monstrous bathroom, and the play-room. They opened off a wide, picture-hung gallery, at the center of which was the head of the grand staircase. She knew about the playroom, for after she'd been sent upstairs earlier that afternoon to deliver linens, the cook had begrudged her a bit of its history. The playroom had originally been just that—a place for the recreation of the former owner's children. Miss Liz had converted it into a private gaming room, and two large, felt-covered card tables, a billiard table, and a private bar had replaced hobby horses, dollhouses, and a miniature battleground for tin soldiers.

Precariously balancing the clumsy tray, Jenny tapped at the door. A man, his face cloaked in shadows, answered and ushered her in. "Food's here," he said, and as she followed him into the light, she recognized him as Andy Dodge.

All five outlaws were in the room, and all five were armed. Baby-faced Billy, a gun strapped to each thigh, was at the closest table, leaning back in his chair. His boots were propped on the tabletop, and he was nursing a bottle of rye. Another man sat beside him, his back to her, casually twirling an empty shot glass in one hand, dealing out sets of faceup poker hands with the other: Rafe Langley.

In the far corner, half in the shadows, she could see Scar Cooksey. He was sitting in a narrow rocking chair, and he was slowly rocking back and forth. Meg Sweetwater was sitting on his lap, straddling him. They were kissing.

Ace Denton was across the room, standing against the bar. He was leaning on one elbow, and he was smirking at her. He was dark, like his posters, and their description of him fit: six feet tall, lean muscular build, mid-thirties. He had the cruel, cold look of a born killer. It was even more intense here—close up and in the light—than when she'd first seen him across that deserted barn. Something in the way he stared made her skin crawl, her stomach lurch. She knew then that if she could only find the opportunity, she could gladly send this man to the gallows.

She looked away, afraid that hatred was shining from her face, and turned toward the table where Billy and Rafe sat. Without speaking, she put down the tray and removed its red-checked cover.

"Hey Scar!" Billy yelled toward the dark corner. "Food's here!"

"Hold your water, kid," she heard him mumble, and she could hear a new sound from the corner, something louder than the chair's wooden rockers moving rhythmically back and forth on the oak floor. It was Meg, breathing heavily, as if she were running hard.

Jenny stole a peek. She liked Meg, and she was afraid she might be hurt or ill. But she didn't look ill.

70

She looked, from what Jenny could see through the murk, exceedingly strange. And Scar had the oddest expression on his ruined face. Under her breath, Jenny mumbled, "'Curiouser and curiouser . . . ,'" then another voice sounded, and her eyes were irresistibly drawn toward its owner.

"Well, what have we here?" It was the man across the table—Rafe Langley. The sound of his voice was even deeper, more melodious than she remembered, and she was drawn toward it. She felt herself leaning a bit further over the table as she raised her eyes.

And then she saw his face. His hair was dark, nearly black, and his eyes were like coal, as if he had no irises—only black, bottomless pupils. He was deeply tanned and his hands were large and finely made: clean-knuckled with long, strong fingers. His face was freshly shaven—not stubbly like Ace Denton's—and there was the deep crease of a dimple in each cheek. His cheekbones were high and wide, and his jaw was square and strong with muscle. There were tiny lines at the outside corners of his eyes, and when he suddenly, disarmingly grinned at her, she knew they'd been put there not by time but by laughter.

He was the most handsome man she had ever seen.

He devoured her in one long, intense look: the rich, straw-gold hair pulled back from her face and trailing down her back; the fine, high forehead and daintily arched brows; the full, pink, pouting lips that seemed to beg for kissing; the creamy, flawless skin and those huge, thickly lashed green eyes . . . He couldn't imagine where Liz found her—she was far too pretty and too virginal to be working here.

He watched the way her full, high breasts pressed against the confines of her shirtwaist, and suddenly he was seized by an overwhelming desire to hold them in his hands, to see just what shade of pink their nipples might be. He never took advantage of the eager and chronically available girls here at Liz's place. Well, almost never. There had been that one night he was too drunk to know better and somehow, the next morning he'd awakened in Iris's bed. The memory still made him shudder.

But this girl was something entirely different. She seemed too delicate, too perfect to be real. And he'd caught that little phrase she'd mumbled. It would appear that she'd read more than dime novels in her short life. He knew the book. He had a smudged copy of it himself, on the bottom of the pile of books he kept down below . . .

He'd make an exception for this girl, he decided. He'd have her, no matter how much she cost.

Jenny could feel color rise and burn in her cheeks as he looked at her. How, she wondered, could just a look from a man make her feel so . . . She had nothing with which to compare it. She only knew it made her feel strange and warm, and somehow naked.

She dropped her eyes and nervously began to unload the tray. But as she set the last plate onto the table, a noise from the shadowed corner made her turn and look.

Meg Sweetwater was writhing on Scar's lap. Her head was thrown back. Tiny wheezing, cooing noises issued from her mouth. Her back was arched, and her hips wriggled and squirmed as Scar rocked her back and forth, his hands clutching at her petticoated hips.

Jenny's blush burned brighter when Meg suddenly began to trill: a short-lived, high, keening sound that was followed by an abrupt, gasping intake of air, and from Scar, a series of short, muffled grunts.

"Crikey, Scar, how come you always got to take dessert afore dinner when Meggie's around?" Billy laughed drunkenly. "Maybe if you ain't tired yet you could take on this little—"

With a horrible feeling that she had just witnessed something terribly, incredibly personal, Jenny unceremoniously abandoned the empty tray. As it clattered to the floor, she darted past a leering Andy Dodge and out into the dark of the hall.

She slammed the door behind her and ran ten feet down the gallery before she leaned against the wall and pressed her hands to burning cheeks. *Oh, God,* she thought, *I've got to do it soon. I've got to turn him in and get away! They're all crazy here!*

She was horribly out of her element. Meg's inexplicable gyrations had both shocked and frightened her, and even now, in the dimness of the corridor, she was surrounded by the muffled sounds of passion: sounds she did not understand. And the face of Rafe Langley—and more so, the way he had looked at her across that table—had made her feel somehow sinful and wrong, joyous and expectant all at once, and she didn't know why.

"Waiting for me?"

The voice—*his* voice—spoke next to her ear. He had followed her out, crept up upon her. Although she was startled, his low, sensuous tone made her legs feel too insubstantial to carry her away.

She looked up into those endlessly deep, dark eyes. His face was inches from hers, and he was smiling. It was not so much a friendly smile as an expression of intent.

"No, I . . . Excuse me," she stammered. "I was just going downstairs. Back to the kitchen."

"No need for you to leave so soon, little one," he said, still smiling. He put his hands against the wall on either side of her shoulders, casually but effectively blocking her exit, caging her between his arms.

"Why don't you and I find an empty room and . . ."

Her eyes grew even rounder and she gasped. He thought she was one of *them:* one of Miss Liz's girls! He wanted to look at her and touch her and maybe even . . . She swallowed hard. She could call out to Mac, but he was downstairs, too close to Harvey's incessant piano to hear her. She was on her own.

"Oh no! You don't understand! I don't work here. I mean, I do work here, but I don't—I mean, I'm not—I mean—"

He lifted one hand from the wall to gently brush a stray wisp of flaxen hair away from her face.

"'I just work in the kitchen," she finished.

"Of course you do," he whispered. He stroked her cheek with his knuckles. "It's much more provocative to be the only clothed female in a house of whores, isn't it? And such a beautiful girl, too . . ." He dropped his hand to finger the collar of her shirtwaist. "Are you as pretty under these things as I imagine?" He continued to smile, but his eyes swept down to linger at her bosom before they came back to

74

meet her gaze.

"I don't care how much you cost, little one. I'll pay." He bent to kiss her forehead, brushing it with his lips.

She felt her spine turn to jelly, but she pushed against his chest with her palms, trying to make him understand.

Instead, he grinned down at her. "That's very good," he remarked. "But you can drop the act."

He trailed two fingers along her shoulder. "What's your name, little one?"

"J-J-Jenny. And please—really, I—"

Without warning, he kissed her quite forcefully, cutting off her protest as he covered her mouth with his. He hadn't much patience with games and he'd had enough of this one.

But when he realized that her teeth were clamped together against him, that her eyes were wide and frightened, and that she was shivering not with passion but with fear, he pulled away.

It was true then. This was no sweetly cunning act of virginal seduction put on for his benefit. She truly was innocent. She didn't even seem to know how to kiss—or be kissed.

"You really are Alice in Wonderland, aren't you?" he whispered. "I'm sorry, Jenny. I didn't believe you." His fingers soothed her brow. "But I *am* going to kiss you."

"Please—please don't," she breathed. Despite his mesmerizing voice, Jenny was terrified. This was no Minnesota schoolboy asking to walk her home from church or offering her a few marbles for a peek inside her panties—this was a grown man: strong, experi-

75

enced, and undoubtedly quite dangerous.

She wanted to get away from him, to be by herself. She was confused enough already without adding this to it, but she seemed incapable of flight. The dark intensity of his gaze, the silky sound of his voice, and his subtle, musky scent were flooding her with trembling waves of a mysterious new anticipation. "I-I don't—" she stammered, "I couldn't—"

He kissed her once more, this time gently brushing her closed lips with his. He flicked her pout with his tongue, teased and tickled the corners of her mouth, nipped gently at her lower lip. He felt her submitting gradually to his attentions as she began to kiss him back: chaste maiden's kisses that slowly became longer and more leisurely as he coaxed her untried mouth.

His fingers gently stroked her throat and the line of her jaw, and finally she began to relax, parting her lips the tinest bit. Artfully, he slipped the tip of his tongue within her pout, teasing her until her small white teeth separated just enough to grant him access to the moist warmth inside.

Jenny's senses reeled as the outlaw sweetly, leisurely plundered her mouth. He tasted faintly of a sweetness she thought must be bourbon, and she wondered if just this secondhand trace of whiskey could be responsible for the giddy trembling in her limbs. Warm shivers began to tingle their way up and down her spine, and unconsciously she reached out to him, gently touching his waist with her fingertips. And when she did, a small inner voice told her that as heady as his kisses were, there was something else: something secret and ancient and primal that would follow quite naturally, something that would make her shiver and quake even more than the bliss he had already given her.

Slowly, he pulled his lips from hers, whispering, "So now you've been kissed, Jenny."

Breathless, she could not speak. She could only look up at him with half-lidded eyes. Her swollen lips were slightly parted, still tingling; and she leaned heavily against the wall behind her.

He traced the line of her lower lip with his fingers as he slipped one hand between her back and the darkly paneled wall, curling it around her tiny waist. "There's much more I could teach you, little one. There's much more I *am* going to teach you. But only me, Jenny, only me."

His fingers slid from her lips to the collar of her shirtwaist and began, deftly, to free the row of buttons there. Once again she was afraid, and she squirmed against his encircling arm. "No," she whimpered, "please don't!"

But her pleas had no effect. He tried to tell himself that he was pushing his luck, that he was moving too quickly, but the need to touch her—just touch her—was stronger. As he slipped the last button free and gently tugged her shirttails and camisole from her skirt, he whispered, "Hush, little one. Don't worry, I won't hurt you. I promise I won't make love to you until you're ready. Until you ask."

Make love to me? she thought as he laid back the halves of pale blue blouse to expose her camisole. *If this isn't making love to me, what is?*

Just the thought that he was seeing her in her undergarments and that he was so near and that he was going to kiss her again at any moment had brought on a new and unexpected sensation: a burning, tingly warmth high between her legs, and with it, a strange, nameless yearning. Her breasts, so near his long, deft fingers, felt swollen; and her nipples had suddenly become so sensitive that it seemed she could count every thread in the weave of the thin fabric that covered them.

He kissed her again.

This time, without thinking, she opened her mouth to him readily. And as she did, she felt him gently cup her right breast through the thin cotton of her camisole. Her bosom heaved slightly at the touch, and she took a deep, sudden gulp of air as rippling shivers spread through her, their source the warmth of his hand. Unbidden, her arms floated up to rest lightly on his broad shoulders, and he took this as a signal to proceed with his seduction.

She felt his hand slip downward, abandoning her breast to boldly slide beneath the hem of her camisole. She shuddered as his warm, sure fingers brushed the bare skin of her stomach, traced the line of her skirt's waistband, then trailed higher to stroke the full underside of her breast. She gasped as he cupped her again, this time with the full heat of flesh upon flesh, and began to gently manipulate her swollen, aching nipple.

Suddenly there was the sound of laughter, of approaching footsteps.

Her lidded eyes jolted open, all passion flooding away at the thought of discovery. Frantically, she dropped her hands to push at his chest.

But he did not release her. Neither did he stop his

kiss, nor remove his hand from beneath her garment. He merely tightened his grip about her waist and effortlessly lifted her off her feet, taking four long steps that carried them around the bend of the corridor. No one would interrupt them here. No rooms opened off this hall. There was only the second floor landing of the service stairs.

Slowly, he felt her begin to relax as she realized what he had done. He eased his lips from hers and began to rain soft kisses on her eyelids, her forehead, and down the sleek column of her throat; and then, there in the darkness, she felt him lift her camisole up over her breasts and gently, sweetly, take the nipple his fingers had just abandoned into his mouth.

A tiny sound escaped her as he gently teased the tight, throbbing tip with his lips, then laved it broadly with his tongue. His fingers sought and found the other nipple, and brazenly he conquered and inflamed it to a tight, pounding bead.

As he began to suckle her breast as might a child, she felt herself approaching something undeniable and unknown: something for which she had no explanation or definition.

Something beyond words.

As if struck deaf and blind, she was oblivious to her surroundings, sensing only his nearness and his touch and their mesmerizing effect. She began to slump against him, but he lifted her, steadied her, held her in position upright against the wall, gauging her rasping breaths as he alternately lapped, nipped, and sucked at the swollen summit of her shuddering breast. *She could not be more perfect,* he thought, *more beautiful, more responsive . . .*

With a wave of longing that he knew he would have to control, at least for the present, he realized that she was the one. He'd wanted her the instant he'd seen her face, but now, after hearing the sultry music of her voice and looking into the clear emerald of her eyes; after witnessing her response to him and feeling her writhe beneath his touch . . .

He'd had many women in his life—more than he could count or remember. But never had he been more certain of anything than that he had to have this girl, this child-woman, forever; and by whatever means were necessary. And he knew that when the time was right to take her, he would fit within her as perfectly as if she were molded for him.

For the moment, he would be content to bring her, gently and without trauma, to her first fruition. He would make her dependent upon him for this feeling. He would make her want him, need him; and finally, he would make her love him.

Above him, her breathing became more rapid and frenzied. She made a tiny cooing sound and he thought, *It's time, little Jenny*. Slowly, he rolled one nipple between his thumb and forefinger, deftly twisting and compressing it nearly to the point of pain; then releasing, only to repeat the process as his lips and tongue teased the other.

And when he was certain she was tottering helplessly on the brink of rapture, he pulled his hand away, pulled his head back; so that nothing touched her except the barest tips of his thumb and middle finger as they gently tethered one pebble-hard tip, and just the edges of his front teeth where they restrained the other.

He heard her moan softly: a little whimper. And then simultaneously and with great care, he bit and pinched those precious pink beads of flesh.

She could never have anticipated her body's reaction to that last sublime pressure. Her body seemed to simultaneously burst, melt, solidify; and for a moment, she was certain that she had died: that her spirit was exiting her body and that God, in his infinite wisdom, had saved the best for last.

She opened her mouth to cry out, only to find it suddenly covered by the outlaw's lips as he swallowed her surprised, ecstatic moans. As well as, she thought, her soul.

He held her there in the night-filled hallway until she recovered herself, and then he brushed her lips with his and smiled down at her. She suddenly realized that she was not only still alive, but that she was partly naked and, in a tardy fit of embarrassed confusion, she tried to cover herself. But he stayed her hands, cupping a breast in each hand and brushing a kiss over her forehead before he lowered her camisole and carefully rebuttoned her shirtwaist.

"Next time, Jenny," he said softly, "we'll go further."

"N-next time?" she managed to whisper. *Further?* she thought. *Can there be more? Is it possible that a person can feel this way more than once and live?*

"Don't be afraid," he whispered, misjudging the perplexed look on her face. "I won't make love to you until you ask. That's a promise. But remember: for you, there is only me."

He was slipping his fingers beneath the waistband of her skirt, neatly tucking the tails of her blouse

81

inside, when bootsteps rounded the corner.

"Ace," came a whisper in the darkness. It was Billy Dodge. "Ace, you out here?"

The man she had identified as Rafe Langley—the man who had just touched her, pleasured her in an incredibly intimate manner, the man who was reclothing her in a dark hallway—stood up.

"Yeah, Billy," said the man who had murdered her father. "Be right with you."

Four

Miss Liz tapped on Mary-Rebecca's door for the fifth time in as many minutes. "Time's up, Frank. Mary-Rebecca, you have another caller downstairs, and he's impatient. I mean it this time!"

From the other side of the door there came a muffled giggling, followed by Mary-Rebecca's flutey voice. "Yes'm, Miss Liz."

Arms folded across her bosom, the madam waited in the dimly lit gallery. A moment later a tousled young man, intently tucking shirttails into half-buttoned trousers, opened the door and nearly crashed into her.

"Oh!" he gulped. "Sorry, ma'am."

She steadied him with a spangled hand. "Now you listen to me, Frank Mitchell. 'Sorry' isn't going to do it. This is the third time running you've overstayed with Mary-Rebecca. Next week, why don't you do the right thing—pay her for a whole hour so you can take your time." She tried not to smile. Frank, who wasn't more than twenty (and who was obviously smitten with Mary-Rebecca), blushed bright red. In his hurry, he'd buttoned his shirt unevenly, and now he was trying to figure out what to do with the extra fabric and button hole at his collar.

"I'm sorry, ma'am. I'd love the spend the whole evening with her, but . . ." He was still fiddling with his shirt front. Miss Liz made a little clucking sound, brushed his hands away, and began rebuttoning it for him.

"Honestly, Frank," she chided softly. She rebuttoned him as far as his waist, then patted his belt buckle. "There. You can do the rest of it yourself."

"Yes'm." He tugged out the tails and began to work at them. "I'd like to, really I would. But you know Old Man Heirrick don't pay me hardly nothin' at the hardware. If he did, I'd . . . I'd . . ." He tucked the repaired shirt back into his pants and hoisted up his suspenders. "I'd marry her, that's what I'd do!" He announced it with more gusto than she'd expected.

"Of course you would, Frank." She patted his shoulder. "But for the time being . . ."

"Yes, Miss Liz. I won't overstay next time."

"That's a good boy, Frank," she said as he walked away, toward the stairs. "Regards to your papa."

"Yes'm."

"And Frank?"

His hand was on the balustrade. "Ma'am?"

"Would you tell Gus Larson that he can come on up?"

Crestfallen, young Frank nodded and started slowly down the stairs. He wouldn't need to pass the message along. Gus Larson was already bounding up the steps two at a time.

A wide grin splitting his sunburnt face, Gus skidded to a halt in front of Mary-Rebecca's door, nodded to Miss Liz and, clutching his floppy farmer's hat to his chest, tapped at the door. "It's me, baby. Gus," he announced.

"C'mon in, honey," came the answer. "I've been pinin' away all evenin', just hopin' you'd drop by."

Gus scurried inside and firmly latched the door behind him. As Mary-Rebecca's giggles floated out into the gallery, Miss Liz shook her head. "If I were you, Frank, I'd start saving my money," she muttered.

"You busy?"

She turned toward the voice. The playroom door was open a few inches, and when she saw him peering out, she smiled. "Never too busy for you, honey."

She walked toward him, but before she could enter the playroom, Ace stepped out into the gallery and squired her around the corner to the spot where, a few hours earlier, he'd held Jenny in his arms.

"The new girl," he began with an eagerness that made Liz a little nervous, "the little blonde you've got working in the kitchen. Who is she?"

Liz sighed. "Now, Marcus, I don't think you ought to—"

"What do you know about her?"

The madam pulled herself erect, tilted her head back, and stared at him down her patrician nose. "Why?"

He grinned. "Don't pull that Queen of the May act on me, Lizzie. Doesn't work, you know. Who is she?

What's she doing here?"

"Oh, all right," Liz snorted. "I don't know much really. She showed up yesterday, looking for work."

Ace arched a brow.

"Kitchen work. She says she's eighteen, and she seems a bright child, except . . ." She made a small sound of disgust and began to tug distractedly at the bangles on her bracelet. "She's not from around here; least, I've never seen her before. Neither has Mac, although you'd never know it." She pursed her lips. "He's spent the last two days hovering over her like a long-lost uncle . . ."

Ace leaned back against the wall, rocking slightly on his heels, and grinned at her. "Good for Mac. She's beautiful, isn't she? I mean, really beautiful. And there's something about her, something behind those eyes . . ."

Miss Liz pursed her lips. "Honestly, Marcus. She *is* a pretty child; almost astoundingly so, I'll admit. But I should think she's just a tad too naive for your tastes. A tad too young, too. But she does have a certain quality about her, doesn't she? A lovely, well, *freshness*. I imagine she'll turn quite a pretty penny for me."

His smile vanished. "I thought she worked for Bertha. Period."

"For now. Remember whose job she's taking over."

Just then they heard Pearl's high titter approaching from around the bend in the hall. "Easy, Slim!" she was giggling. "Wait'll we get in the—" And then there was the sound of a door clicking closed.

Ace scowled. "No. Jenny's different."

"They all seem different in the beginning, Marcus." Liz touched his brow, brushing black hair away from his forehead. "I'll grant you that this little Jenny is innocent now. In fact, I have to admit that I've never met anyone quite so . . ." She looked faintly disgusted. "Well, frankly, I'm not entirely certain that she understands what business we're in. But that'll change. And when it does, well . . . I've already had several offers for her. One that I'm giving some serious consideration."

"No, Liz. You can't—"

She pulled herself up straight, hands on her hips, once again regal and fully in charge. "It's none of your damn business, Marcus Denton. This is my place, not yours. Though God knows, the way you and those others pop in and out of here, a body'd think you owned a part interest. Forget about her, Marcus. If what you want is a little sport, you know that any girl here'd give her eyeteeth for an hour with you. Besides, I can't see what her future matters to you, considering the way yours is headed."

He looked away. He hated it when she was right.

"When the time comes—and trust me, it always does," Liz continued, "Jenny'll make her own decision. You may be long gone by then. Besides"— she smiled coldly—"if that reward on you goes up much higher, I'll be tempted to turn you in myself. And I can't see that your little Jenny would be much good to you after you've kept an appointment with the gallows."

"That's not funny, Liz."

"It wasn't meant to be. It was meant to remind you of who you are. Of the way things are."

His face was grim now. "You're right. But maybe not much longer. You and Mac been watching the papers?"

Her brow furrowed. "Yes, but—"

There was a crash of shattering glass. Miss Liz stepped back into the main corridor as shouts followed the sounds of breakage: muffled at first, then loud and furious. Keeping to the shadows, Ace followed her in time to see Iris run out into the gallery. She was stark naked and screaming, and she was followed directly by a pot-bellied, half-drunk, pantsless cowpoke.

"Goddamn worthless slattern!" he ranted, red-faced. He was hopping on one foot, forcing his boot through a trouser leg. "Stinkin' whore! You bit me, you rotten—"

"I'll bite you again if you don't pay up, you ugly toad-sucker! Nobody walks out on *me* without payin'! 'Specially after I was all cordial-like and took it up the—"

"I told you to say them words, you cheap piece'a baggage!" He'd gotten both boots through and worried his pants up to his knees. "You didn't say the words while I was doin' it, and I ain't payin'!"

Iris dove at him again and clawed at his pants pocket. She didn't get his wallet, but she did succeed in knocking him to the floor.

"You fat jackass!" she shrieked. She slapped at him wildly with open hands. "How the hell you expect me to read them stupid words when you've got my face all shoved down in the pillow, and—"

"Judas Priest!" Liz muttered before she shouted, "Mac!" She touched Ace's arm as she turned toward the combatants. "We'll have to finish this later, honey. Mac!" she shouted again, but Mac was already there, pulling a flailing Iris from atop the howling cowboy. She'd bitten him again, and his left buttock bore the fresh imprint of her teeth.

"Judas Priest is right," Ace muttered. He started back toward the playroom, but the fracas was coming his way and he didn't want to be seen. Besides, he decided, he didn't want to rejoin the others. He wanted to be alone. He had some thinking to do.

Quietly, he turned and walked back into the shadows, back down the narrow hall that led to the service stairs. But instead of turning again to take the stairs, he walked straight ahead, stopping where the hall dead-ended. He raised a practiced hand and carefully slid it along the edge of the paneling. There was a muted click, then a soft *whoosh* as a section of the wall tilted, then slid aside. Plucking a match from his shirt pocket, he flicked it with his thumbnail. As it burst into sulphury flame, he stepped into the darkness beyond the wall. The panel whispered shut behind him.

It was hours before the rowdy crowd thinned. Long after Mrs. Bramley officially closed the kitchen and retired for the night, Jenny finished drying the last dish. Mac wandered out to the kitchen just as she was struggling to lift a stack of dinner plates to the cupboard.

"Here, angel, give me those." He was beside her in two long steps and took the plates from her hands. "There," he said, sliding them onto the shelf. "You shouldn't try to lift so many at one time." He smiled at her, but she was looking down, studiously tugging at the dish towel she'd tied over her skirt. He pulled a chair away from the table, flipped it around, and straddled it, his elbows propped on the high back.

"You see to your mare yet?"

"Thank you, Mac. And no, I haven't." She was careful not to meet his eyes. "I thought I'd go down as soon as I finish here."

Any other time, she would have liked a talk with him. She wanted to ask him just how he had come to be here, to work in a place like this. He didn't seem to fit, somehow. Neither did Miss Liz, really, even though she owned the place. But there was too much on her mind right now, and she didn't want to start a conversation, not even with Mac. She was afraid that if he caught her eye, he'd see the turmoil and shame she felt; afraid he'd ask a question she didn't want to answer—couldn't answer. She turned her back and began gathering the jumble of flatware she'd just dried, dividing it into separate stacks of knives, forks, and spoons.

"All right, Jenny." Mac scratched his head. She usually had a smile for him. But then, it had been a long day. Maybe she was just tired. He sure couldn't blame her for that. Old Bertha could be a real pistol.

"Your little mare. What is it you call her?"

"Fancy." She didn't look up.

"Pretty ring to it." It was just the sort of name she'd pick. "Well, your Fancy's in season, if you didn't know. She's gonna be a little cranky for a while, so you keep your eyes open. She may try to use her teeth or her heels on you. And if you don't want her bred, you'd better keep her inside 'til I tell you different. We've got a stud horse down in the corral right now—probably be here for a few days, anyway. I'll let you know when it's safe to turn her out."

She slipped the sorted flatware into its drawer. *Perfect,* she thought. *Something else I don't understand. In season? Do I want her bred? Doesn't anybody here speak English?* But all she said was, "Thank you, Mac. I'll leave her in her stall, then."

He stood up, flipped his chair the right way round, and shoved it under the table before he walked out into the back hall. Jenny heard a scrape and a rattle and a clink of glass, and a moment later, Mac reappeared. There was a lighted kerosene lamp in his hand.

"Here," he said, and placed it on the kitchen table. "Carry this down with you, angel. It's near full moon and pretty bright outside, but it'll be darker than the inside of a black hog in that old barn. I keep a lantern down there, but you'll never find it if you don't know where to feel. And if you want to slip downstairs and take a carrot or two for Fancy, I don't think anybody'd mind."

"Thanks," she managed to smile. She reached for the lamp as he lit a second to light his way home. Mac did not live in the house with the others. Hidden from view by the back yard's drop-off was an old log cabin, and it was there that Mac chose to live in part-time Spartan isolation.

Jenny scurried down the basement steps and quickly requisitioned two carrots from the root cellar. She'd made several fetch-and-carry trips for Mrs. Bramley during the course of the day, but it was scary in the cellar when the house was this dark and this quiet.

When she emerged in the back hall a few minutes later, she looked for Mac—to thank him again and say good night—but he had already gone.

She walked down the long, gentle slope to the barn. But before she entered, she turned to gaze up at the house. A drowsing behemoth, it loomed to monopolize the crest of the hill; and now, at half past four in the morning, all the lights were out except for two second floor windows. They glowed dimly, like the veiled eyes of some creature of darkness. Harvey's piano was silent, and even the crickets seemed to have stopped their music for the night. All but a few of the customers had gone home, and only two dozing saddle horses and a buggy mare remained tied to the hitching rail out front. From where Jenny stood, the horses, waiting for masters that would not emerge until the light, were tiny black silhouettes in the silent distance.

Here, at the base of the hill, a wide, white-fenced corral ran the length of the west side of the barn. The stalls on this side of the stable opened into the paddock, but tonight the doors were all firmly closed, locking the horses out in the balmy night air. As Jenny turned to go into the barn, she counted five horses milling within its confines. They were the gunmen's mounts, the horses she'd seen that night during the thunderstorm: a buckskin, a bay, a black, and two sorrels. One of them would be the stallion Mac had warned her about.

She walked past the corral and entered the barn. Mac had been right: it was pitch dark. She lifted the lamp overhead to get a better look.

The stable was wide and low and well-kept. To her right there were two enclosed rooms, probably for feed and tack. Several bales of alfalfa were stacked along the wall, and Mac's barn-lantern hung on a nail between the doors. The barn's broad central aisle was flanked by roomy stalls—box stalls to the right; narrower, open-ended tie stalls on the left. Most of them were unoccupied, but all were clean and deep in fresh bedding. Mac was a good steward.

Two milk cows, little more than murky outlines at the dim edge of her lantern's glow, drowsed at the far end of the wide aisle, near the silvery silhouettes of a buckboard and a hooded buggy. A gray saddle mare and a matched pair of chestnuts were turned into airy boxes a little closer.

Fancy was in a tie stall two cubicles down from the feed and tack rooms. At the sound of her mistress's footsteps treading over the straw-strewn floor, the mare roused from a fitful doze and lifted her head. Jenny went to her and patted her neck.

Uncharacteristically, Fancy reached out to nip at her, pinning her ears and stamping a foreleg. In season, Mac had said. He'd also said the mare would be cranky, and it appeared he had been right. Jenny moved to touch Fancy again, but this time the mare jerked away from her, tugging at her tie rope and whinnying. A deeper, plaintive neigh answered her from outside in the corral: the stallion.

It was obvious that the horses wanted to be together. Jenny wondered if "in season" meant that Fancy was feeling something akin to the urge she herself had felt in that dark, upstairs hallway: the mysterious, overpowering need to press her flesh against Ace Denton's, female against male.

She sank down on a bale of straw in the empty stall next to Fancy's, and with her shoe, cleared a little space on the floor. This accomplished, she put the lantern down on bare earth and pillowed her face in her arms, her forehead touching her knees.

Now what was she to do? It seemed impossible to her that the man who had caressed her so wondrously could be a murderer. Worse, a cold-blooded monster who had callously cut down not only her own sweet father, but many others.

It made no sense at all. Yet despite the longings he had awakened in her, she could make no excuse for him. And although, at this moment, she was no longer certain that she was capable of taking his life, perhaps tomorrow or the next day she would find both the opportunity and the courage.

For now, she would bide her time. Above all, she would stay beyond his grasp, beyond the touch that had already proved capable of reducing her to submission.

"You're up awfully late, little one."

Her head snapped up. Ace Denton stood not ten feet away, slouched against a post. There was a grin on his face, and although he must have walked right past her, she hadn't heard a sound.

She did not return his smile. Instead she glared at him, unconsciously crossing her arms across her bosom as if to keep not only his fingers, but his eyes away.

He took a step toward her. "What's the matter, Jenny? You don't look like you're happy to see me."

She scrambled off the straw bale, putting it between them. "Stay away from me," she hissed. "You keep back!"

He paused, puzzled. The smile evaporated from his lips. "What brought this on, little one? I thought you enjoyed my company . . ."

She took another step backward. "I didn't know who you were then. Now I know your name."

He grinned again, shaking his head, and came toward her. *Sweet, silly little Jenny,* he thought. A virgin's first passion might be forgivable in an upstairs hallway with a nameless stranger, but give the stranger a name and it suddenly became too real, too sinful. He chuckled to himself. She had a lot to learn about the attitudes of love as well as the mechanics, and he had determined to be the one to teach her.

She backed away from him again, but this time she dead-ended against the narrow stall's manger. Ace closed the final distance between them and took her firmly by the shoulders.

"No!" she hissed. "Get away from me!" But when he kissed her, she felt her resistance melting and cursed herself for her weakness. She managed, at least, to keep her teeth closed against him, to prevent his entrance to—and conquering of—her mouth.

Puzzled, he pulled back. He knew she was capable of passion; she'd proven that earlier. But now, when he'd expected her to have been more relaxed—even eager—she was cold, remote. Perhaps he had taken her too far too soon. He'd thought, at first, that she understood: that while she might be inexperienced, she had, at least, realized what he'd done to her and why. And he'd thought Liz was exaggerating, just being her old cynical self, when she'd talked about the extent of Jenny's naïveté, but now . . .

He still leaned over her, his face inches from hers. She was staring up at him, shivering, and all he wanted to do was fall right into those green, green eyes. No, Liz wasn't going to have a chance to turn Jenny into another Pearl or Mary-Rebecca if he had anything to do with it. Jenny was for him, and him alone. But first, he decided, he might need to explain a few things to her. Judging from her reaction to him now, it seemed likely that she knew even less than the little with which he had credited her. But where to start?

His lips hovered above her ear. "What do you know about love, Jenny?" he whispered.

The rich timbre of his voice stroked her almost as effectively as had his fingers earlier, but she shoved at him anyway, pushing ineffectually at his chest.

"I only know that I don't want you to kiss me, or to—to—" She blushed hotly and looked away.

Surely she couldn't be *that* naive . . . "Do you know about men and women?" he continued softly. "Do you know why they need each other? Do you know how they love?"

"I don't know what you're talking about! Please just . . . just leave me alone."

Her brows knitted with confusion and embarrassment, and Ace suddenly realized that she really had no idea, no idea at all. "Jenny," he said quietly, "didn't your mother, didn't anybody ever tell you—"

She shoved at his chest again, then put her hands

over her ears. "Go away." She'd meant to shout it, but it came out as a whimper.

Jesus, he thought. *Why didn't somebody . . . ? Oh hell.* At that particular moment, he wanted nothing more than to find the poor girl's mother and give the old bat a good shake. But instead, he gently took Jenny's wrists and pulled her hands away from her ears. She didn't fight him. Her arms dropped to her sides, limp and useless.

He took a deep breath and reconsidered what he was about to do. It was an entirely new situation for him. He was accustomed to more experienced women: women who knew by a touch or a glance just exactly what he intended and what he wanted from them; women who enthusiastically welcomed his advances. He'd never known a woman to react to him in any other way. He didn't know how to "sweet-talk" a girl, because he'd never had to do it. He didn't know how to "court" a girl, for, until now, he'd never met a girl he wanted to court.

He was a master at demonstrating the facts of life, but he had absolutely no idea how to tactfully explain them.

For a moment he considered asking Liz to have a talk with her, but decided against it. Any lecture she received from Liz would be somewhat colored by ulterior motives. No, he'd have to do it himself. He cleared his throat and began tentatively, "It's like your mare, Jenny. She's in season. Do you know what that means?"

"Leave me alone." She whimpered it so softly that he could barely make out the words.

"It means that she needs to mate," he continued. He began to softly stroke her cheek. "She wants to be bred."

She'd turned her face from him, but even in the lamplight a hot spot of red was highly visible on her cheek.

Ace had been nervous before, but quite suddenly he was glad. He found he *wanted* to be the one to tell her, to open her eyes to a world which, until now, had not existed for her. He brushed his thumb over her cheek's bright flush, then began to stroke her temple.

He heard her whimper again: no words this time, just an embarrassed little squeak of sound. He felt an overpowering urge to just shut up and take her in his arms, but he made himself keep on talking, never taking his soothing fingers from her averted face.

"Jenny, do you understand any of what I'm saying?"

She shook her head, just a little.

"Do you know how people make love?"

She shook her head again and bit at her lip. No, she didn't know, and though she desperately wanted to be away from him, away from his dangerous closeness, she wanted to hear. She'd wanted to hear this since that summer when she was ten years old and her mother had washed her mouth out with soap.

"Animals?" he whispered. "Do you know how they . . . ?"

Again, that slight, flustered shake of her head.

"But you do know that males and females have certain . . . certain differences. Physically, I mean."

There was a tiny, affirmative nod.

It was a start, anyway. But how to begin? Horses, he decided. That was fairly safe. "Well, when, say, a stallion and a mare mate, those parts that are different, they sort of . . . They . . ." Damn. Now even *he* was embarrassed. He looked at her, searching what he could see of her face. She still didn't understand, and she'd gone bright red. He took a deep breath and cleared his throat.

"You see," he continued, "a mare can't make a foal by herself. She needs a stallion's seed, and a stallion keeps his seed inside his body just like a mare keeps the beginnings of a foal inside hers." He could barely keep his voice from cracking. He concentrated on his fingers, softly feathering up and down the side of her pale neck.

"And when she comes in season, she signals him that she's ready to accept him. Ready to conceive." He took a deep breath. "So the stallion breeds her. Puts his seed inside her."

Silently, Jenny started to cry. She felt so stupid, so inadequate. "I don't understand," she wept. "Let me go, please!"

"No, Jenny. I'm trying to make you understand. Somebody should have told you about this a long time ago."

He wanted her badly. He wanted to touch her, hold her, see her in the light: see the pink of her nipples, to watch them swell with desire, to see them bead between his fingers.

His left hand slid from her shoulder to cup her chin. He turned her face toward him, making her look into his eyes. "You see, a stallion . . . A stallion carries his seed in an organ between his hind legs.

99

And when he's near a mare that wants to be bred, he gets . . . excited." Unconsciously, he began to toy with the top button of her shirtwaist.

"When he gets excited," he continued, his voice little more than a husky whisper, "that part of him—the male part—begins to grow larger." The button came undone, and his fingers went to the second.

"And when the mare is ready, he mounts her"—he bent slightly to brush his lips across her forehead, her temple—"and he puts himself inside her, in a special place under her—"

"No—" Jenny whispered. She didn't understand what any of this had to do with the way she'd felt in the hallway.

"No, Jenny," Ace soothed, misunderstanding her alarm. "The stallion doesn't hurt her." The third button. "It's pleasurable." He nuzzled her ear, breathed in the scent of her hair. His warm breath wafted over her skin as his lips moved to the pulse spot in her neck. "Very pleasurable."

"It feels good for both of them, little one," he whispered. The fourth button came undone. "If mating didn't feel so good, well, it wouldn't be long before there wouldn't be any more horses. Or anything else, for that matter." The fifth button. With fingertips, he traced the soft V between her breasts, flicked at the edge of her camisole, tugged teasingly at the ribbon that held it in place. If she had been any other girl and any other time or place, he would have simply ripped it away. But then, any other girl would have ripped it away herself, and long before this. His jaw tightened with frustration.

Jenny looked into his face then, and his expression

both frightened and thrilled her. His gaze caressed her almost as palpably as had his hands, and a part of her reveled in it.

The muscles of his jaw rippled as he ground his teeth, and at last, with great difficulty, regained his self-control. It was too soon. She wasn't ready. He wondered how long he could restrain himself.

He still held her face in one hand, and with the other he now began to stroke lazy circles over the partly exposed top swell of the breast his lips had teased only hours before.

With difficulty, he spoke again.

"People—I mean—" He flushed, and he was glad when she turned her head away. He cleared his throat and started over. "Animals seek their mates as the seasons turn, Jenny, but people . . ." He kissed her downy, golden temple, his lips as soft and gentle as a whisper. ". . . people are luckier. People can be together in . . . in that way . . . whenever they want. Because they care about each other, need each other."

His fingers teased her gently: barely touching her skin, skimming delicately up her bosom's plump swell, then up along the line of her collarbone, then down again. Through the fabric of her camisole, he could see the outline of her nipple's beaded tip. He swallowed hard.

"Animals mate for the need of it, Jenny," he whispered, "but people make love to one another for the joy of it, as well as the necessity." His thumb moved down over the fabric to gently rub a wide, lazy circle around her breast's swollen peak. She shuddered again and clutched at the manger behind her.

"Men and women who're in—who care about each

101

other can please each other in all kinds of different, wonderful ways." His thumb moved closer and closer to the throbbing crown. "Not just by climbing on top of each other like livestock. Not like what goes on up the hill."

She averted her eyes: tried to look away, tried to keep what little control she had remaining. She was fully, excruciatingly aware of the heat of his hand. The throbbing in her breasts and between her legs was a reverberating reminder that she was submitting to him again, and willingly. She was shocked that she'd permitted it, and even more shocked that she could be so excited by the knowledge that he was touching her.

Something in the back of her mind, her last vestige of reason, was telling her to run; that as miraculous as that last interlude had been, another might be too much, might *really* kill her. But she was mesmerized by the touch of his fingers and the compelling baritone of his voice: as mesmerized as a rabbit caught in the lantern glare of an oncoming train.

"I gave you pleasure earlier tonight, didn't I, Jenny?"

His fingers hovered near the peak of her breast. They were so near—a hair's breadth away from touching her where she most ached to be touched—but she couldn't answer, wouldn't answer.

He lifted her head, forcing her to meet his eyes. "You loved it, didn't you, Jenny?" he demanded. His nostrils flared with a barely controlled passion that she, suddenly more frightened than confused, read as anger.

"And even now . . ." He paused and stilled those

102

lazy circles over her bosom to cradle its soft weight in his palm. He held it motionlessly, as if by the simple act of cupping her camisole-clad breast he could tether her there forever. Then finally, mercifully, he pressed the flat of his thumb over the tight bead that crowned it. A thin, uncontrollable whimper escaped her, and he breathed, "It feels good, doesn't it, Jenny?"

"Yes, d-damn you," she hissed, the words foreign in her mouth. She hated him for bringing her to this: not only was she half-undressed in the night in the arms of a murderer, but he'd made her swear out loud for the very first time in her life. Her face was wet with silent tears of impotence and shame. His touch was maddening, intoxicating. She was fully aware that if he were to shift his thumb the merest fraction, she would be lost, and she detested him for it.

"Don't damn me, little one," he whispered. "You may as well damn yourself for being human. Because tonight was only the beginning. Men have something between their legs, too, Jenny, just like stallions."

Still cupping her breast with one hand, he trailed the other down her arm to take her wrist and press her palm to the front of his trousers, low on his belly. She could feel something hard there, something that pressed back. Alarmed, she tried to pull away, but he held her hand quietly, firmly, against himself. He smiled down at her.

"You see, Jenny? You can excite me, just like your mare excites my stallion. And one day, you and I will make love, and I promise I'll make you happier than you can imagine."

She began to struggle again, and this time he released her hand. Perhaps he'd pushed her too fast.

"No," she hissed, repulsed. "You'll never do that to me, never!"

"Yes I will, Jenny," he answered, a self-assured smile on his handsome face. "And you'll ask me to do it." His hands were on her shoulders again. His bottomless, obsidian eyes seemed to narrow with intent.

"Never!" She wrested away, barely aware that she'd been able to pull free only because he'd allowed it. The spell broken, she snatched at her open blouse, then ran past him out of the stall and down the aisle.

She stopped in the doorway, her distance from him giving her courage. "You're lying!" she spat. "You made it all up!"

"No, Jenny." He stepped out into the aisle. "It's true." No smile graced his lips now. He looked deadly serious. "Grow up, Jenny. I don't know what kind of game you're playing, but it's time to call a halt. You want me. You want me to make love to you. You can't deny that. You couldn't respond to me the way you do if you didn't—"

"No!" she screamed. "It's not true, not any of those things you said! And even if— You'll never do that to me, Ace Denton. You'll never put that—that—that *thing* inside me. No man will, let alone the likes of you!"

He cursed under his breath and balled his hands into fists, his frustration turned to rage. "You're wrong, Jenny. You'll beg me to. And next time we meet, I won't waste time with explanations."

Stumbling, the fluttering shirtwaist clutched to

104

her bosom, she backed up another ten feet before she shouted, "Lies! There won't be a next time, you—you—you—" She quickly searched her newly expanded vocabulary. "—you *bastard!* You'll never touch me again!"

He looked furious. Eyes narrowed, and he took a step toward her, his arms outstretched as if he intended to throttle her with his bare hands. She fled, buttoning her shirtwaist as she ran up the slope in the moonlight, and only after she reached the back porch did she remember her lantern. She turned around, certain that she would see Ace Denton striding up the lawn behind her, the lamp in his hand and God knew what on his face.

But he was not there. The yard was empty except for the gently rippling grasses that grew there, and no light came from the barn. Somehow, he had vanished into thin air, and he had taken her lantern with him.

"What the hell's the matter with you?"

"Nothing." Ace scowled and jerked the blankets down to the foot of his cot. The soft *snap* echoed through the cavern. He sat down and began tugging angrily at his boots.

"Well for somebody who ain't got nothin' the matter, you're awful dang—"

"I said, nothing's wrong, Scar." He kept his voice low with great difficulty and ground his teeth. He wasn't in any mood to talk about it. He was furious with her, and nearly as furious with himself for mishandling the situation. Why in God's name did she have to be so ... Well, so *everything?* So beautiful and so blonde and so fragile and so voluptuous—and so damned naive!

Scar knew better than to press him. He changed the subject. "Horses okay?"

"What?" Ace unbuckled his gun belt and laid it aside, sat down on the edge of his cot, and picked up a worn deck of cards. He shuffled and began dealing out face-up poker hands. "Oh. The horses. They're fine. Where're the others. Their cots aren't set up."

Scar reached across the low, flat-topped rock between them that served as a table. He picked up the stray lamp Ace had carried in, blew it out, and set it down on the smooth limestone floor. The other lantern shed plenty of light.

"Rafe's up with somebody. Pearl, I think," he said, "and Andy managed to make it as far as Agnes's room 'fore he keeled over. Billy passed out in the playroom. Figured I might's well leave him be—he's too dang heavy to drag all the way down here."

Ace was snapping the cards down on the stone hard enough to echo sharply through the cavern. Scar watched him a little nervously. It had been a while since he'd seen Ace quite this agitated. When Ace looked up, Scar half expected him to fess up to whatever was on his mind, but all he said was, "Why aren't you up with Meggie?"

Scar shrugged. "We was together earlier. And I don't much cater to the idea of bein' with her after, well, after all them others. She don't like it neither. We both like it better if we can make it kinda, you know, special."

106

Ace almost said something sarcastic: almost asked if "special" included that little rocking chair demonstration the two of them had given in the playroom, but he refrained. To each his own, he guessed. He reshuffled the deck and started over. He was still too angry to sleep.

Scar yawned and climbed under his covers. "That was a purty little gal that brung up the food tonight," he said conversationally.

Ace slapped down the four of diamonds, busting the hand he was sure was going to be a heart flush. "I thought you were too busy to notice." He hadn't meant it to sound quite so cutting, but Scar didn't seem to take offense.

"Oh, I seen her. I also seen you follow her out." He grinned. "You didn't come back for quite a while, neither. You and her—?"

Ace didn't let him finish. "No," he answered, too vehemently.

Scar held up his hands. "Crikey!" he whispered. "Take it easy! You want to bring the roof down on us?"

Ace glanced overhead. His denial still echoed faintly through the pillars of stone that surrounded them and the spires of limestone suspended over his head.

"Sorry."

"Yeah, well . . ." Scar pulled the blanket up to his chin and rolled over so that his back was toward Ace. "Turn the lamp down before you go to sleep, will you?"

"Yeah." He shuffled the deck for the third time and

began dealing out a new set of hands.

"You gonna do that all night?"

Ace clenched his jaw and groped along the slick rock floor at the far end of his cot. There was always a bottle waiting for them there. He found it and glared at the label. Gin. He'd have to bring down a bottle of bourbon.

Gin or not, he twisted out the stopper. He didn't bother with a cup. He tilted the bottle and took a healthy swig before he reached down to the jumble of books on the floor. He began digging through them, flipping the topmost volumes aside. There were several of Scar's battered dime novels: *Buffalo Bill, the King of the Border Men* went by the wayside, along with *The Arkansas Kid: Cavalier of the Open Road*. There was even one about them. He picked up *Ace Denton: Battle at Blood Creek* and scowled. Damn things. He'd never even heard of a "Blood Creek," let alone fought a battle there. He flung it aside and dug down through the rest until his fingers found the slim volume he sought. Lewis Carroll.

He stared at it a minute before flinging it aside, too—but not so far he couldn't reach it later—and retrieved his cards. He began slapping the pasteboards down again. When he looked up, Scar had twisted toward him and was staring impatiently, waiting for an answer. He sighed and said, "What?"

"I said, you gonna do that all night?"

He considered it for a moment. "Probably."

Scar jerked the blanket up over his head. "Great."

* * *

After she locked herself in her room, Jenny lay awake until the light, deep in thought and clutching the little half-completed wooden horse her father had made. She'd come here predisposed to hate Ace Denton enough to want him dead. He'd killed her father, and tonight he'd nearly killed her, or so it had seemed at the time. And then there had been that confusing lecture/seduction in the barn. After she cooled down, she managed to fit together the jigsawed pieces of what he'd said to her.

It still didn't quite make sense, but she understood enough to decide that Ace Denton seemed determined to take her for a mate, and that the way he'd made her feel in the corridor had quite a lot to do with that. Well, he'd have about as much chance of doing *that* to her as . . . as . . . She couldn't think of anything impossible enough to match *those* odds. She simply would not allow it. This mania he seemed to have for taking her clothes off and touching her (as well as the mindless response she had to him) were entirely unforeseen—and unforgivable.

Originally, she had planned to turn him in to the sheriff in Green Mule, but soon discarded that notion: Sheriff Wallace appeared to be a regular patron of Miss Liz's establishment. She'd seen him in the bar last night, with Pearl draped across his lap, his badge pinned to the bosom of Pearl's camisole. He'd be no help. This was the Denton gang's home territory, and despite the band's nasty reputation, the locals seemed not only to tolerate their presence, but to be strangely proud of their own close, if clandestine, association with the outlaws.

The law, at least the local variety, seemed out of the question. Which left things up to her. She could not, for the life of her, imagine actually taking him prisoner and leading him somewhere out of the county, where the law might be more diligently enforced. And it also seemed unlikely that she'd be able to actually do away with Ace Denton herself unless she could accomplish it from a distance. Even then, she was no hand with a gun. She'd never pulled the trigger—when it was loaded, anyway—and she'd had a hard enough time just getting the cartridges into it. She couldn't even pretend that she'd be able to hit something more than ten feet away.

And when it came down to it, could she actually kill a human being, even one as reprehensible as he? It suddenly struck her that she'd never so much as killed a hen for the table. Her hatred for Ace, for what he had done to her father, had not lessened. But growing alongside that hatred, and strangely intertwined with it, was a nearly irresistible, completely undeniable—and totally damnable—attraction.

She began to think that it might be better if she just forgot about him and went back to Minnesota and Aunt Victoria. Ace would trip himself up one day. The law would eventually catch up with him without her help.

She had to admit defeat. She'd been a fool to imagine that she could do what the law could not or would not, a fool to think that she could just sashay into his world equipped with nothing but her indignation and outrage, a gun she couldn't use, and

110

some vague notion of evening the score. How could she kill a man when she hadn't even the courage to slap his face?

She decided to leave. Unfortunately, she'd spent most of the last of her meager legacy tracking down the gang. She hadn't enough cash to get herself out of Missouri, let alone all the way back to St. Paul. She'd have to stay on until her two weeks were up, long enough to earn her fare back to Minnesota. It wouldn't be enough to get herself—and Fancy, for she wouldn't desert her little mare—there on the train, but it would buy her supplies for the long, lonely ride north. She prayed that Ace Denton would stay away until after she was gone.

Ace had been good for one thing, anyway: if nothing else, he'd given her some inkling of what the "girls" did upstairs. The picture she'd formed was still quite fuzzy, of course, but now she understood that there was more to Iris and Belinda and Pearl's line of work than just letting the customers look at them naked. She was positive, now, that it had to do with mating—that the customers paid Mary-Rebecca and Agnes and the others for the privilege of sticking their "things" inside them. And, in a way, she began to feel sorry for the girls. It sounded painful, horrible; and it must be wretched, she thought, to have no way to earn your living except by letting stranger after stranger invade your body: to have a constant stream of faceless men treat you like a mare in season. But she still didn't understand just how they did it, or why there were no babies.

She held the little wooden horse to her bosom,

remembered a sunny spring morning when her father had boosted her, all of four years old, to the strong wide back of his old plow mare and led her round and round the yard while he sang a little made-up song: *Jenny's my pretty darlin', Jenny's my cherub girl, Papa loves his darlin', The best in all the world . . .*

She cried herself to sleep.

Five

Sunday

When Mrs. Bramley rolled her out of bed at ten o'clock for another round of laundry duty, Jenny was still exhausted and confused. But later, when she stood in the back yard hanging out row after row of sheets, underdrawers, chemises, camisoles, and petticoats (and even, here and there, a stray dress or blouse), she was pleased to see that the five horses in the corral had been reduced to two: a big sorrel and a tall, thin buckskin.

They must have gone during the night, she thought, smiling. *They've gone, or at least three of them have. But would they split like that? No*, she decided. *They probably wouldn't. They must have replaced the sorrel and buckskin with fresher horses.*

When she got a chance, she even slipped up the back stairs to peek inside the playroom. She'd been right: it was silent and deserted. She didn't know how long their absence would last, but seeing as how Meg

113

Sweetwater was still on the premises, it seemed certain that they would return sooner or later.

Later in the day, about mid-afternoon, Jenny found herself in the dining hall, waxing tabletops. The mammoth room was open and airy—about twenty feet wide and thirty feet long, with a sleek, brass-railed mahogany bar at one end—and like each of the other rooms in the old mansion, it had a flavor very much its own. Its whitewashed, plastered walls, decorated at random intervals with framed prints of horses or naked women, seemed stark compared to some of the other rooms. Stark that was, until you looked upward. The vaulted ceiling was decorated by an incongruous fresco of floating cherubim. An army of airborne cupids—bows in their chubby hands and quivers on their backs—they floated lazily overhead through a pale blue, wisp-clouded sky framed by ornate, gilded-plaster moldings.

She was rubbing at another of the seemingly thousands of white rings on dark wood when she happened to glance back toward the kitchen. Mac was just coming through the swinging door, and as he did, Jenny looked past him to see Meg Sweetwater pick up a linen-covered tray. Mac was talking to Mrs. Bramley, and he stood in the open doorway just long enough for Jenny to see Meg bear the tray away—not up the service stairs toward the second floor, but down to the cellar.

As Meg disappeared through the cellar door, Mac came the rest of the way into the dining room. As the door swung closed behind him, he walked toward the bar, a wooden crate in his arms.

"How're you doing today, angel?" he asked,

smiling pleasantly. She looked very pretty today, he thought to himself. She wore a long white skirt and a simple white blouse with narrow green piping at the collar. Her hair was pulled just off her face by a green ribbon, and it cascaded over her shoulders and back in soft golden waves. Her hair style and attire made her look even more childlike and virginal, if that were possible. His smile widened. It made him feel good just to look at her.

She grinned back. Mac was the one, unvarying touchstone of sanity in this house, and she was grateful he had become her friend.

"I'm all right, I guess," she shrugged. "My shoulders are going to be sore tomorrow, though." She swept a hand toward the dining area, where the difference between the tables she had polished and ones she had not yet reached was glaring.

Mac laughed and nodded.

He pried the crate open and pulled out several handfuls of excelsior. Next came bottle after bottle of clear liquid. From across the room, Jenny squinted at their labels.

"Stomach bitters?" she grimaced.

Mac chuckled and held a bottle aloft. "'Dr. Hostetter's Stomach Bitters,'" he chanted with the singsong ease of a carnival pitchman. Then he grinned and added, "It'll cure what ails you, I guess. Actually, it's gin. They just label it that way to get past the liquor tax."

Smiling, Jenny shook her head and began rubbing at the table again. "This is a beautiful room in the daytime, isn't it?" she asked absently.

"Yes, it is. A grand room, you could say. They used

to take out the furniture and hold formal balls here in the old days. Folks came in from all over." He pulled out the last few bottles, stuffed the packing back inside the empty crate, and set it aside. "You had a chance to see much of the rest of the place yet?"

Jenny smiled and shrugged. "Some of it. Mrs. Bramley had me carry up towels yesterday."

Mac's brow furrowed. "Oh? Did you . . . did you go into the girls' rooms?"

"Yes. They were all downstairs, though. It's . . . It's *different* up there, isn't it?"

Mac ran his fingers through his hair. "I don't have much reason to peek in the girls' quarters unless one of 'em's having trouble with a—with, well, a gentleman." He began to slide bottles of Dr. J. Hostetter's Stomach Bitters between the rye, bourbon, scotch, and dusty bottles of liqueurs on the mirrored back bar. "What'd you think of your tour?"

She told him how Mrs. Bramley had shoved the huge wicker basket of folded linens into her arms. ("A dozen apiece, 'cept Iris and Belinda each get twenty," the cook had grumbled. "And Shirley Mae don't get more than four or five, though if you ask me, two'll be too many.")

"They sure must take a lot of baths," she mused, and Mac didn't know whether he wanted to burst out laughing or drop through the floor. But before he had a chance to do either, she said, "There's something I don't understand, Mac."

He squirmed apprehensively. *Here it comes,* he thought, and pretended to be very busy polishing an already sparkling tumbler from the bar-top tray. "What's that, honey?"

116

"Well, there should have been other rooms on the second floor. I knocked at a couple of doors—the ones with no nameplates—and when nobody answered and I opened them, there weren't any rooms at all. It was just solid wall! And that little short corridor toward the back of the second floor? It doesn't go anywhere! There's a linen closet where a room should be, and a room that should be a closet, and . . ."

So that was what she was curious about! Mac was monumentally relieved. "I think," he chuckled, "that I need to explain to you about Elmer Sweeny . . ."

Briarbirth, Mac said, had been constructed in the late 1850s by an old friend of Miss Liz's: a man both wealthy and somewhat—at least in his concepts of interior decorating and architecture—eccentric. The gentleman in question, a widower named Elmer Sweeny, had been father to a large family, but before his death he'd fallen out with his surviving children. Sweeny, it seemed, had felt a great compassion for the downtrodden slaves of the southern states, and had expended large amounts of both time and money in aid of their plight. Much to his shame, his children—brought up with money and servants, and more accustomed to ordering than asking—were pro-slavery, and for that reason they had sided with the Confederacy. The feud had been bitter and unresolvable, and Sweeny had disinherited them. He left his very grand (and very out of place) estate—furnishings, outbuildings, Onan the parrot, and all—to his old friend from Kansas, Liz McCaleb. The surrounding rich farmlands he bequeathed to three

Negro families he'd taken under his protection before the war.

In his heyday, Mac told her, Sweeny had played with Briarbirth like a huge, private toy, altering its design and fittings according to whim.

Jenny nodded. It began to make some sense now. Because her duties included housework, she'd been able to see a good deal of Mr. Sweeny's handiwork. The front parlor (now the "gentlemen's receiving room") was architecturally appointed (as well as furnished) in a particularly bilious form of the fashion of the day. Sweeny's former study—now Miss Liz's office—had a sort of mongrel Oriental flavor, complete with ornately crafted andirons shaped like snarling dragons. The turreted gaming room, where the roulette wheel turned on weekends and where the customers played cards before or after their assignations upstairs, was painted a dark, hunter green that matched the felt tops of the card tables. There was one rock-faced wall, in the center of which was a huge carved stone fireplace complete with gargoyles. The big room at the rear of the house, opposite the kitchen and behind Miss Liz's office had once, she thought, been a library. Now it served as a store room. It was piled with crates of a wide variety of liquors and foods, from home-canned vegetables and sweet preserves to French champagne and tinned oysters: everything and anything that didn't need to be kept cool down in the root cellar was here.

The other rooms in the house were appointed in a variety of styles that ranged from farm house plain to palatial. Her own little room seemed to be only a remnant of a larger chamber: three walls had walnut moldings at the floor and ceiling, as well as large, rectangular, wallpapered insets, but the fourth had no such detailing. It was crooked, in that it took two jogs of about three feet each on its way across the room; and it was constructed of raw, plasterless wood panels that had been given only a cursory coat of whitewash. Judging from what she'd seen of the house so far, Jenny had decided that the jury-rigged room she'd been assigned by Mrs. Bramley was never intended as a living space. The cook, for whatever reason, had given her a disused storeroom for a bed chamber.

Of course, the entire third floor was very odd, with its zigzagged hallway and mismatched walls. The enterprising Mr. Sweeny seemed to have done more than his share of haphazard remodeling, but on the third level he'd been sloppy about hiding his tracks. Mac agreed with her that portions of Briarbirth were in a mysterious shambles.

"I reckon there are parts of rooms he forgot about or didn't think he needed. I guess nobody but the spiders remember those. Old Elmer was a good soul, one of the kindest men I ever met, but he never quite finished anything in his life. His house wasn't any different."

"You knew him then. I thought, I mean, I just assumed that you came here after Miss Liz owned it."

He twisted a shot glass in his fingers. "I knew him. I sort of worked for him. And when he died, I just stayed on. Like that damn parrot." He put the glass down and grinned at her. "I even helped with a little wall-moving in my day, but most of it was done before I got here. I really liked Elmer—you couldn't help likin' him—but he was an eccentric old cuss. Half the town folks thought he was crazier'n a loon, and that was without their knowing what he was doin' to the house."

"That explains a great deal" Jenny smiled. She had stopped her polishing, and was sitting at one of the tables, chin cupped in her hands, listening intently. "I was beginning to think it was me."

"Not hardly, angel. In fact, you might just be the sanest one here." He came out from behind the bar and plopped down in the chair across from her. "I think I have to agree with you about this room, though. That front parlor is so ugly it scares the hell outta me, and Liz's office, well, it's not to my taste. But this room . . ." He stared up toward the ceiling and smiled. Sunlight streamed in through the banks of diamond-paned windows to sparkle on gold leaf and dance over fat cupids.

Jenny was on her feet again. She began to rub at another white ring on the tabletop. "How'd you come to be here, Mac? To work for Mr. Sweeny?"

He ignored the question. He didn't want to have to lie to her. "You'd better stop doin' so much, sweetie. You're gonna spoil that old dragon in the kitchen. She won't tell you, but she's never had anybody work so hard for her before."

"Oh, I don't mind hard work," Jenny grinned, "but I could certainly use a little more sleep than I've been getting."

"Don't worry, angel," Mac assured her. "If you have trouble sleeping, tell Bertha. She's got a shelf full of remedies out there in the pantry. Everything from salves for cuts and burns to powders for—" He

120

looked aside and cleared his throat. "For, um, female troubles. She's got sleeping drafts, too. All home-made, from herbs and things. But I wouldn't worry. You've made it through the Friday and Saturday night crowds. They're the worst of it. It's pretty slow around here the rest of the week, and—"

Iris Jakes stormed into the room. Her step was quick and hard. She shot a withering look at Mac before flouncing up to Jenny.

"You bitch!" Her blue eyes crackled with cold fire. "You rotten little goody-goody!"

Startled, Jenny took a step backward and clutched the polishing rag to her chest.

Mac shot out of his chair and grabbed Iris's shoulder. "Hold it! Just calm down. What's *your* problem?"

"Let go of me, old man!" Iris twisted away, snarling, "It's her, that's what's wrong with me!" Her twang had risen another octave. "She's after my man!"

Mac shook his head. "Now, I really doubt that, Iris. What on earth would Jenny want with one of your—"

"Not one of *them*, you fool! I mean *my* man! Ace!" She was on the edge of hysterics. "I just heard Miss Liz say he was askin' about her!"

Openmouthed and wide-eyed, Jenny stared at her. No one noticed as Belinda Critchley slipped into the room and went behind the bar to pour herself a morning bracer.

"I—I—" Jenny stuttered.

"See?" Iris screeched, cutting her off. "She can't answer that! She's after him, I tell you!" Her twang grew more shrill and nasal with every syllable. More than anything, Jenny wanted to cover her ears and run, if only to get away from the noise.

"Calm down, Iris," Mac interjected. He caught her arm just as she lifted it to swing at Jenny. "I'm sure there's an explanation—"

"Let go, you old fool!" she screeched. "Little Miss Innocent's hot on his trail, all right!"

Jenny stiffened, suddenly terrified that Iris had discovered her real reason for being at Miss Liz's. *How could she know?* Jenny thought frantically. *How could she know why I tracked him here?* But the prostitute's next sentence put her mind at ease.

"She's out to bed him, Mac, an' by God, I'm gonna snatch every one of those blond hairs outta her head!" She made another lunge toward Jenny, but Mac stepped between them.

"Will you just shut up?" he shouted back, exasperated. "Honest to God, Iris, sometimes I think that voice of yours could cut glass!" He turned to Jenny. "All right, let's settle this. Jenny, you have any idea what she's talkin' about?"

Jenny twisted the rag in her hands. "I—I—the only men I talked to were—I just carried up a tray last night. There were five men upstairs and I took them sandwiches. That's all." She would rather die than admit the rest.

"Then why's he askin' about you?" Iris demanded. Her tone had calmed, but she was far from pacified.

"I don't know," Jenny replied shakily. "Really, I don't know why anyone would ask about me."

Iris straightened and shook free of Mac's restraining arm. Self-consciously, she twisted her hair and sniffed, "You'd better not, you filthy little—"

Mac shook his head. "Enough, Iris. And watch your mouth."

"I'll talk anyway I damn well please, old man." She tossed her snarled, dark red mane haughtily. "And you, Miss Innocent, Miss Fairly-*Reekin'*-Of-Virginity, you keep your hands off Ace! He's always been mine and he'll always *be* mine, so you stay away from him." Her voice dropped to a hiss. "If you don't"—she glared straight into Jenny's eyes—"I'll see you dead."

"That's *enough*, Iris." Liz McCaleb, regally attired in a deep purple, high-necked print, stood at the foot of the stairs. She was flicking the charms on her bracelet. "One fistfight a week is all I'll stand for from you, young lady, and you used up your quota last night. And I suggest you stop eavesdropping on conversations that don't concern you. Now go collect your laundry and put your clothes away. And *do* comb your hair. You look like you just rode out of a cyclone."

Iris snorted one last time in Jenny's direction, then pivoted on her heel, and stomped out of the room.

The madam's attention turned toward Belinda. She was behind the bar, tossing back her third or fourth drink of the day. Her robe was hanging open again, and last night's makeup was smeared and blotched on her face. Right now she looked nearly as ruined as Shirley Mae Vinton.

"You too, Belinda," the madam added. "Get cleaned up. You look like the wreck of the Hesperus. And both you and Iris get dressed. The weekend's over. There's no reason for you two to traipse around all day in your work clothes."

Belinda rubbed at her mouth with the back of her hand. "Agnes is hoggin' the bathtub again," she whined. "Been in there least an hour."

Liz tapped her foot. "Well, make sure you're next," she said curtly. "Oh. And the next time that cowboy comes in—the one Iris took a chunk out of last night?—I want you to turn him. More your specialty anyway, from what I heard."

"I would'a, but he *picked* Iris. And how come *I* always end up with them guys? Let Shirley Mae take a few of 'em. She can use the money, and God knows nobody'd wanna look her in the face while they was—"

"You're good at it, that's why," Liz said, cutting her off. "Just like Mary-Rebecca is my best girl at—" Her eye fell on Jenny, frightened and bewildered. "Well, you know," Liz finished, frowning. *Good Lord*, she thought. *I've either got to get that child working on her back or out of this house. She's got me nearly as sappy as Mac, and in my own place, too!*

With that, she nodded curtly at Mac, then disappeared down the hall. Jenny heard the office door slam behind her.

"I'll be damned," Mac chuckled. "I'll be double-damned." Shaking his head, he started toward the kitchen.

"Reckon I'd better get down and tend to the livestock," he said. "I'll take your mare out and work her on the lunge line, but you'd better not try to mess with her for a while yet. She's rank today, and that stud horse is still down in the corral." He paused, studying Jenny's pale, perplexed face. "Don't pay

Iris too much mind, honey. She's got some funny ideas where—well, where this certain fella's concerned. But that's nothin' you need to worry about. Iris is more screech than she is stomp, anyhow." He started to walk away, then turned back and added, "Just the same, maybe you'd better try 'n stay out of her way for a while."

"All right, Mac. Thank you." She managed to smile at him, and he grinned back. Before he left, he propped the kitchen door open.

"Give you some breeze," he said, securing it.

A moment later, through the diamond-paned windows, she saw him heading down the slope toward the stable.

Jenny turned her attention back to the half-polished tabletop, but before she could take a swipe with the waxy rag, Belinda's voice brought her up short. She hadn't realized the girl was still there.

"She will kill you, y'know," Belinda said softly. She lifted the tumbler, tilted back her head, and gulped the last swallow of rye. "Her stepdaddy taught her how to shoot. Use a bull whip, too. Course, that was in between trips to the hayloft. I hear she finally used his own whip on him: sliced the family jewels right off the ol' crook 'fore she skinned him." She dipped a bar towel into the glass she'd just drunk from, gave it a cursory rub, then slid it back with the clean glasses. "I'd keep clear of Ace Denton if I was you."

She stumbled out from behind the bar, her short silk robe gaping from throat to hem. She seemed heedless of her exposure as she pranced—with that odd, strutting walk—to the hall door. She turned when she reached the stairs and leaned heavily against the newel, her open robe revealing half a drooping, fried-egg breast. "She'll be watchin' you from now on out, missy. An' I'll be watchin' you, too."

Swaying slightly, she clumped up the stairs and out of sight.

Jenny stood there, rag in her hand, staring after Belinda and wondering if being a whore made you crazy, or if the reason you became one was that you were crazy in the first place. She was so lost in thought, in fact, that when the cellar door creaked, she jumped. She had forgotten all about Meg's mysterious trip to the basement, and now Meg was emerging, empty-handed and humming. She didn't see Jenny and went on her way, smiling and softly singing to herself as she climbed the service stairs.

Why would Meg be taking food to the cellar? Feeding the mice? They'd have to be awfully large mice to finish off as much food as Jenny suspected had been under the linen drape, and it seemed that they'd eaten the platter as well.

Mrs. Bramley was still safely out in the backyard, and the kitchen was empty. Jenny walked through to the back hall and put her ear to the cellar door.

She heard nothing, and quietly opened it a crack. Silence.

The cellar was about twenty feet square and had three half-windows along the stairwell side. They were placed at ground level, high along a retaining wall of mortared rock, and enough of the afternoon sunshine came through them to flood the basement with warm, filtered light. The wall opposite the

126

stair's landing had been paneled with dark walnut planks, and she could plainly see its dark, rich grain. She'd thought it quite odd, this bizarre finishing touch, but now that Mac had told her about Elmer Sweeny it made perfect sense.

She slipped through the door and crept downward. But when she reached the smooth, packed dirt at the bottom of the steps, she found the cellar empty save for the same old stacks of crates and boxes piled here and there along the walls. The root cellar door was in the center of the right hand wall, and she crossed the cellar to press her ear to it. Once again, silence. She peeked inside.

There was nothing within except stored food-stuffs, kept cool by their entombment deep under the house. The missing tray was nowhere to be seen. It was exceedingly curious, but she had work to do. With a shrug of her shoulders, she clicked the door shut and went back upstairs to finish her tables.

The sun was close to setting when Mac knocked at Miss Liz's office door. As usual, he didn't wait for an invitation to enter, but this time he only stuck his head in.

Liz was sitting at her desk, scratching numbers into that ledger again. She was wearing her reading glasses, but when she saw Mac, she took them off and tucked them into her pocket. "What is it?"

"Nothing. I just wanted to say hello."

She stared at him for a minute. "Well, you've said it."

"And to tell you that you're getting soft, you old

harridan." He grinned at her maddeningly.

"I'm sure I don't have any idea what you're talking about," she said haughtily, although she knew exactly what he meant. After all these years, Mac could read her like no one else, with the possible exception of Marcus.

"Oh, that's all right, Liz. I didn't expect you to actually admit it. But it's a step in the right direction. I think there may be hope for you yet."

She slapped her palms on the desktop and angrily jolted erect, but Mac had ducked back through the door and closed it before she could think of anything to say.

Hope for me? she seethed. She sank back into her chair and twisted slightly to stare at the row of framed pictures on her bookshelves. Her eye fell on a formal portrait of a man who, although he looked uncomfortable in his Sunday suit, was quite handsome. Her gaze lingered there a few moments before it moved to the image of a small boy hugging a terrier.

She shook her head, retrieved her glasses, and bent back over her ledger. "Old fool," she muttered under her breath. "Doesn't he know there's no hope for any of us?"

By nightfall, it was clear that Mac had been right about Sundays. Only a few farmhands trickled into Briarbirth during the early evening, and by ten o'clock, the dining room was abandoned except for a solitary farmer leaning against the bar. Only three or four additional customers were in the house, and for the first time, the raucous pounding of Harvey's knotted fingers was not overshadowed by shouts and rowdy laughter. She decided, after a while, that Harvey's dubious musical skills had been enhanced by the clamor of the previous night. He did not play the old upright so much as attack it, and by ten o'clock she could bear it no longer.

Mrs. Bramley had long since closed down the kitchen and retired for the night. She knew there would be no more requests for food this evening and had gone up to bed with a sandwich, a glass of buttermilk, and a dime novel, leaving a tub of dishes and glassware for Jenny to wash and put away.

But the relentless, off-key clatter of the piano had given Jenny a headache, and she longed to get out of the house and away from the noise, if only for a few minutes. She lit a lantern, popped down to the root cellar, and appropriated three crisp carrots.

She blew out the lantern and left it in the pantry. She'd need no lamp to guide her to the stable, for the moon was close to full and the night sky cloudless and filled with stars. She tucked a few matches into her skirt pocket along with the carrots, and slipped out the back door.

The big red horse was alone in the paddock now, and the yard in front of the house was empty save for a lone farm wagon and three saddle horses tied to the hitching rail. By the time Jenny reached the outbuildings, the sound of the piano (which she knew Harvey was banging hard enough to rattle the upstairs chandeliers) was reduced to a faint and fleeting whisper: a background for the music of crickets and the occasional cry of a night-hunting bird.

The stable door was closed, and it wobbled and creaked as she slid it open. Carefully, her hands stretched out before her, she walked into the darkness. She found Mac's barn-lantern almost immediately, lit it, and slowly turned up the flame.

The gray and the chestnuts were still in their stalls, and she frowned. She'd expected to find two of them absent—taken by the outlaws to replace the mounts they'd left behind. They must have had other horses hidden somewhere—perhaps down at the old cattle barn or in a pasture beyond the trees—for they certainly weren't in the house any longer. She shook her head and started down the aisle.

Fancy was in her tie-stall, nosing distractedly at her hay. On the mare's far side, two stalls down, was tethered the tall buckskin she'd seen in the corral earlier. Mac must have brought him in, and that would mean that the big sorrel horse outside was the stallion he'd warned her about. Ace's stallion. Outside, the red stud snorted. The sound carried into the barn, and Fancy stamped her foot and tugged impatiently at her tether.

The mare's ears were laid back. She was hard in season now, and she looked testy and out of sorts. Pulling the carrots from her pocket, Jenny entered the empty stall next to Fancy's and offered her one. The little grain trough in Fancy's stall was still full. As she crunched, Jenny patted her neck and offered another.

"It's all right, girl," she said, comforting the mare as best she could. "I think I know how you feel." The stallion outside whickered again and Fancy raised her head, tugging against the halter rope and whinnying softly in reply. Jenny rubbed the star on her forehead, then broke the last carrot into pieces, feeding them to the dainty mare one at a time.

"Mac says you'll be fine again in a few days, girl," she said as the dark mare lipped the last sweet chunk of carrot from her palm. "You'll get over that big red stud, I—"

Hands clasped her from behind, covered her mouth, encircled her waist. Ace Denton pulled her roughly back against him.

She struggled, squirming in his arms, but he held her fast.

"So you know how she feels, do you?" He didn't sound like he was smiling. She could feel his breath, hot against her temple. He took his hand from her mouth.

"Leave me alone!" she spat. "Let go or I'll scream!" She twisted against his restraining arm. His only response was to crush her more tightly against him.

"Fine," he said. The hand he had taken from her mouth moved to capture her breast. "Scream all you want. Who's going to hear you all the way down here? The best you'll do is spook the horses." Beneath the layers of blouse and camisole, her nipple beaded at the first brush of his thumb. *No*, she thought, *I will not let this happen again . . .*

"Stop it!" she hissed. She tried to turn to strike at him, to prevent him from taking control of her as he had the night before. But he restrained her effortlessly with one hard arm, easily imprisoning her wriggling body against his chest.

"I'm tired of games," he said flatly.

The previous evening, her verbal assault had

angered him more than he wanted to admit. And though he'd later decided that nervous fluster was probably responsible for her outburst, he still stung from it. She was like a maiden filly: skittery and shy and maybe even prone to kick or nip on her first visit to the breeding shed. But a filly could be gentled and coaxed—teased along—and sooner or later, she'd stand willingly, even eagerly. All it took was patience and a firm hand. He knew he had the firm hand. It was the patience he wasn't so sure of.

"Admit it, Jenny," he whispered into her hair. "You want this."

"No," she cried, though not as convincingly as she wished.

He still held her tightly to him, and she could feel his hardness pressing against her hip. He began to stroke the outside swell of one breast through the fabric of her blouse, and instantly, both her traitorous nipples contracted to aching, pounding points.

"Please, please don't do this," she moaned, though a growing part of her yearned for the firm caress of his large, powerful hands, wanted the touch of his sure, warm fingers; his soft, insistent lips. She wanted him to make her feel the way she'd felt that first time, in the dark, in the corridor.

But he did not slip his hand beneath her blouse as she both dreaded and prayed that he would. Instead, quite abruptly, he spun her out and away from him and, clasping her wrist, dragged her further into the stall.

With his free hand, he reached over the partition

and untied Fancy. Jenny began to fight him again, but he held her fast, half dragging her behind him as he led the mare out of the barn and toward the paddock gate.

"What are you doing?" she demanded as she twisted against the uncompromising grip he held on her arm. "You're crazy!" How she wished she had her father's old Colt with her at this moment! She might never have slaughtered so much as a hen, but she could cheerfully shoot Ace Denton here and now, as much for the helpless way he made her feel as for what he'd done to her father.

"Let go of me, you . . . you . . . you son of a . . . a . . . a bitch!"

"Jenny, Jenny!" he chided her as they approached the gate. "Is that any way to talk to the man you love?"

"Love you? You're insane! Let go!" She twisted again, but it was no use. His hand was as unrelenting as an iron shackle.

The big red stud horse in the corral saw them coming and cantered to the fence. He arched his neck over the top rail and snorted at Jenny's mare. His nostrils were flared and quivering, his eyes ringed with white. Brazenly, Fancy flagged her tail and pranced in response. She trotted in place and whickered softly as Ace opened the gate and turned her in with the stallion.

"Merry Christmas, Trooper," he muttered as the horses wheeled to dart and dance in the moonlight.

Ace pulled her into the shadows. He hugged her against him once more, her back snug against his

133

hard, broad chest. Her buttocks pressed against his pelvis, and again she could feel that stiff, ominous outline.

"Watch them, Jenny," he breathed. "It's time you learned about the natural order of things, little one. Obviously, I'm not much good at explaining this, so now I'll have to show you. Watch and learn, because soon that's what you're going to ask me to do to you. *Beg* me to do to you . . ."

"You're crazy," she hissed. She pounded at his arm, shoved at his hand. "You'll never do that to me, never! I'll never let you, much less beg!"

"Yes you will, Jenny. A Thoroughbred filly in heat, that's what you are."

She craned her head to see him, to answer him, but before she could he covered her lips with his and, at the same time, tugged free the tails of her shirtwaist. He slid one hand beneath the blouse, tugged free the chemise's ribbon tie, and pushed it aside. At last, mercifully, his warm hand touched her quivering flesh. His fingers tugged softly at her swollen nipple before he gently rolled the hard, pounding tip between his thumb and forefinger.

"You want me, don't you, Jenny?"

"Never," she groaned, even as she felt bubbling waves of pleasure—a pleasure he was bringing her to need as much as air or food or water—spread through her shivering body. "I hate you." Her denial was husky, sensuous, and not at all convincing.

"No, Jenny. You love me. You were made for me."

His hand upon her breast was like fire. His breath was hot on her cheek and the side of her neck as he

134

nibbled and teased at her earlobe. He traced the contours of her ear with his tongue; and despite her firm resolve, her head lolled back against his strong shoulder. She felt suddenly weak. She knew she could not stop him from doing whatever he wished.

She did not want to stop him.

One hand still fondled the soft weight of her breast, but the hand that had imprisoned her relaxed, then crept up to stroke her cheek. He had gauged her point of no return perfectly, and he knew there was no longer any need to forcibly hold her. When he tilted her face up and to the side, she remained tight against him; and when he kissed her, long and sweet, she slid her own trembling hand beneath her camisole to cover his as it cradled her bosom.

"You're mine, Jenny," he whispered in the darkness. "Your lips, your breasts . . . Your body and your spirit—everything you have belongs to me." He tugged a little harder at her engorged nipple, driving home the weight of his words and his dominion: complete and undeniable.

There was no fight left in her. She was overcome by his nearness, his touch, and the aphrodisiac that was his voice. And as he once again covered her mouth with his, she took the hand he held to her cheek and guided it downward, then up under her clothing to embrace the other breast. Right now, she needed—more than anything, more than life itself—to feel the heat of both his practiced hands beneath her garment, inflaming her as he had the night before.

When both her breasts were encompassed, Ace's fingers performing miracles upon their turgid peaks, she sighed and closed her eyes, oblivious to everything but the waves of pleasure emanating from his hands.

"No, Jenny," he whispered when he saw her lids had fluttered closed, "Keep your eyes open. I want you to watch the horses." As if to underscore the command, his petting, plucking fingers slowed their manipulations, easing away from her nipples in silent warning.

She obeyed.

As much as she hated him, she could not bear the thought that he might take his hands away. Her breath came in little gasps as she forced herself to raise her lids and look toward the moonlit paddock.

The stallion and mare had completed their dance of love, and now the mare was ready to stand for him: eager to be bred. Jenny could see that Fancy had flagged her tail to one side, and that Ace's stud was teasing her: whickering softly, soothing her, nuzzling first at her flank, then beneath her raised tail as Fancy snorted and impatiently shifted her weight from one hind leg to the other. Jenny could also see that the stallion's member had emerged from its sheath and was engorged. Unconsciously, she wiggled her hips against Ace, and flushed hotly when she realized that he was in much the same condition.

The thought of it was almost more than she could bear. She drew in a ragged gulp of air and clutched harder at his breast-filled hands.

"Keep watching, Jenny," he breathed into her ear, his voice deep and sensuous in the night. "Don't take your eyes off them. I want you to remember this night always. I want you to remember how you spent it, and with whom."

With that, he slid his hands from her breasts. At first she tugged at his fingers shamelessly, but he whispered, "Now, now, little one. There's no need to be greedy. You'll have it all soon enough."

When she reluctantly relaxed her grip, he quickly unbuttoned her blouse, slipped it from her shoulders, then slid away the straps of her camisole, so that it puddled about her waist. At this moment, she felt no shame. She *wanted* to bare herself to him now, *wanted* to be naked in the moonlight for him: only for him.

She heard him whisper, "Jenny . . . Jenny," and he began to stroke her bared torso, feathering strokes up her sides, along her rib cage. His broad knuckles gently teased the full undersides of her breasts; crept around the outside swells, leaving waves of pinpoint, thrilling shivers in their wake. Fingertips laced along her neck and shoulders, then down between the V of her breasts to tease at the waistband of her skirt. It seemed his touch, his heat, and the sweet musky scent of him was everywhere. Adrift in an effervescent sea of sensation, Jenny whimpered with pleasure.

In answer, he rained soft, warm kisses over her shoulders, the side of her throat. And all the time, his hands never ceased to work their subtle yet powerful magic over her flesh.

She leaned back against him, closing her eyes, wanting only the sensations of his touch and his nearness. But he whispered, "Watch, Jenny. You *must* watch."

She obeyed.

The red stallion mounted Fancy. He craned his

head forward to grip the crest of her neck in his teeth, taking her prisoner, steadying her while he jockeyed for position. Jenny heard Fancy squeal as the stallion held her hostage, clamped between his muscular forelegs; and as he moved about, shifting himself on the mare and grunting in the heat of rut, Jenny felt Ace unbutton her skirt, then loosen the ties that secured her petticoats and underdrawers. With a whisper and a subtle flash of moonlit white, the rest of her clothing slid over her hips and pooled about her feet.

Even as her mare groaned beneath the weight of his stallion, Jenny moaned as Ace's fingers slid slowly down the flat of her belly to briefly brush the blond curls at the apex of her legs; then out to sweep broad, slow, hot circles over her belly and hips. She shivered in his arms, reveling in his touch, the heat of his nearness, his hot breath against her ear, his lips at her throat, murmuring her name. The moonlight was her lover, too: washing over her in a soft blued veil, touching her everywhere, even as did Ace.

And just as the stallion found his mark and, with a primordial, ground-shaking grunt, plunged deep inside the groaning mare, Ace eased his hand between Jenny's thighs. He did not invade her, but only cupped her womanhood softly, applying the slightest of metered pressure that followed, exactly, the driving rhythm of the mating horses.

Jenny writhed against him. One arm was thrown back to curl about his neck and shoulder, her fingers clutching at his shirt or twining briefly through his hair. Her other hand clasped his wrist, riding atop the hand that pleasured her below. She was as swept away by lust and raw animal heat as the sweating, groaning, coupling horses only yards distant. Then, just when she knew it was impossible, that she could stand no more and that she was surely dying of ecstasy, her entire body convulsed violently in a frenzied, volcanic climax.

She called out something that might have been his name or might have been the Devil's, and then she emptied her lungs to scream what was not a word, but a primal shriek; and then she knew nothing.

When she opened her eyes, she found herself inside the stable, propped comfortably against a stack of hay. He'd managed to neatly reclothe her, and Fancy was tied back in her stall, contentedly grinding a mouthful of oats.

Ace was gone. The only things left to mark his passage, to prove that he had been there and that she had not dreamt the episode, were the throbbing aftershocks she still felt high between her legs, and the drying smear of his stallion's semen on Fancy's hindquarters.

Six

Monday

Mrs. Bramley put her to work scrubbing the kitchen floor, and Jenny welcomed the mindless monotony. She toiled in a daze: crouched on her knees, working a soapy, stiff bristle brush into the bleached oak planking in wide, firm circles. Her body seemed far away, her labors performed by someone else, someone she didn't know. She succeeded, for a while, in keeping her mind a void, empty of the painful internal debate that had kept her tossing and turning until the cock's crow at first light. But the arguments crept in upon her again. She hated him. He'd killed her father. But the way he made her feel . . .

There was always that "but . . . ," and there seemed no resolution.

Early in the afternoon, she caught a glimpse of Meg slipping furtively down the cellar steps with another tray, only to emerge a few short minutes later, empty-handed. Jenny waited for her chance, and again she checked the cellar, first peeping downstairs, then descending to find the earth-floored room deserted. As before, she found no tray, no food, no diners: only stacks of boxes and crates and a cool and silent root cellar. It was a mystery, and although it was most likely not an important one, it served, at least, to distract her from her dilemma.

She was still puzzling over the missing dinner trays as, an hour later, she dusted the deserted front parlor. She heard a quick, decisive step in the corridor, and Miss Liz, bracelet jangling, swept into the room.

"I believe you're the hardest working kitchen girl we've had here, Jenny," the madam said smiling.

"Thank you ma'am," Jenny answered. She tickled her feather duster over a genuinely ugly red glass lamp. The dangling, cut-glass pendants made a soft tinkling sound. "I like to do a good job."

Miss Liz gracefully lowered herself into one of the big, overstuffed armchairs. "It doesn't pay too well, though, does it?"

Jenny shrugged and went on with her dusting. "I suppose it pays as well as anything else, ma'am."

The madam's lips set into a hard line. "Jenny, I'm trying to talk to you. Will you please stop fussing with that and sit down?"

Something in Miss Liz's tone told her that she was about to hear something she'd rather not, but there didn't seem to be any escape. "Yes'm," she said, and perched on the divan. She held the feather duster in her lap, her hands folded demurely over it.

"Jennifer," Miss Liz began, "you realize don't you,

142

that the girls who work here make a good deal of money?"

Jenny shrugged.

"Well, dear, I have a business proposition for you."

"Ma'am?"

"There was a man here a few days ago, Jenny. A man who'll be back later in the week. He saw you, dear, and he's taken quite a fancy to you. Such a fancy, in fact, that he's offered a rather large sum for the privilege of spending a night with you." Miss Liz ground her teeth as Jenny blushed and turned her head away. "That is, Jenny, provided you're untouched. I'm assuming that's the case."

Jenny didn't answer. She stared, blankly, out the window.

"Damn it, girl—I mean . . . Jenny, look at me."

Jenny's wide, ingenuous eyes met hers.

Liz began again, softening her tone. "Tell me the truth, dear. Have you ever been with a man?"

"I . . ." Jenny's cheeks were nearly scarlet. "Do you mean . . ." She thought about what Ace had told her the night before, about the horses and what he'd shown her. "Are you asking if I've ever—ever—"

"—slept with a man, Jenny." Miss Liz retained a facade of patient concern, but—not that she'd ever admit it to Mac—her feelings were mixed. Normally she'd never give a second thought to enlisting a new girl for the house, but there was something about this child . . . *Stop it*, she chided herself. *You're getting soft. Jenny isn't a child, she's a young woman. A beautiful young woman who's otherwise most likely*

143

destined to marry some farmer, pop out eight or ten brats and die before she's forty. Besides—this is business, and the child is literally sitting on a gold mine . . .

But still, Liz felt a little guilty. Not guilty enough, however, to refrain from trying to recruit the girl. The man in question had offered one hundred dollars, but she could probably coax him up to two hundred, maybe more. He could afford it, and he'd be, well, an *instructive* first client for her. The same man had deflowered Pearl (although he'd certainly paid a lot less for the privilege than he'd pay for Jenny) and when he'd gotten through, well . . . He had used her in every possible way. No matter what a client requested of Pearl after that night, it would come as nothing new to her. Probably better to get it over with all at once like that.

Jenny was far too pretty to waste herself. She could work here four or five years and build herself a nice stake; maybe move on to one of the bigger houses in Chicago or St. Louis or New Orleans, or retire. The prostitute's life was hard for most women and deadly for some, but Jenny was beautiful and, other than this baffling innocence, intelligent. Liz McCaleb herself had been (and still was) both bright and beautiful, and the sporting life had been reasonably good to her, all things considered. She had no reason to believe it would be any less kind to Jenny.

She toyed with her bracelet. "I'm asking if you're a virgin, dear."

"I—yes, ma'am." Jenny stared at her lap.

"Well, that's excellent, Jenny, just fine." Miss Liz reached across the space between them and took

Jenny's hand. She smiled warmly. "That's just about the best news you could've told me.

"Now, the gentleman I mentioned, he's taken a shine to you, dear, a real shine. Between you and me, he told me that you're just about the prettiest girl he's ever seen. And he told me that if you were pure, he'd pay"—swiftly, she deducted her commission—"fifty dollars just for the privilege of being the first one."

Jenny's horrified eyes grew even wider as she sucked in a gulp of air. "Oh!" She pulled her hand from Miss Liz's. "Oh no, ma'am! I just couldn't! I wouldn't know—"

The girl's naïveté was exasperating. Liz sighed heavily, but she managed to keep smiling. "Now, now, dear, don't you worry about a thing. I'll tell you all about what to expect, and the gentleman will show you. It's all very natural, very easy, really. You'll catch right on." Her smile widened, became almost motherly. *You'd think,* she mused, *that fifty dollars would mean a lot to this girl. You'd think she'd jump at the chance . . .*

"Really dear, you'll enjoy it a great deal. Of course, there'll be a little pain at first—"

Jenny's pale brows furrowed. She bore the expression of a small, snared animal, and the madam quickly amended her statement. "Not even pain, really, my dear. Just a tiny discomfort. Every girl has it her first time. It only lasts a second or two, and after that, it's very nice." Liz oozed reassurance.

"Th-thank you, ma'am," Jenny finally managed to stutter, "but I don't think I . . ." She cursed herself for being such a ninny, then squared her shoulders and lifted her chin. "No, ma'am," she said as firmly as she could. "I don't think so. I'd rather stay in the kitchen if you don't mind." She stood up and took a step backward.

"Don't make a hasty decision, Jennifer," Miss Liz purred. "Think it over. It's the only sure way for a girl with no family to better herself financially. You did tell me you had no family . . ."

"That's right, ma'am." There hadn't seemed to be any need to bring Aunt Victoria and Uncle Homer into this.

The madam smiled, reassured. "You're a pretty girl, my dear, and you have certain qualities that many men find quite desirable." *Not like the rest of the rabble I've got working here,* she thought. Jenny wasn't like the others. She was beautiful, true, but she had something more: there was a look of quality, of breeding about her. She'd save Jenny back for the special clients that would hire her for the night and pay through the nose for the privilege. She'd teach her about wines, how to dress, how to carry herself like a grand courtesan . . . She might even knock out a wall or two upstairs and give the child an entire suite of her own.

It would be the beginning of what Liz wanted: a genuinely "quality" house. Briarbirth would become not just the best house in three counties, but the best in the state—St. Louis and Kansas City included.

"Think it over," she repeated. "The gentleman in question won't be back for a few days yet, and fifty dollars is fifty dollars."

"Yes, ma'am. I will," Jenny mumbled. She was almost to the door when Liz stopped her.

"Jennifer?"

Jenny sighed and turned around.

"You shouldn't wear such dark colors." The madam nodded toward the navy skirt and blouse Jenny had chosen that morning. "I know they're all the rage, but a body'd think you were in mourning. A young, fair girl like you should stay to pale colors. Pastels. Keep it light and pretty."

"Yes'm."

Miss Liz stood up. "I'll be waiting for your answer, dear. About the other. I hope you won't disappoint me."

Jenny nodded and scurried gratefully out into the hall. She knew there was nothing to think over. She'd be more likely to leap naked into a bonfire than work upstairs like Iris and the others. But still, she wondered who the "gentleman" in question had been. Fifty dollars seemed a truly huge sum of money to her, especially for someone to spend on one night of doing . . . well, of doing *that* to her.

Her first thought had been that it was Ace Denton. After all, Iris had said (or rather, screamed) that he had asked Miss Liz about her. But somehow she knew it couldn't be him. She realized that any man so obsessed with coercing her to beg for his favors would not be likely to try and buy them. So she searched her memory for another face: a face that had followed her more covetously than the rest.

None sprang to mind.

There were no customers that night, and the house remained blissfully free of Harvey's musical assault and battery.

Supper was reasonably quiet. Only two cat fights broke out at the table: one between Mary-Rebecca and Belinda over the ownership of a pair of red high-heeled shoes, and another in the long-running series of spats between Mrs. Bramley and Shirley Mae. As had become her custom, Iris glowered at Jenny throughout the meal, snidely demanding faster or better service from her, and purposely spilling things for Jenny to mop up.

After the girls finished their dinner, most of them adjourned upstairs to the playroom for billiards. Mac gave her a wink and disappeared down the hill to his little house. Harvey vanished into his room on the third floor, but not before Jenny saw him filch a bottle of Hostetter's Stomach Bitters from the back bar.

While Jenny gulped down as much as she could stomach of her own dinner of burnt pork chops, cold mashed potatoes, and congealing gravy, Mrs. Bramley scraped and stacked the dishes. Jenny was just about to immerse her hands in a tub of hot, soapy dishwater when Meg, dressed in a pretty yellow print dress, appeared at the kitchen door.

When Mrs. Bramley saw her leaning nervously against the frame, she turned to Jenny. "Just wait a minute before you get too intent on them dishes, missy," she growled.

Jenny froze, wondering what she had done (or not done well enough) this time. Mrs. Bramley, whose tirades she had at first taken with a grain of salt, was beginning to irritate her.

"You dust in the receivin' parlor today?"

"Yes ma'am," Jenny countered quietly. "You

know I did."

"Ain't so sure about that." The cook hung up her soiled apron and smoothed her skirts. "I was in there a bit ago, and it don't look like nothin's been touched."

That's a lie, Jenny thought angrily. She had dusted and swept—and nearly been bitten by Onan to boot. And she knew for a fact that Mrs. Bramley hadn't been anywhere near the parlor all day. She stared back at the cook.

"Don't you look at me that way, missy. You get your fancy little butt out there and take another look at what you was supposed to be doin' this afternoon." She planted doughy hands on hips wide enough for two women and glowered threateningly.

Jenny was halfway to the parlor before she realized what a fool she'd been.

Quietly, she turned on her heel and crept to the back service hall. She approached the kitchen on tiptoe and peeked around the corner. Meg was loading a tray with leftovers and a small pot of coffee.

"That'll keep her outta your hair long enough, I reckon," Mrs. Bramley was saying. "Me, I'm goin' upstairs. I got me a new mail-order catalog I'm wantin' to read. An' by the way, bring back up some'a them platters. They're startin' to get scarce."

As Meg added the last items to the tray and Bertha Bramley poured herself her nightly glass of buttermilk, Jenny took her chance. Silently, she crept to the cellar door and opened it a crack. The basement was in total darkness but she wasn't afraid. She knew the steps and railing were sturdy and safe. She slipped through the door, eased the latch shut behind her, and felt her way deeper into the darkness.

By the time the edge of Meg's lantern-light appeared at the top of the stairs, Jenny had reached the packed-earth floor. She took advantage of the soft advancing glow to scurry behind a tier of crates stacked along the paneled wall. From there she had a good view of the entire room.

The lamp held out at arm's length, Meg reached the cellar floor and marched straight toward Jenny's hiding place. Terrified she'd been discovered, Jenny pulled back into the shadows as far as she could. But Meg walked past her and right up to the paneled wall, about four feet away from where Jenny cowered against it.

She held her breath as Meg, smiling faintly and humming a queer little tune, set her tray and lantern aside. She studied the wall for a second or two before her smile widened.

Fascinated, Jenny watched as Meg ran the tip of her index finger down a slender groove between two glossy boards. Reaching a spot roughly even with her shoulder, she appeared to dig her fingers into the groove, first pressing, then curling them slightly.

There was a soft click, then a gentle grating sound. An entire section of the wall slid back and to the side to reveal a narrow doorway. No light glowed within. Meg, humming softly, smoothed her skirts, retrieved her lamp and tray and stepped through. The panel slid shut behind her, leaving Jenny immersed in total darkness.

Of course! she thought. *This is how he manages it!* She remembered the story about old Elmer Sweeny, builder of the house, and what she'd been told about his sympathies for the slaves. It would only stand to reason that this house had once been part of the underground railway. It must be honeycombed with secret rooms and passages—places where men and women could hide or rest in safety before moving on to the sanctuary of the north. And it stood to reason that there could be a tunnel down to the barn.

She was about to try to feel her way across the cellar and back upstairs when she heard a low rumble. Just in time she slipped back against the wall, expecting to see Meg emerge with the lantern.

But Meg was not alone.

Scar Cooksey was with her, and it was he who carried the lamp. Tucked under his arm were four of the missing trays. Without a sidelong glance he reached back and tripped the lever that sealed the hidden door, then followed Meg to the bottom of the staircase. The saber-scar that crossed his cheek seemed softer in the lamplight, less threatening.

"Meggy," he said, and touched her arm.

She turned to face him, a sweetly distant smile on her lips. He grinned at her a little wickedly and set the lantern and trays on the bottom step before reaching for her.

"Not out here, honey," Meg whispered, tugging at his sleeve.

Scar kissed her roughly and squeezed her buttocks through the thin summer dress. "You don't wanna go back in there an' do it in front of Ace, do you?"

Meg lowered her head. "Well ... no," she admitted.

"And you keep tellin' me how much you hate bein' down below . . ."

Meg sighed resignedly.

Jenny didn't care where they went, as long as they went somewhere else. She looked down and noticed that the hem of her skirt caught the lamplight. Slowly, she reached down and eased it back into the shadows.

"But it's a dirt floor," Meg was saying, scraping a line with her toe and making a face. "I don't want to do it on no dirt floor, Scar."

That's right, Scar, Jenny thought. *Whatever it is, do it someplace else . . .*

But Scar had no intention of leaving. "Don't worry Meggy," he said. He was already tugging impatiently at the closures of her dress. He lifted it over her head, tossed it to the top of a crate and kissed her nose before he tugged the ribbon that secured her camisole. It came off easily, baring her to the waist and revealing pale, heavy breasts tipped with rosy brown. Scar quickly cast the flimsy garment aside and began untying Meg's petticoats. Meg simply stood passively, smiling faintly, watching him as he undressed her.

Embarrassed, Jenny tried to look away, but found she couldn't. Some part of her had to see what would come next.

She hadn't long to wait.

Scar pulled off Meg's petticoats, and then her lacy underdrawers, leaving her naked except for her shoes. Then he stepped back and looked her up and down, appraising her as if she were a horse he was thinking of buying. Meg just stood there, unashamed, quietly waiting.

The silence was unbearable. Jenny, blushing hotly

152

in the shadows, pressed herself harder against the wall as she attempted to keep her breathing as shallow and as quiet as possible. She found that her eyes were glued to the outlaw's face as he stared at Meg's body. His expression had altered from one of cool detachment to something more intense.

Finally, he moved back toward Meg. He didn't say a word to her. He merely picked her up and lifted her to sit on the edge of the crate where he had tossed her clothing. Her bare fanny protected from splinters by the layers of rumpled petticoats, drawers and yellow frock beneath her, she was perched just above him, so that her bosom was even with his face.

"You're a beaut, Meg," Jenny heard him whisper. "A real beaut." He parted Meg's thighs and stepped between them to kiss her lips, her throat, her bosom. Meg tilted her head back and began to make a small, pleased humming sound in the back of her throat. She twined her small fingers through Scar's dark hair and clamped her legs tightly about his leather-vested torso.

Jenny watched, mesmerized. Part of her wanted desperately to put her fingers in her ears and screw her eyes shut. But her lids seemed glued open. Her cheeks burned as she began to fantasize that Ace was touching her again, touching her the same way Scar was touching Meg not more than fifteen feet away. She knew that if he were to suddenly appear before her, she would tear off her own blouse and guide him to her. Never before had she known such yearning— or such self-hatred.

Then Scar stepped back. Meg remained atop the crate, her bosom rising and falling rapidly. Scar stood looking at her for a long minute before he approached her again. He was breathing heavily.

He pulled her down from her perch and drew her naked body to his clothed one. They wrapped their arms about one another and kissed slowly and deeply, with the practiced ease of longtime lovers who know the best ways in which to please one another.

Jenny watched as Meg's pale hands slid down Scar's sides to his waist, then slipped deftly between their bodies to free his belt buckle. Nimbly, she unbuttoned his trousers to free his manhood and take him in her hand.

Jenny gasped, but the lovers were too intent on each other to hear her sudden, amazed intake of air. Neither did they hear her little moan when Meg slipped to her knees to kneel before Scar, and softly pressed her lips to him.

What happened next both shocked and thrilled Jenny. She would not have believed that people did such things, but as Meg administered that most intimate caress to her outlaw lover, Jenny could see by the look on his face, the way he softly touched Meg's hair—and the low, groaning sounds he made in between the whispers of her name—that it pleasured him immensely. This must be as wonderful for a man, she thought, as the thrill she had received from the touch of Ace's lips upon her breasts and his gently pressing fingers between her thighs. Perhaps even more so. Somehow, it was difficult for her to imagine any feeling as intensely gratifying as that, but it seemed that this must be.

Suddenly, Scar reached down and pulled Meg back

to her feet.

"Wait, baby," Jenny heard him whisper. "Save a little for yourself." His voice was cracked and throaty, and when he tipped his head down to kiss his breathless little Meg with a passion both sweet and intense, Jenny could see that his forehead was glossy with sweat.

As he kissed her, he stroked her back and buttocks, running his hands up and down the length of her naked body, kneading and rubbing her pale, freckled flesh. At last Scar eased his lips slowly from those of his swaying mistress, and Jenny thought, *Now they are finished. Now he will pull his pants up and Meg will put her clothes on and they will go away and I can go back upstairs.*

She devoutly hoped this would be the case. She had moved forward, away from the wall, and found she was gripping the edge of the crate before her so hard that her fingers had cramped.

Surely they are finished now, she thought.

But they were not.

Scar stood for a moment looking down at Meg, then gently took her by the shoulders and turned her around so that her back was toward him. He lifted her hair and kissed the back of her neck, then put his arms around her, cradling a breast in each hand. He lowered his head, and Jenny heard him whisper into Meg's ear, "Bend over, Meggy."

Oh, God, Jenny moaned inwardly. *Oh, God, he's going to breed her! Breed her just like . . . just like . . .* She gripped the crate even tighter, her eyes widening in a kind of horrified curiosity.

"I don't wanna do it that way," Meg murmured.

"You know I don't like it when you do that, honey. You promised me you wasn't never gonna do that to me again." She remained standing, and Jenny could see she had tensed.

"I know, baby," Scar said gently. He licked at Meg's ear. "I ain't gonna, I promise. I just didn't wanna do it on the floor and get you all dirty. I'll do it regular, honest I will." He kissed her neck, stroked her breasts.

Meg's head lolled back. Jenny could see that her eye were closed and that the tip of her tongue was licking slowly at her swollen, parted lips. So softly that Jenny could barely hear, she breathed, "You promise?"

"I do, baby," Scar said, "I do." He slid his hands to her waist in encouragement, and she bent forward until her back was almost level. Gripping the edge of the petticoat-covered crate upon which her lover had placed her earlier, Meg braced herself.

Scar took his hands away from her only long enough to worry his trousers downward from his thighs to his ankles. Jenny watched, openmouthed, her own breath coming in tiny little pants, as he reached between Meg's thighs and began to rub her gently and rhythmically. *The way Ace touched me*, Jenny thought. Moaning softly, Meg swayed her back and thrust her hips out and up.

Then the outlaw took his member in hand, and a transfixed Jenny watched as he positioned himself between his lover's thighs.

Meg let out a groan of pleasure, tightening her grip on the petticoat-strewn crate as Scar moved into her again and again. He gripped Meg's hips tightly, using them to steady her, and Jenny could see that Meg's face was contorted in passion.

Jenny's heart beat faster with the couple's every gliding movement. Ace had been right when he'd told her that mating was a fine thing, a pleasurable thing: that making love felt good. In spite of herself, she wished more than anything that at this particular moment Ace would suddenly appear; that he would rip her clothes off, touch her and kiss her everywhere, then do to her what Scar was going to Meg not four yards away.

Meg's moans had turned to a high keening wail, the same sound Jenny had heard her make in the playroom that first night. But this was stronger, louder, and growing more intense by the second. At last it erupted into a muted scream as Meg, gulping for air, began to twitch and spasm uncontrollably.

Scar held steady for a moment. He rubbed Meg's shivering back with one hand and slipped the other beneath her waist to steady her, to ensure that she would not fall. Gradually, Meg seemed to regain some control. She tightened her grip on the crate, and Jenny could hear her whisper, "Yes."

Scar began to move again, and then he, too, seemed to lose control of his body. The rhythm of his thrusts, smooth and cadenced before, suddenly became jolting and savage. With a monumental groan, he thrust one last, volcanic time before he slumped forward onto Meg's sweat-slicked back.

The cellar was suddenly close to silent, the stillness broken only by the ragged, sated breathing of the lovers. Jenny clamped both hands over her face to muffle the sound of her own shaky respiration. She felt terribly, desperately in need of release—a release she knew she would not, could not have—and hot silent tears of frustration began to slowly trail down her flushed cheeks.

Scar withdrew, then stood up and brought Meg with him. She leaned back against him, and he hugged her like that for a few minutes, kissing her shoulders, her turned and uplifted face and the back of her neck, stroking her still-quivering belly before he turned her to face him. They kissed again: a long, slow kiss which was not a gesture of passion so much as one of gratitude and tender affection.

He released her at last and tugged his trousers back on. As he buckled the belt, Meg began to gather her clothes.

"Don't get dressed, baby," he grinned at her. "Not yet."

Meg cocked her head and paused, one foot already inserted into a leg of her drawers.

Scar shook his head. "Wait'll I'm gone, Meggy, OK? I wanna be able to think back, after I get into bed tonight, that the last time I seen you, you was naked."

Meg smiled at him and tossed her pantaloons back on the crate. She stood up and faced him, her hands clasped demurely. Scar went to her one last time. He reached behind her, cupping her buttocks in his hands and stroking the crease between them as he kissed her nose.

When he brushed Meg's lips in farewell, Jenny suddenly realized she had moved as she watched the lovers. She was standing almost directly in front of the hidden door. Just in time, she slipped to one side, crouched and flattened herself into invisibility against the deeply shadowed wall. Scar passed by her less than an arm's length away, and after sliding the panel aside, disappeared into the tunnel.

When the door clicked shut behind him, Jenny had to stop herself from breathing a sigh of relief. It was not until several minutes after Meg had dressed and gone upstairs that she allowed herself to relax.

As she slowly felt her way through the darkness and up the steps, she was still shivering with desire and wondering just what kind of a monster Ace Denton had unleashed in her.

The kitchen was deserted.

Jenny was thankful that there was no one there to see her in what she knew was a bedraggled state. She had nearly soaked her blouse through with perspiration and she was still a little breathless. She went to the big kitchen sink and cranked the pump handle.

When cool water gushed, she splashed handfuls over her face and the back of her neck. It helped some, but she yearned to get upstairs and bathe completely, even if it would be only a sponge bath at her little enameled basin. Mac had seen to Fancy for her, so there was no need to make a trip to the stable. Part of her was seized with a pagan desire to go down the hill anyway: to strip off her clothes and plunge into the spring-fed water tank, to wait for him in the barn, naked.

But the other part of her—the part that was growing just a little stronger every moment that she stood at that kitchen sink dashing cold water against her face—detested Ace Denton for making her feel this way: lost and unfulfilled and aching for things that she'd never known existed. She hated him for taking away her father and all that he represented: her last close family, her farm, her future, the only tenderness and genuine love she had ever known.

She would not go to the stable.

She plunged her hands into the now-tepid dishwater and began to scrub intently at the crockery. It was inevitable that he would appear again. He was still somewhere in the house. It was more likely that he would emerge in the barn to seduce her, but if the house was as warrened with passageways as she now suspected, he might come for her anywhere.

It would be impossible to avoid his advances. Without exception, he'd managed to seduce her at their every meeting, and there was no reason to believe he would change his pattern—or that she could change hers. Therefore, she decided, further seductions were inevitable, and would continue to be so until one of them left the house. It would be another week and a half before she would have the money to go home. He might be called away or chased away first, but she couldn't depend on that, so she would have to count on another ten days of his impending presence, during which he was bound to find her and seduce her again and again. Of this she was certain.

That maddening smile of his! That handsome, beckoning smirk that reeked of confidence, of control, of sexuality . . . That smile that was ready to open and gobble up her body, her mind, her soul: to swallow her whole. He was like the little crocodile in that poem in *Alice*:

> . . . *How cheerfully he seems to grin,*
> *How neatly spreads his claws,*
> *And welcomes little fishes in*
> *With gently smiling jaws!*

And while she knew from recent experience that there would come a moment during each encounter when she could no longer resist him, she made a solemn pledge to herself. She would allow him to touch her—she really had no choice in the matter, when it came down to it—and she would allow herself to take pleasure from his caresses. Once again, she had no choice. His touch always brought her bliss.

But she would give him no satisfaction. She would continue to tell him no. She would not offer him pleasure such as she had just seen Meg give Scar. Above all, she would never make the request he most wanted to hear. She would never beg her father's murderer to strip her of her virginity.

Then there was Iris. Obviously she had some sort of history with Ace—at least, Iris would have her think so. Jenny wondered if the outlaw came to Iris's room after her clients had gone, if he kissed Iris and held her and touched her in the same way . . .

Maybe one day, one day when she was much stronger, she would confront Ace Denton with the truth about her identity. She would tell him just exactly what she thought of him. And then she would spit in his face.

Smiling a hard little smile that was an entirely new expression for her, she finished her work.

It was around eleven when Jenny arrived in her misshapen, windowless bedroom. Miss Liz's girls seemed to be wide awake, for when she passed the second floor landing, she could hear the sound of raucous female laughter, the crack of billiard balls, and the clatter of glasses.

She had carried up a pitcher of water, and the first thing she did, after securing her door, was to pour it into her wash basin. She pulled off the dark skirt and blouse, stripped to the skin and scrubbed herself from face to toe. She had washed her hair early in the morning, before Mrs. Bramley put her to work on the kitchen floor. It had been tied up in a knot on top of her head all day, and after she dried herself and donned a fresh white nightgown, she released it from its prison of pins.

It cascaded down her back, as fresh and fine as spun gold and wavy from being twisted all day. She glanced in the mirror, and for a second saw herself much younger: *Papa's Golden Cherub*. That's what her father had called her.

Sighing, she sat down on the edge of her narrow bed and leaned forward, brushing her hair from side to side and over her head until it shone even more brightly.

She had risen to place her hairbrush back on the shabby dresser when she heard a whisper of move-

162

ment behind her.

It was Ace, dark and wickedly handsome. Tonight he wore no gun belt over his tan trousers, and the sleeves of his crisp, white shirt were rolled to just below his elbows. He was standing near the wall at the foot of her bed, and he was smiling that handsome, deadly crocodile's smile.

"How—how did you get in here?" she demanded after a quick glance proved her door was still firmly latched. For a moment she wondered if he'd swum under it.

He ignored the question. "You didn't go to the barn tonight," he said quietly, his black eyes twinkling. His voice reached across the narrow room to touch her as effectively as might any stroke of his hand.

"I—I was busy." *Why do you begin to collapse so easily?* she scolded herself. *Be strong, Jenny!*

"Yes, I know," he said in a purring baritone. He leaned back against the wall, maddeningly casual, and crossed his arms. "I know you were busy. That's why I thought you'd come to see me."

"What's that supposed to mean?" she demanded nervously.

"It means, little Jenny, that I know you were in the cellar earlier. Those walls are full of peepholes." He straightened and dropped his arms to his sides. "I know what you saw. I know because I saw you watching. You seemed to find it quite fascinating." He took a step toward her. "I saw your face, Jenny. I know what you want." Another step.

"You don't," she stated flatly. She tried to move away from him, but the room was tiny and the dresser

163

was already hard against her back. "You can't possibly know what it is that I want."

Ace took a final step to close the distance between them. He began to stroke her upper arms through the cotton of her nightgown. "Really Jenny? Then why don't you tell me just what that might be?"

Dear God, she moaned inwardly as she felt her treacherous body respond dramatically even to this slight, almost pristine touch. *Why this man? Why is he the only one to make me feel this way?*

"I want you to leave me alone," she hissed, even as she felt her nipples tighten with desire. At least the fabric of her simple farm-girl nightgown was heavy and voluminous. She hoped it was dense enough to prevent him from detecting her response.

"That's not true, Jenny," he whispered as he took her in his arms and pressed his lips, firm and warm, to hers.

At first she clamped her teeth against him, but then she remembered the conditions of her newly sworn vow. It was all right to enjoy this, all right to take his gifts as long as she gave nothing in return; at least, nothing he really wanted. It was her one and only lever. She opened her mouth to receive him, allowing herself to revel in the warm silk of his kiss. She danced her tongue along his: darting, playing, daring him to kiss her even more passionately.

By the time he took his lips from hers she was quivering with want, and it was all she could do to keep from grabbing his hands and clasping them to her bosom. Her nipples ached and pounded even more insistently than they had in the cellar, and she desperately wanted his touch.

But there was the vow, the stupid vow she had made to herself. And having broken her original lethal promise, she could not break this second pledge. It paled in comparison to the first, but the bargain she'd made with herself was fast.

She balled her hands into fists at her sides, digging her nails into her palms in hope that the pain would distract her from her aching breasts.

It didn't.

Ace was fully aware of her discomfort. He took her shoulders, holding her far enough away from him that the crests of her bosom just missed brushing against his chest. He kissed her temples, her forehead, her eyelids.

"Tell me what you want, Jenny," he whispered, then nipped at her earlobe.

She whispered something, some barely audible word.

"Tell me, Jenny," he repeated.

"I want you to go away," she breathed weakly.

His tongue seared a trail down the side of her throat, then up again, and he kissed the line of her jaw. "No, you don't, Jenny. You want me to touch you. You want me to lift your nightgown and kiss you, pet you, stroke you. Isn't that right?"

She couldn't answer. She could only groan. hearing him say it, hearing him form the words for what he had done to her before only made the ache worse. And somehow, hearing him say it had started a blaze of longing between her legs. Her breath had become rapid and shallow. She clamped her eyes shut and turned her head away.

He spoke again, purposefully torturing her.

"That's it, isn't it Jenny? You want me to take off your nightdress. You want to be fondled and kissed. You want my lips and hands at your breasts. I know they pound, Jenny. I know they ache." He ran his tongue around the edge of her ear, then tugged gently on the lobe with his teeth. "I can't see them Jenny, but I know they're pink and swollen and so tight they hurt."

She whimpered, her head lolling back and away, and he ringed her throat with a line of tiny kisses just above the high neck of her gown.

"So few buttons, little one." He kissed the point of her chin, then the corners of her mouth. Her cheeks wer flushed and the first hot tears were squeezing from the inner corners of her tightly closed lids.

"It would be so easy, Jenny." His lips were at her ear, his breath hot against her face, her hair. "So easy to slip free these five little buttons and slide this gown over your head. So easy to cup those beautiful, silky breasts of yours in my hands. So easy to kiss them, to suckle them, to take the ache away."

He felt Jenny arch her back, unconsciously pushing toward him, trying to make even the slightest contact with his chest. But he tantalized her, holding her just far enough away that it was impossible. He began to tickle her ear with his tongue.

"Do you know what it's like for me when I nurse at you, my little Jenny? You taste of salt and sweet, and you fit into my mouth perfectly. I can feel your every response, your every thought through just that pink bud of flesh, Jenny. And when its tip hardens just right in my mouth, if I bite down just so . . ." He nipped at her earlobe, and she gasped for air, her knees giving way.

She couldn't stand much more. Her entire body was pounding, as if all her blood had rushed to just beneath the surface of her skin and pulsed there, hot and bright. *Don't bother to unbutton it*, she thought. *Just rip it off of me, damn it. Rip it off and touch me, kiss me, do what you want, anything you want . . .*

"Jenny," she heard him whisper. "Tell me you want me to touch you. Tell me you want to be naked in my arms."

Someone in the room—Jenny was certain it could not have been her, although she felt her lips move—said, "No."

Ace sighed heavily. He was close to exasperation, but he refused to give up on her. Two could play this game.

"All right, then," he said resignedly, suddenly sweeping her up, lifting her into his arms.

Her lids popped open in surprise, and she found herself looking directly into the glossy jet of his eyes. They were narrowed, and she could see that his nostrils were flaring again. It was a look that she had once mistaken for anger and now knew to be passion. And perhaps his passion was more to be feared than his wrath.

"You win," he said. The muscles at the back of his jaw clenched with frustration. "Tonight I won't hold your breasts. I won't kiss them. I won't even *look* at your precious damned breasts."

He stood in the middle of the room, hugging her against his chest, staring deep into her eyes. She couldn't read his face now. She didn't know if he was going to hit her or kill her or bend her over and breed her like a filly in season. And at the moment she didn't care: anything would be all right if it ended this agony of frustration.

Finally he broke the silence.

"I have something else in mind tonight, Jenny," he whispered huskily, then took two steps to the foot of the narrow bed. He sat her down, perching her precariously at the edge.

"Lie back," he said.

By the tone of his voice, Jenny knew it was not a suggestion, and somehow she found it strangely thrilling. She complied, and watched as Ace reached for her pillow and snugged it under her head.

He stared down at her for a moment before he walked to the foot of the bed to stand above her bent knees and reached down to pluck at her gown. Slowly, he lifted the white fabric higher and higher until he floated it halfway up her slender thighs. His fingers dropped it there, then feathered along the crease between her tightly clenched legs to her knees.

"Relax, Jenny," he whispered. "Just relax. I'll take care of the rest."

His voice was music, his touch the merciful caress of a dark angel, and Jenny obeyed. Ace slipped first one hand, then both between her knees, cupping each inner surface gently and gliding his hands up and down the lower half of her thighs, easing them apart so gradually that Jenny was barely aware of their movement. She was only conscious of the tingling warmth spreading from his skimming fingers: a warmth that pulsed strongly between her legs and spread to engulf her in warm, liquid sensation.

She closed her eyes again as those shivering surges traveled through her: delicate shimmers at first, then quakes and rumbles along her limbs and deep in her belly. Her breasts seemed to strain at the fabric covering them, and she moved her torso slightly from side to side, unconsciously abrading their sensitized peaks against her cotton gown.

Then she realized that Ace had slowly pushed her nightgown even higher. It was pooled about her waist now, and Ace was kneeling between her legs. His fingers feathered delicate strokes higher and higher on the tender inside surfaces of her upper thighs.

She could not imagine what he planned. She only knew that the closer he came to their juncture, the more excited and abandoned she felt.

Then his heated lips and tongue began to follow the trail his gentle hands had blazed, leaving a lazy, wandering line of kisses as he lipped and licked at that sensitive flesh. Higher and higher came his meandering, shameless mouth, until she could feel the warmth of his breath filtering through the golden curls at the base of her belly.

Her breathing deepened and her pulse quickened in delicious, unnamed anticipation.

"What . . . what are you doing?" she heard her own voice whisper as she felt him slip his hands beneath her thighs, then slide up to cup her buttocks. He shifted his arms, and she felt her hips, buoyed by his encompassing hands, rise slightly above the mattress as her upper thighs slid in some perfect, natural way along his arms.

Moving even closer to the throbbing heat that had possessed the base of her belly, he slipped his hands from her buttocks and brought them up around the outside of her hips, angling her legs even wider apart with his shoulders. From either side, she felt his fingers comb her curls. "Sweet Jenny," he whispered before, gently, he parted the curtain of ringlets to expose the pink silk within.

And then he kissed her.

Fire surged through her body. Incoherent, distant, babbling noises seemed to issue from her lips as he caressed her in an intimate and perfect manner she had never imagined possible. Where his fingers had failed to delve the night before, his warm, insistent tongue traveled tonight, and Jenny began to twist her hips, squirming against him, wanting more, always more of this potent new magic.

It was exquisite torture that he administered now. No other sense existed for her except the heat of his breath, the hot silk of his tongue. Jenny gripped blindly at the sides of her mattress to keep from jolting off it as, abruptly, she erupted into ecstasy.

She gulped for air as her back arched high off the bed in spasm after shattering spasm. At last she eased back onto the sweat-drenched mattress. Low purring sounds came from the back of her throat as she lolled there, panting and only partly conscious. Ace lowered her nightdress, then went to her side to scoop her into his arms again.

As he sat on the bed, an exhausted Jenny half on and half off his lap, he stroked the beads of perspiration from her forehead. Her eyes were closed, her lips swollen and parted, and every few seconds she shuddered slightly with what he knew were the aftershocks of her shattering release. Never had a woman responded so powerfully to him as did his little Jenny, he thought. And never had he responded so strongly in return.

But why would she give nothing back to him? He didn't understand her reasons, and at the moment, he wanted, more than anything, that she should give him some sign. He also needed a release of his own quite badly. His fingers moved to his belt and the buttons of his trousers.

Gently, he took the hand of the sated blond angel on his lap and pressed it to himself. Automatically her fingers curled about him, and Ace took a jagged breath as she gently squeezed, then released his swollen member.

Swimming in thick, pulsing honey at the edge of awareness, Jenny felt him take her hand, and at some primal level, she knew where he had placed it. At that level, it seemed the most natural thing to do, and when she felt him kiss her forehead in encouragement and whisper her name, she continued to move her hand upon him. It seemed the easiest thing to do. It seemed to be what she *wanted* to do.

Ace groaned and shifted slightly. Her fingers burned an exquisite trail along his shaft, shooting welcome tongues of flame through his groin. Her touch was uncannily perfect, and he knew that the sensuous way she fondled him came naturally to her: this was no learned, carefully contrived caress from the jaded hand of a prostitute. It was the sweet, natural, ingenuous expression of a girl who was born to pleasure and to be pleasured.

"Jenny," he whispered as she stroked him. "Yes, Jenny."

But as he kissed her brow and shuttered lids and murmured her name, Jenny began to swim closer to awareness. She recognized that he was showering her face with kisses, that she was on his lap, and that he had lifted her gown again to cup her buttock.

She was also aware that her hand seemed to be moving of its own accord.

Her eyes fluttered open when she realized what she was doing. Immediately, she ceased the movements of her fingers. She still held him—she seemed unable to let go for some reason—but she halted the motions which were giving him so much pleasure.

Suddenly, she hated herself. She couldn't even keep that one weak pledge—couldn't even keep it for two hours. Silent tears welled in her green eyes and streamed down her cheeks even as she stilled her caress, and Ace, very near his own release, dug his fingers into the bare flesh of her bottom.

"Jenny," he hissed through clenched teeth, "don't stop now."

Through tear-filled eyes she looked up at him and saw beneath his features the face of primal man, ancient and possessed by lust. She barely understood that she had taken him too far, too close to the edge, and that she must finish what she started or pay the consequences.

"Jenny!" he growled, pinching her buttock even harder. "Jenny, please!"

But despite the genuine danger in which she might

be placing herself, she managed to whisper, "I can't."

She began to pull her fingers away from him, but the hand that had clutched her bottom suddenly clasped her wrist, staying her hand.

She froze, and for several long moments they stayed like that: her fingers curled motionlessly around him, his hand clamped hard about her tiny wrist, their eyes locked as they waged a silent battle of wills.

At last, he released his grip on her wrist. He had not spoken, but his eyes accused her furiously. Without breaking that damning, terrifying eye contact, he buttoned himself back inside his trousers.

With a final, disgusted sigh, he suddenly stood up, unceremoniously dumping her to the floor. She landed with a thud on the thin braided rug, legs akimbo, her nightgown hiked up around her waist where he had shoved it. Mouth agape, she stared up at him.

"I've had it!" he snarled. "You will and then you won't. You take, but you won't give. Why, Jenny? Why are you such a teasing little bitch?"

She would take a lot of things from him, and had. But she wouldn't take *that.* "I'm sick of you!" she cried as a sudden influx of adrenaline made her too brave, too foolish. "I'm sick of you all! It seems to me that by now you've completed that one corner of my education you found lacking. You've proved your point, so why don't you just get out and leave me alone!"

He was seething, glaring at her, his hands clenched into fists, but she was drunk with anger and couldn't stop. "You all think you're so damn smart because

173

you know about—about—*that*. But you're not as smart as you think. Outlaws and whores, that's all you are! No better than animals!" She yanked open the bottom drawer of her bureau, jerked out her copy of Cicero, and threw it at him. It missed.

"Can you read that?" she snorted. "Can any of you read that? I'll bet there isn't one person in this house who wouldn't translate *sic transit gloria mundi* to 'Monday, Gloria was ill on the train'—and it'd take them a week of thinking to get that far! And furthermore," she spat, "maybe the reason I'm such a 'teasing little bitch,' as you so very *graciously* put it, is because you're such a son of one!"

With a guttural roar, he reached down, hauled her into the air by one shoulder and cast her to the bed. She landed on her back, and before she could move or think, he jabbed two fingers beneath the collar of her nightdress. With one mighty jerk, he ripped it from neck to hem. The entire front of her gown came away, and he stood over her, angrily balling the fabric in his fists.

Her fury drained abruptly, leaving her in the icy clutches of cold terror. She'd gone too far this time, and she was suddenly certain that he was going to kill her—he looked angry enough, and perhaps she'd given him justification.

But maybe he wouldn't. Maybe if she gave him what he wanted he would go away, be satisfied and never come back. Maybe. She managed to pull her eyes away from his. Wordlessly, the remaining half of her nightgown falling from her shoulders, she slid to the edge of the bed.

She barely heard him say, "Jenny, Jenny, I'm . . . I

didn't mean . . . Damn!'' Shivering with fear and confusion, she couldn't look at him.

She put her legs over the side, then twisted to bend over the edge of the cot: her knees on the floor, her torso flat on the mattress. He would have to do it to her on his knees, too, she thought, but she was too drained and too frightened to stand up for him as Meg had for Scar.

Her weeping was audible now. She screwed her eyes closed and hoisted her fanny into the air as she had seen Meg do. She braced herself for his first thrust.

Nothing happened.

He did not speak again, nor did he touch her.

She waited another minute, still crying. Why did he torment her so? Maybe she wasn't doing it right. She moved her knees further apart and tilted her hips as high as she could, but still he did not touch her.

"Do it! Just do it, get it over with!'' she finally cried, opening her eyes and twisting her head toward him.

The room was empty except for the discarded rag that had been the front half of her nightgown, lying crumpled on the rug where he had dropped it.

Ace strode into the circle of light, flopped on his cot, wrested a bottle of bourbon from the pile of books and newspapers at the end of the stone table, and gulped nearly two fingers of it, straight down.

Scar had his nose stuck in *The Arkansas Kid: Cavalier of the Open Road.* He looked up. "Who put the burr under *your* blanket?''

Ace didn't answer. He shot Scar a filthy look before he raised the bottle again. The dent he put in it this time was smaller, but still substantial.

"Don't you ever get tired of that damn book?" he snapped. He started to recork the whiskey, then thought better of it and took another swallow. "You've read it at least a dozen times."

"It's real excitin', that's why. Even better than the one 'bout us." His face screwed up a little. "Say, you think Mac's ever read this?"

Ace snorted derisively.

"Christ!" Scar scowled. "What the hell's wrong with you lately, anyhow? Two nights ago you come in here ready to take on a rabid grizzly with your bare hands. Then last night you was so silly I nearly had to put lead in your pockets 'n tie you to the floor. And now you—" Suddenly he brightened. "You got yourself a girl, ain't you?"

Ace's head snapped up. If looks could kill, his expression would have put Scar at least twelve feet under.

Scar's grin widened and his eyes sparkled. "Yeah, that's it all right." He chuckled and leaned back against the pillar of stone behind his cot, lacing his fingers behind his neck. "I'll be damned. Ol' Mr. Ice-Water-For-Blood Ace Denton, Mr. Love-'Em-And-Leave-'Em has gone and fell in love."

Ace put down the bottle and reached for his deck of cards. "Shut up."

With great difficulty, Scar suppressed most of a giggle. What got out echoed through the cavern, and he shot a nervous glance upward before he added, "So who's the lucky girl? Agnes? Naw, not her, not

Pearly neither . . . Sure as hell ain't Shirley Mae, and Belinda? Not a chance . . . Jesus, don't tell me it's Iris! Now wouldn't *that* just—"

"Shut up." Ace hissed it through clenched teeth, and the look in his eyes told Scar he meant business.

"Jesus!" Scar's narrow lips twitched with the effort of suppressing the curl of a smile. "Sorry! But Crikey, Ace, I don't think I ever seen you quite so—" The grin fairly exploded across his features. "It's that little blonde, ain't it? That little gal in the kitchen. What's her name—Penny?"

Ace was shuffling the deck, but something went wrong and they sprayed up into the air. Scar muffled his laughter with *The Arkansas Kid* as Ace, in the center of a shower of pasteboards, sighed, "Jenny."

But before the last of the cards had fluttered to the ground, he stood up and stalked off toward the house tunnel. *The office*, he thought. *The books in the office. It'll be in one of those, goddamnit.*

Scar, still tittering, shook his head. "Where the hell you think you're—" Ace turned to swear at him, and he added quickly, "And don't tell me to shut up again."

But, "It's gotta be Latin," was what he snarled before he disappeared.

She was dreaming she was lost in a great, dark forest. She was all alone—even Fancy had deserted her—and she was crying. She began to run through the trees, and as she did, their branches turned into hands that plucked at her hair, her clothes. On and on she ran, and just as she thought her lungs would burst, she came into a clearing.

In its center there was a very large oak, and on a gnarled, low-hanging branch sat the Cheshire Cat.

"Hello, Jenny," he said. "Or may I call you Alice?"

"Go away!" she screamed. "You're all crazy here!"

He smiled, spreading cat lips wide over an endless row of razored cat teeth. "That's right," he said.

"I don't want to be here," she cried as a Gryphon with a long scar on his cheek landed high in the playing-card branches. *Bend over, Meggie,* it wheezed. *Bend over, Meggie.*

She ran, screaming. Her feet tangled and she fell, but hands plucked her up into the air. Ace's hands. While the chanting Gryphon circled overhead, Ace looked deep into her eyes. "Teasing little bitch!" he snarled, and dropped her to the forest floor.

She woke abruptly, soaked in cold sweat, her quilt knotted in her hands, every muscle in her body tensed and aching. There was a light in the room, the light of a single candle. Ace was standing over her and she cringed.

"It means," he growled, " 'So passes away the glory of this world.' " He blew out the candle. There was a soft grating sound, and then he was gone.

Dear God, she thought, pressing her palms to her throbbing forehead, *what am I doing here?*

Seven

Tuesday

Although Jenny had never heard the word "addiction," she was now bitterly aware of its definition.

It seemed impossible to quell her longings for this man she so despised. After he disappeared, leaving her shivering and confused, her nightmares, then her dreams, had been filled with him: his face, his voice, the sensation of his touch were overpoweringly compelling. And while her hatred of him—and everything he stood for—had not lessened in the slightest, she realized that he had somehow managed to mark her, to claim her as his own: that no matter where she went, no matter how far she ran, he would always be there—tormenting her, pleasuring her—if only in her unceasing, shameless dreams. And the dreams were not enough.

Despite the bright morning sunshine flooding the kitchen, her dilemma crushed down on her like a dark, enveloping cloud.

Mrs. Bramley had collected every lamp and lantern in the house. She'd filled the kitchen with them— table lamps, hand lanterns, storm lamps—and now she was on the back porch trimming wicks and refilling reservoirs with acrid kerosene. In the kitchen, Jenny listlessly scrubbed and polished the sooty shades and chimneys.

The white-curtained window over the kitchen sink looked down toward the stable, and it was there that she stared, rather than at the glass and metal in her soapy hands; and not at the barn so much as the big red stallion pawing the ground, prowling nervously in the corral. Jenny seemed unable to ignore him, and though she detested herself for it, the sight of that big sorrel stud horse—and the memory of what Ace had made her watch—brought back the tingling. He'd told her that he wanted her to remember that night always, and with whom she'd spent it.

Well, you got your wish, she thought, and scrubbed a little harder at the chimney in her hands. She wondered if Fancy tugged at the tie rope in her stall, if she needed to be mounted by that prancing, pacing stallion as much as Jenny herself needed to be held once more by his master.

Why couldn't this man, for whose touch she so maddeningly ached, have been a rancher or a shopkeeper or a bank clerk? Why couldn't he have come to her in the guise of some nice Minnesota schoolboy or Iowa farmer? Why did he have to be an outlaw, a murderer?

Why did he have to be Ace Denton?

He was a devil, and somehow, he had possessed her soul. She knew, all too well, how close she had come to breaking her vow last night; and how difficult it had been, spent and sated and cuddled in his strong, safe arms, to still the hand that held him. She hadn't wanted to stop. She'd wanted to press her lips where her fingers rested. She had wanted to make him groan with the same ecstasy with which he had gifted her.

But she couldn't break that promise. Beneath it, underlying the want of him, the need of him, were two pictures that relentlessly returned to her mind: the sight of her father's gravestone, and the image of that half-carved chunk of cherry wood in his battered trunk.

She knew she was sinking into a quagmire of emotion from which there might be no escape. Knowing he was near, that he might be watching her, and that at any moment he could appear to tempt her again, each time more exquisitely, more irresistibly than the last . . . Every minute she stayed in the house was an agony for her.

There was no question of her staying with him. It was impossible. But she realized that unless he left within the next few days she would be lost. She could not go; not yet. She had no money except less than a dollar of her "inheritance" and seventy-four cents she'd taken in tips over the weekend. There was no hope that Miss Liz would give over her wages to date and let her depart. The madam had made it all too clear that she was on trial. No money would be paid to her until she had finished her first two weeks for Mrs. Bramley.

Once, for almost an entire minute, she'd even considered taking Miss Liz up on her offer of the "gentleman's" fifty dollars. But even though the gentleman would have been nice and anonymous, and though its end result would be to get her away from Ace Denton, it would have been wrong, so wrong.

If only she didn't want Ace so badly . . .

She was still staring down the slope at his stallion when she heard voices in the dining room. The day was unseasonably warm and sticky, and the communicating door was propped halfway open to aid ventilation. She could hear their voices clearly: Mac, Meg Sweetwater, and Miss Liz. Mac had gone into Green Mule right after breakfast, and must have just returned.

She heard chairs scrape the floor, then the rustle of paper.

"Here," Mac was saying. "Right on page two."

"Move your damn shoulder," Miss Liz grumbled impatiently. "I can't see."

There was silence for a moment, then Meg's voice chirped, "Ma'am, could you say it out? I ain't one for readin'."

"Sorry dear."

There was another rustle of paper, then a short pause before Miss Liz spoke again. "Basically, it says there was another hold-up three days back, down in Winston. Says Ace and the Dodge brothers held up the bank. Wounded two people in the street, killed the bank guard, and got away with close to twenty-five hundred dollars."

"But that can't be," Meg's little voice trembled. "That's two days' ride! They was—"

"That's right," Mac cut in. He sounded disgusted, almost angry, but not with Meggy. "You better take

182

this paper down with the next tray, honey. I got a feeling Ace is gonna be real interested in—"

Glass shattered, exploded in the kitchen.

From the back porch, Mrs. Bramley bellowed, "What the hell you doin' in there, missy!"

Dumbly, Jenny looked down at the soapy shards at her feet. She had unconsciously moved toward the door as she listened, and now she was nearly halfway across the room, staring stupidly at the remains of a glass chimney she had just let crash to the floor.

Mac was there in an instant. He took her arm and backed her away from the splatter of water and shattered glass on the oak boards. "You cut, angel?" he asked. "You bleedin'?" He didn't voice it, but he might as well have added, *You listenin'?*

Jenny was shivering, although at the moment she couldn't think why. "No, I—I'm fine, Mac. I was just taking it to the table and—"

"Well, at least she ain't wrecked more than one," Mrs. Bramley snapped. She had bustled in from the back porch, and her expression was nearly as indignant as her tone. "You remember this, Liz," she called into the dining room. "You remember to take that busted chimney outta her wages!"

She turned her rage back on Jenny. "And as for you, missy, you just git back over there 'n finish up and don't you dare break nothin' more. If you ain't the laziest, worst excuse for—"

"Shut up, Bertha." Mac's tone was low, but his voice had taken on a mysterious command. "You never had it so good and you know it. Go trim your wicks. I'll see to Jenny."

The cook screwed up her bloated face as if to say

183

something scathing, but at the last moment thought better of it. With a snort, she clumped back out to the porch. Mac sat Jenny down on a chair and went for a broom and dustpan.

She sat numbly, her hands in her lap, watching in silence while he swept up the last of the glass splinters. When he had finished, he peeked out into the dining room to make certain Meg and Miss Liz had gone. The bar was empty, and he let the connecting door swing shut to further ensure their privacy.

He pulled out a chair next to Jenny's, then reached over and took her pale hands in his. "You were listenin', weren't you, honey?"

She looked up at him, wan and confused. There were tears forming in her eyes, but they had not yet spilled down her cheeks. It seemed she had cried more in the last week than in the whole of her life put together.

"Iris said he asked Miss Liz about me," she whispered. "What . . . what did he ask, Mac?"

"He just wanted to know who you were, angel." His voice was as quiet as hers. "That's all. He just didn't figure you belonged here."

"He . . . I . . ." Jenny's voice broke, and Mac squeezed her hands in his.

"You saw him again, didn't you, honey? After that first night you served 'em, I mean." His voice was paternal and soothing, and he lifted a hand to brush away one escaping tear with a big rough thumb.

Jenny nodded. "He's in the house, Mac," she whispered. "I know about the secret door in the cellar, and—" She was about to say *and the passages*

184

*in the house, and the tunnel to the barn, and how
Meg is taking them food, and that everybody in the
house seems to know about this but me, and he
doesn't just see me Mac—he touches me, touches me
all over until I go out of my mind and I can't make
him stop and I don't want to make him stop
anymore . . .* but he hushed her before the words
could tumble out.

"I wouldn't mention that again if I was you,
Jenny, not to anybody." He patted her hands, then
squeezed them until she looked into his eyes. "You
understand what I mean, angel? Not anybody."

She nodded. "I won't, Mac."

He smiled and rubbed her arm. If she said she
wouldn't tell, he believed her. "See, Miss Liz don't
take kindly to anybody knowin' her secrets unless she
tells 'em herself. She takes, well, a real personal
interest in Ace. You gotta understand that Miss Liz,
she grew up with Ace's daddy, and she's known Ace
since he was a boy back in Kansas, before the war, and
before he got mixed up with Quantrill and ended up
on the wrong side of the law . . ."

Poor little thing, he thought. *Ace probably came
out and talked to her, and she's scared to death
having an outlaw in the place—especially one with
Ace's reputation . . .*

He stared at Jenny's soft profile. She had looked
down and away, but Mac kept talking, his voice low,
almost as if he were talking to himself. "Ace, he never
should'a thrown in with Quantrill. It was foolish-
ness, all of it. He'd been driftin' around like a lot of
young fellas do, tryin' to figure out just what he
wanted to do with his life. He didn't want to be a

185

farmer like his pa—didn't have the want or the knack of growin' things. Thought maybe he might want to ranch, though . . . Guess he was an odd sort of kid. Liz told me once that when Ace was a tad, he always had his nose in a book or his hands on a horse. Said he was a better hand with a bronc than most anybody she'd ever seen . . .

"So he took off. Went west. I guess he must've worked a few different outfits in the Territories out Colorado way. That's where he met up with Rafe Langley. But when the war broke out he came home, and he brought Rafe with him.

"There was a lot of grief in Kansas in those days, angel, just like in Missouri. Neighbors against neighbors, families splittin' up and the like. Sometimes certain folks would take it on themselves to sway their neighbor's opinions, and some of the ways they used weren't very nice.

"Now, Ace's daddy'd never owned a slave in his life. Never could've afforded one even if he believed in it, which he didn't. He was a plain, honest farmer that gave nobody any trouble and expected none in return. But when Ace came home, he found his pa dead."

Mac sighed as the sadness of those war-torn times flooded back into his heart. "It was Jayhawkers that did it. A mistake, pure 'n simple. They rode in late at night with torches and guns, and they were too liquored up to notice they were burnin' out the wrong farm. Ace's pa died in the fire, and when young Roy came runnin' out, they shot him. He was only fifteen. I heard that one of the bunch that did it hung himself a few days after, once he realized what

186

they'd done. Anyway, that all happened 'bout a week afore Ace 'n Rafe rode in.

"Ace was pretty broke up. Said he didn't want to get mixed up in somebody else's war—he'd been west for a few years by then, and a lot of the westerners, well, they didn't feel like it was their battle to fight—but he was by-God gonna get the ones that killed his pa and kid brother."

Jenny had turned slowly toward him as he talked, and was listening intently. Mac paused, and Jenny squeezed at his hand, urging him on.

"It was Rafe Langley talked him into joinin' up with Quantrill. Rafe knew some boys that'd gone to ride with him, and he told Ace that the Union army'd never do anything to stop the Jayhawkers—they were all one and the same, he reckoned—and that the Rebs were too hard-pressed to mess with 'em. Quantrill was the only way, Rafe told him, 'cause his boys could do things that the regular Confederacy wouldn't or couldn't."

"But why?" Jenny whispered. "Quantrill's men, they did horrible things! My papa told me—"

"Ace didn't know any of that, angel. Not then. Nobody did, really. It didn't start to come out till later. Anyhow, he 'n Rafe joined up. He met Andy Dodge 'n Scar Cooksey 'round that time. Cole Younger and Frank James were there, too. Young Jesse—Dingus, they called him in those days—he came later, and there was a few other fellas whose names you'd recognize. Anyhow, by the time Ace realized what was goin' on, well, it was too late. What really did it was the Lawrence raid. Ace 'n Rafe 'n Scar, they were all there. Turned Ace's stomach, what he saw, and he deserted Quantrill on the spot. Couldn't stand it anymore when he realized that the men he was ridin' with were just as bad—maybe worse—than the boys that burned out his pa. But by then the law had his name, and there wasn't any goin' back to a regular life, not for any of 'em . . ."

He squeezed her hand, adding sadly, "Don't believe everything you hear about Ace, angel. Don't ever believe everything you hear about anybody."

They sat in silence for a minute or two before Jenny asked, "What you were reading from the newspaper, Mac—"

"Don't ask me any questions I can't answer, honey." He pushed back his chair and got to his feet. "You best just forget all about this. And steer clear of Ace. You're better off that way. Trouble rides on him like fleas on a blue tick hound."

The day wore on. Jenny's mind was far away, and she tended to her duties like a sleepwalker. Mac's story had evoked an emotion she wouldn't have suspected she was capable of feeling toward the outlaw: sympathy. Additionally, it was clear that Ace was being blamed by both the law and the press for a crime he could not possibly have committed.

Was it possible that it hadn't been him in Fowlersville? That someone else had murdered her father? The questions gnawed at her. She wanted desperately to believe it had all been some kind of horrible mistake; that Ace had been miles away, and that all those witnesses in Fowlersville, Iowa, had been drunk or blinded by the sun or incompetent . . .

No. That couldn't have been the case and she knew it. Too many people had seen him, and that many witnesses couldn't be mistaken. Perhaps this last hold-up had been at night—maybe someone had just seen a tall, dark man and two blond boys and assumed it was Ace and the Dodge brothers. Maybe, just this one time, somebody had traded on Ace Denton's reputation. Because it happened once didn't mean it had happened before.

The last meal of the day had been served and the kitchen tidied before Jenny came to that conclusion. Mac mentioned to her during dinner that she might want to check Fancy. The mare was off her feed. She was still in season and probably just cranky, but he thought that she might eat for Jenny what she would not eat for him.

"I'll go down right after I finish the dishes, Mac," she had answered. She was actually anxious to go. It would be a way of testing her newest theory: she'd become convinced that Ace had found her in the barn because of the carrots.

Both times she'd visited the stable, she'd made a trip to the root cellar before she went down the hill. He must have seen her through one of those cellar peepholes.

Tonight she'd visit Fancy empty-handed. And she strongly suspected that she would not be visited by Ace Denton.

The house had received only two customers so far this evening: a cowboy drifting west had chosen Mary-Rebecca as his lady of the hour, and Iris was upstairs with her regular Tuesday all-nighter: one of Green Mule's three attorneys. The other girls

189

wandered around the house or lounged in the receiving parlor.

Belinda Critchley, slouched drunkenly against the bar in the empty dining hall, was the only one of them to see Jenny stride purposefully down the long slope to the red barn.

Fancy *was* out of sorts.

Jenny offered her a measure of grain, which she refused, and a fresh bucket of water, which the mare immediately sent flying with one well-placed kick.

Operating on the theory that one good grooming was worth a full measure of oats most any day, Jenny decided that whether Fancy wanted it or not, she was about to be curried within an inch of her life.

She hauled out a currycomb and body brush and began to work on the obstreperous bay in earnest. She started at the little mare's head. At first she split her time between dodging Fancy's teeth and hooves, and glancing furtively over her shoulder for Ace. But as the mare became resigned to Jenny's ministrations, Jenny, too, began to relax.

She'd been right: the carrots had been the giveaway, after all. If he was not here by now, he wasn't coming.

At first, she was delighted. She had managed to avoid him. She'd finally won a round. But as she worked on Fancy's coat, scrubbing out the grime with the currycomb and flicking it away with the bristly body brush, she found that she was actually a little disappointed he hadn't made an appearance. By the time she had curried her way back to Fancy's hip she was almost missing him.

She rubbed harder at the mare's seal-brown coat, working out the dust and dirt, unconsciously attempting to dispel her frustrations with physical labor. This new feeling—this feeling she had experienced for the first time only a few evenings ago in a darkened hallway with a stranger—had taken such a hold on her that less than twenty-four hours after her last encounter with Ace, the yearning within her had become almost unbearable.

She worked her way back around Fancy's rump, and was embarrassed when at the pressure of the brush, Fancy flagged her tail to the side and whickered, calling to the stallion.

She felt herself blush and whispered, "Stop that, Fancy."

"Why should she?"

She wheeled toward his voice. At the edge of the circle of lantern light, he leaned against the feed room door, blue-shirted arms crossed over his rawhide vest.

He wasn't smiling this time.

"She wants it just as bad as you do. She's just a little more honest about it, that's all." He closed the distance between them and stopped less than an arm's length away. "That's something we could all use a little more of, don't you think, Jenny?" he said, his eyes as flat and hard as his voice. "Honesty, I mean."

Her knees began to buckle at the sight and sound of him, but she took a deep breath and curled her fingers even tighter around the brushes in her hands. He was only two feet away from her now, and she could just catch the clean, musky scent of him. *I will not give in this time,* she told herself in what was already a halfhearted lecture.

"I shouldn't think that honesty was something you'd know very much about," she blurted.

Immediately, she wanted to snatch back the words. A part of her meant them, certainly; but another part—the larger part now, and growing stronger all the time—understood why he had gone the way he had, or at least what had started him toward it. And then, there was a certain guilt on her part for having taken a moment's satisfaction, fleeting though it had been, when Mac first told her about the murder of Ace's father. For a fraction of a second, she had been pleased that he had felt pain of the same sort he had made her suffer.

"Really?" he said. His voice was cutting, his tone just short of cruel. "Maybe not. Maybe I don't know much about *your* kind of honesty, Jenny. What kind is it that lets you say 'no' when you mean 'yes,' and 'go' when you mean 'stay'? What makes you think you're so much better than everybody else?"

"I mean what I say." It was a lie, but she was stuck with it now.

"I don't believe you, Jenny. Not for one single, solitary minute." His eyes were narrowed, their black and bottomless irises indistinguishable from the pupils. The intensity of that gaze locked her there more effectively than any rope or chain. The sheer force of his nearness seemed to envelop her in waves of heat, of sensual energy. It was all she could do to keep from pressing herself against him.

"Believe what you want." What she meant to come

192

AFFIX
STAMP
HERE

HEARTFIRE HOME SUBSCRIPTION
SERVICE
P.O. BOX 5214
120 BRIGHTON ROAD
CLIFTON, NEW JERSEY 07015

GET 4 FREE BOOKS

Heartfire Romance

FREE BOOK CERTIFICATE

GET 4 FREE BOOKS

Yes! I want to subscribe to Zebra's HEARTFIRE HOME SUBSCRIPTION SERVICE. Please send me my 4 FREE books. Then each month I'll receive the four newest Heartfire Romances as soon as they are published to preview Free for ten days. If I decide to keep them I'll pay the special discounted price of just $3.50 each; a total of $14.00. This is a savings of $3.00 off the regular publishers price. There are no shipping, handling or other hidden charges. There is no minimum number of books to buy and I may cancel this subscription at any time. In any case the 4 FREE Books are mine to keep regardless.

NAME

ADDRESS

CITY _____ STATE _____ ZIP

TELEPHONE

SIGNATURE

(If under 18 parent or guardian must sign)
Terms and prices subject to change.
Orders subject to acceptance.

HF 101

MAIL THE COUPON BELOW.

4 FREE BOOKS

TO GET YOUR

ENJOY ALL THE PASSION AND ROMANCE OF...

Heartfire

ROMANCES from ZEBRA

After you have read HEART-FIRE ROMANCES, we're sure you'll agree that HEARTFIRE sets new standards of excellence for historical romantic fiction. Each Zebra HEARTFIRE novel is the ultimate blend of intimate romance and grand adventure and each takes place in the kinds of historical settings you want most...the American Revolution, the Old West, Civil War and more.

Zebra's HEARTFIRE ROMANCES Are The Ultimate In Historical Romantic Fiction.

Start Enjoying Romance As You Have Never Enjoyed It Before...
With 4 FREE Books From HEARTFIRE

SUBSCRIBERS SAVE, SAVE, $AVE!!!

As a HEARTFIRE Home Subscriber, you'll save with your HEARTFIRE Subscription. You'll receive 4 brand new Heartfire Romances to preview Free for 10 days each month. If you decide to keep them you'll pay only $3.50 each; a total of $14.00 and you'll save $3.00 each month off the cover price.

Plus, we'll send you these novels as soon as they are published each month. There is never any shipping, handling or other hidden charges; home delivery is always FREE! And there is no obligation to buy even a single book. You may return any of the books within 10 days for full credit and you can cancel your subscription at any time. No questions asked.

Now you can get Heartfire Romances right at home and save
Heartfire Romance
Get 4 Free Heartfire Novels.
A $17.00 Value!
Home Subscription Members can enjoy Heartfire Romances and Save $$$$$ each month.

out as a flip rebuff was instead expressed as a weak whisper. The battle had not yet begun, and she was already giving up the fight despite all her resolutions to the contrary.

He took her by the shoulders. At the instant his fingers came to rest, she somehow lost control of her hands. The brush and currycomb slid from her grasp to thud softly on the strawed floor. She hated herself for her response, but she was powerless to control it.

"What I believe, Jenny, is that right now you need to be kissed."

She found she couldn't form the word "no," and she tried to shake her head, but before she could, his lips had already found hers. There was only a fraction of a second's pause before she gave herself wholeheartedly to his embrace. She felt her arms drift up to hug his muscled neck. Her fingers laced into the dark forest at the back of his head as he pulled her more tightly against him.

The kiss was deep and long, and it left her breathless and shaken and wanting more. But to her surprise, he stepped away from her and sat down on a bale of straw, leaving her to sway weakly next to Fancy's stall.

He sat there for a long minute, staring at her in a silence broken only by an occasional rustling movement of the livestock. He still looked deadly serious, and something about his manner frightened her. Sitting there quietly, watching her wordlessly, he seemed somehow more threateningly sexual, more dangerously primal than when he had entered her room last night. She could only stand and stare back at him, feeling her heart race. More strongly with each passing second, she wanted him to come to her, to touch her and make her his. But she could not admit it to him, at least not in words. She had her promise to remember.

Finally, he spoke. "Well," he said. His voice was a low, resonant murmur. "It seems we've reached an impasse."

She wasn't quite certain what he meant, and nervously waited for him to continue. More and more, she hoped he would do so standing, with his arms about her.

He didn't. He stayed where he was, not moving except to lean forward to rest his elbows on his knees.

"The lady wants to, but she won't," he mused. "The lady says no when she means yes." His gaze, which already bored into her, intensified.

"Maybe we need to leave words out of this entirely," he continued. "At least, your words. Except for one thing, Jenny, and you know what that is."

He stood up slowly and came toward her, stopping an arm's length away. "You know that I want you. And I know that you want me. But the last thing, little one, the final act—for that, you'll have to ask. I won't break my word, no matter how much I'd like to." He reached out to touch her soft, golden hair. "You're so beautiful, Jenny, so sweet, so bright. I don't understand why you're doing this. But for now, no more questions, no more answers."

He kissed her again, very sweetly, and felt her shiver as he barely brushed her lips with his. Then he stepped back again, less than an arm's length away, and looked down at her.

"Take off your blouse, Jenny," he whispered.

It was not a request. It was more on the order of command, although the words were not callous or demanding. It was more as if he had given her permission to do something they both knew she wished to do, but could not instigate.

Slowly, her trembling fingers went to the bottom of her shirtwaist, her eyes never leaving his. The first two or three buttons came undone clumsily, but the last few she freed rapidly. She tugged the tails free, slipped out of it, and draped it over the side wall of Fancy's stall. She turned back to him, her bosom rising and falling, straining against the fabric of her camisole. Why didn't he touch her? He had to know how badly she wanted him.

He knew. But he wanted her to give herself to him, freely and uncoerced. If tonight she could bare herself to him willingly, even eagerly, perhaps what would come later would be easier for her—a natural next step. He hoped. For the time being, for tonight, he had decided that he would not yet take her; not here in the barn. But he would have her naked in his arms, and of her own volition. There would be time for the other later.

He reached out to lightly run his fingertips over her shoulder, then took another step away—far enough that he could see every inch of her—and in a deep tone that bathed her in prickling waves of expectation, whispered, "Now the skirt, little one."

She seemed unable to stop herself. She fumbled with the closure, then let the skirt fall to the straw. She stepped out of it and picked it up, laying it atop her shirtwaist before she turned to face him again.

Her breath came in quickening little bursts, and she found that the act of disrobing before him was incredibly exciting to her. She desperately wished that he would come closer to her and kiss her once more.

But he didn't.

"Petticoats, Jenny." The sound of his voice, low and intimate in the circle of lamplight, was as evocative as any physical caress. She felt as if the two of them had been somehow lifted out of time: that nothing existed beyond this golden orb of light in the middle of a lonely stable; that outside it, where the darkness ruled, there was nothing but void and empty space.

She untied her petticoats, one by one, and placed them atop her discarded skirt and shirtwaist.

Now she faced him wearing only her shoes, stockings, and underclothes. Why didn't he come to her? Why didn't he kiss her? She needed him desperately now: her breasts ached for his touch, and the apex of her legs burned with moist heat.

But "shoes and stockings, next, Jenny," was all he said.

She complied, kicking off her shoes without bothering to unbuckle them. Rolling her stockings down her legs and off her feet, she cast them aside in wadded little balls.

She looked at him expectantly, her breathing almost labored by now. This time he didn't speak. He just shifted his gaze to the ribboned neckline of her camisole and nodded slightly.

She understood.

Very slowly, she slipped free the ribbon and slid

the flimsy cotton from her torso, revealing her creamy breasts to the soft glow of the lantern and the waiting, hungry eyes of Ace Denton.

As to the rest, he did not have to speak. She laid her camisole aside, and with hands that shook with anticipation, untied and pulled off the last thin barrier to the outlaw's hands and eyes. She placed her drawers atop the pile of her discarded clothing and taking a deep breath, turned to face him.

Slowly, luxuriously, his eyes wandered down the contours of her body, learning every soft swell, shadowed hollow, and lush, inviting curve. He took his time, letting his gaze linger here and there as the line of his vision traveled from her face to her feet and back up again to rest at her wide, green, beckoning eyes.

"God, Jenny," he whispered, his voice breaking. He felt awed by her symmetry, by the perfection of her form, and for a moment, she seemed unreal to him. She seemed the creation of some long-dead, divinely inspired sculptor: a masterpiece, irreplaceable and precious beyond all kingdoms, suddenly transported here to him and placed in his stewardship.

At last, he stepped forward and reached out to her. But he did not take her into his arms as she hoped. Instead, he began to explore her, silently and almost reverently. His fingers slid over her warm, waiting skin, gently tracing the milky contours of her throat, her shoulders, the hollows of her collarbones. His hands cast her adrift in a sea of sensation as they skimmed over her lightly, brushing the full swell of her breasts, the soft bell of her rib cage, the pale flatness of her belly and the shimmer of golden curls at its base. He moved behind her and she felt his fingers glide down the line of her back in a tingling cascade of shivers, then up again to flutter over her shoulder blades. Slowly, his fingers drifted downward once again to sweep lazy, spidery circles over the pillowy softness of her buttocks.

Jenny's lips parted, and the tip of her tongue flicked slowly back and forth between the sharp white edges of her front teeth. If he had meant to tease her to the brink of madness, then he had succeeded admirably. Her nipples were swollen and tight, her belly twisted with an aching emptiness which she knew only he could fill.

He was still behind her. One hand tickled at the crease between her buttocks, the other lifted her shimmering blond hair. And when she felt his lips brush the back of her neck and heard him whisper her name, she whimpered and turned to face him.

This time it was she who kissed him, stretching upward on tiptoes to reach his mouth, locking her arms behind his neck, and pressing her vulnerable flesh against the muscular solidity of his denim and leather-clad body. Her mouth opened wide, and she drew him into herself, rejoicing in the moist, heady warmth of his plundering kiss. Abraded by his rough leather vest, her bare, sensitized nipples shot streams of pleasure outward through her body and down to her throbbing belly. Suddenly she knew she wanted more than to just be fondled and petted—she wanted him to own her: to do with her whatever he pleased.

She couldn't break her vow. She wouldn't ask him to make love to her. And then there was the promise he'd made: he'd said he wouldn't take her virginity until she asked. But he was an outlaw. What could such a vow mean to him? Surely tonight he would put himself inside her and fill the aching void.

Their kiss deepened as each took nourishment from the other; first he played the aggressor, then she, then he again. She felt him slide his hands further down her back to cup her bottom, sensuously kneading that bare, tender flesh as their kisses grew wilder, more frenzied. He stroked the crease between her buttocks then slipped his hand lower, between her legs, to caress her from behind. At the instant she was invaded by his touch, desire, like liquid flame, swept through her. She tilted her hips back toward his rapacious hand, all the while greedily drawing his tongue further into her mouth.

Yes, she thought, *now he will do it without my asking. Now he will love me.*

As she writhed, naked and wanton in his embrace and giving herself wholeheartedly to his kisses, Ace blessed the fates for her. She was perfection, and she was his for the taking. But he would not steal her virginity. She must make him a gift of her innocence. And it wouldn't be long before she would do just that. Of this he was certain.

Her breathing had grown labored, and he broke off the kiss momentarily. His fingers slipped from her just long enough to slide around the curve of her hip and down her belly. She sighed when he began to pet her again, and when her head lolled to the side to rest against his shoulder, he whispered into her ear, "Touch me, Jenny."

She offered no resistance; there was not even a

slight hesitation as she withdrew one pale, slender arm from his neck and slid her hand to his broad leather-vested chest. Down his side her fingers traveled, then slipped between their bodies to rest at his belt buckle. Here she paused, and when she did, he slowed his intimate caress, waiting for her to continue what she had begun.

He kissed her temple, now damp with perspiration, and repeated, "Touch me."

When he felt her fingers tug at his belt, prying the leather free from its silver buckle, he kissed her forehead again and resumed his gentle, tender massage.

She was engulfed with the want of him. His touch and his kiss were all that mattered now. She was not the spent and sated girl of the previous night—she was intoxicated by desire and the heat of the moment, and she *wanted* to touch him: to hold his hardness in her hand before he pushed himself inside her, as powerful and driven by primal lust as his stallion.

She released the buckle, then the buttons of his trousers, and felt exhilaration—strange and new and wonderful—when he moved against her hand. He groaned when her fingers, not quite meeting, curled around him; and as overcome with desire as she was, a part of her wondered if there would be room inside her for all of him.

"Oh, Jenny," he moaned before taking her lips again to kiss her with a passion even more intense. He was close to the edge—very close, he knew. Always before, he had managed to control himself with her. His lingering caresses were calculated to keep her poised on the brink of rapture without toppling her over the edge, but as he kissed her and held her softness in his arms and felt her fingers dance over him in the most perfect way he could imagine, he realized that he had to pull away. At any second, her slender hand would plunge him over the same precipice at which he kept her so carefully balanced.

He thought how easy it would be to just lift her off the ground; to lift her into the air and slide her down upon himself; to push deeply inside her warmth while she wrapped her legs about his waist and called out his name . . .

He pushed her way.

Jenny knew that something had changed, something was either terribly wrong or terribly right. As close as she was to her own release, something within her told her to wait, to be still and quiet.

Finally, he pulled her close again, pressing against her so tightly that she could feel the rapid beating of his heart.

"Sweet Jenny," he murmured into her ear.

"Are you—are you all right?" she managed to whisper.

"Yes, angel," he whispered. He tilted her face up toward his and pressed his lips to hers briefly before saying, "And now I'm going to make you better than all right."

Quickly, he buttoned his trousers. Then he scooped her up and carried her to the big bale of straw at the edge of the circle of light. He sat down upon it, cradling her on his lap.

He looked down at her for a moment as she lay across his thighs: compliant and aching for his touch, her intelligent but naive eyes full of longing and desire. He bent his head and took her lips again, at the same time cupping one perfect breast in his hand and teasing its swollen crest. When the flat of his thumb found her nipple, she moaned and he toyed with the tight, pounding bud a minute longer, rejoicing in the fierceness of her pleasure.

Then his lips took their leave of hers and began to trail a wandering line of kisses down her throat, then lower, until his mouth replaced his teasing fingers upon her breast and his hand slipped down her body to brush her golden delta. Even before he had begun to slide his fingers lower, she parted her thighs: inviting him to touch her, to possess her, letting him know she would deny him nothing.

Jenny's head lolled backward. Her eyes were closed, her lips swollen and parted as she took in air in ragged little gasps. One hand was curled about his muscular shoulders, clawing and plucking at the fabric of his shirt; the other cradled his head, her fingers artlessly entwined in his gleaming hair as he raised his head again to kiss her lips.

She knew nothing but this realm of exquisite sensation now. She was obsessed, and there was nothing for her but the fiercely compulsive want of his touch, his nearness. His heated kisses, gentle yet urgent, sent almost convulsive quakes of sensation traveling back into her spine, shooting down along it to her belly and upward again.

"Jenny," he whispered between long kisses, "sweet Jenny . . ." And when his fingers dipped lower to invade her, she could imagine no sensation more perfect, more right.

The convulsive throbbing in her body grew, quickening in meter, deepening in intensity; and never, never before had she felt such perfection of being, such safety and *rightness* as she felt at that moment, naked in the night in the outlaw's arms. *Forever*, the last rational part of her brain rejoiced. *I want this to last forever: to never, ever stop, to always be this way...*

But then, impossibly, the intensity of sensation elevated, and even that last small thought was lost to her as she was swept by an explosion of mind and body that shattered her into a thousand shards of sparkling crystal—bright, blinding, gleaming; spinning outward into infinity.

Gradually, she floated back to an awareness of her surroundings. Ace still held her on his lap, rocking her softly back and forth. The hand between her thighs had withdrawn to cup her buttock, hugging her to him protectively. His lips brushed tiny, tender kisses against her forehead and temple, and his palm gently cradled one breast.

Her eyelids fluttered, and he whispered, "Welcome back."

Now that it was over and the delirium of sensual heat gone, she was suddenly overcome by the shame of being here with him, naked and so completely under his control. More than anything, she wanted to curl into a ball and disappear.

"I—" she began falteringly, but he hushed her.

"No, you don't," he said with a grin. "Not this time. Absolutely no words. From you, anyway." He took his hand from her bottom and slipped it under her thighs. Then he stood up, still holding her, and carried her back to Fancy's stall.

"For right now," he smiled, "we're just going to get you decent again, little one." He released her legs, and she slid gently to her feet.

Her brow furrowed with that wave of latent modesty, she crossed her arms over her bosom to cover herself; but he chuckled softly and pulled them back down to her sides.

"Don't be embarrassed, Jenny. You're beautiful; more than beautiful. Don't ever be ashamed to let me see you." He kissed the tip of her nose as he reached to the pile of clothing and picked out her drawers.

"Just don't let anybody *else* see you that way," he added as an afterthought.

He could not have been happier. He was certain now that everything was fine, everything was perfect. She needed him, she wanted him, she trusted him. And the next time she'd need no coaxing: she'd ask him to make love to her. He helped her step into her drawers, then began to tie the petticoats about her tiny waist.

She blushed deeply when he gently pushed her hands away, refusing both her assistance and her mute protests, and he was delighted to see that the flush of color bloomed not only in her cheeks, but on her chest as well, tinging the tops of her breasts with a faint rosy glow.

She wished fervently that she could, by some magic, vanish like the Cheshire Cat and reappear alone and fully clothed in her own room, away from Ace Denton, away from her guilt, leaving nothing behind but her fading shadow. "Please . . ." she began, but he held a finger to her pouting lips.

"No, Jenny. I told you. No words." The last petticoat in place, he reached back to the dwindling pile of clothing and picked up her camisole. He stared at it a minute before discarding it in favor of her skirt. *Not yet*, he thought. *Not quite yet.*

He dropped the skirt over her head, watching her breasts vanish, then reappear as the waistband passed over them. And before he buttoned the skirt into place, he couldn't resist pausing to sweep a slow circle over one upturned nipple with the wide flat of his palm.

He kissed Jenny's forehead before reaching reluctantly for the camisole. But just before his fingers touched it, he pulled back his hand.

"Oh, hell," he muttered, and bent instead to collect her shoes and balled stockings. Kneeling before her, he slid the stockings up over her legs and buckled her shoes. On the way up, he nuzzled for a moment at the deep V between her breasts; then he rose to kiss her lips.

Jenny responded to the kiss in wonder, for as he had reclothed her, she had felt a surprising resurgence of desire. And now, as he held her for what she knew would be the last time this evening, she was tempted to stay with him a little longer, to begin removing the clothing he had only just replaced. She hated herself for it, true. But it seemed that her body was not at all impressed with any of her lofty promises and resolutions. Her body only wanted his touch.

But this evening she'd have no cause for further

recriminations. His lips pulled away from hers, and with a sigh, he slipped the camisole over her torso, tied the ribbon into a clumsy little bow, and helped her into her shirtwaist. Brushing her hands away when she tried to help, he buttoned it carefully, then tucked it into her skirt.

"Tomorrow," he whispered before he kissed her one last time. Then he grinned at her wickedly: the crocodile once again. "Maybe you'd better groom the other half of your mare."

He bent down, plucked up her brush and curry-comb and presented them to her. She took the implements numbly and stared at them. Groom her mare? Now? He was crazy, he was—

—gone. When she looked up again, she was alone. He had vanished again. Disappeared into thin air: thin air, being, of course, his secret passage—wherever *that* was.

She dropped the brushes on the floor, plopped down on the bale of straw, and rested her forehead against the heels of her hands. Now that she was alone, she felt her strength returning and along with it, a full measure of anger and self-recrimination. *Tomorrow is right*, she thought. *But not for what he thinks. Because tomorrow I will come down here and find the entrance to that blasted tunnel. And I'll make sure he never gets out of it again!*

She rose, rescued the grooming tools from the floor and set them aside, then picked up her lantern. "Tomorrow," she said aloud, and started for the door.

So engrossed was she in her plan to foil Ace Denton's next seduction (and her own inevitable capitulation) that she did not notice a little flurry of movement outside the circle of lamplight, just past the open stable door. By the time Jenny walked out into the night breeze, a grinning Belinda Critchley was nearly to the house, happily planning the most effective way to break this most interesting news to her friend, Iris Jakes.

Ace slid back the panel and stepped into Liz McCaleb's bedroom. Dressed in a long, white silk wrapper, she sat, reading, in the high-backed ultramarine chair beside her bed. It suited her, he mused, the way a throne suits a queen.

At the sound of his boot steps she looked up over her glasses. "I expected you some time ago."

He grinned at her almost foolishly. "Oh. Sorry."

"I don't know what you think you have to smile about, Marcus." Grimly, she folded her spectacles into her book and set them aside.

"I'm not sure you want to know, Your Highness." Still grinning, he flopped down on the bed, rolled onto his back, and clasped his hands behind his head.

"Marcus!" She stood up and stared down her nose at him. "What the Devil's gotten into you? And get those boots off my bedspread!" Lips pursed, she slapped at his legs.

"Oh, c'mon Lizzie!" he laughed. "They're not even close." He wiggled them in the air.

Liz folded her arms and shook her head in disgust. "I must say I'm having a hard time understanding your attitude. Didn't you read the newspaper I sent down today?"

He sighed, and his smile twisted into a grimace. "Of course I read it. It didn't tell me anything I wasn't already fairly convinced of."

"What are you going to do?"

He didn't answer.

"Marcus, something has got to—"

"What?" He sat up quite abruptly, and it startled her. "Any suggestions? Have you come up with a formula to turn Ace Denton into a model citizen overnight? To make him beloved by the masses? Welcome at the Farmer's Association mid-week and the First Baptist come Sunday? If you have, I'd love to hear it." He swung down off the bed to face her. "I mean, I'd really *love* to hear it, Lizzie."

"Stop it, Marcus. I'm not your enemy."

He took a deep breath and tried to smile. "I know. I'm sorry. Too much of my mother's temper in me, I guess."

She didn't smile back. "It's just that you don't seem to be taking this very seriously."

"Seriously? Trust me, I am. But there's not a damn thing I can do about it tonight, is there?"

"Well then, why did you bother to come up?" She tugged angrily at her dressing gown's belt.

"I wanted to— Oh, never mind." He walked back across the plush blue carpets and put his hand on the sliding panel. He'd wanted to tell her that he'd fallen in love with Jenny; that he wanted to care for her and have children with her. But not now. Not when she was in this mood. It would keep.

The wall slid open. Ace struck a match and stepped through. "'Night, Lizzie."

"Marcus!" she barked as the panel clicked shut. "Marcus Denton, you come back here!"

He made his way down through the warrened maze of hidden hallways. He had reached the cellar passage and was turning the corner into the cobwebbed resting room when he saw the soft glow of a lantern peeking from beneath its door. He blew out his own candle and crept to it. It had to be Scar in there, but a man couldn't be too careful, especially a man with a five thousand dollar price tag on his head.

He cracked the door and peered inside. It was only Mac. He sat on one of the old, spidery benches, the lantern on the dirt floor between his feet.

Ace opened the door and went in.

"There you are," Mac said. He stood up.

Ace jerked his thumb toward the ceiling. "I—"

"Yeah, I know. I was just down below, and Scar told me you were goin' up to talk to her. But I wanted to have a word with you myself."

"All right, Mac." He closed the passage door behind him and leaned against the wall next to it, crossing his arms over his chest. "What is it?"

Mac sighed heavily. He genuinely liked Ace, but the boy—for Mac always thought of him that way—made him a little nervous. Maybe it was because Ace reminded him too much of the way he had been all those years ago: a little too callous, little too cocky, and a little too handsome and lawless for his own good.

"It's about Jenny."

Ace stiffened defensively, and Mac knew immediately that his hunch had been right. At first he'd thought that Jenny was simply afraid to have the outlaws in the house. But later he'd reevaluated her manner and decided it was something more than that. Something he might have to look into.

"What about her?" Ace said.

"What have you been up to with that girl, Ace? If you've . . . If you've hurt her or frightened her or done—done *anything* to her, so help me God . . ." His hands curled into fists at his sides. Ace was younger, true, but Mac knew he could still give him a good thrashing if need be.

Ace held up his palms. "Take it easy, Mac. I'm not about to go man-to-man with you."

Mac relaxed, but only slightly.

"She's not like the others, Marcus," he continued, "and I don't want anything bad happenin' to her, if you get my meaning. If your intentions are anything less than honorable—"

Ace laughed. "Honorable? I'm sorry, Mac. Just seems like a funny sort of word for anybody to use in this house. But yes. My intentions are 'honorable.'"

"I'd like to know how you plan to pull *that* off," Mac grumbled. "The way things are goin', you'll be lucky to go another year before some bounty hunter hauls in your carcass. And even if you're lucky enough to talk or shoot or run your way out of that, where you gonna be in five years? Or ten? Or twenty? Playin' bouncer and hog-slopper in some two-bit whorehouse like me? I used to think I was pretty damn smart, too, you know."

Ace slouched and stared at the dirt floor. Mac was right. He hadn't thought that far ahead. If anything, he'd envisioned some sort of nebulous, fairy-tale future where everybody lived happily-ever-after, and suddenly he realized how stupid that was. But he would think of something. For Jenny—for the life he wanted to make with her, share with her—he would think of a way.

He raised his head. Mac was staring at him impatiently.

"I'll find a way, Mac. I promise you that."

The older man shook his head and sighed, "I wish I could tell you it'd be easy. I wish I could tell you that it's even possible." He ran his fingers through his hair before he added, "You just better not hurt her, Ace. You just better not ever give that child grief."

"I won't, Mac. She's . . . she's not like any girl I ever met. She's like Alice in Wonderland, only all grown up."

Mac scowled. "Who's this 'Alice' girl?"

Ace smiled a little. "Nobody, Mac. It doesn't matter. What matters is that I love Jenny. I'll be damned if I understand her, but I love her."

Mac picked up his lantern and walked past Ace to open the door. He stepped through it, but before he turned down the short passage that would lead him to the main cellar, he added, very quietly, "Sometimes love isn't enough, boy, and that's the truth of it."

He walked away without bothering to close the door, and Ace watched as Mac MacCauley, who had once been feared in three states as the Arkansas Kid, disappeared down the passage.

Eight

Wednesday

Morning came none too quickly for Jenny. She had slept uneasily the whole night, tortured by doubt and self-recrimination. Her dreams, both erotic and terrifying, had been filled with him. First she had dreamt of him as Malory's Lancelot: a handsome and tragic hero in gleaming armor, come to carry her off to a fairy-tale castle. But then Lancelot became the Black Knight, and in her dream she quaked and screamed with terror when she saw him pull his dagger, driving it through her father's heart, then her own.

So when she was roughly awakened by Bertha Bramley, she was almost grateful.

"Breakfast to get, missy!" the ill-tempered cook growled as she shook Jenny's shoulder. "Cookin' and chores to do! Nearly ten o'clock!"

"Yes'm," Jenny managed to mumble, and a few minutes later, she was down in the kitchen numbly

213

setting the table for breakfast.

She finished just as the girls began to wander in. Meg was the first to arrive, doe-eyed and distracted as usual. Pearl, Mary-Rebecca, and Agnes wandered in a few minutes later, followed closely by Shirley Mae Vinton, who immediately instigated another in the escalating series of verbal battles with Bertha Bramley.

"You call this slop food?" Shirley Mae hissed over her flapjacks. "I wouldn't eat this garbage if I was starvin' to death!"

"You don't have to eat my cookin' if you don't want to!" Mrs. Bramley's face twisted into a grimace. "Go ahead an' starve. See if I give a damn!"

"By the size'a your backside, I don't reckon you'd know much about starvin'," Shirley Mae sniffed disdainfully.

Mac let them run on until Bertha Bramley picked up the big wooden batter spoon and lunged toward the grizzled redhead.

"Enough!" he moaned, snatching the makeshift weapon from the cook's fingers. "Honest to God! Just *one* mornin' could we do without this?"

The combatants snarled at each other, silently agreeing to pick up tomorrow morning where they had left off today, and got on with the meal.

Iris Jakes had not yet come down for breakfast. Her regular Tuesday all-nighter, Attorney John Q. Lacey, had spent the night.

"Still up there," Belinda Critchley informed them when she finally made an appearance. It was obvious she had come to the kitchen by way of the bar. She already reeked of rye.

214

"I come down the hall past her room, and I could hear them li'l ol' bed springs creakin' away to beat the band. I hear he sent down for a bottle of champagne last night, too. Bastard musta just won himself a real big court case to be so free with his time 'n money . . ." She flopped down into a vacant chair about the same time Mrs. Bramley slid a plate of eggs and wheat cakes under her pug nose.

She took a couple of bites, then in a voice dripping with sugar and pitched to carry over the jabbering conversation of the other girls, she said, "And how are *you* this morning, Miss Jenny?"

Jenny flinched. She would have expected nothing more from Belinda than a terse order for more sausages or eggs; certainly not this strangely couched inquiry as to the state of her health.

"I—I'm fine, thank you," she stammered.

Mac, too, had noticed the exchange. He arched one caterpillar brow and looked from Belinda to the kitchen maid and back again.

"Well, gracious, sugar," Belinda continued as she helped herself to a cup of coffee. "I should think you'd be better than just *fine.*"

"I don't understand what you—" Jenny began, but Belinda cut her off.

"Oh, I should think you'd be practically *radiant,* sugar!" Belinda's smile held all the sincerity and benevolence of a rattlesnake. She reached across the table for the salt. "Why, I half expected to find you just floatin' on a pretty pink cloud this morning."

Jenny, openmouthed, stared back. She had absolutely no idea what to say, but Mac, noting her fluster, stepped into the breach.

215

"You're drunk, Belinda, and it's not even noon," he warned. She was getting crazier all the time, and she was apt to say almost anything when she'd been into the liquor. Lately, that was most of the time. As a rule, he was prone to just let her spring wind down when she got like this—it was easier than shutting her up—but he didn't like the insinuations she was making about his Jenny. *Stupid little cow*, he thought. *She's just out to stir up trouble, and Jenny's handy*.

Belinda turned toward him and grinned far too innocently. "Oh, I'm not drunk, *Mister* MacCauley," she drawled. "Not by a long shot. I have important things to do today . . ."

With that, she dropped the subject and, still grinning smugly, devoted her attention to breakfast.

Jenny looked toward Mac gratefully, and he gave her a reassuring wink. She was certain Belinda could have no way of knowing what she and Ace Denton had been up to, but the prostitute's thinly veiled accusations had not only hit home, they'd unleashed a fresh torrent of guilt. Jenny decided that Mac must be correct: Belinda was drunk. Maybe she was just trying to stir up trouble. The girl had a reputation for engineering explosive situations between the house's other inhabitants as a way of entertaining herself. Perhaps she was just testing the water, trying to find the kitchen maid's Achilles' heel.

Thank God for Mac. Much more of Belinda's needling, and Jenny would have burst into tears and given away her guilt, if not the details of her secret.

At last everyone, with the exception of Iris Jakes, had eaten their fill and wandered out of the kitchen.

Iris was still upstairs, hard at work accommodating the libidinous lawyer. Jenny stared out the window toward the barn as she soaped the breakfast dishes, and when they were done, she dried them hurriedly. She had plans.

The last plate, the last dish, the final pieces of flatware polished and put away, Jenny slipped from the kitchen and out the back door. Today she would uncover the entrance to his passage, and she would find a way to block it. As she marched resolutely down the slope, she did not glance back at the house. If she had, she would have seen Belinda Critchley standing at the big dining room windows, whiskey-filled tumbler in hand, chatting with surprising animation to a tousled and increasingly furious Iris Jakes.

It had to be here someplace.

When she entered the barn, the tack room door, bracketed by chest-high single-bale stacks of alfalfa, was directly to her left. She searched there first. The dusty cubicle was hung with harness and ropes. Toward the back were leather trappings—ancient, cracked, and spiderwebbed—along with riggings in current use: soft, pliant, well cared for and smelling of neat's-foot oil. Hung along one wall were buggy whips, riding crops, spare reins, bits and girth straps, and a wicked-looking bullwhip. Fancy's saddle and bridle were there, too, and looked to have been recently saddle-soaped by a thoughtful Mac. But the walls yielded no secrets. They were solid and silent.

Next she investigated the feed room, feeling

carefully along the dusty, cobwebbed boards. Two walls were merely thin partitions, and revealed no hidden doors or panels. The other two were hugged by long, low, covered feed bins, above which were hung wobbly shelves crammed with grime-caked bottles of patent veterinary remedies and disused miscellany. Nothing.

Jenny swore softly. She had been certain the tunnel's mouth rose to an exit in one of those two rooms. The outer walls of the barn itself were single layers of board, incapable of concealing the width of a passage. There could be no trap door in the floor. She had tramped hard in both rooms, hoping for a hollow echo. But there was none. The floors were solid, packed earth.

No. She had missed something. She decided to start over.

She was coming out of the feed room when she heard the slam of the barn door. There was no time to turn around or think before a deafening *boom* nearly pitched her to her knees. Beside her, the topmost bale of alfalfa exploded in an angrily churning cloud of dust and debris.

"Filth!" The voice was a rusty blade scraping the shattered air.

Jenny pressed back against the feed room door. The air was a miasma of whirling dust and furious bits of hay, but she could see a woman—first just her outline, as if through smoke, then the tangle of red hair. Jenny coughed and rubbed at her burning eyes. Iris was still there, clearer now. Her feet were planted wide. She was livid, and she had the bullwhip from the tack room.

218

"You filthy little slut!" she snarled through clenched teeth as she flipped the thick, lethal lash to one side. "I told you to stay away from him!"

Her arm snapped with unbelievable speed and force. Even as Jenny ducked to one side, the sound of the impact numbed her eardrums and a shower of splinters and wood chips rained down into her hair.

"I warned you." Iris's face was twisted with cruelty. "I warned you, and you went with him anyway." Glaring, she reeled the whip back in. It hissed through the straw, slithering toward her like a trained snake.

There was no doubt in Jenny's mind that Iris meant to kill her. "Please," she began, "I didn't—"

"Don't give me none of that goody-two-shoes act, Little Miss Sugar Drawers," Iris hissed. "I know you was down here with him last night, and buck naked to boot! I know what y'all were doin'." She flicked her wrist with almost casual ease, and the whip's lash flipped out next to her in a straight sinister line.

Jenny hugged the wall.

"I warned you," Iris repeated. "I told you he was mine. He's been mine for years. He loves me, an' I love him." She shook her tangled, setter-red mop defiantly and twisted her wrist again. This time it sent a sinuous wave down the black, braided lash.

"Me 'n Ace, we're gonna get married some day," she sneered. "We don't need some teasin' little virgin messin' with us." Her voice, which had been raised to nearly glass-shattering volume, sank to a low growl. "Less you ain't no virgin no more . . ." Her lips tightened into a thin, reptilian smile that did not reach her narrowed eyes.

219

She was blocking the entrance to the barn, but Jenny knew there was another way out. If she could get to the rear door in time . . . She'd never seen anyone use it—it might be padlocked or nailed She shot a quick glance down the aisle.

Iris read her mind. "You'll never make it." She shifted the lash again anxiously. "I'm gonna teach you a lesson. A real permanent lesson. And even if you live, you teasin' little man-stealer, I'm gonna make you so damn ugly, nobody's gonna want you, least of all Ace Denton!"

Her arm snapped back, then out, and Jenny heard a sickening swoosh as the lash cut the air. She threw herself to one side, but not before the leather thong at its tip sliced the sleeve of her blouse. It left behind neatly sheered fabric and a burning line of red on the flesh of her upper arm.

"God*damn* it!" Iris bellowed as Jenny scrambled further away to duck behind a thick support post. "You let him touch you all over, you filthy little—" The whip cut the air again. This time it struck the timber just above Jenny's head. With a roar that resounded through the stable, the impact released a thick cloud of dirt and splinters and tore away a fist-sized chunk of whitewashed pine.

Jenny jumped forward and dodged across the aisle. On both sides, terrified horses reared and bucked in their stalls as she searched frantically for something, anything, with which to defend herself. The horses strained at their ropes, their nostrils wide, their eyes frightened and white-ringed.

"—had his hands all over you!" Iris screamed over the frantic whinnying of the horses. She strode purposefully down the aisle, furious past all reason. "I warned you—you can't say I didn't warn you!"

She struck out again, and this time Jenny didn't dodge quickly enough. She jumped back and to her right, giving a wide berth to Fancy's flashing heels as the tip of the lash ripped a jagged tear in the front of her blouse and raised a hot, blood-beaded welt above her left breast.

Jenny hit the floor and rolled, scrambling to her feet again before she finally found the quavering remainder of her voice.

"Iris, please! I didn't ask him, I never wanted—"

"Liar!" The whip snaked out again. It missed its target and whacked murderously against a partition. The thin boards shattered with a thunderous crack.

Too frightened to weep, Jenny dodged another three yards down the aisle before she tripped and stumbled. Every step she'd taken toward the rear door seemed to carry her further away, but she scrambled to her feet again.

"Dirty lying—" Iris was closing in again, a triumphant gleam in her eyes and glory in her twisted face. "Nobody's ever gonna want you again, with or without your clothes, 'cause when I finish with your face, I'm gonna slice the rest'a you into rawhide strips!"

Jenny was on her knees, gasping for breath and trying to push herself upright on rubbery legs. The paralysis of terror had nearly taken over, but somehow she found the strength to twist herself to the side before Iris's arm moved again.

She got as far as the plunging buckskin's stall before the lash reached toward her. It struck the frenzied animal instead. Blood spurted in a dark line across the gelding's narrow rump. Squealing and pulling uselessly at his tie rope, he bucked frantically in pain and terror.

Jenny saw the flash and felt the rush of air as his iron-shod hooves narrowly missed her rib cage. But as she lurched away she tripped again, falling flat only inches from the maddened gelding's stall.

Iris closed the distance between them. Grinning, she prepared to send out the lash again; this time knowing that if her weapon did not strike home, it would at least drive Jenny into those plunging hooves.

Jenny knew she'd never make it past Iris. There was only one small, slim chance for her, and that was through the gelding's stall. She would have to land next to the partition at his far side, drop quickly, then roll through the two-foot gap beneath the bottom board to the empty cubicle beyond.

Mustering all her strength, she dove headlong into the buckskin's narrow stall.

She hit the ground just before the gelding's rib cage could crush her against the partition. She twisted and tumbled blindly, cringing and crying out as her arm scraped the bottom board. All about her, the screaming horse's sharp, pistoning hooves drove into the ground.

She pulled her hand away as a hoof barely missed her fingers. On her back, she shoved herself halfway into the next stall and momentary safety. Her head, her shoulder, then one leg were clear; but before she could drag herself the rest of the way through, the whip rumbled and cracked again, this time lashing

222

into the empty stall. Straw filled the air as if snatched up by a cyclone, blinding and choking her as Iris's laughter mingled with the bellows of the frenzied gelding.

Too close, hooves crashed down again on her right, now her blind side. She heard her shoulder seam rip as a hoof spiked her sleeve to the floor, pinning her arm momentarily before shredding the fabric and grinding it underfoot. To her left, Iris cracked the whip again in a strike calculated to drive her back toward the horse. Once more Jenny's eyes were burned and blinded and her nose filled by dust and pulverized straw. To her left, the buckskin's rear hooves glanced her shin. She heard her skirt rip.

Eyes screwed shut against the whirling dust, she dug in her heels and shoved herself the rest of the way into the next stall. Her knees buckled, and she curled herself into a ball, braced for the sound and scorch of the lash. But instead of the booming crack and searing pain she'd expected, there was a shriek of exasperation and a dull thud.

Coughing, Jenny opened her grit-tortured, burning eyes. In the aisle, Iris struggled against the strong grip of Ace Denton. Her bull whip lay in the straw beside her like a dead blacksnake.

"Let me go!" Iris kicked and twisted against him as violently as the tortured buckskin still fought against his rope. She stared daggers at Jenny. "I'm gonna kill her!"

"Damn it, Iris," Ace growled between clenched teeth. She squirmed angrily in his grasp even though he'd hauled her nearly off her feet. He looked up at Jenny. Her dust-grimed face was streaked with hot tears, her blouse and skirt were ripped, and the flesh of her arm and upper chest bore angry red welts.

"Jenny?" he said, even as Iris lurched against him again, painfully landing a sharp heel against his shin. "Jenny," he repeated, a whisper this time. "Are you—"

She didn't wait to hear him out. Sobbing convulsively with anger and relief, she darted past him. With a last burst of strength, she tugged open the barn door and hurled herself outside. She ran, stumbling blindly, toward the house.

With Jenny safely out of harm's way, Ace released the thrashing, kicking prostitute. She wrenched away from him, rubbing the red places on her arms where his fingers had dug into her flesh. She glared reproachfully. "You shouldn't'a stopped me, Ace," she screeched. "I was teachin' her a lesson."

"A lesson on what?" he sneered. "How to be a lady or how to beat a horse?"

She made a move to slap him, but he caught her wrist and held it in midair. "We've been over and over this," he said. He made himself control his voice, lower it. "I'm sick of it, Iris. I've tried to be nice, but you don't listen. You never listen. You only shout and scream and go on dreaming."

She twisted against his hand, but he held her fast. This time he was going to make her understand, once and for all. If cruelty was the only thing she understood, then cruelty it would have to be.

"You love me, Ace," she insisted. "I know you love me!"

224

"No." He said it firmly, quietly.

"But we're gonna get married, you and me!" She aimed the words at him like a loaded gun.

"No, Iris. Not now, not ever. I never gave you any reason to think—"

"Liar!"

She looked as if she could kill him, too, and suddenly he was very glad he'd tossed the bullwhip out of her reach. "It's all in your head, Iris. It always has been, and that foulmouthed girlfriend of yours feeds more of it to you night and day." She twisted again, and he dug his fingers harder into her wrist. He'd leave red marks, he knew, but it would just have to be that way.

"I don't love you, Iris," he said. "I don't even like you."

Suddenly, she ceased her struggle and just stood there, staring at him. Her eyes were still angry, but the mindless tantrum was over. He decided it was safe to let go of her, but he was careful to keep himself between her and the whip.

"I don't understand, Ace," she said finally. "I don't understand how you could want that—that—virgin!" She spat the word as if it were the most vile of curses.

"I don't expect you to understand."

The fury came back into her face and he half expected her to make a lunge for the whip. But instead, she lifted her hands to clutch at her ruffled, rumpled bodice.

"Why?" she cried. "Why do you want her when you could have me?" Her fingers curled into the flimsy material, and in one motion, she ripped it

225

open to expose herself. Cupping a breast in each hand, she pinched her protruding nipples—still bruised from the attorney's enthusiastic but clumsy attentions—and took a step toward him.

"For you, Ace," she whispered. "For you—"

"And every drunken farmhand in the county with two bits to spare," he said. Now, perhaps, she would finally understand.

She stopped, dropped her hands to her sides and faced him, bare-breasted and furious. "You bastard son of a—"

"Don't ever bother her again, Iris."

Jenny washed, dressed her wounds and changed her clothes. She wanted nothing more than to stay barricaded in her tiny room, but Mrs. Bramley searched her out. Huffing and puffing, the cook dragged Jenny back down to the kitchen. The cuts on her arms and chest still smarting, she stood at the kitchen sink, peeling the first potatoes for the midday meal.

She stabbed at them, twisting out the eyes with that short, sharp blade, first wishing it was Ace beneath her knife, then Iris. Mostly Iris; Ace had stopped her, after all. But still, she found she was furious with him, too, a fury over and above the hatred she already bore him. For now, as loathe as she was to admit it to herself, she was jealous. It must be true, what Iris had said. There must be a shared past between them, a bond of some kind. Surely Iris could not have concocted a passion so strong out of thin air.

She shuddered as the vision of Ace, his arms about

226

a younger, less-used Iris, sprang into her mind. She really knew next to nothing of Iris's history. Had Ace come to her, too, once upon a time? Had he seduced her, touched her, held her in his arms, told her she was for him, only for him?

She was too lost in anger and doubt to notice as Iris slowly mounted the crest of the hill and entered the back hall.

But Iris saw her. She paused in the doorway a minute, her features twisting, and then she straightened and threw her shoulders back. She let the door slam loudly behind her.

Jenny's head jerked up. Involuntarily, she backed away, the paring knife clutched in her hand. But Iris did not enter the kitchen, nor did she look angry.

She smiled.

It was a sensuous, feline smile, dripping with cream, and as she leaned provocatively in the doorway, her grin widened.

"I'm real sorry, darlin'," she purred. "Truly I am. I must've had it all wrong. I never shoulda doubted Ace." She let her hand, which had been clutching the two torn halves of her bodice, casually drop to her side.

"He just couldn't wait to get his naughtly little ol' hands on me again," she confided with a wink. "Law!" she grinned, rolling her eyes to the ceiling. "He does fill me up, that nasty, wonderful man . . ."

After a moment, she looked back at Jenny. The girl's eyes were brimming with new tears. Good.

"I need to lie down for a while after *that*," Iris continued with great relish. She took a step toward the stairs, then hesitated. "Like I said, sugar," she added, "I'm real sorry. I thought he had a hanker for you, but he set me straight. Just doin' you a kindness, I guess. Reckon he felt sorry for you, bein' so plain 'n all . . ."

She smiled again. "I swear, there's nobody makes me feel the way Ace can." She closed her eyes for a moment, as if in memory of his caress, then grinned broadly before she started up the stairs. "Do come up and wake me for lunch, will you, sweetie? That man makes me work up one powerful appetite."

And she was gone, leaving Jenny behind to weep helplessly, silently, into her hands.

The rest of the day was torture.

Agnes picked the hour before luncheon to exercise Onan, but fifteen minutes after the now-familiar slam of the dining room doors and the cry, "Heads up! Loose bird!" Agnes's services were requested upstairs. She managed to catch the disgruntled macaw before she went, but Jenny was stuck with putting the dining hall back together. The bird had not only knocked over three chairs, but had spattered the bar and several of the tables with droppings and feathers.

The midday meal, which Mrs. Bramley served at four o'clock, was saved from total disaster only because of three drifters who happened by at half past two. Selecting the services of Iris, Belinda, and Meg, the cowboys were in a celebratory mood and kept the girls busy until mid-evening. And so, for a little while, at least, Jenny was saved having to face Iris again.

Belinda's client was the first to run out of both energy and money. She appeared in the kitchen at about nine o'clock—a fresh tumbler of rye in her hand—just as Jenny and the cantankerous cook were cleaning up the supper dishes. Plates had been saved back for the girls, and Belinda rapped her fingers on the table impatiently while she waited for Jenny to fetch hers from the warmth of the big iron oven.

"Finish up them dishes, missy," the cook growled. She clumped out to the pantry and took up a lantern to light her path to the privy. "When I get back I want to see 'em all dried an' put up."

Jenny knew she had plenty of time—Mrs. Bramley's visits to the privy were never brief—but the last ting she wanted was to be alone in the kitchen with Belinda and especially Iris, who she knew might be joining them any minute. As dreadful as was the cook's company, at least Bertha Bramley would have provided some sort of buffer between Jenny and the girls.

She turned to her work, drying and stacking the plates as quickly as she could, hoping to finish and take sanctuary in her room before Iris made an appearance. She heard Belinda mumble some new order. *Blast!* she thought angrily, *Whatever it is, get it yourself and leave me alone!*

"I said, I heard you 'n Iris had yourselves an altercation this afternoon," she repeated. Jenny heard the words plainly this time and turned to face her.

"Who told you that?" she half whispered as she felt the color drain from her face. "Iris, I suppose."

"Why sure, honey," Belinda smiled. "Iris tells me

ever'thin'. Specially when it comes to her 'n Ace." She plucked the greasy, heavily breaded skin from a piece of fried chicken and plopped the gooey mass into her mouth, whole. She chewed happily. "My, my," she marveled between mastications, "doesn't that Bertha know just what to do with a hen . . ."

Jenny stood there twisting the dish towel, watching Belinda's rouge-smeared mouth work as she chewed that horrid doughy glob of fried flour and chicken skin. Suddenly, she realized that the dislike she had felt for Belinda and Iris and all the rest of them had grown into hatred.

There sat Belinda—makeup wandering all over her sallow face, robe gaping as usual—teasing and taunting her, trying to goad her into some kind of reaction, and who in creation was Belinda anyway? Just a two-bit whore in a two-bit whorehouse, and Iris was no better!

She'd let them get to her, all of them: Iris with her threats, her assault and then her innuendos; Belinda, who sat there gobbling fried fat and flour and baiting her, trying to get a reaction, any reaction. And most of all, Ace Denton. She couldn't deny that he'd gotten to her the most of all, and that it would be a long time before she got him out from under her skin . . . But she would, by God. Let Iris have him, and he her! Let them all have each other!

She took a deep, cleansing breath and turned back to the stack of damp dishes.

"Well, I must say you're certainly a cool one for somebody who got herself tickled with a bull whip this afternoon," Belinda ventured hopefully. She wondered whether the girl would cry or get angry. Probably cry. She didn't look like she had enough temper (although Belinda liked to think of it as spirit) to get mad.

Jenny did not speak, nor did she look around. She kept on drying plates.

"Why, if that'd been me," Belinda continued, "I swan! I'd'a spent the rest of the day in my bed with the vapors."

The vapors and four cowhands in from Sedalia, Jenny thought, and dried the last dish. She stacked the plates and slid them into the cupboard before turning her attentions to the flatware.

Behind her, Belinda screwed up her face. This wasn't the reaction she'd hoped for. Unless the girl was crying into her dishrag . . . She smiled a little at the thought of it. Maybe she could get the little blonde stirred up enough to provoke a nice cat fight between her and Iris. That was always fun. She was deeply sorry she'd missed out on the skirmish in the barn. Now that must have been something to see! She tried a different approach.

"Oh, our Miss Iris," she purred, "she's terrible jealous of anybody she thinks is comin' between her and her Ace." She put a great deal of inflection on the last two words, and was pleased to see Jenny's shoulders tighten just a fraction. Good. She'd hit the right nerve.

"They're powerful in love, those two. Why, that sweet man'd do just about anything for his Iris, I reckon . . ."

I will not turn around. I will not say a word. I will

not cry. . . . Jenny dried the silver, piece by piece. A few more and she'd be done. Just the pots and pans to go . . .

". . . and Iris's always tellin' us what a darlin' man he is, real good to her, always tellin' her how much he cares and all, sweet-talkin' her an' talkin' about how they're gonna get married some day . . ."

The flatware was finished. She shoved it into its drawer and started drying the first of the big skillets. She was so angry now that her insides felt knotted into a small, tight fist. She had to make a conscious effort not to let the iron skillet slip from her shaking hands.

". . . and the way she says he makes love to her! Y'know, I just can't tell you how pure jealous even *I* get sometimes, just thinkin' about it . . ." Belinda leaned back in her chair. It was time to twist the knife. "She tells me everything, y'know," she purred. "Ways he likes to pet her 'n kiss her, all them private things . . ."

Jenny had finished all but the largest saucepan, which still soaked in the tub of murky dishwater. She reached down to it.

". . . says especially he likes her to take off all her clothes real slow, while he watches. 'N then he likes to hold her on his lap 'n . . ."

Jenny's fingers tightened around the handle. The dishwater was filthy, and she could only see the barest outline of the top of the pot through the scummy murk.

". . . likes to suckle on her, she says, jus' like a baby. Now ain't that just the sweetest li'l ol' thing you ever did hear of? Says he likes to just hold her there 'n . . .''

Jenny lifted the pot. It was heavy, but she could manage.

''. . . heaven when he shoves his way up inside her. That's what Iris says. Says he's a real glory. Makes her feel like she's done died and gone off to heaven, and—''

Belinda let out a bloodcurdling shriek when the water hit. She shot out of her chair immediately, sputtering and gasping, soaked to the waist in gray, greasy water. She stared, gape-mouthed, at her sodden, gaping robe; then at her dinner—transformed into lumps and chunks floating in a scummy sea of dishwater; and finally at Jenny, who was very calmly drying the last pot, now that it was empty.

There was a thud and a scuffle as Mac, followed immediately by Miss Liz and Shirley Mae, crashed through the door.

''What's goin' on out here?!'' Mac thundered. ''Who's bein' killed?!'' And then he saw Belinda—dripping and bedraggled and too furious to do anything but sputter incoherently; and Jenny—carefully folding the dish towel and placing it neatly on its rung.

He began to laugh: great, whooping, thigh-slapping roars that he made no attempt to contain.

'''Bout time, Belinda,'' he finally managed to say before he was overtaken by a fresh burst of belly laughs. '''Bout goddamned time!''

Gray and greasy water beading on her hair and dripping off the end of her nose, the sodden prostitute glared at Miss Liz. The madam looked from Belinda to Jenny and back again.

She started to speak, but no sound came out. Finally, she closed her mouth with an audible click of teeth and shook her head. She exited to the dining room without a word, one hand pressed tightly over her smile. She was followed closely by Shirley Mae, who could only mutter, "Well, I'll be damned . . ."

Jenny gave a businesslike nod to Mac (who was happily clutching his aching ribs) and left the kitchen before Belinda could find her tongue. Once out of sight, she fairly ran up the stairs, then down the hall to her room. She lit the lamp, locked the door, and sat down on her bed.

Now the anger and frustration came pouring out in a torrent of tears. *Blast them!* she raged as the tears streamed down her cheeks. *Blast them all!* Blast that cow Belinda and her scheming and needling! Blast Iris and her threats and snide innuendos! Blast Miss Liz along with her fifty dollar offer, and put a curse on nasty, grumbly Bertha Bramley, wasted Shirley Mae, smug Mary-Rebecca, and drunken, wizened little Harvey and all the others. Let them all roast in perdition together, except for Mac: sweet, kind Mac, who it seemed was the only one here who respected her, who genuinely liked her without wanting something in return . . .

But most of all, blast Ace Denton. And along with him, she cursed herself for her inability to resist him. With a jerk, she stood up, suddenly remembering something important.

Quickly, she doubled-checked the lock on her door. Next, she went to the little dresser and began to

234

half-drag, half-push it across the tiny room. It was heavier than it looked, but within five minutes she had shoved it hard against the opposite wall: the wall he'd appeared in front of two nights before. A little out of breath, she surveyed her work, her hands on her hips and a look of satisfaction on her face. *There*, she thought. *That'll keep him out.*

Satisfied that she had insured herself a safe and solitary slumber, she undressed; and after reapplying a thin veil of Bertha's homemade, smelly salve to the already fading welts on her chest and upper arm, she slipped into a long white nightgown. Within seconds after she blew out the lamp, Jenny had fallen into a deep, exhausted sleep.

She was floating up, up out of the comforting numbness of bottomless black; up toward sensation; up toward light; up toward sound. A voice.

A line of dim light appeared between her lashes and she felt something brush her shoulder. "Aunt Victoria?" she mumbled, half in a dream.

"Shh, Jenny. I'm just seeing to your battle wounds." A deep voice, too near. His voice.

Her eyes popped open. Immediately, they were locked to his. The lamp was lit and turned down so far that it cast only a dim, yellow glow over the room. Ace was sitting on the edge of her bed. He had unbuttoned the top of her gown and pulled it away to expose the red marks above her bosom and on her upper arm. Across the room, her dresser stood exactly where she had shoved it, and she could see that her door was still latched.

For what seemed like the millionth time this week, she began to cry.

The outlaw's forehead furrowed in concern. "Is there something else, Jenny? Did that buckskin kick you? Are you hurt somewhere else? What is it?"

"Blast you!" she finally managed to blurt. "How did you get in here? Why can't you just leave me alone?" Her fingers clawed ineffectually at the bedclothes and she twisted away. Already the sound of his voice was making her tingle, making her want him, and she detested herself for it. "Why are you torturing me?"

He took her by the shoulders and pulled her to a sitting position. "Torture? If anyone's being tortured, it's me, not you."

"Oh, really?" she hissed, anger overtaking her frustration. Her face was still streaked and wet, but the outburst of tears had abruptly ceased. "If all you want is somebody to—to—*breed,* all you have to do is go down one floor!"

"Jenny!" He shook her once, hard, but she still glared at him with narrowed, unblinking eyes.

"Go on!" she hissed. "Go to Iris. She's the one you want, not me! Go to her and leave me—"

He kissed her, cutting off her words—kissed her almost cruelly, as if by the pressure of his lips he could punish her for what she'd said, make her see the lie of it. And though she kept her teeth clamped shut against him, she could tell that he made not even the slightest attempt to invade her mouth. He merely maintained the pressure, mouth against mouth, so that she could not speak again.

At last he released her. This time she was mute,

although her eyes still accused him.

"Don't ever say that again, Jenny," he said at last.

"You can't stop me this time, Ace Denton! I'll say whatever I—"

Again he silenced her, but this time his kiss was intended to convince, to coerce. She twisted, fighting him, but gradually she felt herself yield. She was unable to help herself. Her lips, then her teeth parted, and she felt him slide into her mouth, warm and silky. Soon she was returning his kisses eagerly, forgetting to hate him, forgetting to hate herself, remembering only that she was whole only with him.

She felt him slip free the remaining buttons on her nightdress and slide it from her shoulders, baring her to the waist. Gently, he stroked her throat, her arms, the tender skin of her shoulders, traced his fingertips along the soft ridges of her collarbone, feathered the broadness of his palm over her breasts; and her fingers—seemingly of their own will—went to the buttons of his shirt, freeding them rapidly.

She tugged the open halves apart and slid her hands inside, feeling the silky curls that covered his broad chest. His body was hard and strong, and suddenly she wanted to press herself against him, flesh against flesh.

Ace sensed her urgency, and pulled away only long enough to tug off his shirt. He took her into his arms once more, this time pulling her close so that her breasts rubbed against his chest as he kissed her. His hands floated up and down the soft ladder of her spine, and she happily squirmed against him. Her nipples pressed into the taut breadth of his chest to be tickled and abraded by the black pelt of fur that

237

covered it.

She wanted to mold herself against him, to merge with him, to *be* him. Her fingers flew to his belt. Something beyond reason drove her to hold him again, and more than ever she wanted to feel him inside her. She yearned to be filled with him, to know what it was like to be so intimately, perfectly joined with another human. And she knew that tonight, there would be no turning back. Her fate had been sealed. His intentions were obvious, especially when he stood up to strip off the rest of his clothes and stand before her, naked.

He was beautiful. There was no better word to describe him. His body was perfectly balanced, hard and strong and copper-skinned. Muscles rippled across his flat belly and bulged in his arms, chest, and long, hard thighs. He stood there a moment, letting her look at him, knowing that she wanted to drink him in, learn him with her eyes; and then he stepped closer.

He bent down to pull back her covers, but before he could, she leaned toward him, toward the eager shaft jutting from the dark curls between his legs. But just before her lips could kiss him there, she remembered her vow, and instead, turned her head to rest her cheek against the raised silky underside.

Touched, Ace reached down to stroke her hair, and she hugged his thighs, pressing her cheek to that which she would not let her lips caress.

At last, he gently pulled her arms from about his legs, pushed back her covers and lay down beside her. She still wore her nightgown, although it was puddled about her waist, and after kissing her lingeringly, he reached to remove it. Jenny lifted her hips for him. He slipped it down over her feet and tossed it aside before he returned to her mouth.

Now he gifted her with the sweetest and lengthiest of kisses, all the while stroking her quivering body. Jenny rejoiced in the calm surety of his touch. Each caress of his gentle, skilled fingers seemed more delicious than the last, each place he touched her more sensitive than the one before. She, in turn, explored him, delighting in the strong, animal feel of his body. He was all hard angles and bulges of muscle and sinew: a warm, steely wall of flesh in which she wanted nothing more than to be enveloped.

Side by side they lay in the dim golden glow of the lamplight. Flesh pressed against flesh from head to toe as they leisurely, sensuously discovered each other's bodies, each other's secrets. Being in his arms seemed at the same time both completely safe and exquisitely perilous. Each interlude with him had been better than the last, each occasion of his touch more perfect. She wondered when it would be time for him to enter her.

But when she felt him shift his weight to hover above her, she couldn't imagine what he might be doing. He pressed his knee between her thighs and although she didn't know why, she parted them for him. Then both his legs were between hers, and he lay atop her, propped on his elbows.

She could feel the insistent weight of his shaft press against her thigh as he kissed her again, then dipped his head lower to feather kisses over the top swells of her bosom, then up the column of her throat to her eager lips. In mounting urgency, Jenny arched her back and pressed against him.

He propped himself on one elbow and shifted his weight again to slip his hand between their bodies. Down over Jenny's belly his fingers traveled, until they slipped between her thighs to touch her. He found her luxurious with moisture, and gently positioned himself against her before he brought his arm up again and hovered over her.

Jenny felt a euphoric rush of shivers when he stroked her, and a nearly unbearable ache of want and hunger when she felt him, slick and broad, poised at her threshold. *Lying down?* a tiny voice at the back of her head asked in amazement. *Face to face? How perfect, how miraculous, how wonderful!* And then his lips departed from her bosom. He lifted his head and gazed into her eyes.

There was an almost interminable silence: silence, that was, except for the sounds of their breathing. And then his voice: a husky, baritone whisper in the half-light.

"Ask me, Jenny."

No, please, she wept inwardly, *please don't make me ask! I can't, I won't—please just love me, just love me and don't make me ask!* More than anything she wanted him, wanted him to push forward and make her his—to brand her with his love. But this one thing he wanted her to voice, she couldn't. The doing of it was one thing, but the asking . . .

Her eyes were wide now, and still he hovered above her, his eys locked to hers, his length poised to plunder.

"Jenny?"

Still she could not speak. Her bosom heaved, her

240

nipples grazing—with sensation more excruciating at every breath—the pelt of his chest as he hung, suspended above her.

They stared at each other a long time, engaged in a silent and intense battle of wills: he, aroused nearly to the point of mindlessness, knowing that if he lost control for even one second, he would take her by force; and she, bound by her pledge and unable to say the words he wanted to hear, wishing that he would.

"Jenny!" he finally managed to whisper in a voice hoarse with passion. "Jenny, you have to ask me!"

She opened her mouth, and it was a moment before she could form the words, "I can't."

Ace shifted his weight to one arm and ran his fingers through his hair in complete exasperation. He was angry, and within a split second, his anger had grown to fury.

Jenny saw the change in him, and suddenly felt her arousal turn to terror. She was trapped with him in this room, imprisoned beneath his body. He could do anything he wanted to her, she realized, and her terror became cold fear.

Abruptly he rolled off of her and got to his feet. He snatched his clothing from the floor and dressed quickly, leaving Jenny naked on the bed. She made an attempt to reach for her quilt, but he snatched it away and hurled it to the opposite corner of the room.

"Why pretend, Jenny?" he barked. "You're a tease at heart, aren't you? You might as well sit there naked and see if you can make a fool of me again."

She leaned over the bed and tried to snag her nightdress from the floor, but that, too, he yanked from her fingers and tossed out of her reach.

"Come on, Jenny. Give us a shake. Give us a shimmy. Give us a taste of what you're keeping to yourself. And tell us about it in godamned Latin, while you're at it."

All the hate she'd held in her heart when she first arrived at Miss Liz's came flooding back. He was an arrogant monster, a thief, a murderer; and suddenly, she didn't care if he killed her here and now.

"Get out! I hate you! You're a murderer and I wish you were dead!" She snarled it at him, her hands clenching the edge of the thin mattress.

He started just a little. He hadn't expected another verbal outburst from her—her fists pounding at him, perhaps, but not this. In her anger she had forgotten her nudity. Now she made no attempt to cover herself. She crouched on the bed like a catamount ready to pounce.

"Wish I was dead!?" he growled. "You little— What have I ever given you except pleasure?"

"I don't want you, or your pleasure! You killed my father!" Her eyes were wild with hate and fury, and at last—at long last—it was out.

Ace blinked and stared at her. "I *what?*"

"You heard me. You murdered my father, and I came here to see you hang. Or kill you myself if I had to." She raised herself up to stand on wide-spread knees and balled her hands into fists. "I couldn't do it. I'm not as cold-blooded as you and your friends. But I'll find a way to see you hanged, you murdering bastard, I swear it! Maybe not this week or next, but sooner or later, I'll find a way. So go downstairs to your sweet Iris. Enjoy her while you can and leave me

242

alone!" She was drunk with anger now, fury pumping more and more adrenaline into her shaking body. Her eyes had dilated until their emerald was reduced to only a thin ring of green surrounding huge black pupils.

The way he looked at her was both hateful and thunderstruck. "And just when was I supposed to have killed your father, Jenny?"

"Last month in Fowlersville, when you robbed the bank. He was just walking down the street and you—you—" On the edge of hysteria, she lost the words and glared at him: her nostrils flared, her breasts heaving.

Suddenly, he began to understand. "Jenny, I don't—"

"Oh, that's right," she sneered. "There've been so many, I suppose it's hard to pick out just the one."

Suddenly, he understood. His anger remained, but the growing fury within him was no longer directed at Jenny. Poor Jenny. What hell he must have put her through, with her thinking what she did about him. There was no explaining it to her now: she was too upset, and he had no real proof.

Someone would pay for this, he vowed, and very soon.

He bent to retrieve her nightgown, then held it out to her. She snatched it from him and clutched it to her chest.

"You know the way I feel about you, Jenny. You've felt my touch." His tone was entirely different than it had been only seconds before. "Can't you tell, Jenny? Do you really believe I could . . ."

She looked up at him, and hatred—simple, pure,

and suddenly all-consuming—shone from her face. "Yes! No. Yes—" Her brow knotted in confusion even as she glared at him. "I mean, everybody knows that you— I don't know! Just get out and leave me alone!" The tears came then, and she pressed her hands to her face. "Just leave me alone," she repeated, sobbing.

This time he didn't wait for her to look away before he exited. He took two long steps to her dresser and then, with enough force that he might just as easily have punched it through the wall, he smacked his fist against a paneled seam. The wall behind the dresser slid away, and in one quick movement, he vaulted the little bureau and disappeared into the blackness beyond. She heard another thud of fist against wood, and the panel swung closed again with a barely audible whisper.

Nine

Both Iris and Belinda showed up on time for breakfast, though their attitudes toward Jenny were at opposite ends of the spectrum. Belinda glowered at her throughout the meal, and once went so far as to try to trip her as she walked past. The only thing that prevented the outbreak of fisticuffs was the presence of Mac, who leaned against the cupboards throughout the meal, watching Belinda and periodically sending a warning look her way.

By contrast, Iris could not have been more sweet, more syrupy—or more condescending. She acted toward Jenny as if she were a none-too-bright, unfortunate-looking younger sister who must be spoken down to and pitied.

"Jenny, dear, maybe after breakfast I could help you do something with that hair of yours," she'd purer.

"Jenny, sweet, I know it's hard for you, but do

245

please try to remember that I don't care for cream in my coffee . . ."

"Jenny, you really oughta try to stand up straight. Honest, darlin', you'll never find a man to look at you twice if you're all slouched down like that . . ."

By the time the meal was over, Jenny was ready to slap her, even though she knew that it was just the reaction for which Iris—and Belinda—hoped.

After the breakfast cleanup, Bertha Bramley sent her out front to Miss Liz's office.

"She wants you to dust up in there. Polish up that big desk of hers while you're at it, too, and do a good job for a change! I'll be checkin' after you finish up. Anything ain't done right, you're gonna have to do over. And when you're finished, don't dawdle. There's butter needs churnin', and bread to bake . . ."

Actually, Jenny rather enjoyed being alone in the office. It was on the opposite side of the house from the kitchen and dining room, and its big bay window looked up the road toward town. Of course, town was another three miles away, but the road curved away to the north—the direction in which she would soon be traveling.

And Miss Liz's office was filled with all kinds of strange and wonderful curios; mostly, Jenny surmised, left over from the days of Elmer Sweeny. The majority of the room was decorated in a bastard Oriental fashion. The furniture was a little lighter and airier here than in the rest of the house, although it still suffered somewhat from overstuffing. A heavy brass tortoise, nearly three feet long, crouched between the two green leather wing chairs that faced Miss Liz's desk, and the Oriental carpets layering the floor echoed the deep Chinese red of the walls.

Over the mantel hung a rather wonderful painting of a beautiful dark-haired woman, formally posed in a garden and wearing a stunning gown of deep rose and pearl gray satin. Jenny immediately recognized the model as a much younger Liz McCaleb. The mantel itself was carved marble, and below were the snarling dragon andirons which she had glimpsed so many times through the open door.

On the bookshelves were Buddhas of brass and stone and teak; ornate winged dragons and oriental figures beautifully carved in pink or green jade; and tiny, fragile ivory figurines. Scattered into the collection at random were pieces of a more native and eclectic sort: a wooden dog that looked to have been whittled by a child; a crudely painted ceramic bird's nest cradling four aggies and a purie; several porcelain pieces of varying quality; a blown-glass elephant; a tarnished piccolo; a few small, silver-framed photographs of gentlemen and one of a little boy; a chipped moustache cup; a half-dozen cloisonné paperweights; and a clever and delicate bisque box that contained three faded and unmatched garters.

The books were old and leather-bound, and most of them had titles in Latin or French or German. Jenny, dusting the gold-stamped spines, decided that in addition to the eccentricity of his architectural pastime, Mr. Elmer Sweeny must have been quite a scholar.

The dusting finished, she cleared the top of the heavy mahogany desk and set to work polishing its already gleaming surface. As she rubbed smooth, even circles over the deep and lustrous wood, she stared out the window, to the north. She knew that she wouldn't be able to stay another week waiting for her slim wages. She would have to leave soon and take her chances. Horseback was not the safest, nor the most comfortable, nor the wisest way for a lone young lady to travel, especially a young lady who had over four hundred miles to go and only slightly more than a dollar and four bits to her name. But somehow she felt it was infinitely safer than staying on here.

I'll finish out the day, she thought, *and leave first thing in the morning, before anyone else is up*. By the time she had finished buffing the desktop and drawer fronts she was firm in her decision. She pushed Ace Denton from her mind, at least insofar as his advances were concerned. She knew that if she let her physical responses enter the picture, she might never be able to leave.

She was down on the floor, bringing out the dark shine on the first of the desk's carved legs when the door opened. She twisted toward the sound apprehensively, afraid that it might be Iris or Belinda, but it was Miss Liz. She was dressed in deep hunter green today, and her charm bracelet jangled faintly as she swept into the office.

After breathing a sigh of relief, Jenny looked up and said, "Afternoon, ma'am."

"Good afternoon, Jennifer," Miss Liz replied with a smile. She glanced about the room. "Everything looks just lovely, dear." She put a hand down to Jenny. "Now do get up. It looks finished to me."

Jenny took the offered hand and got to her feet.

"I'm not quite done yet. I still have three more legs to do . . ."

"It can wait, dear. Right now I'd like to have a word with you, if you think you can spare the time." She motioned toward one of the green leather wing chairs, and Jenny perched on its edge, folding her hands demurely in her lap.

"Yes'm."

The madam sat down behind her desk and smiled again in a manner that was motherly but faintly patronizing. "Do you remember our little chat, Jenny? The one we had the other afternoon in the parlor?"

"Yes ma'am . . ." So it was about *that*. She'd been afraid she was about to be lectured for dousing Belinda.

"Have you thought it over?"

"Well yes, and while I'd like to thank—"

Miss Liz was irritated, but with some effort she managed to broaden her smile. She waved a hand and cut Jenny off. "Don't be so quick to answer, dear. I wanted to tell you that I've spoken to the gentleman in question since our conversation, and he's really quite insistent. So insistent, in fact, that he's raised his offer."

Jenny waited for her to continue. She had no intention of accepting, even if the "gentleman" was offering the entire state of Missouri and part of Iowa, but she knew that Miss Liz would not be satisfied until she'd said her piece.

"He's willing to pay you, Jenny—and I hope you have some concept of how much money this is—

seventy-five dollars. For just one night out of your life.''

Miss Liz paused dramatically to let the words sink in. Actually he had raised the offer to one hundred and fifty dollars, an unprecedented sum for this establishment, but she had her expenses and overhead to consider. As she looked at Jenny, she saw not so much the girl herself, but what she represented: a grand house, a great house; and an eventual retirement in style—back East, maybe, where no one would know where Liz McCaleb had come by her money . . .

"Do you understand, Jennifer?'' The girl was just staring at her. Could she really be so stupid?

"Yes ma'am, Miss Liz. I understand. And seventy-five dollars *is* a lot of money—"

"That's right, dear. It's a small fortune. And if you decide to stay on, it's just the beginning. I can make you a very wealthy young woman.'' She could see the girl was about to turn her down and, quickly, she altered her approach.

"I'm going to confide in you, Jennifer," she continued, lowering her tone conspiratorially. "The rest of my girls are not . . . Well, they're not in your class. You have something special, something past that pretty face and lovely golden hair.''

Jenny blushed slightly, and Miss Liz, deciding she'd pushed the right button, purred ahead. "You have a certain quality. It's hard to describe, but maybe it's a kind of innocence. The kind that you won't lose even after . . . After you've been with one man or many. It's just part of your nature, that sweetness. And that's a rare quality—a quality that men are willing to pay for, and pay dearly. Do you understand what I'm saying, Jenny?"

Jenny nodded. "Yes ma'am. I understand. It's just that I couldn't— I don't think, I mean I know that I could never—"

"Honestly Jenny!" The madam's grin twisted into a scowl of exasperation. She tugged angrily at the spangles on her bracelet. "Don't be such a little fool!"

Frightened by the madam's sudden change of tone, Jenny cringed against the cushions, her eyes wide. Immediately, Miss Liz took a breath and lowered her voice to its previous familiar and coercive purr.

"I don't think you realize what I'm offering you, Jennifer. You told me when you came here that you don't have any people. You're alone in the world. That's a bad way for a young girl—a young, pretty girl especially—to be in. The world is a very large, nasty place. What are you going to do out there? Wait tables or scrub floors until you work yourself to death? Teach school in some backwater and retire an old maid? Marry some farmer who'll work you to the bone until you have the good sense to die in childbirth? What else is there except what I'm offering? And I'm offering a life of easy work—not work at all, really—where you'll be admired by rich, powerful men. You'll have beautiful clothes and fine things, and more money than you'll know what to do with."

The girl's expression had softened and she seemed to be listening intently. Good. Miss Liz lowered her tone even further, almost to a whisper, and leaned across the desk.

251

"I'm not asking you to be like these girls here, Jenny. You and I both know that most of them are trash. They're beneath you. And I'm telling you that what you can become is as distant from what they are as a dove is from a toad. You can be some*body*, Jenny. Somebody elegant and wonderful and desirable. And I can help you become her." She leaned back in her chair and waited.

Jenny had been listening, and she knew that most of what the older woman was telling her was true. She herself had lied, of course, about not having anyone—there was Aunt Victoria, waiting in Minnesota—but what kind of a life would she have there? In terms of fulfillment, it wouldn't be much better than waiting tables in a nunnery.

She weakened for a moment, as a picture floated through her mind of herself, newly sophisticated and witty, dressed as elegantly as Miss Liz had been when she posed for her portrait. . . . But then the reality of it, of a life spent allowing strange men touch her, use her, replaced that vision until all that was left was a picture of Shirley Mae. . . .

It was impossible. She knew that if she turned down this offer, Miss Liz would not let her leave the room until she relented. She decided to stall.

"Thank you for explaining it for me, ma'am," she began. "I guess I just hadn't thought about it like that. It's just that, well, do you mind if I take a little more time to think about it? It's a pretty big decision." *There,* she thought. *That will hold her until tomorrow, and by then I'll be gone.*

Miss Liz smiled, quite genuinely this time. "Of course, dear," she said, rising. "You think it over very carefully and see if you don't decide I'm right. And tomorrow you can give me your answer."

Jenny got to her feet. "Yes'm. I'll do that. And I'll just get back to the furniture now, if you don't mind. I have some thinking to do."

"Certainly, Jennifer. I'll leave you to it." Smiling with satisfaction, she left the room, closing the door softly behind her.

Not too long afterward, Jenny was back in the kitchen finishing up the butter Mrs. Bramley had already churned. She sat at the table, pressing and turning butter in a wide bowl with the wooden paddle, working out the last of the buttermilk, working in the salt. The smell of baking bread and biscuits flooded the room, and the cook was bent over the sink, snapping beans and talking to herself. Jenny thought that they seemed to be fixing an awful lot of food—certainly not the gargantuan amounts they'd prepare for a Friday or Saturday night, but a great deal more than usual.

The puzzle was solved after she carried the pale, finished butter to the counter; because it was then that she looked out the window.

The corral was crowded with horses again: *their* horses. They must have come in while she was dusting the office. Suddenly she was very happy that she'd made the decision to leave in the morning, although she regretted that she hadn't made up her mind a day earlier. She wished she could wipe the events of the last twenty-four hours out of her mind.

Jenny jumped when the cook growled, "Let me see

that," and snatched the bowl from under her nose. She gave the mass of soft, fresh butter a cursory poke with the paddle before she grumbled, "S'pose it'll do. Get it put up."

While Jenny packed the butter into round, embossed molds, Mrs. Bramley checked her already overcooked roast and finished snapping the beans. By the time Jenny carried the butter to the cool cellar and returned to the kitchen, the cook was frying up sliced potatoes and onions in a huge iron skillet.

"Piece'a bacon wrapped up over there," she barked when Jenny finished with the packing. "Throw it in with them beans, cover 'em with water, and set 'em to heat."

Jenny complied and slid the heavy saucepan at the back of the stove.

"You do a decent job in Liz's office?"

"Yes ma'am," she said flatly, knowing that no matter what she had done, it would not be good enough. Bertha Bramley was someone she'd be delighted never to see again.

"Well, we'll see about that after we get this mob fed. Ever'thin' in there better be spic 'n span, missy. Spic 'n span!" With quick jabs of her spatula, she turned the potatoes and onions in their sizzling butter.

"Now get to settin' that table."

Jenny nodded resignedly, and with a sigh began pulling out plates and silverware.

"We got extras today," the cook muttered as Jenny folded and placed the last napkin.

"Ma'am?"

"Extras! You deaf or somethin'?"

"No ma'am."

"Well, pay attention, then." She scraped the last of the potatoes, golden but still swimming in grease, into a heavy serving dish, and pulled down another bowl for the green beans. "Get out five extra settin's and fix up a tray."

Oh Lord, she's going to make me take it up to them, or down to them, or wherever they are . . . Jenny thought. She obeyed, however, and with shaking hands arranged a tray and brought it to the table. Mrs. Bramley had loaded the sideboard with food by then. She began filling the five plates, heaping them with fried potatoes, soggy beans, and dry, overcooked slabs of roast beef. Over each, she ladled a healthy dollop of her ever-present gravy, then waved the dripping spoon at Jenny.

"Get this up to the playroom, missy. They's already got somethin' up there to drink it down with." With that she turned her back. As Jenny struggled up the back stairs with the heavy tray, she heard Mrs. Bramley's hollered version of the dinner chime: "You lazy whores better get your butts down here and eat this afore it gets cold. I ain't responsible!"

When she reached the second floor landing, Jenny stopped to balance the heavy tray on the railing while she waited for the ache in her arms to ease. Finally she decided that it would take more time than she had for the pain to go away, so she took a deep breath and, hoisting the tray again, started down the hall. The girls had, by then, all gone down for dinner. The only sound, aside from the echo of her footsteps, was the murmur of male voices coming from behind the

255

playroom door.

She tapped at it with her foot. It seemed forever before Billy Dodge, a silly smirk on his baby face, ushered her in.

She had half-expected to find Meg with them, but Scar Cooksey's girlfriend was nowhere in sight. Scar was, however. He was at the bar with Andy Dodge.

"—glad to get up outta that hole in the ground, even for—" she heard him say before he saw her and silenced himself. Both he and Andy turned to watch her as she self-consciously carried the tray toward one of the felt-covered card tables.

"Let me help you with that, miss," said a voice, *his* voice, at her elbow.

She nearly dropped the tray, but caught herself just in time. She looked toward him. His face was expressionless, betraying neither emotion nor recognition.

"No, thank you," she said, gathering herself. "I think I have it." She took the last three steps to the table and with numb hands, slid the tray onto its green, cigarette-scarred surface. Behind her, she heard his receding footsteps as he joined Andy Dodge and Scar Cooksey at the bar, and then his voice mingling with the others as the men began to talk.

One at a time, she set the steaming plates around the table, then began laying out the silver and napkins. *There is something to be thankful for,* she thought. *At least there's enough gentleman in him that he hasn't told them what he did. Or what I did . . .*

She had finished and was picking up the tray when

256

from behind, an arm closed around her waist. She knew immediately it was not Ace, and she let out a little yelp as she tried to twist away.

It was Rafe Langley. He was leering at her, and when she struggled he only gripped her tighter. "Ain't you gonna stay on a bit, little darlin'?" he whispered. His breath was foul with whiskey and cigar smoke.

"No!" she cried, suddenly wishing that Ace had told them all that she was his girl, lie or not. Rafe would never have dared touch her then. "Let me go!" She wiggled against him, the big oval tray clutched to her breast. "Please!"

He tugged the tray out of her hands and let it clatter to the floor. "Let's jus' see whatcha got under there, honey," he smirked. She could hear young Billy Dodge laugh as Rafe's dirty fingers went to the top button of her blouse.

"That's enough, Rafe."

Ace Denton's hand stayed his arm.

"Aw c'mon, Ace. What's'a matter? Her 'n me's jus' havin' us a little fun. She looked a little icy to me. Thought maybe I'd take her over to the corner and take some'a the chill off the merchandise." His fingers went back toward the buttons.

Ace grabbed his wrist again. "I said quit it. The lady doesn't want to play."

Rafe snorted and turned her loose. "Hell," he argued. "Ain't no 'ladies' in *this* house! She's just puttin' on, like they all do. I was just—"

Jenny didn't hear the rest. Scooping up the tray, she darted from the room. She took the steps two at a time and nearly flew down to the kitchen and the near-comfort of Mrs. Bramley's curses.

Dinner was relatively uneventful. Agnes and Pearl did not join them for the meal, being otherwise occupied with a pair of teenage farm boys who had appeared at the door, a knotted bandanna full of coins between them and conspiratorial looks on their smooth, eager faces.

For once, there was no mealtime argument between Bertha Bramley and Shirley Mae Vinton. Earlier in the afternoon, after her little talk with Jenny, the madam had taken it upon herself to give Shirley Mae her walking papers. She'd been putting it off for months. The other girls were averaging thirty or forty "callers" a week, but the aging prostitute was lucky to turn five, even with the busy weekend crowds; and those men that took her upstairs did so only as a last resort.

Miss Liz had spoken to her as kindly as she could, never mentioning the obvious—that Shirley Mae was just too old and too unattractive to continue.

"I'm so sorry, Shirley," Miss Liz had said, "having to let you go like this. But things are tight, and I just can't afford to keep on a girl who handles less than twenty gents a week. You've been in this business a while. You know how it is."

"Yeah, I reckon I been in it some kinda while, all right," Shirley Mae sniffed, her usual facade of crude bravado gone.

"I'd offer you a job in the kitchen, but knowing how you and Bertha—"

"No, you're right, Liz. That ain't for me. I couldn't work with that old cow for five minutes, an' we both know it . . ."

Miss Liz saw the tear cutting a hot path through the thick makeup caked over Shirley Mae's premature wrinkles, and said softly, "Of course, you'll have your severance pay. That'll give you a good start somewhere else."

"Sev'rance pay? What's that?" Shirley Mae brightened somewhat.

"That's what I give my girls if I have to let them go," Liz McCaleb lied. She had never in her life given a girl severance pay, but now seemed like a good time to start.

"Let's see, now, Shirl," she continued, pulling down a three-year-old ledger from the shelf. She knew it didn't matter which book she drew out. Shirley Mae couldn't read. "How long have you been with me?"

"Five years last April," she sniffed, leaning forward eagerly. Maybe being fired wasn't as bad as she'd thought.

Liz opened the book at random and appeared to study it intently. "Yes," she said finally. "That seems right."

She turned a few pages, running her fingers down random columns while she thought, then snapped the ledger shut and returned it to its place on the shelf. Quite businesslike, she sat down behind her desk and clasped her hands.

"According to my calculations, Shirley Mae, your severance pay amounts to eighty-six dollars and seventy-five cents." She picked an odd number on purpose. It was less likely to arouse suspicion. After a moment she rose with great dignity and crossed the room to the mantel, then reached up to touch the frame of her portrait. There was a soft click before the painting swung out to reveal a wall safe. She worked the combination quickly and, pulling out her battered cash box, said, "That should give you a good stake, Shirley Mae. Let you start fresh. It's a goodly sum."

"Yeah," she answered, smiling wanly now. "It sure is." She had never seen so much money all at once. "I never knowed you done this sorta thing, Liz." She watched intently as the madam carried the metal box back to the desk and opened it. Carefully, she counted out the gold pieces and change before she slid them into a small white envelope.

"I don't like for it to get around, Shirley Mae. This severance pay business, I mean. I'm counting on you not to say anything to the other girls." Miss Liz handed over the envelope and the other woman accepted it happily, sliding it inside her ruffled top to ride against her sagging bosom.

"Thanks, Liz," she said as she went out the door. "I mean that. You run a good house here. I was treated square while I worked for you, and this," she said, touching the cash-filled envelope through the fabric of her blouse, "this here's more'n fair." She straightened, tugging—out of habit—at her bodice. "I reckon I'll be leavin' tomorrow, if you can spare Mac to drive me to town."

By supper time, word had gotten around. And

although no one mentioned it to her face, everyone in the house knew that Shirley Mae had been asked to leave. There was little conversation during the meal other than an occasional and unnaturally polite "Pass the salt," or "Biscuits, please."

Even Belinda and Iris were somewhat subdued, although it was due to the solemn atmosphere created by Mac, Harvey, and the girls more than any compassion on their part. Although Jenny felt sorry for Shirley Mae, she was probably the happiest person in the room, for she knew she'd be away from them all by tomorrow. An additional cause for joy was that she hadn't had to face the outlaws again. She'd spent the hours between the dinner cleanup and the supper service scrubbing the dining room floor, and Meg had taken up their supper tray in her stead.

Mary-Rebecca left the table halfway through the meal. Her regular Thursday-nighter arrived early and eager, and so she missed the gooseberry pies Bertha Bramley had baked for dessert. The remaining diners—with the exception of Belinda, who gobbled down her own piece and half of Iris's— weren't able to do much more than pick at their portions. Considering that Mrs. Bramley had baked them, they were excellent pastries, for as heavy-handed as the cook was with nearly everything else that emerged from her kitchen, her baked goods were close to heavenly. Gooseberry was Shirley's favorite, and it was Bertha's way of doing something nice for Shirley Mae without having to actually admit it. They all understood, and although Shirley Mae was as reticent as the cook to speak a kind word, she rested

261

her hand on Bertha's shoulder for just a second when she left the kitchen.

It was enough to bring tears to the cook's eyes— after Shirley Mae was out of sight, of course. For Bertha Bramley knew, better than anyone, what the world held in store for a woman of Shirley Mae's ilk once she was too old or too ugly or too fat or too tired to continue. Bertha had been extraordinarily lucky to find a position with Miss Liz. Most others were not so fortunate, and she was well aware that it would only be downhill for Shirley from now on out: a sinking spiral that would continue until she died, more than likely penniless and alone in a gutter or the back room of some sod shack of a saloon in the middle of nowhere . . .

So when Shirley Mae left the kitchen to go upstairs and begin packing, gruff, headstrong, abrasive Bertha Bramley began to cry. The remaining girls quietly trickled out of the room as Mac went to her.

"Now now, Bertha," he soothed. "She knew what she was getting into . . ."

"Maybe she could stay on, Mac. Do somethin' around here. God knows I can't stand the sorrowful ol' bitch, but I hate to see anybody—I mean, I wouldn't wish it on a stray cur . . ."

"Come on, Bertha," Mac said softly. "Liz said she asked her to stay, but she was of a mind to move on. Besides, you know damn well you'd kill each other inside a week. . . ." He took the dishrag from her hands, put his arm about her broad shoulders, and ushered her out through the swinging door to the deserted dining room. "Let's just you and me go out

262

here and sit down and have us a talk. We don't get to talk much, do we, Bertha . . .''

Ace and Scar had been oddly quiet since Meggie brought their supper. The only real chatter had been from the Dodge brothers, and now that Billy was pretty well drunk, even their conversation had lapsed into an occasional nonsensical burst of laughter. No one had come to pick up the dinner debris, and dirty plates were stacked in the center of the second poker table. Rafe had tried to get up a game just to kill some time, but neither Ace nor Scar seemed interested. Andy was lousy at cards—he was too easy to beat. And Billy wasn't much good for anything when he was this far in his cups. Downstairs, Harvey was back at work at the old upright providing atmosphere for an unexpected party of card players, and the resultant vibrations rattled the floorboards under their feet.

Rafe shoved his chair back. "You boys're 'bout as excitin' as a day-long church service. Believe I'll stretch my legs a bit, then hit the sack.''

Ace, slouched in the chair across from him, shoved his hat back from his eyes. "What? Oh. Reckon we'll be along pretty soon. Those damn dinners of Bertha's do me in every time." He rubbed at his eyes. "Harvey doesn't help much, either.''

Rafe smirked. "Yeah," he muttered as he opened the playroom door a crack and peeked out into the gallery. It was clear. He nodded to the others and slipped out.

Ace sat quietly for a minute or two, staring at the

closed door before he looked toward the bar. Scar was leaning against it, watching him expectantly.

Ace nodded, just slightly, and Scar slipped quietly from the room.

He returned much more quickly than Ace had expected, and went back to his spot at the bar. He pulled out a fresh bottle of rye and tugged out the cork.

It was less than a minute before Agnes sashayed in. She was wearing a low-cut cerulean dress that showed off the golden highlights in her usually drab, light brown hair.

"Evenin', boys," she smiled. "Things're a little dull downstairs, so I thought . . ." Her eye came to rest on Andy. He was sitting next to Billy, at Ace's left, and he was staring at her intently. Agnes was his favorite, though he didn't treat himself to her as often as he'd like. For all Andy's roguish aspirations, he was a miser at heart.

"Hello, sweetie," she purred, and poured herself into his lap. He grinned foolishly and stared down her cleavage.

Ace pulled his hat down over his eyes, crossed his arms over his chest, and leaned back in his chair. Scar poured himself a shot of rye.

"Y'know, Andy," Agnes cooed softly, "I been thinkin'. What with it bein' such a slow night and all . . ." She dipped her head and whispered something in Andy's ear, something that made his face light up like Christmas and the Fourth of July all rolled together.

"Sure!" he said, and stood up so fast he almost dumped her on the floor. Billy, watching with dull

264

eyes, managed something like a chuckle.

"Easy, Andy boy," she giggled as Andy took her arm and fairly dragged her from the room.

As Agnes pulled the door closed, Ace caught her eye and silently mouthed, "Thanks."

She smiled and winked at him before Andy tugged her out into the hall behind him.

Bottle in one hand and three glasses trapped between the fingers of the other, Scar sat down in the chair Andy had just vacated. He slid one glass to Ace and one to Billy Dodge and began to pour.

Ace leaned forward and nudged Billy's brimming glass toward him. The boy grinned lopsidedly and hoisted it into the air. It sloshed on the way up, and half of it ran down his arm. He didn't notice. "To—to—" He cocked his head and looked at Ace. "Wha's it *to?* Gotta be *to* somethin'."

Ace nodded solemnly. "You're right, Billy." He lifted his own glass, not nearly so full as the boy's, and Scar followed suit. "To . . . Let's see. To adventure. How's that?"

Billy smiled. He liked that. "'Venture!" he mumbled, and drained his glass. He was the only one who drank, but he didn't seem to notice.

Scar refilled Billy's glass almost before it hit the table. "So, Billy," he said. "Adventure. That's a mighty fine word."

"'Venture," the boy repeated. He drank again.

Ace waited until Billy gulped the whiskey before he twisted toward him and said, rather sadly, "Course, I don't suppose you get too much of that." He shook his head as Scar tilted the bottle again. "Too bad. Adventure's a grand thing, Billy. It leads to fame."

"Like in them dime novels," Scar interjected.

"Exactly." Ace nodded solemnly. "Course, the time for adventure is gone, I guess. It's not like the old days. It's too hard, anymore. Too many bank guards, too many Pinkertons, too many citizens who want to be heroes. . . . Oh, I'm not complaining, mind you. I've had my share. I've had a whole book written about me, that one Scar's always reading—"

Scar frowned. "I ain't always read—"

Ace kicked him under the table, and Scar, rubbing at his shin and trying not to swear, corrected himself. "Yeah," he said through clenched teeth. He glared at Ace. "That's the one I'm always readin', all right."

Ace shook his head sadly as he curled Billy's limp fingers back around the glass. "You and Andy weren't in that book, and well, it's a shame, that's all. A real shame that the two of you won't ever be—"

"Wrote up," said Scar.

"Immortalized," said Ace.

"Well, now, I dunno," Billy slurred. He lifted the glass and emptied it. Half went down his throat: the other half decorated his shirt. "I done things in my time. Things you boys don't . . . don't . . ." His head wobbled, and Scar grabbed a fistful of his hair.

"That better, boy?" he asked, still hanging on.

"Thanks."

"Any time."

Ace ground his teeth, then forced himself to smile. "What sort of things, Bill? If you've done something, well, something you're going to be *famous* for, I think you owe it to me and Scar to let us in on it before the general public. Don't you, Scar?"

"Hell, yes!" Scar still had a fistful of Billy's yellow hair, and it was only because of this support that the boy hadn't gone facedown on the table. "If Billy was gonna be *famous* an' he didn't tell me first, well, I reckon I'd be right hurt . . ."

"Not s'posed to say . . ." Billy rolled his eyes from Ace to Scar, then back again. "But I s'pose I could tell you boys, if you promise not to . . . not to . . ." His eyes started to drift shut, and Scar shook him by the hair.

". . . not to say nothin'."

"We promise, Bill." Ace smiled his best. "Now what have you gone and done?"

Jenny, alone now, began clearing up the rest of the dishes. Although she'd only known Shirley Mae for a few days and they'd barely spoken during that time, she couldn't help but feel badly for the woman. In Shirley Mae, she saw the future of every girl in the house with the exceptions of Miss Liz and herself, and it made her ache with helplessness that this sort of thing could happen. She understood the madam's reasons for letting Shirley go and she knew it was the way of their world, but she hated the unfairness of it. There should have been somewhere for Shirley to go, something for her to do. There should have been, in the beginning, some other alternative.

She wondered if years ago, when Shirley Mae was young and pretty, someone had promised *her* fine clothes and fawning men and a life of luxury: the things Miss Liz had told Jenny were in store for her.

As Harvey's discordant version of the "Minute

267

Waltz" stretched interminably in the background, she scraped the last plates into the slop bucket for Mac's hogs and cleared off the counter. She refolded the greasy bacon paper—Bertha frowned on waste—and tucked it beneath the lard can at the end of the sideboard, then wiped away the gravy spatters and tidied up the spilled flour and sugar that dusted the pink marble. Then, using both hands, she lifted the ponderous copper kettle from atop the stove and emptied it into the big dishwashing basin. She refilled it before she wrestled it back stop the burner.

She worked quickly, taking some measure of happiness in the knowledge that this would be her last stint in Mrs. Bramley's kitchen. She washed the glasses, flatware, and most of the dinner plates before the water grew cool and scummy, and she tipped the heavy basin to pour the rest of the dirty dishwater into the sink and down the drain. She stacked another load of dirty dishes in the empty tub: two iron skillets, a handful of serving utensils, the rest of the plates, and on top, Bertha's big butcher knife. Then she shook out another measure of soap flakes, and poured out the entire contents of the simmering kettle over the top.

The butcher knife turned blade up when she added the water, and she reached into the tub to wash it first and get it out of the way. But before she touched it, she jerked back and popped her scalded fingers into her mouth. The water had been close to boiling. Silently cursing herself for her carelessness, she was reaching over to pump some cooler water when she heard footsteps in the back hall.

268

Belinda slouched drunkenly against the door frame. "Well," she smiled cruelly. "It don't look like Mac is here to protect his li'l angel, does it?"

Before Jenny could answer, Iris appeared behind Belinda. "Sure looks that way." She smiled a honey-coated viper's grin. "Appears our sweet Miss Jennifer is all alone, doesn't it?" She took a step into the kitchen. "You know, sugar, me an' Miss Belinda been talkin'. We been worried about you." She walked past Jenny to block the dining room door.

Jenny stole a glance back toward Belinda. The women had covered both the kitchen's exits, and Jenny was suddenly quite frightened. She knew the depth of fury of which Iris was capable, and she had a fairly good idea that Belinda, if pushed, would be able to match her. She fervently wished she'd controlled herself yesterday with that pan of water . . .

"Anyway, darlin'," Iris continued, the sugary, put-on sweetness of her drawl sliding further, with every word, toward the nasal twang that was her natural voice, "we thought that—us bein' your *friends* an' all—we might jus' take it on ourselves to kinda teach you how things work 'round here." She smiled again, but this time her eyes were narrowed and her lips were twisted and tight.

Jenny opened her mouth, but before she could form words, Belinda spoke.

"Won't do you no good, hollerin' for your precious Mac," she said. She had dropped all pretense of good humor. "Him 'n Miss Liz're closed up in the office with that cow, Bramley. Seems she's

269

takin' ol' Shirley's leavin' terrible hard. Between that and the old geezer at the piano—"

"Ain't nobody gonna hear nothin'," Iris cut in, taking a step toward her. "Not nothin' at all."

Jenny felt the cold marble countertop pressing into her side as Iris closed the distance between them. Behind her, she heard the click of Belinda's approaching heels.

"Good Book says an eye for an eye." Jenny jumped, pivoting toward Belinda's voice. "Or so they tell me." Another step. "Reckon that means a dousin' for a dousin', don't you, Iris?"

"Sounds right to me, Miss Belinda." Iris was only five feet away now. "Course, that water looks pretty hot, don't it? Saw you burn your fingers, Miss Jenny. I wonder what that tub'a water'd do to your pretty little face. . . ." Three feet away, an arm's length. "Seems to me a baptism by fire ain't such a bad idea."

"Full immersion, Sister Iris?" Belinda's voice, right behind her.

Iris Jakes shook her head solemnly. "Not enough water. Just the head, I think . . ."

"No!" Jenny shrieked, and lunged forward, away from the basin.

As one, the girls reached for her. Each grabbed one of Jenny's arms, and they hauled her, kicking and screaming, back against the counter. She fought hard against them, twisting and turning her way out of one grip, only to find it replaced by another. The girls, especially Iris, were stronger than she would have imagined, and they had the force of calm, cool assurance on their side.

Panicked, Jenny flailed wildly, crying out for help

270

as she fought to put distance between herself and that deep tub of scalding, soapy water. Then Belinda planted a spiky high heel in her shin, and pain—intense and immediate—shot up her leg. Her knees buckled.

"Got her now," she heard Iris mumble as the girls lifted and shoved her in a half-circle to face the steaming basin.

"Stop it!" she cried. "What's the matter with you!" She put her hands on the edge of the counter, trying to push herself away from the hot, acrid lye fumes already assaulting her eyes and nostrils. "Mac!" she cried, choking, "Mac! Somebody!"

She felt Iris's hand on the back of her head, pushing her closer to the tub. Through the rising steam she could see what they could not—the upturned blade of the butcher knife, its point just below the surface.

With unprecedented effort, she forced her arms to straighten, hoping to lock her elbows. But Belinda moved too quickly. She threw her body against Jenny's, to shove her back against the edge of the counter with a thud that nearly crushed her chest and left her breathless.

Iris's hand was still at the back of her head, her fingers twisted painfully through Jenny's hair. As Jenny gasped for air with lungs that refused to inflate, Iris sadistically yanked her lolling head back and forth.

"Mess with *my* man, will you?" she hissed into Jenny's pale, terrified face. "We was interrupted yesterday, but I keep my promises. I told you I'd fix your goddamn face so nobody's want it any more.

271

And one way or t'other, I'm gonna make good on it."

Jenny could no longer fight back. She seemed incapable of pulling any air into her collapsed lungs, and could only stare into Iris's evil face. She was dimly aware that her jaw had gone slack, and that the room was beginning to swim around her.

Iris wrenched Jenny's head sharply and gave her a good shake before she pushed her face toward the scalding basin. Again, Jenny saw the looming, razored point of the butcher knife. She heard Belinda's inebriated titter as Iris tightened the grip on her hair and pushed her further over the tub. The burning fumes seemed to be eating into her eyes, her face; but in a second, it wouldn't matter anymore, because Iris was going to shove her face into that searing water, down upon the blade of the knife.

"I baptize thee," Iris intoned with mock piety, "in the name of the Father, the Son, and the Holy—"

"Hey!" Abruptly, Jenny felt a slight ease in the girl's painful grips as Rafe Langley's voice boomed through the kitchen. She could see nothing now but the surface of the water and the tip of the blade beneath, but she heard bootsteps enter the kitchen.

"What the hell you two whores doin'?" he demanded.

"None of your business, Rafe!" Iris snarled, giving Jenny's wobbling head another shake. "It's between us."

More bootsteps, coming nearer now, and just when she had given up all hope of ever drawing breath again, blessed air rushed into her lungs. She gasped it greedily in huge, thankful gulps, and felt both reason and strength returning. She shoved herself backward, only to be rudely jostled back over the tub. Her face bobbed dangerously close to the surface, the tip of her nose burning as, for a fraction of a second, it dipped beneath the suds. The edge of the blade was only inches away from her eye, and she cried out again as she whipped her head back and away.

"Let her go, Iris. Ain't sportin', two agin one like that . . ." Rafe Langley's voice again.

Iris's hand knotted into her hair even more cruelly. "I told you, Rafe—it's none of your goddamn business."

"Ain't so sure about that," he said. He sounded very close now.

Jenny shoved away from the tub. Although she was still trapped between Iris and Belinda, and although they still held her fast, the girls made no attempt to force her back against the countertop.

"Women," Rafe muttered. "They's all she-cats at heart." And then she felt his hand, too. His touch was still repulsive, but it was infinitely better than those vengeful, female grips. He pried Belinda away first.

"I reckon it's any man's business when he sees a purty girl 'bout to get unpurtied." He pulled Iris's hands away next, and Jenny slumped toward the floor between them. Rafe let her drop.

"What's a matter with you two, anyhow?" he said. "Reckon Ace's right about you, Iris. You're a connivin' she-devil, through and through. Now, some fellers like that, but not—"

Jenny scrambled clumsily to her feet, shoved

273

Belinda aside, and scurried, as quickly as her aching shin and sore lungs would permit, out the back door and down the hill to the barn.

The stable was pitch dark when she stumbled through the door. She leaned against the wall for a minute to catch her breath, to wait for the tremors in her limbs to abate before she groped for the lantern.

She struck a match and touched it to the wick, then turned the flame up as high as it would go. She lifted the lantern over her head and looked about.

All was well. Fancy stood calmly in her stall, her head turned toward her mistress, her ears pricked. Scar's buckskin was infinitely calmer than the last time she'd seen him, and as she walked closer, she could see that someone—Ace, or maybe Mac or Scar—had applied a thick coat of salve to the wicked gash Iris's whip had left across his sand-colored croup.

She entered Fancy's stall and rubbed the star on her forehead. The mare snorted softly and affectionately moved her head against Jenny's hand. She was on her way out of season, and acting more like the sweet, even-tempered mare that Jenny knew.

She managed a weak smile.

"What do you say, girl? How about the two of us getting out of here tonight?" She was afraid to go back up to the house. She'd have to abandon her clothing and her meager possessions. She wouldn't even have her father's old clothes in which to disguise herself, let alone her pack roll, blanket, or meager savings. She could take only her mare and the clothes on her back, but so be it.

She gave the mare's neck a pat, then quickly walked back to the tack room. Inside, she looped Fancy's bridle over her arm and pulled the heavy saddle from its berth, lugging it back out into the lamplight and down the aisle toward Fancy. She was fairly certain that Belinda and Iris would come after her as soon as Rafe was out of the way, and she wanted to be long gone before they made it to the barn.

She draped the bridle over the side of Fancy's stall before she settled first the blanket, then the stock saddle on her back. She reached under the little mare's belly for the girth strap, and after looping the latigo through the cinch ring, pulled it tight. She waited a moment for Fancy to blow out the last gulp of air she always swallowed when she was being saddled, then snugged up the cinch with an extra tug and tied it off. Without looking, she reaching behind her for the bridle.

Instead of leather, her fingers met flesh.

She whirled around and jumped back, lurching into Fancy's rump.

It was Rafe. "Didn't mean to scare you," he said. He was on the other side of the partition, leaning against the top rail. His hat was shoved rakishly to the back of his head and he'd clamped a strand of straw between his teeth. He was smiling.

"Ain't it a little late for a ride?"

"My—my mare needs exercise. I never have any time during the day."

"Um-hum," he said, although it was plain he didn't believe her. "Them girls was pretty het up back there."

"Yes, I . . ." She wished he'd move his elbows off her bridle, but he didn't look as if he was planning on it. "Thank you for stopping them," she finished, trying to hide her fear. She remembered the force of his grip when he'd grabbed her in the gaming room, and the way his dirty fingers had plucked at the buttons of her blouse. If he had done that in a room full of other men, what would he do to her here?

"Well," he grinned, twirling that piece of straw between his lips, "It'd be a sin to do perm'nant hurt to a face as purty as yours."

Jenny waited nervously for a few seconds, but he still showed no signs of surrendering the bridle.

"I really do have to exercise my mare," she said at last. "Could you hand me my bridle, please?" She was afraid to reach for it herself. She wanted him to be the one to hold it toward her, wanted him to be the one to extend his arm, giving her the edge if she needed to jump away.

"Naw, I don't think so," he said, his grin widening. "'Cause I don't figure you're goin' for no exercise ride. I think them girls scared you real good, an' you're hightailin' it outta here. That's right, ain't it?"

She stared at him as haughtily as she could, struggling to keep her gaze level, saying nothing, hoping to back him down.

It didn't work.

"Yeah," he said. "Thought so. Well, I tell ya, little darlin', it don't matter to me if you wanna leave. Reckon maybe you think them girls up there ain't as good as you. An' maybe you're right. You got some kinda class, all right. That's why I'm willin' to go so high for you."

Jenny's jaw dropped open. "What?"

He tugged the piece of straw from his mouth, cast it aside, and stood erect, although his forearms still pinned Fancy's bridle. "Been waitin' for ol' Liz to gimme an answer. Been real patient about it, too. A hundred and fifty bucks is a powerful lotta money, girl. Fella's gotta do a lotta robbin' to earn that much." His leer made her blood run cold.

"But I figure you're worth it, bein' pure 'n all. I like to educate a gal right: like to be the first." He moved away from the rail.

Jenny made a grab for Fancy's bridle, but in the time it took her to snatch it up and bring it to her chest, Rafe swung into the stall and locked his hand around her free arm.

"Like I said, honey: you wanna take off, ain't no skin off my nose. But before you do, I'm gonna have what you been makin' me wait for." He pulled her toward him. She dug her heels into the floor and slapped at him with the bridle.

"Stop!" she screamed, nearly as furious as she was frightened. "Stop it! Why can't you people just leave me alone!" She caught Rafe across the face with the bridle. It whipped around the side of his head and the curb bit smacked hard against his ear. More in surprise than pain, he let out a yelp and angrily snatched at the straps, yanking them down and to the side.

Jenny let go, but not quickly enough. She fell toward him. Rafe took advantage of her stumble to jerk her out of the stall and into the aisle. She landed on her knees in the straw, her wrist still tethered by his fist.

He hurled the bridle aside before rubbing at the red mark that crossed his ear. "Dammit, gal, you can't be *that* stupid! Ain't no need to fight for your honor no more: I'm the one! I'm the man with the money, the man you been savin' it for." He hauled her to her feet as he whispered confidentially, "I know how this stuff works, an' I know ol' Liz was gonna take a good chunk of that money for the house. Now that you're leavin' 'n all, I guess we don't need to include her in this little deal, do we? We'll just keep it 'tween the two of us." Digging a finger into his pocket, he withdrew a small leather pouch. He gave it a little toss into the air and caught it again, winking.

"Offered Miss Liz a hundred and fifty for you. Reckon she was gonna give you 'bout half. Got 'round a hundred on me this minute, an' if you're as good as I think, it's all yours. You ever even seen a hundred dollars, all to once?"

He glanced around at the deep straw mounded in empty stalls, then tugged her toward him. "Reckon right here's as good a place as any. 'An after, you can be on your way with nobody the wiser." His grin widened, and he added, "Course, that's if you can still sit a saddle when I get through . . ."

His fingers tugged at the collar of her blouse, and Jenny screamed, "No!" Her free hand curled into a fist. She beat wildly at his chest. "Stop it! I'm not one of them! I'm not for sale!" His boot absorbed most of the impact of the one good kick she got at his ankle. She managed to elbow his hand aside, but not before the two top buttons of her shirtwaist popped off and disappeared into the straw.

He tugged at her wrist again, pulling her hard against his chest. He reeked of stale smoke and cheap whiskey, and the rough stubble on his chin sandpapered her forehead as he growled, "Don't seem to me you got much choice in it, girl. You been askin' for it. I seen the way you walk, the way you fill out that shirt. . . . All you gals is alike anyhow. Pearl come upstairs with me willin' enough the first time, and didn't she start to pitch a fit once I got started!" He smiled sadistically, and a wave of cold fear washed through Jenny's body. "Guess you're just startin' your fit a little early."

He pinched her jaw and angled her face up toward his. "Go right ahead," he whispered, that horrid sneer still on his face. "Complain all you want if it makes you feel like a lady . . ."

Twisting, struggling against him, Jenny kept her teeth and lips clamped shut when his foul mouth pressed clumsily against hers. He did not hold the kiss long. He pulled back and shook his head slightly before his predatory grin widened. "Well, reckon I ain't much one for the kissin' part, either, honey. And I guess there're better uses for that pretty little mouth of yours. Maybe we should just get down to brass tacks. But first I wanna see what I'm payin' for."

His fingers went to her blouse again. He took a grip and yanked. In a shower of mother of pearl, the remaining buttons popped off to leave the two halves of her shirtwaist fluttering. Jenny squirmed, but he tugged her arm behind her back, bending it up and holding her wrist high between her shoulder blades.

279

The pain was excruciating, and Jenny cried out again.

"Ain't nobody gonna hear you, little darlin'," he hissed, and covered one camisole-clad breast with his grimy palm. "Oh yeah," he smiled. "You got nice ones. Not as big as Pearly's maybe, but real nice, real firmlike . . ."

"Let me go, you filthy piece of trash!" Jenny hissed through clenched teeth. She knew she was incapable of physically overpowering him, and every nerve in her captured arm was screaming in agony. She could only pray that Ace would somehow magically appear and save her, but knew she'd be a fool to count on it. Swiftly, she forced her mind away from the pain and toward logic, and suddenly hit on what might—lie or not—be her only salvation.

"I said, let me go!" she barked, making her voice as commanding as she could. Rafe was kneading her breast quite roughly now. "I—I'm not what you think I am. I'm not a—I'm not a virgin anymore. I'm Ace Denton's girl!"

Rafe let up the pressure on her breast, although he did nothing to ease that painful grip on her arm. "Ace's girl?" He studied her for a few seconds. "Liz guaranteed me you was untouched."

"Well, I'm not!" she bluffed, gathering speed and volume when his brow knotted. "Liz didn't know, but he did it to me! We did it a lot, every day, and right here in this barn. And he's not going to like you touching me." The pain in her arm was excruciating. She tried to pull away, but he only jerked it higher, more cruelly this time.

"Oh, he did, did he?" He seemed to mull it over for

a moment before his lusty sneer returned. "Guess that takes some of the fun outta it, but just the same, I reckon I oughta be open-minded. Bet there's a few things even ol' Ace ain't done to you yet, honey."

Through the fabric of her camisole, he found her nipple and gave it a sharp tweak. When Jenny cried out and bit at her lip, Rafe smiled.

"Ace's girl, huh? Guess that explains a coupla things. But I don't reckon ol' Ace'd mind me travelin' the same trail after him. Can't see as it'd bother him none, his girl bein' a whore. What with his mama bein' one."

The pain in her arm was suddenly forgotten. "His mother?"

He leered, amused by her shocked expression. "What'd I do? Let the cat outta the bag? I figured, you bein' Ace's girl 'n all, he woulda told you 'bout Liz." His fingers dug into her breast again, then curled under her camisole's neckline, ready to tear it away.

"Course, this is gonna take your price down a bit . . . How 'bout when I'm done, I just give you what I figure it was worth?"

She slapped at him, but he ducked, laughing.

"He'll kill you when he finds out!" she cried, trying one more time to bully him into releasing her. "He'll be here any minute!"

His hand moved to dig into her shoulder. "Ain't the man been born can take Rafe Langley, little darlin', and don't you forget it. But you know . . ." He looked over her shoulder, back toward the feed room. ". . . maybe you got a point 'bout the other."

With that, he eased her wrist down from between her shoulder blades and allowed her to straighten her throbbing arm. *Thank God,* Jenny thought, and began to move away.

She didn't get far. Instead of releasing her, he redoubled his grip, dragged her toward the lamp and snatched it from its nail. With the lantern in one hand and Jenny's narrow, pounding wrist clamped in the other, he marched toward the far end of the barn.

"Reckon you 'n me need to find us a more private place," he sneered as Jenny kicked and flailed in his wake. "Old cattle barn'll do just fine. Nobody ever goes down there no more. Ain't no tunnel, neither."

He gave the door a savage kick, and it banged open.

"No!," Jenny screamed as loudly as her sore lungs would permit. "No!" He stepped through the doorway and she grabbed at the frame like a life preserver, crying out to Ace, to Mac, to God, to anyone who could hear. But with a mighty tug he pulled her free, leaving her fingers full of splinters.

"Like I said," Rafe Langley smirked over her screams as he dragged her down the hill, "ain't nobody gonna hear you."

Ten

The disused path was narrow and rutted, and she fell twice as Rafe relentlessly dragged her down the slope toward the cattle barn. Its doors, if ever it had owned any, were long since missing; and as he pulled her into the mammoth, yawning structure, it seemed to Jenny as if she were being sucked into the black and gaping mouth of hell itself.

Inside, the barn stank of sour rot and desolation and mold spore. As he tugged her inside and across the wide, dung and dirt-packed floor, she could hear the scurry and squeak of rats rustling through mildewed islands of hay and behind bales of ancient straw just beyond the bobbling ring of lamplight. Better than thirty feet above her head, she could just make out the faintest outlines of the heavy, dust-layered beams that braced the peaked roof. Something scuttered along them: more rats.

Rafe didn't notice, didn't care. He pulled her all the way acros the broad, barren space that was the center of the barn before he released her. He cast her away from him to tumble, in a cloud of gray and spore-filled dust, atop a decaying mound of hay.

She landed on her side with a thud and immediately hugged her bloodless hand as she tried to get to her feet. When her legs finally cooperated and she was able to pull herself erect, she looked up into the steely, leveled barrel of Rafe's pistol. He had hung the lantern on a post and dragged out one rare, sturdy, dry bale of hay. Now he sat upon it. His elbows were propped on his knees. A horrible, expectant grin was on his face. He pointed the gun at Jenny.

"Strip."

She stared at him dumbly. The blood had finally begun to return to her hand, and with it came a dreadful ache to match the one in her wrist and arm. Her struggles had exhausted her, and she realized, with a kind of grim resignation, that he had won.

There was a click, echoing faintly in the cavernous structure, as he cocked the pistol. "I said, *strip!* I wanna see some skin. All of it!"

Slowly, numbly, as if she was far away and only commanding her distant body to obey, Jenny's trembling, pounding fingers came up to pull apart the open halves of her shirtwaist. Clumsily, she pulled it off her shoulders, letting it drop into a rumpled pile on the dirty straw beside her. Then she looked up, back into the barrel of the gun.

"Keep goin' . . ." His black, carnivore's eyes narrowed and he waved the Colt. Just a little.

Next she unbuttoned her skirt, feeling the splinters in her fingers dig deeper furrows as she clumsily worked at the broad, flat buttons. At last it slipped to

284

the floor. She stepped out of it and looked up at Rafe.

Again he wiggled the gun at her—more impatiently this time—and in a daze, she began to untie her petticoats. One at a time, they fell to the floor in a circle about her feet, and as the last layer dropped to join the rest, she realized that she was weeping silently.

Her cheeks were flooded with tears of hopelessness as she stepped out of the pile of underskirts, and she heard her own voice, cracked and alien, whimpering, "Please don't, please . . ."

"Get them drawers off, honey, an' I mean now!" he threatened. She didn't look up at him this time. With fingers that shook so spasmodically that she could barely control them, she freed the waistband of her underdrawers and, crouching in a pathetically unsuccessful attempt to shield her body from his eyes, pulled them down her legs and over her feet.

Now she stared at the floor, seeing only her tears as they fell to spatter on the scuffed tops of her shoes. She stood before him, her hands crossed over the pale triangle of curls at the juncture of her legs, her body clad only in her thin camisole and the cold gooseflesh of terror.

"Shoes, too. I don't want you kickin' me, accidental-like."

She managed to pry them off.

"The top thing, too."

Numbly, she removed it, and cowered in the lamplight: naked, shivering, and staring at the ground. For what seemed like a lifetime, he did not speak. Then she heard a rustle and a thump, and realized that Rafe had stood up. He was dragging the bale closer. She shrank away, but he was close enough to grab her wrist again.

"Goddamn if you ain't purty all over," he whispered as he looked down at her. "I'm gonna have to get after ol' Ace, keepin' you to hisself all this time an' never sayin' a word . . ."

She felt her stomach lurch as he pushed the cold barrel of his still-cocked Colt toward her, and ran it across one of her breasts, then underneath to heft its weight. He trailed the pistol down her torso in a straight line, smiling all the while, to nudge her hands away from the golden ringlets they shielded.

Iris was holding the shears.

"Get all her stuff outta the drawers," she said to Belinda, "an' toss 'em on the bed."

Gleefully, the besotted brunet went to Jenny's little bureau and tugged at the bottom drawer. She began pulling out garments at random, laughing as she pitched them over her shoulder toward Iris.

The first to land was Jenny's best dress: pale green and, until this minute, neatly folded. With a joyful snort of pure meanness, her hair tangled wildly and flying as she worked, Iris made the first stab with the scissors, and the second. Then, with great abandon, she began to slice the material into jagged, celery-colored strips as more of Jenny's meager wardrobe sailed toward her.

Belinda reached the top and final drawer and yanked out Jenny's saddlebags. Still laughing, she tugged at the buckles and dumped the contents of both pouches on the floor, where she'd already dropped *Alice* and Cicero's *Orations.* The racket prevented her from hearing a soft grating sound that came from behind the dresser.

"Hey!" she said, pawing through the small pile of objects. Her fingers touched dull gray metal. "Hey, the little bitch's got a gun hid in here!" She stood up, swinging it out to the side. "What the hell you 's'pose she'd be doin' with—"

A hand snatched it away.

Belinda gave a little shriek and jumped into the center of the room as Ace Denton swung his legs over the bureau and planted his feet on either side of the mess she'd just made of Jenny's belongings.

Iris looked up from her labors. She'd already shredded both of Jenny's dresses and was busily turning a skirt into jagged strips of dark blue fringe. When she saw the expression on Ace's face, she gasped. She took a step away and turned the tips of the shears toward him.

Ace looked at the pile of scraps on the mattress, then at Iris—looking more and more like a mad-woman—and Belinda, her eyes frightened and red with drink. He could have slapped them both, but he took a deep breath, clenching and unclenching his fingers on the grip of the pistol he'd just taken from Belinda. Finally under control, he tucked it beneath his own gun belt.

"Iris, I've never hit a woman in my life, but I've never been closer to it than right now. Just what the hell do you two think you're doing?"

Iris tossed her head and sneered at him. "What're

you doin' here? You come to visit your sweet little Jenny?"

He gritted his teeth. "Where is she?"

"How the hell would I know?" she hissed. "It ain't my job to keep track of your other girls, Ace."

"You just can't get it through your thick skull, can you, Iris?" He shook his head in disgust and tried for the last time. "There are no other girls. Not any that matter. Not now, not ever. Only Jenny. And never—*never*—you."

"Bastard!" she cried. "Liar!" She charged him, the shears raised to stab, to kill, but he caught her arm easily and wrenched the scissors from her fingers. Screaming curses, she tried to slap at him, to claw him, and finally he simply shoved her away. She fell in a tangled heap against the wall next to the headboard.

"Where is she, Iris?" he demanded.

"I hate you," she hissed.

"Fine," he replied. "Hate me all you want. Just tell me where she is."

Iris pressed her lips into a tight line and glared at him defiantly.

"You bitch!" He took a step toward her, his hand raised. "Tell me, or so help me God—"

"She's gone." It was Belinda's voice, slurred by whiskey and meek with fright.

He turned toward the pathetic little whore and grabbed her by the shoulder, nearly lifting her from the floor. Her thin robe was hanging open again. "Gone?" he bellowed. "Gone where? Why?"

"We was . . ." Belinda began to cry. "We was in the

kitchen, and—" Her nose was red and running as fast as her tears, and she pulled up one of the hems of her short robe and blew her nose in the crumpled silk. "—there was a sorta argument, and . . ."

"I can just imagine what kind," Ace growled. He glanced reproachfully at Iris, who still crouched against the wall. He gave Belinda a teeth-rattling shake and her flat little breasts jiggled sadly.

"Where did she go!"

"I don't know!" she wept, terrified. "She just run off to the barn. She's prob'ly long gone by—"

Ace let go of her more forcefully than he'd planned, and she bumped back into the wall with a thud. In two strides he was at the bureau and sliding his fingers into a crack between the wall boards. The panel slid silently to the side and he hopped atop the dresser, swinging his long legs up after him.

But before he could swivel to step down into the passage, Iris was on him again.

"She's gone, Ace, don'tcha see?" She snatched at his clothing, his hair, trying to turn him back toward her. "She don't want you, Ace. I'm the one! I'm the one that wants you!"

He grabbed at her hands, tore them from him, but she only clung tighter. "Don't do it!" she cried. "Don't go after her! I'll kill you! I'll kill you both!"

He slapped her across the face with a blow hard enough to send her hurtling back to the floor and leave the angry red imprint of his hand on her cheek. She looked up in shock and fury as he slid through the opening into the darkness.

"I'll find you," she screeched, "and I'll kill you!

You'll rot in hell together!"

A soft thud as the panel slid back into place was his only reply.

"I said, lie down on it." Rafe pointed at the bale of hay. He'd dragged it to within a yard of the post where he'd hung the lantern.

Jenny stood at the far end, where he had moved her at gunpoint, and now she slowly sat down, wincing as her bare bottom was stabbed by the coarse alfalfa's long-dry sticks and stems.

"Lie down, damn it!"

She leaned back, ready to drown in her own tears, and felt a new rush of pain as her back and shoulders were assaulted by the bale's spiky surface.

"Christ," Rafe muttered. "Didn't Ace teach you nothin? Scoot down!"

Before she could move, he reached down, grabbed her ankle, and savagely jerked her toward him. She cried out as she felt the dry stalks the size of darning needles pierce her back, embed themselves in her flesh.

"Well, ain't you just the little crybaby?" he muttered as he walked behind her. "Put your hands up behind your head."

Somehow, she managed to raise them, and when she did, felt him loop her wrists together with baling twine. Then he walked away toward the post, pulling her arms out as far as they would go, straight back over her head. He ran the twine's end around the post a few times, then secured it.

"There," he said, returning to stand above her.

"Hell, gal, you're makin' this into a lot more trouble than I figured on. But that oughta keep you from scratchin' at me altogether. An' don't it jus' make that fancy little front'a yours stand up to beat the band!" He whistled in appreciation and Jenny turned her head away, sobbing helplessly as he dropped to his knees beside her and clamped a hand over each of her breasts, kneading them crudely. She tried to twist away, but he planted an elbow firmly in her groin to pin her and quickly replaced one hand with his lips. Before she realized what was happening, he slurped her nipple into his mouth and bit down.

She whimpered with the pain, which now seemed to be everywhere in her body. He raised his head—dark, oily hair hanging in his eyes—and said, "You know, girl, you ain't never gonna make no money in this here business if you don't learn to cooperate."

Although she'd believed it was impossible for her to weep any harder or more mournfully than she had been, she did so now. Rafe paid her no heed. He got to his feet and moved to stand over her knees.

"Spread 'em," he said.

Lost in her own grief and terror, Jenny didn't hear him. But she felt, a split second later, and new and searing pain as the toe of his boot caught her just below the knee.

"I said, spread 'em!"

Somehow, she managed to ease her knees apart a few inches before she froze again.

"Judas, you're a coy one," he muttered before barking, "All the way! I want to see what I'm gettin' into." Then he laughed loudly, obscenely.

But she couldn't do it. She could only lie there, crying and wishing she was dead.

Finally, she felt his hands on her knees, and then pain as he thrust her thighs so widely apart that she thought they would pop from their sockets.

"That's better," he smiled.

His fingers went to his gun belt, and slowly, taking his time, he unbuckled it and dropped it to the straw. Then he slipped free his belt and began to unbutton his trousers. His shaft loomed toward her as he worried his pants off over his boots.

Naked from the waist down, he walked around her to stand over her face, the impending implement of her torture gripped in his hand. "What'd'ya say, little darlin'?"

She twisted her head away, burying her face against her aching, outstretched arm.

"Well, I reckon you're right," she heard him mutter. "You prob'ly ain't trained good enough yet so's I can trust you to not bite down. It'll wait 'till later, after I take the edge off them high spirits of yours . . ."

Jenny snapped her legs shut, but before she could roll to the side and off the bale, he was back and kicking at her knees. "Dammit, girl, when I tell you to do somethin', I mean it!"

This time the toe of his boot drew blood; and slowly, Jenny made herself obey.

He dropped to his knees, shoving her legs even wider apart. He touched her, sending a shiver of revulsion through her.

She cried out, and he cursed.

"Judas," he muttered in disgust. "Drier'n the salt

flats in summer, an'—". He pushed his finger further inside, jabbed at her painfully once, then twice, then drew it out with a smile. "Well I'll be damned," he grinned. "Ain't you the sly one? Tellin' me Ace'd been at you all week, when you ain't even been popped yet! Savin' it for a surprise, was you?"

He reached into his shirt pocket and brought out a greasy packet of paper—the same kind Mrs. Bramley used to wrap bacon scraps.

"Yeah, you're dry all right," he continued, "but ol' Rafe can take care'a that." He unfolded the packet. "Helped myself to some pork fat outta the kitchen, just in case . . ."

Jenny began to scream.

Ace came up from beneath the last feed bin and dropped the lid shut behind him with an unaccustomed bang. He groped his way through the darkness, found the door, and stepped out into the barn. He felt for the lantern, but it wasn't on its nail. Swearing softly, he dug into his pocket for a match. He only needed enough light to claim his saddle and bridle from the tack room—there'd be enough moon outside by which to saddle up, but God only knew if there's be enough light for him to track Jenny.

He figured that she'd be heading toward town. It was the last place in the world he needed to show his face. The locals might put up with having the Denton gang in the county, as long as they didn't know exactly *where*. They might even secretly be a little proud of it. But if he was brassy enough to actually ride down Main Street . . . He knew that such an act would be another case entirely. He'd have to hope he could catch her before she got that far.

He struck the match and yanked open the tack room door, pulling down his bridle and tugging the saddle halfway off the rack before the flame burnt too low and scorched his fingers. He shook it out, cursing fluently under his breath, and tucked the stub into his pocket. There was straw scattered on the floor even in the tack and feed rooms, and the last thing he'd need right now would be to have to stop and put out a fire.

In the dark, he hoisted the heavy saddle up to his shoulder and looped the bridle's headstall over its horn, then groped his way out into the aisle.

He was heading toward the main door and the paddock beyond when he heard an odd scraping sound. He turned toward it, but could see nothing. The sound had stopped. Shrugging, he took another step toward the yard.

Then he heard it again.

"What the . . . ?" He reached into his pocket and, walking toward the sound, pulled out another match and flicked the sulphur tip with his nail.

It was Fancy, saddled but not bridled. Irritated at being tacked up and deserted, she was rhythmically rubbing one of the stirrup leathers against the side of her stall. Ace dropped his own tack and went to the mare. Then he saw Jenny's bridle, discarded in a jumble of twisted leather further down the aisle.

"Jenny?" he said aloud, then raised his voice. "Jenny! Are you in here?"

Then distantly, barely distinguishable from the

cry of a night-hunting bird, he heard a woman scream.

"There now," Rafe said, satisfied with his labors. "Reckon that'll do 'er."

Jenny screamed again when he stood up on his knees and moved forward, pushing his pelvis against the juncture of her outflung thighs and reaching out with one hand to take a grip on her breast. He gave the nipple a hard twist and grinned even wider when Jenny opened her mouth to cry out again.

Her last scream had sapped her strength and ruined her throat, and this last cry of pain and fear came out only as a hoarse bellow of rushing air.

"Yessir," he grinned as his grimy nails dug into her pale flesh. "Like I said, them's real nice ones. Real nice to hang onto, durin'."

She used the last bit of strength in her legs to kick herself to the side in a feeble attempt to bounce off the bale. But she only succeeded in jolting her body up into the air and straight back down, hard enough to embed a fresh new crop of twigs and bristles in the flesh of her back.

"Whoa, there, little darlin'!" Rafe laughed. "You just hang on! I know you're anxious, but you're s'posed to wait 'till I get in the saddle a'fore you start buckin' . . ."

He slid his free hand between them, and with a hopeless, nauseated rush of loathing, Jenny shuddered as she felt him position himself against her. "OK, honey, here we go," he smirked. "Y'know, you oughta be payin' *me* for this. I'm gonna get you broke in real good—make a real pro outta you."

He was bringing his hand back up, ready to dig his fingers into her other breast before he made that first, piercing thrust, when the explosion came.

It echoed through the barn with a boom that shook the ancient rafters and sent flying a swarm of bats. Rats squealed and darted in terror, raised clouds of dust as they burrowed into hay or fell, shrieking thinly, from the rafters. Rafe leapt to his feet as Jenny screamed again—a hoarse bark of rattling air that was lost under the deafening squeaking of rats and bats and the whooshes of air fanned by their frightened wings.

A lone man stood in the broad doorway, silhouetted against the moonlit sky. His gun was drawn. A faint curl of smoke rose from its barrel.

He strode forward, to the edge of the circle of light. Jenny couldn't make out his face, but she'd never been so glad to see anyone in her life.

Then he spoke, and she had no doubt as to the owner of the voice.

"Back off, Rafe."

The surprise left Rafe's face. "Christ, you 'bout scared me to death."

Smiling, pantsless, and still kneeling between Jenny's legs, he grinned.

"Quit playin' around with that gun, will you? I'll be with you in a few minutes." He leaned back toward Jenny. "In fact, you can go next if you want. First time's mine, though."

He turned his attention toward Jenny. "Big night for you, honey," he grinned. She shuddered as he

296

clamped a hand on her shivering thigh. "Somethin' to tell your gran'kids about—the night you got it from both Rafe Langley *and* Ace Denton. Oughta make you a real celebrity." He leaned in toward her.

There was a click as Ace cocked his gun.

"Get away from her, Rafe, or so help me God, I'll splatter your skull all over the barn."

Rafe hesitated, but made no move to pull away from Jenny.

"I'm awful damn close, Rafe. Don't push this any further."

Rafe stared up into Ace's shadowed face for a long minute before he slowly got to his feet, using Jenny's outflung legs for leverage. As he reached down to scoop up his trousers, she let out a hoarse whimper and somehow managed to roll herself off the side of the bale. Her back was bloodied and brought away twigs and stems that sprouted from her once-creamy skin. She scrambled behind the post to which her numb hands were tethered, and curled herself into a naked, quivering ball.

The bats ceased the last of their hysterical flight as Rafe struggled back into his trousers. "I get it," he was saying. "You wanna keep her all to yourself."

He fastened the last button and threaded his belt through the buckle. "Shit, I didn't know you had your eye on her," he lied, an apologetic smile on his face. "If I had, I never woulda—"

"You'd have taken her anyway." Ace took a step forward into the light. His face was terrifying in its stony wrath. "Seems to me," he continued, "that lately you've been taking a lot of things that belong to me. Like my name."

For a fraction of a second Rafe looked uneasy, but he quickly controlled his expression, forcing it toward one of injured bewilderment. "I don't know what you're talkin' about, Ace."

"Really?" Ace wasn't buying it for a minute. "I know about Norwalk and Fowlersville and Vista Springs and Winston, Rafe. Your little friend Billy came clean."

Rafe looked at him in disbelief, then irritation. Ace was a fool to try and bluff him. Billy would never say anything. Andy wouldn't let him, not—

"See, after you went downstairs, we arranged for Andy to get a little, let's say, *involved* with Agnes. And once he was out of the way, well . . . Billy never could hold his liquor. You should have known that, Rafe. He was pretty far gone when you took off, and it didn't take much more whiskey or encouragement for him to start bragging. . . ."

Rafe took a tentative step away. He was genuinely frightened now, but he tried to smile, to bluff it out.

"How many more, Rafe?" Ace continued. His eyes were flat and hard. It was an expression Jenny had never seen on his face before, and hoped she would never see again. "How many more people have you killed in my name? How many more are there for me to find out about?"

"Now, Ace—" Rafe began, holding up a hand.

"How many!"

As the two men glared at each other, the forced smile evaporated from Rafe's lips. The only sound in the barn, apart from the occasional soft scutter of a rat, was Jenny's muted weeping. It floated between Ace and Rafe like a child's dare line, toed in the dirt.

They were both painfully conscious of her presence and her plaintive whimpering, each for his own reason. But neither man would risk even a glance in her direction.

"You gonna shoot me or not?" Rafe's voice was low and serious. "Make up your mind, Ace. Or did you plan to keep us standin' here like this all night?"

Ace didn't answer. He just held that flat, deadly stare.

"I don't even got my gun. You owe me that, anyway."

There was a pause before Ace said two words.

"Get it."

Rafe looked down. His rig was behind him in the straw, where he'd dropped it earlier.

"Hold on," he said, holding out his left hand, the flat of his palm toward Ace. "If you got your mind set on it, let's at least do it right."

Slowly, his palm still outstretched, he twisted his body away with a deliberate motion and began to bend his knees, easing his right hand toward his gun belt. "Just hang on, there, ol' pal," he said. His face was turned away, in shadow. His fingertips touched the leather. "Lemme get this strapped on, and we'll—"

Abruptly he threw himself to the ground, twisting as he jerked up the pistol, holster and all.

He fired.

Ace went down and Jenny screamed, certain he was dead. But he hit the ground rolling and fired immediately, his arm outstretched.

Rafe's second shot went wild. By the time his

finger could squeeze the trigger again—and less than three seconds after he had first touched his gun—he was dying.

As Jenny wept in the shadows, Ace slowly got to his feet. His gun cocked, a faint curl of smoke rising from its barrel, he stepped toward the body.

Rafe lay in a tangled sprawl, his arms outstretched, his head propped slightly against a mound of straw. Half his face was gone, and a dark red stain was rapidly draining down the front of his shirt, turning the pale plaid felt to dark burgundy madras. There was a hoarse, bubbly rattle as the final breath exited his lungs. Only then did Ace reholster his pistol.

Quickly, he abandoned the body and went to Jenny. He fell to his knees and put his arm around her, but at the instant his fingers touched her back they were pricked as if by needles, and a look of agony twisted her tear-stained face. Gently, he took her shoulder and turned her back toward him.

She looked as if a porcupine had been using her for target practice.

"Oh, Jesus," he whispered, and began to cry with her. He yanked a pocket knife from his vest, and hurriedly cut her wrists free. Then, as carefully as he could, he pulled her exhausted body across his thighs.

"It's all right, baby, it's all right," he soothed as he began sliding the biggest straws and sticks out of her flesh.

She clutched at his shirt, knotting it into her fists and whimpering as he worked. He talked softly all the while, trying to take the pain away with his voice as well as his fingers. Within seconds he had removed the largest of them, and gently he turned her over, then hugged her against his chest, rocking her as if she were a lost and terrified child.

"Oh, Jenny," he wept. "Poor Jenny." He cradled her like that for several minutes, both of them crying: his tears those of anguish and remorse, and hers of relief and exhaustion.

Finally he whispered, "Can you stand up, do you think?"

She nodded, and carefully, he helped her get to her feet. He put her hands on the post to steady her, leaving her on the shadowed side, away from the lantern's glare. If nothing else, he could give her the shelter of darkness. Then he began to scoop up her clothes.

"Somebody will have heard, Jenny. Those last three shots made a helluva blast. They'll be coming any minute." He picked up her blouse. It had no buttons left, and he discarded it in favor of the camisole. He dropped it as gently as he could over her torso, but she still shuddered when its light weight whispered over her back.

"I know it hurts, baby," he said softly, "but we've got to get something on you. When we get back to the house, I'll get the rest of that stuff out and get you something for the pain."

He kicked her petticoats and drawers aside and snatched up her skirt. Already he could hear voices and the sound of running feet coming up the path. "Here," he said. "This'll do for now. All that other stuff is too damn heavy."

He had just secured the last button when the light of a second lamp entered the ancient barn. Miss Liz held the lantern high with her left hand. There was a pistol clutched in her right. Mac was two steps ahead of her with a shotgun.

They stopped stock-still when they saw the body, and Liz let out a gasp. "Oh God, Mac, is it—"

"I'm all right." Ace stepped out of the shadows, trying to support Jenny as best he could without causing her further pain.

Mac was standing over the body. "Reckon this is going to make it hard to get a confession out of him, Ace," he muttered. He gave the corpse a little shove with his toe, as if to prove to himself that Rafe was really dead. Then he looked up at Jenny. Her face drawn, her body limp, she slouched against Ace.

"Angel!" he cried. "Jenny darlin', what did he do to you? Are you—"

"It's all right, Mac," Ace said softly. He helped Jenny away from the shadows and toward the center of the barn and Miss Liz. "But if I'd got here any later, it wouldn't have been." He bent to retrieve her shoes, and as she leaned against him, he slid them onto her feet.

The madam was looking back and forth between Rafe's body and the battered girl, and there was horror and disbelief on her face. As Ace brought Jenny closer, Liz reached out to touch her cheek. "I'm so sorry, child. So very sorry. I never thought he'd . . ." And then she ran out of words.

"Bertha still got plenty of her remedy left?" Ace asked. "You know, that stuff she uses for cuts and kitchen burns?"

Liz nodded. "Why?"

Gently, Ace turned Jenny just a little to the side

302

so that above the line of the girl's camisole, Liz could see the bloodied and punctured skin between her shoulder blades. The madam winced in sympathetic pain.

"Tell her we're gonna need about a pint of it," he said. "Agnes still keeping Andy busy upstairs?"

Liz nodded.

"How about Billy?"

"Still passed out in the playroom, where you and Scar left him."

"Good. I'll take Jenny down through the tunnel. Nobody'll bother us there while I get her fixed up." He looked down at Jenny again—her blond hair tangled and full of bits of dirty straw and hay, her back a bloodied map of insults, her wrists ringed with the angry red marks left by her bonds—and his eyes welled once more.

Miss Liz saw his anguish and tightened her lips to hold back her own emotions. So Marcus really did care for this girl. He'd found someone at last. Nodding, she said, "I'll bring some of Bertha's salve to the cellar."

She raised her lamp and turned toward the door.

"Ma?" he added softly.

It's true, then, Jenny realized, as the madam stopped and faced him. Yes, now she could see the little similarities, more telling than the dark hair and eyes of both: the same strong line of jaw, the proud way both carried their heads . . .

Ace raised his voice, bringing Mac back in the conversation. "Don't let any of the girls see the body."

"Why not?" Miss Liz lifted a brow.

"I've got my reasons," he said, then addressed Mac. "After I get Jenny fixed up, maybe you could ride into town and get the sheriff."

"What the hell you want him for?" Mac asked loudly. "I'd think he'd be about the last person you'd want to see right now."

"I don't want to see him, Mac. Just tell him Ace Denton is dead." He looked down at the body. "And when he gets here, give him that."

Mac scratched his head and smiled. "Guess you got a point there. Plenty of people'll be linin' up to identify him. Or what's left of him . . ."

"Say that Rafe killed me, then took off and stole my horse on his way out. That's why I want you to keep the girls away. They all know Rafe well enough to identify him, even with, well, even the way he is now. Ace Denton needs to die tonight, forever and all."

Mac, still standing over the body, nodded solemnly. "OK. I'll take your stud outta the corral and tether him back of the barn 'til you're ready. Nobody'll see him out there."

"Thanks. There's a good reward, Mac. It was up to five thousand last time I heard. You and Ma split it."

"But what about you?" Miss Liz broke in. She was standing alone now, in the center of her own lamp's circle of yellow light.

Ace smiled. "I'm cuttin' out of here as soon as Jenny's fit to travel. That is, if she'll come." He looked down at her, and she smiled back, her green eyes wide and full of love.

Eleven

He gave Miss Liz a head start up the hill, and with the rest of Jenny's clothing tucked under his arm, began to help her along the path to the horse barn. Several times she tried, in a voice still cracked and raspy, to ask him about Liz or about Rafe, but he hushed her at each attempt.

"Later, Jenny," he said as he gently guided her along the overgrown path. "Later I'll answer all your questions, but right now, we've got to get to the tunnel before one of those girls sticks her nose out . . ."

At last they gained the smaller barn, and, lighting a match in the welcoming sweet smell of its darkness, he led her along the aisle and into the feed room.

"I knew it!" she managed to whisper as Ace lit a fresh match and lifted the lid of the last feed bin. This one contained no grain. Ace grinned at her, then bent to run his fingers along the rear join of the wooden box's floor. The *click* was so soft that Jenny barely heard it, and was followed by a gentle *whoosh* of air as the feed bin's floor swung down from hinges at its rear.

Ace held his match over the black hole he'd just uncapped, and she could see steps: the top few of a narrow flight of worn wooden stairs, walled on either side by mortared stone.

"I'll go down first and light a candle," he whispered, brushing a light kiss over her dirt-smeared forehead. "Then I'll be back up for you."

She nodded, reaching fingers out in the gloom to find a wall against which to lean. Then he disappeared over the side, and she was suddenly alone and engulfed in blackness.

There was a frightening moment in which she could see nothing and hear little but the sound of her own breathing, but the void was dispelled when a soft glow sprang from within the tunnel. She could see the steps more clearly now, and in a few seconds, the top of Ace's head came bobbing up the staircase to rise from the feed bin like the finale of a magician's best trick.

Halfway emerged, he leaned his arms along the top edge of the bin and grinned at her. "Ready to pop down the Rabbit's hole?"

She nodded, and held out a hand to him.

Gently, he helped her step over the side wall and put her feet safely on the top step.

The staircase was steep and narrow, and must have led down at least twenty feet. Once they were at its foot, he went back up to close the lid and trap door behind them, and Jenny looked about her.

The tunnel was narrow—just wide enough for two people to walk abreast—and it seemed that great care had been taken in its construction. About eight feet overhead, the ceiling was boarded with wide planking, but so heavily beamed and trussed that very little of the planking showed through. It looked to have been whitewashed long ago, and some of the chalky stain remained, reflecting and magnifying the light of their single candle. The walls were rock and mortar, and here and there slightly damp. Beneath her feet, the floor was deep in a gravel of small, smooth river rock.

Just then, Ace rejoined her. Silently, he took the candle from its niche in the wall and began to lead her along the tunnel toward the house.

She'd been certain that their path would be a fairly straight one, angling gently upward until it reached the cellar room of the old house. But instead, the passage began to slope down, deeper into the hillside.

"Where are we going?" she asked as their footsteps crunched and echoed along the narrow passage.

"You'll see," he grinned.

She realized now that the walls had changed from man-worked mortared rock to sheer, smooth limestone, and that the tunnel itself had widened. The ceiling, too, had changed to a yellow-streaked, light gray limestone, and its height varied to such an extent that several times Ace ducked to avoid a low hanging ledge.

Then the tunnel veered lazily to the right, taking them even farther away from the house. Jenny knew they must be deep within the hill now, and she was about to ask why the tunnel meandered in such a roundabout way when it turned left again. Suddenly she could see light ahead, and hear the echoing drip of water.

"Where are we?" she whispered, leaning a little harder into the warm strength of Ace's guiding arm.

He stopped and smiled down at her. "Welcome to Wonderland, Alice." In two steps, he swept her around the final bend in the corridor and into the light.

The cavern was gigantic. Jenny and Ace were standing on a wide, flat ledge of nearly white limestone, and before them stretched a vast underground lake of indeterminate depth. Its far shore was lost in the darkness, and its black, glassy surface, illuminated in streaks and abstract swirls of pale light, was disturbed only by occasionally falling droplets of water. These, she saw, dripped from the dimly lit tips of the massive stalactites that loomed from a barely visible ceiling of vaulted stone.

To her left, along the edge of the lake (or at least the portion that was visible to her), was a solid sheet of limestone that sloped gradually downward to form the lake's bed. As the stone beach retreated from the water, its surface grew buckled. It swirled and swelled in soft, multicolored undulations, growing more otherworldly and fantastic before its boundary, too, was lost in darkness. Stalagmites grew upward, sometimes meeting stalactites reaching down from above to form damp and massive pillars of pink or white or soft yellow calcite, giving Jenny, for a moment, the feeling of standing in some ancient and dreamlike Greek temple.

Echoes of droplets falling to the lake filled the cavern with an eldritch music, and when Ace whispered, "How do you like it?" the walls murmured his words over and over.

The pain in her back, her wrists, and her wounded knee momentarily forgotten, Jenny could only smile up at him, her mouth agape in wonder. He took her expression for an answer, and grinning widely, whispered, "I thought you would."

He took her, then, along the shore toward the light source that illuminated what she could see of the cavern. Forty feet around the curve of the lake's edge and just back into the forest of stone, a large lantern sat on a low natural table of rock. The floor of the cave was level for several feet on three sides of this limestone table before rising in the hillocks and spires of stalagmites, and in this clear space sat two cots and a wooden chair. Books and newspapers were stacked in haphazard heaps on the stone floor, and another pile of volumes rested next to the lantern, on the tilted, irregular surface of the table.

He led her to the first cot.

"Can you sit down?" he asked, remembering the thornlike stems of hay still embedded in her body.

Jenny lowered her eyes and blushed slightly, although in light of everything else that had happened tonight, she didn't know why she should.

"All right." Ace led her to the edge of the small clearing in the forest of stone, and pressed her hands against a thick, breast-high stalagmite. "Here," he said. "Lean on this if you need to. I'm going to go get a few things from Liz, and I'll be right back, OK?"

Jenny nodded gratefully, and he was gone.

*   *   *

Ace wove quickly through the limestone jungle until he reached the far end of the cavern. There, he relit his candle and entered another passage.

This one was far shorter than the first, and led sharply uphill for about fifteen yards before ending at a wide-brick-walled shaft. The shaft, about six feet across, contained a circular metal staircase which was secured not only by the heavy pole in its center, but by iron spikes connecting it firmly, at five-foot intervals, to the brick of its enclosure.

He climbed it two steps at a time, and some fifty feet later, gained the top. He stepped off the stairs to the floor of a small cubicle—bricked on three sides, wood-paneled on the fourth—and pulled down the lever that extended from the paneling. It slid aside softly, and he stepped through.

Now he was in the large windowless resting room. Cobwebbed oaken benches sat along three sides, and in the center of the room was an ancient potbellied stove, long disused. The stove and the wooden benches were all that remained to mark the passing of the countless slaves sheltered by this room as, before the war, they had bided here on the road to the North and freedom.

He did not linger. He opened the room's only visible door and exited into yet another dark passage. This one was narrow, dirt-floored, and walled in unpainted pine. Although it continued onward for several yards to a steep rise of wooden steps, he stopped after proceeding only ten feet. Lifting a hand to the wall, he pulled aside one of the small hinged blocks of wood that were placed randomly along the way. Through the peek hole beneath, he first saw nothing but blackness. But a moment later, light blossomed as the cellar door opened and feet appeared at the top of the staircase.

It was Scar Cooksey, and with him, Meg Sweetwater. They crossed the cellar toward his hiding place and swung open the panel immediately to his left.

Meg came through first and gave a shriek when she saw Ace. She clamped a hand over her own mouth, then hissed, "You scared me to death!"

Scar slipped through after her and sealed the wall behind them. As the three walked back into the wide resting room, Scar handed Ace a small paper-covered jar.

"Liz said you wanted this."

"And this stuff, too." Meg handed over a cloth bag. He peeked within, and found two washcloths and a towel, a roll of bandages, scissors, soap, and a pair of tweezers.

"Thanks, Meg," he said as he rebundled it. Then he noticed that she was carrying a worn carpetbag. He looked at both Meg and Scar questioningly.

"We're hightailin' it, too," Scar said. "Seems as good a time as any, you know?" He gave Meg's shoulder a little squeeze and she grinned. "'Bout time I made an honest woman outta Meggy here. Figure we'll head out west. Maybe California. Maybe south to Mexico . . ."

Ace smiled at Meggy quite warmly and gave Scar a broad grin of congratulations before he asked, "What's going on upstairs?"

Scar scratched his head. "Purty amazin' stuff, if you ask me. Ol' Agnes's fairly got Andy barricaded in

311

her room—he don't know squat yet, 'ceptin' maybe he ain't never had such a good time. Agnes told him it was on the house tonight, 'n he's takin' full advantage of the management's generosity.

"Billy's still passed out, but Mac locked him in the gamin' room so's if he comes to, he won't be goin' nowhere."

"What about the rest?" Ace pressed. "Didn't anybody else hear the shots?"

"Just Mac 'n Liz, far as I know. They was in the kitchen, so they would'a been closest. Iris's actin' a little proddy, like she knows somethin's up—but then, she always acts a mite strange if you ask me. . . . Belinda's took to her room with a case of the vapors, an' Bertha 'n Shirley Mae are sittin' out in the parlor, drunker 'n two skunks and cryin' over old times, actin' like they been best friends since who laid the rail." He shook his head. "Never seen nothin' like it."

Ace nodded. So far, so good.

"Mac says he'll go for the law soon as you give him the word," he added before asking, "You leavin' tonight, too, are you?"

"I was going to, but I don't think Jenny can ride yet. I may have to wait down in the cave for a while. Can you do me a favor?"

"Sure, Ace. Anythin'. You know that."

"Thanks. I want you to take Trooper and Jenny's mare with you as far as the big bend in Briar Creek. You know the place. By the old roundup pen. If I remember right, there's plenty of water, and it ought to be grassed in pretty good."

"Yeah, I know it. Be happy to oblige. I'll take

Rafe's horse outta the way too. Figured Meggy could have him—Rafe sure ain't gonna be needin' him no more."

Ace nodded in agreement, and the three of them began to make their way down the circular staircase to the cavern.

Jenny heard them coming long before they reached her. Even the tinest noises traveled quickly in the cavern, although it was impossible to determine their origin. Sounds echoed back and forth, bouncing randomly off the damp walls, the still, dark water, and the spires and pillars of rock, creating a humming murmur, as if from a far-off throng. Although the random refraction of sound turned their low conversation into a blurred murmur of tones and trills that made it impossible to understand any of the whispered words, she was able to recognize all three voices.

She waited, watching in the direction he'd taken when he left her, and before long she saw a gradually nearing glow: crazed patterns of quickly shifting beams and sparkles of light, then shadow, then light again as the lamp snaked toward her through a maze of stalagmites and stalactites.

The light came closer and grew brighter, and suddenly Ace (along with Scar and Meg) appeared beside her in the little clearing.

Except for Scar's whispered, "Miss Jenny," as he nodded slightly and touched the brim of his hat, neither he nor Meg talked to her. Scar quickly scooped up his clothes, dime novels, and pack roll, and Meg, a happy glow on her fair, freckled face, simply put one hand atop Jenny's. She gave it a little squeeze before she took Scar's arm and disappeared once more into the muted calcite jungle. A minute later, Jenny saw them emerge further along the limestone shore and vanish into the mouth of the far tunnel. She never saw them again.

Ace was at her elbow. "Jenny?" he whispered.

She turned toward him. The sound of his voice was so quiet and reassuring that it actually seemed to ease the pains she'd felt more and more acutely while she waited. And she was suddenly more tired than she could ever remember being. More than anything, she wanted to sleep.

Ace knew she was exhausted, but his first priority was to clean her wounds. Gently he took her arm and led her toward the nearest cot. He supported her with one hand, and pulled back the covers with the other.

"I know you want to sleep, Jenny, and you'll be able to in just a few minutes. Liz sent down some salve and bandages and things, all right?"

She nodded, and he reached for the bottle of bourbon. He pulled the cork with his teeth and poured an inch of the dark golden liquid into an enameled cup, then held it under her nose. She made a face when the fumes assailed her nostrils.

"This'll help, I promise," he whispered as he tilted the mug, forcing the whiskey into her mouth. She swallowed, gagging just a little, but after the first sip it didn't seem to bother her so much. She finished it off obediently, and within seconds, felt the whiskey's warmth diffusing through her body.

"Better?" he asked.

"Better."

"Good." He began to help her out of her skirt and camisole. This time, as he undressed her, she was neither embarrassed nor aroused. She recognized that he only wanted to help her, and besides, she was too tired to protest.

Her skirt fell to the floor first, and he winced when he saw the gash below one knee where the toe of Rafe's boot had caught her. The skin around it was already blooming with angry color. There was a good-sized bruise on the other shin, too, which he also blamed on Rafe. He could not know that she had received this particular battle scar from the heel of one of Belinda's best green pumps.

He shook his head sadly before, very carefully, easing the camisole away from her torso. Her back was a peppered, bloody mess, and there was a streak of dried blood above her right nipple. He bit at his lip and hoped that she could not see, from his expression, how battered she looked. He helped her lie down on the cot.

"On your tummy, Jenny," he murmured in a voice that was as hoarse with emotion as hers was with fatigue. "I want to get this stuff out of your back first, okay?"

"All right." With his help, she eased herself down upon the cot.

Once she was settled, he pulled the blanket up to cover her legs (and as much of her lower buttocks as he could without touching the field of splinters) and set to work.

Poised over her body with the tweezers, he said, "Now some of this is going to hurt, baby, but try not

315

to cry out or make any noise. Sound bounces around down here pretty bad, and a loud enough shout might just bring the roof down on us. Do you understand?"

She nodded. "But is it safe to stay here? Shouldn't we . . . you . . . You shouldn't be here!"

He smiled. "Don't worry, Jenny. It's safe, and I'm not going anywhere without you. Now get ready, because Old Doctor Ace is about to perform a little surgery."

"All right, but still, I . . ." Quickly, she jammed the pillow into her mouth as he drew out the first of many splinters and twigs.

He worked as quickly as he could, making certain that he removed even the tiny bits of dried matter that had broken off and lodged under her skin. It was nearly an hour before he worried out the last fragment. Jenny had managed not to cry out, but her pillow was wet with tears.

"There," he said at last, getting to his feet. She reached behind her to pull her covers up, but he cautioned her, "Not yet. Let me get you washed up first. Then I'll give you a treatment with some of Bertha's magic salve. That'll kill the pain for a while so you can turn over and let me see to your knee."

He went to the other cot and pulled a covered enameled basin from beneath it. After removing the cracked mirror and shaving kit it held, he wended his way to the still surface of the underground lake. There he filled it, and after returning to Jenny's side, wrung out a clean white washcloth. This he rubbed on the bar of soap Miss Liz had sent down, and very gently began to wash her back and fanny.

316

Jenny gritted her teeth. She didn't know which was worse: a back full of splinters, their removal, or the cold bite of spring water flooding onto the raw cavities they left behind.

At last he was satisfied that her wounds were clean. After he rinsed her skin, he set the basin aside, then opened the jar of ointment. A foul odor rose almost immediately, and Jenny wrinkled her nose.

"What does Bertha put *in* that?" she whispered as she watched him scoop out a handful with the obvious intention of rubbing it into her screaming back. "It's *awful!*"

"Pretty rank, isn't it?" Ace chuckled. "But in a minute you won't mind . . ."

With that he began to spread the off-white goo between her shoulder blades, and almost immediately she felt a cooling, blessed relief from the stinging pain of her injuries. She sighed happily as he gently worked his way down her back to her bottom.

He pulled the blanket up to her shoulders and asked, "Do you think you can turn over now?"

"Yes," she smiled. "It's much better." She eased herself over and looked up toward the half-visible vault of the cavern's roof. She'd been a little afraid that she might come eye-to-eye with the looming point of a stalactite, but the cot had been positioned so that it sat safely under what must be one of the few clear spots in the cave. Above her, so high that the lantern's light could not invade it entirely, was only a faint, smooth arch of stone.

"Jenny?"

Ace helped her to sit up a little, and poured two

fingers of whiskey into her cup. "Try to get a little more of that down. It'll help."

She tilted, then emptied it, coughing a little.

He took the cup away and she lay down again, sighing happily as new warmth bathed her aching limbs. "Yes," she said. "You were right." Then thinking back over the last few days, added, "Are you ever wrong about anything?"

"Hardly ever," he grinned, his black eyes twinkling. He tugged the covers from her legs. Now that she was on her back, he removed her shoes, then washed and medicated her knee.

Next he took her hands one at a time, checking her wrists for broken skin. Luckily, the twine had not cut her, although she would probably have a few bruises. After removing the wood splinters from the hand with which she had clung so tenaciously to the back door of the horse barn, he bathed and salved her palm and fingers.

She was half asleep. Her lids drooped as she watched him tend her wounds, and by the time he eased the blanket down from her shoulders to clean the bite mark Rafe had left on her breast, she had fallen into a deep, dreamless sleep.

Very gently, so as not to disturb her, he washed and medicated the tender pink of her nipple. Fortunately, only one tooth had broken the skin (and so shallowly that he was certain there wouldn't be a scar), but as he looked down at her sleeping body, he began to cry. The tears were silent, and two of them spattered on her breast as he bent over her.

He wanted to wash her all over: to scrub away the last traces of Rafe's touch. He knew it was stupid to think that some of Rafe might linger on her skin, her hair; and he knew that he had, thank God, arrived in time to prevent the son of a bitch from doing the worst. But it still pained and angered him that Rafe had seen her, hurt her, that he'd ever put his filthy hands on her . . .

Though there was no one there to see his tears, he rubbed at his eyes, and after tucking Jenny's covers under her chin, he carried the basin of soapy water back to the black lake's shore and emptied it. There was more current here than one would think, and he knew that it would not be long before the soapy cloud would be dispersed and carried away to Briar Creek.

He looked back at Jenny: sleeping like the dead, her blond hair knotted and full of twigs and straw, but still looking angelic despite tonight's insults to her body and her soul. If he had been able to kill Rafe Langley ten times over, he would have done it gladly.

"She's asleep," he said, in answer to Mac's question. "I'm going to wait at least a day before I take her with me. She's not ready to travel yet."

Mac nodded. The two men were on the second floor of the house, standing in the symphony in blue that was Miss Liz's richly appointed bedroom. Ace had entered through the panel. Mac, being the conventional sort, had used the door.

Miss Liz was sitting on the wide canopied bed, her back straight, her hands folded neatly in her lap. Somehow, Ace thought, she always managed to look like exiled royalty.

"And Scar is taking the horses?" she asked.

"Yes, to Briar Creek. They'll be fine there for a day or two. I thought that when we're ready to go, we could borrow Daisy," Ace said, referring to Mac's gray saddle mare. "She'll find her way back, won't she?"

"Yeah, she always comes on home," Mac smiled. "Guess this means it's time for me to go for the sheriff."

Ace leaned against a tall bureau, hooking his elbow over its corner. "Pretty soon."

"What about the Dodge boys?"

"I've been thinking about that," Ace answered. "I don't figure they'll have the nerve to do much on their own in the way of crime, once they hear Rafe's deserted them. Besides, if they're here for the sheriff to take in, he might just ask them to identify the body . . ." He paused for a few seconds, drumming his fingers against the highboy's top drawer.

"So maybe somebody ought to pry Andy off Agnes," he grinned, "and give him the bad news about me being dead and all. If I know Andy, he'll throw Billy over a saddle, drunk or not, and be out of the county in two shakes."

Miss Liz shook her head. "I don't know, Marcus. What if the two of them try to track down Rafe and wind up finding Scar and Meggie?"

"I wouldn't worry about it. Neither one of 'em are any great shakes as trackers, even in the daylight. They're going to be too scared to do anything but put as much distance as possible between themselves and this place."

Mac went to the door and put his hand on the knob. "Guess I'll go break the news to Andy, then.

320

And I'll give the boys a healthy head start before I leave for town."

Softly, he slipped from the room.

There was a long pause before Miss Liz spoke. "I'm sorry, Marcus," she said.

"Sorry?"

"About Jenny."

"She'll be all right, Ma. It looked a lot worse than it—"

"No, not about that." She stared down at her hands, took a breath, and then raised her dark eyes to meet his. "All week I've been trying to . . . I've been trying to talk Jenny into working for me. I didn't take you seriously. I didn't know she was something special to you, and she's such a pretty little thing . . ."

Ace smiled. "Yes, she is that, isn't she? Don't apologize, Ma. I mean, she didn't take you up on it, did she? Besides," he teased, "I guess I can't blame you for wanting to give the place a little class." Then he frowned, pretending to scold. "Just don't try it again!"

The madam smiled faintly. "Where will you go, you and Jenny?"

He slouched against the chiffonier and began to fiddle with the edge of the doily that covered its marble top. "I don't know yet. Guess I haven't thought that far ahead. But you can bet it'll be someplace where they've never heard of Ace Denton."

"Marcus?" She looked a little strange: somehow frail and vulnerable. He didn't think he'd ever seen her quite like this before, except for that one day, long ago, when he'd called her "mother" for the first time.

"What is it, Ma?"

"Will I ever see you again?"

He crossed the room, his boots sinking into the deep powder-blue carpets, and sat next to her on the bed.

"Of course you will. I'll always let you know where we are." He put his arm around her, and she began to cry. "What did you think? That I was just going to vanish into thin air forever? From you?"

She pulled a lace-trimmed hankie from her sleeve and daubed at her eyes, embarrassed to weep in front of her son. She'd always taken pains to shield her softer side from the world, even from him, but now she didn't seem to be able to stop the tears.

He rocked her for a little while, then said, "You know, Ma, half that reward money, plus what you'd get if you sold the house, would set you up pretty nice back East. And knowing you, I'll just bet you've got a tidy little sum stashed away someplace, too. Don't you think it's about time you—"

She sniffed angrily. "You sound just like your pa!"

"That shouldn't surprise you."

She pulled away from him, although not very far.

He waited for a moment, then asked quietly, "Why didn't you ever marry him? And don't give me the runaround you usually do. I think I have a right to know."

She looked at her son with those dark, piercing, eyes, and studied his somber face for a few seconds before she said, "All right. I guess you do." She took a deep breath and looked away from him before she began.

"He was the first for me, you know. The first ever, and I loved him like crazy. We were just kids then. He was sixteen and I was thirteen." She smiled to herself. "Thirteen. Was I ever really that young?"

She fingered her bracelet and found a tiny, tarnished heart. "He gave me this," she said, turning it over. It was clumsily engraved J.D. & E.McC. "I used to wear it on a long fine chain around my neck. . . ."

Ace had heard parts of this before in little dribs and drabs, but somehow he needed to hear it again, needed to hear the missing bits. He squeezed her hand, and she continued.

"His folks moved away before I knew that I was carrying you. That was back in Illinois. I didn't even know where they'd gone for certain. They just joined up with a wagon train headed west. Anyway, my ma and pa were fit to be tied when I started to show. Disowned me on the spot. My father gave me four dollars and told me to be on my way and that was it.

"There wasn't really any place for me to go, but finally this lady took me in. Well, I thought she was a lady—that's how naive I was. I worked for her. Miss Sharon Virginia Clancy was her name, and when you were about two, she took me and three other girls on the road with her. We had a covered wagon, and we figured we were going to work our way west. I guess somewhere in the back of my mind, I thought that maybe, just maybe, I'd run into your father again. Pretty silly of me, I know. I didn't know the west was such a big place . . .

323

"Anyway, we didn't make much progress. We just meandered over into Iowa and down into Missouri. That took us nearly two years. You were past four by the time we wandered into Kansas."

Ace stroked the back of her hand. "You know, Ma, when I was a kid, I used to have dreams about sleeping on the front seat of a Conestoga, looking up at the stars and eating peppermint candy."

She smiled a little wistfully. "It wasn't a dream, honey. That's where we'd put you to bed, the nights we had customers. And one of the other girls, Lilly, she always kept a big bag of peppermints on hand, just for you. Always gave you one when we bedded you down for the night. They were all crazy about you, you know. You were such a beautiful baby . . ."

"But what about Pa?" he asked.

She began to fiddle with her bracelet again. "Like I said, we finally made it to Kansas, and we were going from town to town, or at least the outskirts of them. And one day, I saw him. He was driving a buckboard full of grain sacks, and there was a girl on the seat beside him. A real pretty little blond girl—younger than I was, and I wasn't past eighteen yet—and she had her arm laced through his.

"He saw me about the same time I saw him, and he gave a start. I could see the girl asking him what was the matter, and he kind of patted her hand and just drove on. But he came back that evening, and he and I had a talk.

"He cried, he did, when he found out he'd left me in a family way, and when he saw you it was about all he could do to keep from hugging you to death. Course, it turned out he was married to that little

324

blond girl I'd seen him with. They'd only tied the knot about three weeks before. We had a long talk about what to do, and we decided that you ought to go and live with him.

"I guess he and his wife had a real donnybrook over it, but she finally agreed to take you if he'd keep to the story that you were an orphan they'd taken in, not kin at all. Your pa wasn't too happy about it, but since it was better than you being raised up in a wagon full of whores—"

"Ma!"

"That's what it was, like it or not, Marcus."

"I just don't like you calling yourself that, that's all . . ."

She patted his hand this time, then tucked her frilly handkerchief back into her sleeve. It felt good, after all these years, to say it out all at once like this. "Anyway, in the next few years, I raised myself up some. Oh, I was still a whore—" She placed two fingers over his lips before he could protest the word, and continued. "—But I'd gotten to be a high-class one. I was pretty fancy, all right. Worked in Chicago, in a real toney house. I had beautiful clothes. I got my portrait painted. Oh, I was elegant, all right. I'd taught myself not to talk so much like a hayseed, and I had enough wealthy clients that I was finally able to save up enough money to start my own place. Chicago didn't have room for another fine house, so I decided to try Kansas City.

"That's where I ran into Elmer Sweeny. I was just coming in at the depot, and there he was. He was from back home in Illinois, too, and while I remembered him as just another grown-up, he knew me right off. Well, he took me to lunch, and it wasn't long before he had me figured out. He was a pretty smart old cuss, that Elmer, and by the time we'd finished our roast beef, I felt like I'd known him since Adam.

"I was still wondering what to do and where to set up shop when he turned to me—he was right in the middle of paying the check—and said, 'I know where Joe Denton is.'"

She laughed and said, "Elmer was like that, you know, always saying things just *so*, for effect, always taking in strays. Just like he took in Mac years later, after he moved out here and built this house. He found Mac lying out in the south pasture one day, all shot up and half dead with his old bay horse standing guard over him. Elmer recognized him right away as the Arkansas Kid because of that fancy rig he used to wear. But Elmer, he decided on the spot that any man who could inspire enough loyalty from a dumb horse that it wouldn't even wander off to graze was probably all right in his book. Mac just stayed on after he was up and around. Guess he was tired of the running and the hiding. And well, when Elmer passed on, I guess Mac was just used to living here . . ."

"Ma?"

She patted his hand. "Sorry, honey. I guess you knew all that already. Anyway, I went out to Clinton, Kansas, with Elmer, and he sent word to your Pa that I was there. Joe came up the very next day with you and your half brother Roy—I remember, Roy was just a bit of a thing, then, and he was sitting on your lap—and told me how his wife had passed on with

326

fever just before he'd moved to the new farm. He wanted me to marry him real bad, I could tell. Not just because he was saying so, but by everything about him. But, Marcus, I just couldn't."

"Why, Ma? Why not?"

"Oh, honey, if you'd seen us then ... Elmer Sweeny couldn't even take me home with him. His wife wouldn't let me in the house. He put me up at the hotel, and there I sat, all silk and satin and perfume and pearls and practically shouting my profession; while your daddy sat across from me, so plain and honest and decent. . . . I knew I couldn't do it to him or to you."

"So that's when you set up the house in Fisher?" He remembered it well—two towns away and the focal point of every local boy's dream once he entered puberty. He'd lost his own virginity there when he was sixteen.

She nodded. "I never worked again, myself, after that day, but I ran a good, clean house. Still, I was surprised when I heard your father had told you about me. I asked him not to, you know."

"I know. But I think I had it figured out long before he said anything, Ma . . ." They sat in silence for a few minutes, then Ace said softly, "You going to marry Mac?"

"What?" She reared up, suddenly indignant and regally offended.

He grinned and stood up. "Don't pull that on me, Lizzie. You know Mac loves you. And you love him too, if you'd ever get down off that high horse of yours long enough to admit it."

She snorted at him.

"Besides," he added with a wink, "now that I'm dead, you're practically rich!"

"I want to talk to you about that." She'd once again assumed the mantle of Her Majesty, Elizabeth McCaleb, sovereign of all she surveyed. "Just what do you think you and your Jenny are going to live on?"

He bent down and bussed her on the cheek. "We'll be all right, Ma. I've got nearly a thousand stashed away in a bank in Kansas. Been putting it in a little at a time over the years, under the name of Marc McCaleb. Ought to be a nice-sized nest egg by now. That is, if Rafe and the Dodge boys didn't knock it over while I was looking the other way . . ."

He grinned at her impishly, and she shoved at his chest with both hands, laughing in spite of herself. "Oh, honestly, Marcus!"

When he returned to the cavern, Jenny was still sleeping, and so soundly that she had not shifted an inch from the position in which he'd last seen her. He turned the lamp down to a feeble glow, then quietly undressed and slid beneath the covers of the second cot.

He watched her for a very long time before he fell asleep.

Twelve

Friday

She dreamt that she was Alice at the tea party: a tea party held not in a forest of trees, but a forest of stone. The March Hare and the Dormouse were there. So were the Mock Turtle and the Cheshire Cat. A large flamingo, an ace of hearts clamped in his long, curved beak, sat in the center of the table. The Mad Hatter banged his teaspoon against a bronze bust of Bertha Bramley before he raised it aloft and intoned,

> *Twinkle, twinkle, little bat!*
> *How I wonder where you're at!*

Then he looked straight at her and said, *You know the song, perhaps?*

Something touched her shoulder, and the Cheshire Cat began to fade away into nothing but a grin. She opened her eyes.

"Welcome back, little one."

Sleepily, she smiled up at Ace, and stretched luxuriously before she realized that her back was free from pain.

"Bertha ought to bottle that salve and sell it," she whispered. "Just that one treatment, and—"

"Three, actually." He was sitting on the edge of the rough stone table, and he turned the lamp's wick a bit higher before he leaned back toward her.

"Three?"

"You've slept almost twenty hours, Jenny. I did your back early this morning and again this afternoon. You didn't so much as mumble when I rolled you over."

"Oh." She smiled sheepishly, then hoisted herself up to lean on her elbow. "What time is it now?"

Ace pulled a pocket watch from his vest. "About seven-thirty."

"Friday night?"

He nodded, grinning. "That's right." He jabbed a thumb toward the cavern's ceiling. "Business is pretty brisk up there. I hear that Bertha's cursing you more than she's mourning me . . ."

"What did—"

"Liz told everybody that you ran off last night. That you were frightened by the gunplay."

"Well," she smiled, "the last part's not a lie. What happened to the . . . to the body?"

Briefly, he recounted the events she'd missed, both last night and this morning. After the Dodge brothers were given adequate time for a healthy head start, Mac had fetched the law. Sheriff Wallace had arrived swiftly and asked few questions. Although he seemed somewhat saddened at the loss of a local hero, he'd

330

been "right honored" to haul "Ace Denton's" body into town to the undertaker, and had done so with little fanfare. Shirley Mae had stayed on to help Bertha with the weekend crowds, although considering the amount of shouting and swearing coming from the kitchen, he didn't know how either of them had any time left over to cook or serve.

"Our horses are waiting for us at Briar Creek," he said, after he'd told her about Scar and Meg. "Provided you still want to come with me . . ."

"You know I do," she whispered.

He leaned forward then, and kissed her quite sweetly, just brushing her lips before he pulled away and said, "I'll bet you're half-starved. You probably want to get cleaned up, too." He touched her tangled hair and gently drew away a nettle. "I think you'll find everything you need in here," he said, pointing to the basin. It sat on the stone floor beside her cot, and had been refilled with the toiletries he'd removed the night before. On top, he'd placed a comb and brush.

"You can bathe in the lake if you can stand the chill," he added. "It's shallow. And don't worry about fouling it with soap. The current'll carry it out and away."

"Thank you," she whispered.

He winked at her, then got to his feet. "I'll go on up and see if Liz has had a chance to set us out some dinner yet. I'll, um, take my time, all right? And there's a, uh . . ."

She couldn't believe it, but he looked a little embarrassed.

"A, uh . . ." he faltered, then waved his hand

toward a hedge of stalagmites behind her. "Well, it's back there," he finished. Quickly, he lit a candle, and then he was gone.

Slowly, she sat up. She was still a little stiff and sore. She knew those symptoms would abate once she began to move about. But the sharp pains in her knees, wrists, and back had vanished. Standing up, she wrapped the blanket around her and stepped curiously toward the area he'd indicated. She peeked behind the rise of stone, wondering what might possibly have been so embarrassing to him that he couldn't say the words, and then she saw it—completely, ridiculously out of place in all its painted porcelain splendor: a chamber pot.

She couldn't help but giggle, but she remembered to cover her mouth with her hand. Even so, the echoes of her muffled laughter rang through the cavern, magnified to the chuckles of a large and strictly female crowd.

A few minutes later, she was kneeling at the barely lapping bank of the cavern's lake. She tested the water with her fingers. It was on the chilly side, but not so cold that she wouldn't be able to stand it. She needed to immerse herself fully, needed to completely obliterate any and all traces of Rafe Langley's touch.

After painfully but completely combing the last of the burrs and sticks of straw and hay from her dirty hair, she let her blanket fall to the stony shore and waded into the lake. The clear, nearly still water was more than bracing, and she broke out in gooseflesh before she had walked in up to her knees. But she did not pause, and before long was immersed past her waist and happily, despite her chattering teeth, soaping her hair.

Once her long blond tresses were squeaking between her fingers and clean enough to suit her, she began to scrub at her body with soap and a washcloth, unconsciously rubbing most savagely at those places Rafe had touched. Somehow, no amount of soap and water seemed adequate, and deep within her, she knew that there was something else she needed to make her clean again, to make her right and whole.

But whatever it was, it was not within her power. Finally deciding that she was as dirt-free as she could make herself, she left the water's chill and toweled herself dry.

The only clothes she could find were those she'd worn the previous night. She couldn't bring herself to put them on. They seemed ruined beyond the surface damage of the blouse's missing buttons or the bloodstains dotting the camisole and skirt. They smacked too much of Rafe, and seemed soiled just by his having seen them. So she left them where they were, wrapped herself in a soft wool blanket, and perched on the edge of her cot, brushing the last of the snarls from her damp hair.

It wasn't long before she heard Ace returning, and not much longer before she could smell the dinner he was bringing with him. Her stomach growled angrily at the first scent, suddenly reminding her of how badly she'd treated it. A few minutes later Ace appeared from behind the last columns of stone, a napkin-covered tray balanced before him.

He put it down and grinned at her. She looked scrubbed and bright and beautiful, and her cold-water bath had put the bloom back into her cheeks. "Better?" he asked.

"Much," she smiled. "And you were right. I'm *starving!*"

He lowered the tray to the floor, scooting it to a level stretch of the streaked limestone. "Well, since Bertha made this, I can't promise it'll taste like much, but I *can* guarantee that there'll be plenty of it"—he whisked away the covering napkin and made a face—"whatever it is."

They sat side by side on the edge of Ace's cot while they ate. He poked into the gravy morass with some suspicion, but Jenny dove in headlong. Although she finally decided the solid thing beneath the gravy was chicken-fried steak, she didn't much care. She was ravenous, and for the first time since her arrival at Miss Liz's, she cleaned her plate with gusto.

Afterward, she slid her plate back on the tray and sighed. "I feel almost human again," she said with a satisfied smile.

"Glad to hear it, ma'am," he grinned. He put his plate down on top of hers, then pushed the tray away with the toe of his boot. He stood up and walked away toward the house tunnel.

"Where are you—?"

"Just a second."

He returned in a moment carrying her saddlebags and one of her frayed satchels. "Thought I'd pack these up for you and bring them down." He deposited them at the foot of the cot atop his own pack roll and gun belt before he sat down next to her again.

334

She looked at him questioningly. "I have two carpetbags."

"I know. I'll explain later." He sat there looking at her.

"When do you think—" she began, suddenly self-conscious. "That is, when should we . . ."

"Leave?"

She nodded.

"Soon as you're ready to travel, I guess. Too busy up there at the moment for us to take a chance for a while, though. Somebody'd be bound to see us leaving the barn. We can leave just before dawn, or wait until just after sunset tomorrow. It's up to you."

"Either one." Now that she had agreed to go, she began to wonder just what she was getting herself into. He'd made no offer of marriage, and even though she wanted nothing more than to go with him, what was her guarantee that he wouldn't grow tired of her? What would prevent him from abandoning her somewhere along the way to who knew where? But yet, when she looked at him and heard his voice, she knew that she had no choice but to follow him and suffer the consequences, whatever those might be.

On the pretense of checking her fingers for splinters he took her hand, but after giving the pink, healing wounds a cursory inspection, he began to stroke her palm lightly. Somehow just that whispery touch was enough to send an unexpected shiver up her spine. She lowered her eyes and bit at her lip, hungry for him and ashamed that she was, in the light of last night's attack. She wondered if perhaps it would be more ladylike to be taken by a case of the vapors and refuse his attentions. But then, she'd never claimed to be much of a lady . . .

As one hand traced serpentines over her palm, he slid the other across her bare shoulders, playing with the damp, golden coil of hair that hung down her back.

"Jenny?" he whispered.

Slowly, she tilted her head up toward his, certain that he was going to kiss her, but just before their lips met, he said, "Maybe I should take another look at your back."

"It's fine. Really, it is," Jenny muttered, wondering if he planned to spread some more of Bertha's goo on her, just when she'd washed the last of its stink away.

"I'll be the judge of that," he smiled. He stood up, and as he did, pushed her shoulders back and to one side until she was stretched out on his cot.

"That's better." He twirled his index finger in a circle. "On your tummy now . . ."

Obediently she turned over and reached beneath herself to loosen the blanket, which she'd knotted just above her breasts. Considering Ace's behavior over the past week, his reticence now was somewhat disappointing. She wondered if somehow the rules had changed without her knowledge.

She lifted herself up just a bit so that he could slip free the sides of the blanket, and waited for him to pull it down and bare her back. But instead, he rested his hand on the soft wool over her shoulders, and said, "Do you understand, now Jenny? About Fowlersville? It was—"

Gently, she cut him off. "—It was Rafe. I know that now, and I'm sorry."

"There's no need for you to be sorry, little one. There was no way you could have known any different. I'm just glad," he smiled, "that you didn't get around to using *that* on me . . ." He pointed to her father's Colt. It lay where he had left it: on the stone floor beside the other cot.

Jenny's brow furrowed. "Papa's gun?"

Ace scratched his head. "That's kind of a long story. For now, let's just say I rescued it." Somehow, he didn't think this was quite the right time to tell her about Iris and Belinda's little escapade, or about her clothes. "Let's take a look at your battle scars."

She felt the soft blanket slip slowly from her shoulders, then down the length of her back and finally down to her thighs. The last slide, the one that bared her fanny, sent another wave of tremors up her spine. She felt herself break out in gooseflesh, although this time not from the cold. Then his fingers touched her, gently stroking her upper back.

"Looks pretty good," she heart him whisper. "Does this hurt?"

"No, not at all," she answered. She couldn't tell him that her nipples, crushed into his blanket beneath her, were beginning to tighten with want.

His fingers trailed lower, to the small of her back. "How about here? Any pain?"

"I . . . No, none." This she said through clenched teeth, struggling to sound as normal as possible despite the warm tingles racing up and down her spine.

He was taking his time, tracing little circles on her

337

flesh, pressing here and there, as if he had no idea that each second his fingers lingered on her body drove her more mad with longing.

"Here? Or here?" he'd say, and each time she'd answer that there was no pain, although by now there was beginning to be some, if only in her aching, pounding breasts and the lip at which she bit. Her hands were tucked beneath her shoulders, and she curled them into fists. After everything he'd done to her these past few days, how could he not know her torment? What was there to stop him now? Why couldn't he just—

His right hand slipped lower, and she felt the heat of his palm as it rested on one side of her fanny, and then the strong fingers of his left as they began to trace lacy circles over the other buttock.

"Any pain yet?" he asked.

She tried to answer him, but all that came out was a little squeak, half-muffled by the pillow.

"Good," she heard him say. "You're healing nicely." But he didn't stop that feathery stroking, he didn't even break its rhythm. Now he was trailing his fingers along the outside swell of her hip, each time a little lower, pushing the blanket, a bit at a time, completely away from her bottom and halfway down her thighs. His fingers fluttered up now, over the tender backs of her legs, then into the crease between them, and without thinking, Jenny parted her thighs just a fraction.

"Yes, indeed," he said, quite matter-of-factly. "You're looking very good, young lady. Very good, indeed."

She shuddered when she felt him slide the fingers

338

of one hand between her thighs and slowly begin to move it up and down, never quite touching their juncture, but always coming dangerously close. The tingling in her spine had spread lower, to the place he refrained from touching, and was rapidly evolving into an intense throb. It was all she could do to keep from reaching behind her and dragging his hand higher, to touch her there. Then she felt his lips brush first one buttock, then the other: fluttering kisses as light as the touch of a bird's wing, and she whispered, "Ace?"

He did not answer her in words, but slid his hand up and back along the crease of her buttocks.

"Ace . . . Ace, please . . ." she tried to whisper, but the words came out as a hoarse, breathy mumble. Her fists had uncurled, and she gripped the sides of the cot with white-knuckled fingers.

Now his hand moved softly, slowly, dancing spirals on its way up her spine. His lips followed his fingers, feathering silky kisses over her buttocks, the small of her back, her shoulders. By the time his mouth and fingers came to rest at the back of her neck, every inch of her skin tingled.

He lifted her hair away and traced a lazy figure behind one of her ears with the point of his tongue. "Yes, Jenny?" he whispered. "Did you say something?"

She turned her face toward him—he was kneeling very close now—and managed to murmur, "Would you . . . would you please . . . ?"

"Yes, Jenny," he smiled.

He stood up quite slowly, and walked to the other cot. Stripping the rest of the blankets from it with one smooth motion, he laid them out on the level shelf of the rock floor, near the water's edge. Then he came back to Jenny and held out his hand. She rose without bothering to grab for the blanket, finding quite suddenly that her nudity was not the least bit shameful to her. She was excited by it now—excited to be naked with Ace; naked *for* Ace.

He swept the blankets off his cot, too, then carried them to the grotto's shore. He spread them out over the others before tossing the two feather pillows down at one end of the makeshift mattress. Then he stopped and looked at Jenny—so beautiful and young, so trusting, so willing.

That she could so totally trust him—or any man— after last night was miraculous, and Ace knew that the responsibility he bore tonight was a heavy, although joyful one. He would have to be more than careful, he knew, after what Rafe had done—and almost done—to her.

Jenny watched his face as he drank her with his eyes, and she could see something more than lust there. She wanted to think it was something lasting and fine and good: something that would be there not just for weeks or months, but forever. She knew so little about him, yet there was the overpowering feeling that somehow, she knew everything she would ever need to know, and that he was privy to the same depth of understanding about her.

Ace began to undress, never taking his black, piercing eyes from her, and she eagerly watched the gradual revealment of his strong, hard body. He was as powerfully handsome, as ruggedly symmetrical as she had remembered, and when he at last tugged away the final garment, she could no longer be still.

She went to him. He opened his arms to her, pulling her hard against him as they kissed softly, sweetly.

His mouth trailed a sensuous path over her lips, her throat, her temples as she squirmed against him, and when he took her lips again his kiss was long and passionate. She teased his tongue with her own, and as she coaxed him more deeply into her mouth, she felt the naked hardness of him pressing, long and thick, against her belly.

Then they were lying on the blankets, face to face, touching, tasting, exploring each other. She traced the hard angles of his tightly muscled back and arms as, in turn, he claimed the peak of each breast with his lips and tongue: suckling first lazily, then urgently, then lazily again until she wanted to scream with pleasure. Jenny covered his brow and the dark curls of his head with kisses, nipping at his ear or the tanned skin of his shoulder as he pleasured her. His teeth tugged gently at her swollen nipple, abrading it just slightly before he flicked the sensitized tip with the point of his tongue, then suckled again with an impassioned urgency.

His hand slipped between her legs just as hers found his satiny thickness. Shuddering with delight and anticipation, she raised her leg, sliding it atop his thigh to grant him better access; and when she did, he whispered her name and lifted his head to kiss her deeply.

Their lips met with undisguised, full-blown want: she held nothing back from him this time, held nothing in check. He had thought her kisses perfect before, but now he was surprised by the depth of her passion and the breadth of her response. What would she be like, he wondered, once she had learned all he could teach her? Her fingers, stroking him perfectly, were enticing him, inciting him to enter her, but he steeled himself. *Not yet*, he thought, mustering all his remaining self-control. *Not quite yet.*

Gently, he tested, with the slowly probing tip of his finger, the barrier he would soon conquer. It was thin and would offer little resistance, but he knew there would still be some pain. He smiled a little sadly when Jenny drew a ragged breath and arched up to meet his hand. Then slowly, with easy, gliding strokes, his fingers began to prime her for what was to come.

Finally, she could stand it no longer. She was on the brink of falling into that miasma of ecstasy to which he had brought her so many times before. But this time, she wanted to know, at last, what it meant to be a woman. His woman. "Please, Ace!" she managed to whimper. "I want to feel you inside me before I . . ."

And he knew. She was exactly where he'd wanted her: so close to rapture that the pain of that first penetration would be lost in the pleasure of her release. There would be plenty of time—years—to make love fully, to experience its every form and nuance. He would see to that.

Never ceasing his caresses—although tempering them just slightly, enough to delay her climax until he was ready—he rolled her onto her back. She parted her legs immediately, urgently, and he eased himself between them, whispering hoarsely, "Try not to cry out, Jenny. I may have to cover your mouth, all right?"

She nodded as she felt him nudge against her, then push forward slightly to ease slowly, perfectly within. She opened her mouth and craned her head backward, an uncontrollable, glorious smile on her face at the sensation. It was so perfect, so right! How could she never have known she was so empty? He began to rock within her, shallow movements, barely inside, and all she could think was, *He is filling me with himself, he is becoming me, and I am becoming him . . .*

And then she couldn't think anymore. She felt herself floating up off the floor, as if her body and spirit had separated, yet were more fused than ever they had been: her body molded and joined with his; their souls entwined, merged, were made one. She was buoyed by that magical, wondrous conjunction; swept into the air by sensation.

Suddenly he drove forward, filling her completely and sending her into a rushing, whirling current of wind and fire. There was a pain, quick and sharp, but only momentary. It was gone as quickly as it had come, washed away by the torrent of pleasure in which she spun: helpless and adrift in a sea of joy.

Then there was quiet, except for the sound of their breathing. She lay beneath him, shivering, still impaled. She felt her muscles involuntarily caressing him as he rested within her: contracting and releasing with the after-tremors of her violent release. And just as she realized that his hand had covered her mouth to keep her from crying out, he drew it away and kissed her deeply and tenderly.

She drank of him, wanting more and more, urging him to a kiss even more passionate as she ran her hands up and down the straight line of his spine and kneaded the taut, bulging muscles in his back. She wanted all of him: wanted him to love her forever like this. The sensation of him, firm and quiescent inside her, was indescribably gorgeous, and she knew she could never have enough of his touch and the feeling of this rare and intimate joining.

She had been saddened that it was over, and so she was delighted when he slid one hand down to cover her breast. As he kissed her again, he gently rubbed the flat of his thumb over the crown, teasing the hard bud at its peak. A low moan escaped her throat, and he swallowed it as he drew her tongue into his mouth, teasing and tempting her. And then she began to feel him move inside her, creating a new series of sensations for which she had no name.

Her legs opened wider and she slid her thighs up along his sides, rejoicing in the slow, sultry rhythm of his deeper and deeper penetrations. She clutched at the straining muscles of his back. His skin was sleek as heated satin, his sinews fluid steel. And when he dipped his head to pluck at her nipple with his lips and teeth, he whispered her name as if it were a litany and she the goddess he worshipped.

Swept into his rhythm, she moved with him; drawn into the ancient rhythm of lovers, meeting him thrust for thrust, and realizing that *this* was the cleansing she had needed: this willing sacrifice of her maidenhood upon the altar of Ace's body was the purifying act that made all things new and bright.

And then—wonder of wonders!—she felt him

swell within her, growing larger yet; and as he did, Jenny's wave of ecstasy suddenly burgeoned alongside his to dash her, jubilant, upon a sparkling, spun-glass shore. She reached to cover his mouth at the same time he covered hers, and this time they vaulted the heights of splendor together—spinning wildly through the void, beyond the constraints of space or time.

It was several minutes before either could speak.

Hovering above, propped on his elbows, Ace remained embedded deeply; and to her joy, he made no move to alter the situation. He merely brushed a stray strand of still-damp hair from her flushed face and smiled down at her.

"Jenny," he finally whispered, and brushed a kiss over each of her eyelids.

She smiled and raised her head to press her lips against his as she slid her legs back down to the blanket. "Is it always so wonderful?" she asked, her eyes half-lidded.

Ace chuckled into the curve of her throat. "One would hope so, little one." He was more than a little surprised at himself, for he wanted her again already. He was concerned, though, that she might be in pain, or at least a little tender. Lying beneath him, her lips swollen and half-curled into a satiated smile, she seemed in no discomfort; far from it, in fact. He decided he wouldn't make love to her again unless she seemed eager. Still, he was loath to remove himself from within her warmth: it had, after all, taken him a great deal of effort to get there.

He ran his hand under her shoulder and began to slide it down her body, between her back and the blanket, until he had firmly cupped her hip. Without a word, he rolled over onto his back, taking her with him so that she lay sprawled upon his chest, their union unbroken. She brought her knees up a little, glorying in the feel of him inside her, and lifted herself up on her elbows so that her nipples just brushed the pelt of his chest. He took a plump breast in each hand and began to fondle them, teasing their pink and swollen crests.

"Do you want to know something silly?" she whispered. Despite her rapidly rekindling excitement, she felt the need to confess.

"What's that, Jenny?" He raised her a little higher above him and propped himself on one elbow so that, from below, he could ring one rosy crest with the tip of his tongue.

Her spine dissolved into a cascade of shivers as he flicked the tingling crown with his tongue, then took it between his lips.

"I didn't know people could do this like we . . . I mean . . ." He was making it difficult for her to talk, teasing at her like that. "I mean, I thought, after you showed me the horses, and after . . ." He worried her nipple, tugging its tip with his teeth like the gentlest of terrier puppies, and she inhaled sharply before she could continue. ". . . after I saw Scar and Meg in the cellar . . ."

He pulled his head away, letting the nipple plop softly from his mouth, and chuckled. Deep within her, she could feel him growing harder again.

"Oh, sweetie," he smiled, "there are a lot of ways a man and a woman can give each other pleasure." He ran his hands down her back, over her hips to her

346

thighs, coaxing her to pull her knees forward. She knelt upon him now—her thighs gripping the sides of his torso, her forearms resting on his broad, furry chest—and she grinned almost wickedly when she felt her new position further embed his tumescence.

He smiled up at her. "What you saw Scar and Meggie do," he continued, "was just one of those ways. In fact . . ." He drew her down to him and whispered something into her ear.

"Really?" she murmured. A teasing smile flickered at the corners of her mouth.

"Absolutely." Ace lifted himself on an elbow again and kissed the tip of her nose. "Just pretend it's a very *slow* gallop . . ."

Iris was staring at the ceiling. For the millionth time her eyes traced and retraced the hairline crack that crossed the room diagonally through the whitewashed plaster. There was really nothing else to do, except remember to moan at the appropriate intervals and keep moving her hips; not too much, of course—there's probably be ten or twenty or God-knew-how-many after this one, and she didn't want to wear herself out.

It was a busy night. She and Belinda generally took the bulk of the trade, anyway, but what with Meg gone, and Shirley Mae consigned to slinging hash . . . She moved only enough to keep him happy, to let him know she was alive beneath him. She was certain that no matter how slight her response, it would be more than he received from his wife.

She felt him stiffen and groan, and with almost

believable enthusiasm, she gave him the most action he'd see from her tonight: one good strong arch of her back and thrust of her hips that sped him to his climax.

Sweating and white and naked, he collapsed upon her. She had to wriggle fiercely to push him far enough off of her torso so that she could breathe. At least this one didn't smell too bad, she thought, but she still had to make herself count to twenty before she spoke. You couldn't rush them too much, or they'd think they'd been cheated, no matter how many times they'd stuck it to you . . .

"Harry," she said.

He didn't answer.

"Harry!"

This time he moved a little and turned his head toward her. His face was broad and thick, like his body. But unlike his torso and legs, which were pale and flabby, his face and hands were tanned and healthy-looking. *God*, she thought. *Bankers're sure ugly underneath . . .*

Harry smiled at her in a way he never smiled when he was at the bank—or at home for that matter—and rolled the rest of the way off.

"You're a pip, Iris. What do you say we wait a few minutes and do 'er again?" He thumped his chest and grinned. "Think I might just be up to it tonight."

"Time's up, Harry." She glanced at the clock on the dresser and tried to look disappointed. "You know you're the best by me, but if you wanna take another ride, it'll cost you extra." She smiled her best. "I'm just a li'l ol' workin' girl, you know . . ."

He pursed his lips. She could practically hear the

coins clinking in his head as he counted them up. He hoisted himself to a sitting position.

"Well, maybe not. I guess my regular half hour will do me all right." He climbed over her and began to dress.

Her eyes went back to the crack in the ceiling. She didn't move. She didn't bother to cover herself. She lay there on the stained, wet sheets, naked except for her black stockings, shoes, and garters; silk-clad legs casually flung wide; still staring at the ceiling.

Harry dressed quickly, retrieving his clothing piece by piece from the heavy green chair on which he'd thrown them so hurriedly only thirty minutes earlier. He buttoned his vest, adjusted his watch chain, and checked the time.

"You all right?" he asked. She was still lying in the same position. Her thighs were still flung wide, and he could see the imprint his knees had left behind in the bedclothes between her legs. He wished they'd repaper the damn room. After two years, he was sick of the same pink rosebuds, the same pink and green rug on the floor, the same old dresser, wardrobe, bed, and chair in the same old places. Funny how he never noticed them until afterward . . .

"Um. Fine. Never had better, Harry. Just thinkin'." Still staring upward, she furrowed her brow.

Harry, now fully suited and once again assuming the pompous posture of Banker Fielding, asked, "What about?" As if he really cared . . .

"Nothin' much." Actually, she had quite a mystery to unravel, but it was nothing she'd want to share with him. Or anyone. At least, not right now.

"Oh." Banker Harry Fielding reached into his

pocket, pulled out a dollar and four bits in change, and slid it onto the dresser. He wondered how Iris could be so beautiful to him while he was on top of her, and so distasteful afterward. Her hair, fanned out in a red, knotted tangle on the pillow, was a rat's nest. It hadn't looked like that before. Or had it?

"I'll be leaving you then."

Finally, she looked at him. "Oh. Sure. See you next week, Harry." Suddenly she beamed at him, and batted her eyelashes. "You take care now, sugar, you hear?"

He nodded. The smile caught him off guard, like it always did. Every week, he told himself this was the last time, and every week he came back again. He straightened his shoulders and let himself out.

Once he was gone, Iris sat up and swung her legs over the side of the bed. She just couldn't figure it out. It didn't make any sense. She shook her head, then stood up and walked across the room.

A pitcher of water sat at the far end of the dresser top and she poured a few inches into the matching basin. She dipped a cloth into it, and mechanically, began to wash herself as she tried to puzzle it out.

Somebody was down there. Ace was dead, his body hauled away to town. She hadn't cried when she'd heard, but it hurt her nonetheless. It was his own fault, of course. If he'd listened to her, if he'd understood, then he'd probably have been in her room, in her bed, and not down in that old cattle barn with Rafe getting into an argument over God knows what and getting himself killed . . .

And now he was dead, and the rest of them were gone. Even their horses were gone.

But somebody was down there.

No one had seen but her. No one else had seen Miss Liz sneak that tray out of the kitchen and take it to the cellar and come up not three minutes later, empty-handed.

So who was in the cellar?

Iris knew about the passages that honeycombed the house. The secret wasn't that closely guarded, except to outsiders. She guessed that Pearl and Mary-Rebecca and Agnes and that snotty little man-stealing kitchen maid that had run off were probably the only ones in the house that didn't know about the hidden room in the cellar and the passages that led to each floor. The panel that opened into that bitch, Jenny's, room had come as something of a surprise, especially with Ace popping through it like that, but she'd known there were access points—secret panels and sliding doors and all that nonsense—everywhere.

Iris had never braved any of the house passages: it was understood that they were dangerous and full of spiders or rats or worse, and decidedly off limits to any of the girls. But she'd been in the cellar room.

One day last winter when Ace and the rest were away, she'd talked Meg into showing it to her. It had been awful, being closed in like that: under the ground with no windows and only that single door in or out. She'd only lasted a few minutes before she had fled back to the cellar proper and back up the stairs. She'd never gone down there again.

She finished washing, and without bothering to dress, ripped the sheets off her mattress. She wadded them into a ball and stuffed them into the hamper

351

before pulling a fresh set out of the top drawer of her dresser.

When the bed was ready for her next customer, whoever that might be, she shrugged into a frilly petticoat (nothing underneath—it gave them a cheap thrill downstairs) and a flimsy camisole. She tied the ribbons absently. She was still thinking about Miss Liz and that tray. Everybody was gone. Or dead.

So who was down there?

Jenny lay on her back, dozing peacefully beside him. Her lips were curled into a slight, enigmatic smile. Before they'd nodded off after that last incredible bout of lovemaking, Ace had retrieved one blanket from the layers beneath them, and now they lay under it. He guessed that he'd been awake for about five minutes, and—careful not to disturb Jenny—he rolled to one side, and dragged his pile of clothing closer. His fingers snaked into the vest pocket and plucked out his watch.

Two o'clock. Things would still be loud and rowdy upstairs. He put the watch back and rolled toward Jenny, coming to rest on his side. He propped his head on his hand so he could look down at her face. Beneath the blanket, he slid his hand onto her stomach. He could just feel the bottom swells of her breasts, and he was stricken with a sudden desire to pull the blanket away from her sleeping form and pillow his head upon her bosom. But he didn't, because just then, Jenny's eyelids fluttered open.

"Hello, little one," he whispered, and gave her tummy a gentle rub.

She smiled up at him. "I didn't dream it all?"

"Nope," he grinned. "I hope you're not disappointed."

Jenny withdrew a hand from beneath their blanket and reached up to stroke his cheek. "Far from it." And then she blushed; quite charmingly, he thought.

"What did you do before you came here?" he asked. "Schoolteacher or schoolgirl?"

"Neither," she giggled. "Why would you think that?"

"I found a copy of *Alice* in your room, not to mention the Cicero you heaved at me the other night." She blushed, and he tickled her stomach until she smiled at him again. "You have to admit it's a pretty bizarre library," he grinned.

"I suppose you're right," she giggled. "When I was twelve, my father sent me to live with my mother's sister and her husband. In St. Paul. They didn't let me go to school, not for very long, anyway. But they had a lot of books, mostly about religion or what my uncle used to call 'right living.' I taught myself to read Latin, and when I left, Uncle Homer let me bring Cicero along. He thought it would be . . . uplifting."

"And *Alice?*"

"I took care of their little girls, and it was their favorite book. Mine, too, I guess." She smiled sheepishly. "I read it to them over and over. That copy was my official going-away present. And by the way," she grinned, "how does an outlaw get to be familiar enough with *Alice* to call her by her first name?"

He laughed gently and rubbed her belly. "Oh, I

know a lot of people you'd like to meet, if you haven't already. David Copperfield and Captain Ahab; Heathcliff and his Cathy, Jane Eyre, Oliver Twist, Ebenezer Scrooge, the Lady of Shalott—"

"Stop!" she giggled. She'd seen that fanning pile of volumes by his cot, and she'd wondered about them. "How'd you get to be . . . I mean, Mac told me that you were—"

"—a Kansas farm boy. I know he did."

"You know? How could you?"

He tickled her tummy again. "The cellar isn't the only room in the house with peepholes. I caught most of that little talk you had with him. What he didn't tell you was that my father sent me back East for my last two years of school."

Jenny looked at him curiously, and he gave her tummy another rub. The underside of her far breast was fairly calling out to him to reach up and fondle it, but he refrained with difficulty.

"I was sixteen when Pa packed me off to Maryland. I remember, it wasn't more than a week or two after I lost my virginity. At Liz's old house, back in Fisher, Kansas, to a hand-picked girl named Prudence."

"Did you know then? That Miss Liz was—"

"—my mother?" He smiled. "No. Not for certain. I'd had suspicions something was strange, though. Pa seemed to visit over there an awful lot, but all he ever did, far as I could tell, was sit out on the porch and talk to Liz or play checkers. And then there were all those things that disappeared over the years."

"Disappeared? What things?"

"Oh, toys I'd outgrown, things I'd whittled."

"My Papa used to whittle, too," Jenny smiled,

354

thinking of that long-ago carved menagerie, and of the little cherry-wood horse she'd brought along. "He made beautiful things. Toys for me when I was little, and the most cunning little animals."

"He'd've had it all over me then, I'm afraid. I never could come up with much of anything you'd recognize . . ." He grinned at her and brushed his lips against her forehead.

"I think I know where they disappeared to," Jenny said. "When I was dusting in the office . . ."

He chuckled. "Yes. I imagine you came across part of the Marcus Denton Memorial Collection. It's what gave her away to me, you know. The evening I made my first and last official visit to the house in Fisher I wandered into her office by mistake. Nobody was in there. It was early in the evening in the middle of the week, and I guess Liz was off somewhere with Prudence, telling her she better be extra nice to me or else . . .

"Anyhow, I kind of glanced at the bookshelves. She had quite a collection of bric-a-brac even then— she's only got a fraction of it out now—and lo and behold, there were two of my wood carvings. And a bowl full of marbles, my very favorite aggie in with them. There was an old photograph of me when I was little, and a bunch of other stuff."

"Did you say anything?"

"Not then. It was pretty mysterious, all right, but it sort of paled in contrast with the mysteries upstairs, if you get my drift."

Jenny blushed again and dipped her hand back under the blanket to cover his as it lay on her stomach.

"It was a long time before I got to talk to her about it. When I left that night, I was so full of myself that I almost didn't need a horse to get home. It wasn't until the next day that I really started to think about it, and the more I thought, the more the pieces fit together.

"Then Pa announced that I was going back East to school. Right away. That put the capper on it. He didn't have the money for something like that. It was an expensive boarding school, a prep school for rich men's sons. I argued with him, but he wouldn't take no for an answer. He said it had all been taken care of by a 'friend of the family.' He knew I hated the farm, even though I never said so, and after the whole thing clicked in my head, I didn't fight him on it. I went."

"But did you tell her when you came back? That you knew, I mean."

"I couldn't. She was packed up and gone by then. Nobody'd say where, except to someplace in Missouri. I didn't run across her again till after the war."

"But when you did, how did you—"

Ace laughed softly. "Wait a minute! I started out asking about you, and all I've done is talk about me. Tell me about St. Paul. Tell me what you were like when you were a little girl."

She did. She talked about corsetted Aunt Victoria, and straightlaced Uncle Homer who used to hide behind the kitchen door and watch her skirted backside while she was bent over the iron bathtub, bathing his daughters.

Ace interrupted her at that point. "I can't really blame him," he grinned. "It's a backside worth watching."

She told him about the farm and about her mother: perpetually clad in black and stingy with both affection and understanding. She talked about her papa, and how he'd take an afternoon off from spring plowing, sometimes, just to walk with her through the woods; how he'd wink and hold a shushing finger to his lips, then lift her high in the air to peek at bird's eggs.

And then there was the final tale: the letter that brought her to Fowlersville, Iowa, the horrible thing she'd learned there, and her subsequent trailing of the Denton Gang.

"I'm awfully glad," Ace said when she was finished, "that you were a beautiful young girl and not some middle-aged bounty hunter with a shotgun in his hand and that reward on his mind." He paused for a moment, then grinned, "That old Colt of your daddy's . . . Do you know how to use it?"

A bright spot of color appeared in each of Jenny's cheeks. "I could barely load it," she admitted, "and I've never actually fired it."

He smiled, "I guess I can take some comfort knowing that even if you hadn't found out in time, you probably would have missed me." He saw that he'd embarrassed her and, beneath the blanket, laced his big fingers through her slender ones. Then he lay back down next to her, still on his side, and slipped the arm on which he'd propped himself under her shoulders.

They lay there quietly for a few minutes before Jenny spoke again.

"It is Wonderland, isn't it?"

The tips of stalactites sparkled above her, pale and

357

golden and otherworldly. Beyond Ace's shoulder she could see the pastel forest of stone pillars and the soft beams of light from the lantern behind them. Just a few feet away lay the shore of the glassy lake: its surface lit softly here and there by the escaping lamplight, its far bank fading away into the darkness.

She looked into the onyx of his bottomless eyes. "I'm glad we were here," she murmured. "I'm glad I was here with you, the first time."

Ace stretched his head nearer to kiss her. "And the second," he reminded her before he kissed her again. He was itching to move his hand just a little higher: just far enough to fill his palm with the soft weight of her breast.

"And the second," she repeated after him. "Ace?"

"Yes, Jenny?" He was nuzzling her forehead now.

Beneath the blanket, she slipped her fingers from his and lifted his hand to her breast. "Do you think it would be all right for the third?"

He chuckled so loudly that she had to kiss the sound away.

Iris knew the mattress pad must be soaked again by now, but she didn't care. After all, Joe Harper was the one lying on it, not her. He was on his back at the edge of the bed, his pants unbuttoned and all his meager equipment on display, passed out cold. She hadn't even had time to straddle him before the whiskey caught up with him. At first she'd been angry. She'd not only lose the money for the half hour he usually took, but she'd have to go get Mac to haul him downstairs as well. But then a thought struck her, and she brightened.

First she leaned over him. "Joe!" There was no response. She patted his face. "Joe?"

He was out cold. She'd have plenty of time to sneak downstairs and have a quick look before the half hour was up. Then she could just come back up and take the money out of his pocket and holler for Mac. Old Joe would never remember if he'd had her or not.

But he was a little too close to the edge of the bed. She wouldn't want him falling out and waking up before she got back. Swearing under her breath, she managed to roll him onto his side. He looked fairly comfortable as he lay there snoring, and she gave his shoulder a little pat.

Next, she dressed. As usual, she'd stripped off the second they got to the room, and now she hurried back into her camisole. Instead of a petticoat, she pulled on a pair of lace-trimmed pantalets: they'd be easier to hurry up and down stairs in. Then she took off her shoes and stockings. Not that there'd be much chance of anyone hearing her as she went down the back stairs: Harvey was banging that piano loud enough to wake the dead and that damn parrot was in one of his talkative moods—she could hear him screeching *Bugger off! Heave to!* all the way up here. But she'd have to be quiet when she got to the cellar. She didn't know who was down there, but whoever it was, she wanted to see, not be seen.

She peeked out into the hall. Light fanned from beneath Belinda's door, and she could hear Belinda's drunken giggles mixed with male laughter. Across the way, Pearl ushered an elderly farmer into her chamber. He was stooped and gnarled, but he held his hat in his hands and grinned at Pearl like a schoolboy on his first date.

As soon as the door closed behind them, Iris slipped out and hurried to the back stairs.

No one saw her. Bertha was in the kitchen, but she was so busy cursing Jenny's absence and arguing with Shirley Mae that she never glanced toward the rear hall. Quietly, Iris requisitioned a lantern and a match from the pantry counter, and opened the cellar door.

She closed it behind her and stood on the top step for a moment, listening. Except for Onan's cries of *Howdy cowboy!* and *Bugger off!* and Harvey's mangled version of Mozart reverberating through the door, there was silence. She had been right. Whoever Liz had taken that tray to was further back, in the secret room. She lit her lantern and started down the steps.

The latch was easy to find. She'd been careful to memorize its placement last winter, when Meg had given her the tour. One never knew when something like that might come in handy.

At first, she slid the panel only an inch, holding her lantern away from the opening so that her light would not be seen. No sound issued from the blackness beyond. She smiled and slipped into the pine-walled passage beyond the cellar.

Now there was only one barrier between herself and the old runaway slave's way station. She crept to the door and put her ear to the wood. There was no sound, and she knitted her brow. She knew someone had to be in there—phantoms didn't eat.

She dimmed her lantern and set it aside before she

slowly, carefully, lifted the latch and eased the door open a fraction of an inch. Still there was nothing but silence.

She opened it a bit wider. She could see nothing in the pitch black beyond, and she cursed under her breath.

She retrieved her lamp before she braved a step inside. The room was empty: not one single solitary rat in residence. She held the lantern high over her head and turned in a circle. Other than a few spiders, the chamber was vacant.

She cursed again and started back toward the passage and the cellar. But just before she passed through the doorway, she noticed something odd out of the corner of her eye. She turned and lifted the lantern.

It was a black line: a black line on the other paneled wall, to her right. She didn't remember it. The wall should be smooth, flawless paneling. She crossed the room toward it. She reached out to touch it but before she could, she heard the sound. It was a sort of curious murmuring, more a low uneven humming than anything else. And the black line from which it emanated was an opening in the wall.

She grinned coldly. So the game was still on, then. She pushed her hand into the crack and gave the panel a little shove. It rolled back easily and silently, and she stepped forward, to the top step of the circular staircase.

Thirteen

His kisses took her breath away.

They had kicked free the blanket and Ace had pulled her partially atop him. They had kissed and petted, and now she had slipped down his torso. Her lips and tongue flicked over his shoulders, then his chest, then downward to circle his nipples. One at a time, she nipped and sucked at the two erect beads of flesh that crowned his flat male breasts, and she was delighted and aroused when his response to her attentions rivaled her own when he had suckled her.

At last she slipped lower, kissing her way down the line of his belly. Ace saw where she was going, and although he couldn't think of anything he'd enjoy more at this moment, he was almost shocked.

"Jenny!" he hissed through clenched teeth, "I don't think you're ready to—"

She lifted her lips from his midsection long enough to grin and whisper, "This time, there'll be no talking from you, Mr. Ace Denton. No sirree."

The staircase seemed to wind down forever.

The deeper Iris went, the easier it was to hear that low murmuring, but she still couldn't make out the voices. There seemed to be the sound of water, and voices over it, but she couldn't tell how many or who. What did Liz have going down here, anyway? Underground poker games? A secret society? She grinned. *I'll bet it's something good, anyhow,* she thought, just as the bottom of the staircase came into sight. *And whatever it is, I want in on it. I wonder just what in the hell the old bag's been holdin' out on us . . .*

The tunnel sloped downward and she followed it almost gleefully, all thought of rats and spiders and worse forgotten. The further she walked, the more the echoes began to unbraid themselves into separate components. About the same time she saw the glow of light from what looked like it might be the mouth of the tunnel, she was able to identify the low, echoing sound of a man moaning.

I only know one thing makes a man sound like that, she thought. *Just who's working down here?* Her smile was cold and wicked as she set her lantern down. There was light ahead and she wouldn't need it. Besides, she didn't want to give them any advance warning. This might be something she'd want to think over for a while. Something she could use to her advantage later on.

It was when she reached the mouth of the tunnel that she recognized the voice. She was pressed against the stone wall of the passage, staring with openmouthed astonishment at the softly lit grotto and thinking that it reminded her of nothing so much as a gigantic mouth full of stone fangs, when she made out that one word and knew the voice that spoke it.

The word was "Jenny" and the voice belonged to the late Ace Denton.

Fury, pure and untainted, raged through her. So this was the game! Alive! The son of a bitch was alive, and that filthy little blonde was down here with him . . .

She started forward blindly. Any thought she might have had about the surprising beauty—or terror—of this place was gone. But when her foot hit a stray pebble to knock it into the base of a stalagmite with a little *ping*, it echoed. Ace's reverberating mumbles and groans continued, and she knew they hadn't noticed, but still, she stopped to gather herself before she went on.

She was going to kill them. She was sure of that. She'd kill them if she had to use her bare hands, or . . .

She looked down at the grotto's floor. Maybe there'd be a rock, something, anything. And there was, but it was something much better than a rock. Not more than five feet away from her was a scattering of small stalactites that had fallen from above in some earlier year or age. Silently, she crept toward them and very carefully, so as not to make a sound, began to sort through them.

Most were broken and useless—too light or too blunt to do her any good—but then she found exactly what she needed. It was a nearly perfect spire, about fifteen inches long: narrow, solid, and still bearing a sharp, chipped point. A dagger of stone.

Iris hefted it in her hand and smiled. It was an expression that did not reach her cold, hard eyes.

Quietly, carefully, and very slowly, she began to creep toward the light.

It was all he could do to grab at her shoulder and pull her away from him, but he knew that if he didn't stop her now, it would be too late.

"J-Jenny," he stuttered. The whisper rattled in his throat. "Wait. Please."

Reluctantly, she moved back up to lie beside him. "Did I do something wrong?"

He pulled her onto his chest and hugged her. "Wrong? Oh, Jenny, you do everything right. Better than right. We just have to wait a minute, that's all."

"Why?" She rolled those big green eyes at him. He could see that she was nearly as aroused as she had made him, but if he didn't get himself under control, he'd have nothing left for her.

"I'll explain later, Jenny. For now, just trust me." He was feeling more in command of himself, and eased over to position himself above her. Immediately, she circled his neck with her arms, and he felt her legs glide up along his, to his hips.

"My Jenny," he whispered.

Jenny's lips formed a smile, and a long, breathy, "Ahhhhh," came out as he entered to fill her gradually and completely. No feeling was more perfect, more gorgeous, she thought; nothing could ever be better than the sensation of Ace inside her body, inside her soul.

"I love you, Jenny," he whispered.

"Ace," was all she could say.

Iris held the stone dagger high over her head, poised to strike; but when she took that last careful step forward into the stone clearing, they weren't there. But they were close by—they'd have to be. She could hear every panting breath that son of a bitch and his nasty little virgin whore took.

She looked around the clearing: dirty dishes, piles and piles of books, the stone table that bore the lantern, Ace and Jenny's belongings, two stripped cots. She saw the basin and wash things beneath one, along with some crumpled clothing.

And then she saw what was beneath the other, and silently laying aside her stone knife, she smiled.

They lay naked and sated on the blankets, spooned: he behind her, his arms cradling her. She drowsed, her head pillowed on his bicep. He kissed the back of her neck, and it was perfect. Everything was perfect with Ace. She could not imagine how she had lived so long without him, without this.

She closed her eyes again, and there was nothing for her but the faint sound of water lapping the black lake's shore, the whisper and heat of his breath against the back of her neck, and the warm, soft pelt of fur on his chest and belly pressing into her back and buttocks.

Then he was gone. He pulled away from her with shocking abruptness. Her eyes fluttered open in time to see just his shadow as he vanished into the stone forest at the lamplight's edge. It was then that she heard the click of a gun's hammer.

It was Iris: half-dressed, her hair wild and tangled, her eyes deranged. She held Jenny's old pistol, and she was pointing it straight at Jenny's face. She was smiling.

"Let the sonofabitch run, sugar," she drawled. "I'll get to him later. After all, he's dead already, isn't he?" Iris's mad grin widened as Jenny frantically tried to cover herself. "Well, I reckon I can see why he'd want to stick it to you, but that still don't excuse it. Don't excuse it at all . . ."

Jenny stared straight down the barrel of that gun, mesmerized. Could she have been this wrong about him? She had trusted him, loved him; and he had deserted her, run away and left her with this madwoman. But then, she'd been wrong about him several times before.

For a split second, she found herself hating him again: found herself wishing she'd never followed him here. But then Iris's voice grated the air.

"That's right, Mr. Ace Denton," she said. Her voice was raised and under the echoes, Jenny could hear a distant rumbling. "You'd *better* hide, you son of a bitch!" She was talking to the air now. She knew he was there somewhere. "I might have known it, you sneaky bastard. Just who the hell did the sheriff haul outta here, anyhow?"

Jenny was on her feet now, the blanket clutched about her. "Iris please!" she hissed. "Keep your voice down!"

Iris curled her lip disdainfully. "You stupid little

368

snip! Who the hell's gonna hear me?"

"Iris, you don't understand!"

"Oh, I understand, Little Miss Sugar Drawers." Her voice was lower now; not because of Jenny's warnings, but because the echoes were less overpowering. "I understand plenty."

Iris smiled, and Jenny shrank away instinctively.

"I was gonna kill you both," she said, taking a step forward, "but I think maybe I changed my mind."

About twenty feet behind Iris, Jenny caught a glimpse of Ace before he disappeared behind another pillar of limestone. He was creeping slowly forward, into the circle of light; and before she caught herself, she gave a little sigh of relief.

Iris misunderstood. Her cold grin widened. "Oh, I'm still gonna kill *you*, Miss Jenny. But not Ace. No, not him. I'm gonna give him the same sort of present I gave my stepdaddy. I'll fix him, all right. I'll geld that bastard, and he'll never do nobody again."

She saw him again. He was within ten feet of Iris now, and Jenny spoke quickly to distract her. "Listen to me, please! You can't fire that gun down here. You'll bring the—"

"Bring what? The law?" She laughed loudly: too loudly to notice the small clatter of rock her voice brought down in the shadows. Beneath Jenny's bare feet, the cavern floor vibrated slightly, ominously.

"Iris please!" Jenny whispered. Just past Iris's shoulder, she could see Ace creeping forward. He was clear of the rock now, nearly close enough. "Keep your voice down! We can talk about this, we can—"

"Talk?" Iris shrieked. She swung the gun barrel back and forth. "Listen, you little back-stabber,

369

maybe I won't kill you first. Maybe I'll let you live long enough to hear your precious Ace scream when I shoot off his goodies, and then you can tell *him* to keep his goddamned mouth shut—"

Ace leapt forward. He threw himself upon her, wrenching her gun hand up and away from Jenny. "Drop it, Iris," he hissed as she writhed and fought. He had her wrist, but he couldn't get the gun. "And shut up! You don't understand!"

"Bastard!" Iris screamed before Ace could cover her mouth. The pistol waved wildly as she twisted against him.

She pulled the trigger.

The shot went wild, its reverberating explosion and whining ricochets followed immediately by a deep, bone-jarring rumble that did not die with the echoes. Iris stopped stock-still to stare up into the rock overhead. From further back in the cavern came the crash as the first small rocks exploded on the stone floor, and the splash as they pocked the surface of the lake.

Ace yanked the pistol from her fingers. He bent, and in one motion snatched up Jenny's bags and his own, slinging his gun belt over his shoulder.

"Run!" he shouted over the growing din of breaking, falling rock. "Run for the barn!"

Jenny pivoted and sprinted away, Ace close behind her. She tripped on the hem of her blanket halfway around the shore and Ace reached toward her, ripping it from her shoulders and casting it aside. "Just go!" he bellowed.

Just before they ducked inside the mouth of the tunnel, Jenny looked back over her shoulder. Water sprayed back into her face as the first of the big stalactites hit the lake's surface. The air was filled with dust and flying bits of shattered stone. The ground rumbled and shook. It sounded like the end of the world, and in the center of it all stood Iris, just where they had left her.

"Iris!" Jenny screamed. "Iris, run!"

Dully, Iris turned her head to look at Jenny. Just as Ace grabbed Jenny's shoulder and hauled her into the tunnel, she saw Iris disappear under the leading edge of an ocean of stone.

The dust and debris billowed smoke and thunder as it chased them along the tunnel, and they didn't stop until they'd emerged through the feed bin. He dropped the lid after them before he took her arm and said, "All right?"

"Yes, I think so," she panted, but just then they both looked toward the door. It was rattling on its hinges. Around them the feed room walls shivered convulsively, then stopped as suddenly as they had begun. But the sounds didn't stop. They came not from the tunnel below, but from the yard: rumbling, quaking, horrible sounds as the earth broke and collapsed upon itself. Quickly, Ace lit a match and ripped open his saddlebags. He yanked out a pair of trousers. As he tugged them on, he said, "Get into your riding clothes as quick as you can. I think this might be a good time for us to leave."

As she blindly scrambled into her father's old trousers, Ace slipped out of the feed room. A few seconds later, he was back. She was nearly dressed by

371

then, and as she fastened the last few buttons on the old plaid shirt, he towed her, along with their baggage, out into the aisle. The scream of moving earth and shattered rock had faded by then, and all she could hear was an occasional creak of stone and faraway splash of displaced water. And, she suddenly realized, the distant sound of shouting voices.

"C'mon," he said. There was a look of abject amazement on his face. "You've got to see this."

His arm around her, they peeked around the stable door and up toward the house.

"Dear God!" Jenny whispered.

"Exactly."

The long, grassy slope between the crest of the hill and the barn was no more. In its place was a raw, gaping pit of at least an acre's measure, still groaning as rock settled and new stone and earth fell from the sides to sink into the roiling, dirty water below. Amazingly, Briarbirth remained. The house on the hill still loomed against the near-dawn sky, un-harmed and unmoved, poised on the edge of the precipice like a headstone over a plundered grave.

It seemed that everyone was out in the front yard. From where Jenny stood, they were little more than tiny silhouettes, and if she couldn't make out their words, she could pick out the sound of their voices.

Mac and Liz were easy to identify in outline. They stood near the porch. Mac had his hands on his hips, and it seemed he was shaking his head. Miss Liz was turned to the side, watching Agnes chase around the front yard after Onan, who seemed to have effected his own release during the confusion. His words were the only ones which came clearly down the slope.

Bugger off! he squawked as Agnes scrambled after him. He fluttered out of her grasp, landed on the eave, and screeched, *Howdy, cowboy! Heave to!*

Suddenly, Jenny realized that beside her, Ace was chuckling into his hand. "C'mon," he finally managed. "They're okay. Let's get Daisy and cut down the back slope before it gets any lighter."

The sun was well up by the time they reached the roundup pen on Briar Creek. Fancy and Trooper were waiting patiently, grazing enthusiastically side by side through the knee-high yellowing grasses. Scar had piled their tack along a fence rail and covered it with a tarp.

Ace dropped their gear, then helped Jenny down before he looped Daisy's reins through her bridle and sent her home with a pat on her silvery rump.

They saddled up without conversation, and struck out toward the west, Ace in the lead.

"Ace?" Jenny jogged up beside him.

"Um?" He was rolling a cigarette. She'd never seen him smoke before, and she suddenly realized how much she had to learn about him.

"Where are we going?"

"Kansas. I have a little business to take care of." He tucked the tobacco pouch back in his pocket. "Do you think you can learn to call me Marc? Ace is dead, Jenny."

"Marc," she said. She liked the way it felt in her mouth. "Yes. It's a good name." She smiled before her lips tightened. "But what do you have to do in Kansas? You're not going to— I mean, after all this, you wouldn't . . ."

He laughed. "I'm not planning to knock over a freight office, if that's what you're afraid of."

She relaxed visibly, and he reached over to rub her shoulder. "Two things, actually. I have to pick up our nest egg, and—" She frowned, and he added, "Don't worry, Jen, it's my money. What I got out of the farm plus . . . Well, all right. It's not *all* honest money. But most of it is."

She didn't say anything. She just looked at him, her lips pursed, and he broke out laughing.

"All right, all right! I can see I don't have a chance . . ." He finally got around to lighting the cigarette and took a long drag on it. The smoke trailed out behind him in a narrow white plume. "How about," he said, tossing the match to the side, "if I give the, uh, excess to the widow and orphan's fund or something, and we use the farm money and its interest? That ought to give us about six hundred, I guess. Maybe a little more."

She smiled. "Better. But what's the second thing you have to do in Kansas?"

"Not me, Jenny. Us. I think we'd better find a preacher as soon as we get out of 'Ace Denton Territory,' don't you?"

She looked down and bit at her lip, too happy and too relieved to answer him. She'd been terrified he wouldn't ask.

Suddenly, he jerked his horse to a halt and grabbed at her reins. "You are going to marry me aren't you?" he asked. He looked stricken. It had never crossed his mind that she wouldn't.

But the smile that broke over her face calmed him.

374

"Yes," she said, quite simply.

He let go of her reins, and they started out again. "Well . . . well . . . well good, then." Now *he* was the one who couldn't think of anything to say.

"Ace? I mean, Marc?"

He looked over, and she was staring down at her saddle horn once more, her palms crossed over it.

"What is it, sweetie?"

"Will I . . ." She bit at her lip again. "Will I have a baby now that we . . . ?" She kept her eyes down.

He smiled and reached across the space between them to take her hand. "I don't know, Jenny, but I hope so. I hope we have lots and lots of babies."

Epilogue

December, 1879
Oro Blanco, Arizona

Mrs. Haggerty planted hands on her generous hips and grinned as she stared out the window. "Here she comes for the mail. Ain't she just the sweetest little thing? All that blond hair and those big green eyes . . ." She looked behind her, toward her husband. He was dozing in his chair. "Connor!" she thundered.

He lurched forward. "What? What, mother? Wasn't sleeping, you know!"

She smiled. "Yes, Connor, I know you weren't. I was just saying that Mrs. McCaleb's coming across the street. Why don't you get her mail up?"

He stood, adjusting wire-rimmed glasses on his narrow, sunburnt nose. "Got it right here, mother." He pulled it down from its slot just as the little bell over the door jingled.

"Morning, Mrs. Haggerty, Mr. Haggerty," the

young woman said. She carried a baby with silky black hair. An eight-year-old girl as blond as she and a dark-haired, dark-eyed boy of four followed in her wake.

"G'morning, Mrs. Haggerty," said the little girl in singsong fashion. She looked up at the postmistress with huge, gold-flecked, hazel eyes.

"Hello yourself, Miss Alice," she grinned. "Are you helping your mother with her errands today?"

"Yes'm," Alice said. She pursed her bow-shaped mouth into a little pout before she brightened. "Mama's going to make me a new dress and I got to pick out the yard goods. It's going to be pink with little red kittens, and there's going to be a ribbon for my hair, too!"

"Well," the postmistress replied quite solemnly, "that sounds to me like a very fancy dress."

Alice grinned. "My Daddy says I'm a very fancy young lady!"

Mrs. Marc McCaleb smiled and shook her pretty head. "Now, Alice . . ."

Mr. Haggerty handed over the mail. There were two stacks: a fat one, mostly bills and advertisements, addressed to MAD HATTER SILVER MINE, M. McCALEB PROP., and a slender fan of personal correspondence. She tucked the business mail into her bag and leafed through the other, brightening when she came to a long blue envelope.

"Good one?" It was Mr. Haggerty. He was leaning across the counter, staring at her. Jenny McCaleb was, he guessed, the prettiest lady in Oro Blanco. And the nicest, too.

She smiled, and it brightened the room. "It's from my mother-in-law, back in Pennsylvania." She started to tear the envelope open, but felt a tug on her skirts. It was the little boy.

"What is it, Michael?"

"Can we have a cookie?"

She looked from him to Mrs. Haggerty.

"If you wouldn't mind, Mrs. McCaleb. I took some fresh from the oven not an hour ago, and they're just beggin' to be tasted." Alice stood next to the postmistress, nodding and trying to look gaunt.

"I suppose," she said, touching young Michael's dark curls. "Mind your manners!" she called after them, but they'd already scampered ahead of Mrs. Haggerty, toward the kitchen. They knew the way all too well.

She sat down on the long bench under the street window and laid the baby down next to her. Little Elizabeth Jane was sleeping soundly, her chubby thumb tucked firmly between pink lips.

She opened the envelope, slipped out the pale blue pages inside, and began to read.

Dear Jenny and Marcus,

We were so pleased with the photograph you sent of our newest grandchild! I think Mac has showed that poor picture of little Elizabeth Jane to everyone in town. It's a good thing I had it framed right off, or it would be tattered to ribbons by now.

We had a letter from Bertha about two months ago. I think I told you that she and Shirley Mae started up that little bakery in St. Louis? Seems they are doing grand business, although if they still fight like they used to, I don't know how they manage to keep the cakes from falling. She said Agnes had been through to see them. She is married now, to a medical doctor. They have a little boy (although I'll be damned if I can remember his name), and they were moving out to Colorado where her husband has kin. Agnes told her that she'd seen Belinda; not to talk to, though. Just passed her on the street in Kansas City. She said Belinda was in a carriage with a man who is known to have several girls working for him, and does not treat them very well. It's a sad thing.

Bertha also said she'd heard they finally did something with Elmer's old house. After I gave Briarbirth to the county, they just let it sit there for the longest time, but two years ago, somebody went out and shored up the cliff next to the house and built a wall along the rim so nobody'd get killed falling in the pond. Anyway, they turned the damn thing into the county orphan's home. Mac thinks this is just about the funniest thing he's ever heard, and I guess even I think it's sort of poetic.

Mac had a surprise for me the other day. He has been working with that idiot bird for ages, but could never teach him a new word. So I was very surprised when I came down to breakfast Tuesday morning and the damned thing looked me straight in the eye and said, "Lizzie." It was entertaining, I suppose, the first few times, but now we can't get him to shut up. He just sits in the front window, screeching, "Bugger off, Lizzie! Heave to!" all day long.

I know I have said this before and you are probably tired of reading it, but I do so wish that you children would move back here to be with us. We read about the lawlessness of your part of the country and the Indians and bandits, and even though Marcus says he is doing well and making a great deal of money, I worry for your safety. Mac says I'm being a silly old fool—that young people need young places, sometimes. But still, I worry. I am happy to hear, at least, that Marcus has completed your new house. It sounds very grand, and Mac spent a lot of time looking at the sketches Marcus sent for him. I think he half wishes he had been there to help build it. He seems fascinated with what Marcus had to say about making adobe blocks, and when he read that you had made the outer walls three feet thick and solid adobe, he turned to me and said, "Lizzie, they won't be able to fit one blessed tunnel in the whole damn place!"

I'm going to be sending a package for the children (as well their parents) which I hope you will have in time for Christmas. We will be thinking of you.

Much love,
Mother and Mac

Jenny read the letter a second time before she refolded it, eased it back in its envelope and consulted the watch pinned to her bodice. It was time to be off. Elizabeth Jane was still sleeping soundly beside her on the bench, and carefully, she scooped her up.

"Good news?" It was Mr. Haggerty. He'd probably been sitting there the whole time, watching her.

"My in-laws are teaching their parrot to talk," she said.

He looked at her a little strangely before he grinned and called, "Mother! You got those young'uns stuffed full of gingersnaps yet?"

The children came running out, all crumbs and smiles, and Jenny gathered them up along with her parcels and bade the Haggertys good day. When she emerged on the sidewalk, Marcus was just coming across the street.

"Hello, angel!" he boomed as he bussed her on the cheek.

"Me too, Daddy!" Alice cried, and he swept her up into the air while she giggled and squealed.

"Oof!" he said, putting her down. "You're getting so grown up, Alice! You're going to break your father's back one of these days!"

"Me Daddy?" pleaded little Michael.

The former Ace Denton grinned at his son. "Seems to me, Mike, that you've still got a few weeks left of shoulder-size." He boosted the gleeful boy up to his broad shoulder, took Jenny's parcels under his arm, and they walked down the street to where Trooper stood, tied to the back of a wagon.

It was a freighter, and on the side was stenciled MAD HATTER MINE. Jenny frowned. "Still?" she asked.

"Sorry, Jen. He says the buggy won't be ready 'til Friday. Don't worry. By next week you'll be able to hitch up Fancy and one of her daughters and step out in style again." He lifted the packages and children up to the backseat, then helped Jenny aboard. "Anything good in the mail?"

"Letter from your mother and Mac," she said as they started down the street. "Lots of bills."

"As usual," he said with a grin. "Nice to have something to pay them with, though, isn't it?"

382

She smiled at him, and he added, "What's Ma have to say?"

Elizabeth Jane was awake now, and beginning to squall. "She said that . . . Oh, Janie, I know you're hungry, pet. We'll be home in a bit." She soothed the baby's brow. "Well, you can read it when we get home."

They were well out of Oro Blanco by now, and headed down a narrow desert road. Low, pale gray-green scrub pillowed the soft tan sands on either side of the lane. It was a landscape that Jenny had never imagined she would live in, let alone grow to love; but she had.

"Woolgathering again?" Marc's hand was on her knee.

"What?"

He chuckled softly. "I asked you how it went at Doc Peterson's."

"He says she's still the most beautiful baby he's ever seen," she grinned. She'd given Elizabeth Jane the tip of her little finger to suck, but it wasn't working. "Pretty baby," she cooed, "Hush, baby."

"Maybe you should give her her dinner."

"Marcus!" She looked shocked, and he stifled a laugh.

"Well, who's going to see out here? And she'll be bawling like crazy by the time we get back if you don't."

She began to unbutton her bodice. "Do you ever get tired of being right?" she smiled as she pushed her camisole aside and held Elizabeth Jane to her breast. The baby took it and began to suckle with soft, eager smacks.

Marc looked on, a little jealous. "Isn't it about time

for you to wean her?" he suggested hopefully. "I mean, I hate to be greedy, but I'd like to have my—I mean your—I mean . . ." He shot a quick look toward the backseat. Alice and Michael were busy concentrating on the new picture book Jenny had bought them.

"Well, I'd like to have them back," he whispered, winking.

Jenny loosened her bodice a bit more and re-adjusted the baby. "Dr. Peterson said I could start her on solid food any time now." She let Marc grin for a minute before she added, "But I'm afraid you won't have me all to yourself for too long . . ."

"Jenny?"

"How do you like the name *Heathcliff?*"

Chuckling, he shook his head and leaned over to kiss her temple. *"Heathcliff?"*

She made a face, and he laughed.

"We've got plenty of time to come up with a name." He reached over to touch Elizabeth Jane's downy head.

"You don't seem very excited," she said.

He put his arm around both Jenny and the nursing baby, and as they turned down the long lane that would take them to the *Mad Hatter* and home, he whispered, "My dear, I'll be happy to show you just how excited I am as soon as the children are asleep tonight. In fact," he added wickedly, "I may show you several times."